The M   Knives

by

Stephen James Messenger

©2017

Chapter 1 – The Swordsmith

The young Romani woman touched her belly and smiled at the life that kicked there. She sat at the little table in the single room that served as bedroom and kitchen and all the places that were needed in her life in the little house across the yard from the forge. The bright, hot sun hung in the sky, allowing little breezes to scamper beneath it in the hilly countryside near Granada. Like she had done every day, from the first day that she realized that she was pregnant, she prepared to read the story in the cards.

She shuffled the deck, again and again and again and then again, putting herself and her question and her child into the cards until finally, she felt that las tarjetas were ready to speak. If only they would tell her something that she could understand instead of merely whispering the pieces of secrets as they usually did.

She read the Swordsmith's Cards. Her husband, the huge, kind, gifted Moor she had fallen in love with, had taught her these cards. She had been raised Romani and knew the reading of the 'tarjetas gitanos' as well as she knew how to read the sky for rain or her husband's deep, dark brown eyes for the unspoken passion that he held only for her.

The Swordsmith's Cards were something a piece of and apart from all of the other tarot she knew or had ever heard of. She was a woman to whom the cards quietly spoke if she put her questions to them with the greatest care, opened herself to them in their time, and allowed the answers to state their peace. The Romani woman read the cards as assiduously as priests read the Bible, the Torah, or the Quran.

*

The Swordsmith's Tarot has only two suits: Swords and Knives (if the cards of the Suit of Swords are a precisely-constructed musical composition, the cards of the Suit of Knives are a wild improvisation), thirteen cards in each suit for the Minor Arcana (Ace through Ten, Knight, Queen, and King) and fifteen for the Major Arcana: The Master, The Craftsman, The Stabbed Man, The Devil, Fire, Steel, Strength, Justice, Judgement, Death, The Stars, The Sun, The World, The Dungeon, and The Swordsmith (in other decks, this card was known as The Fool) for a total of forty-one cards (a number that the Arab mathematicians called a prime number, the thirteenth prime number).

*

The Suit of Swords represents the element of the Air. And just as the Air is essential to the making of a sword, the cards of the Suit of Swords address the results of the making of a sword: conflict, power, force, change, courage, oppression, ambition, and action. The cards of the Suit of Swords are powerful and dangerous, ready to confront hatred and one's enemies and resulting, sometimes, in violent battle (which, like a sword itself, can be either constructive or destructive).

Just as a sword is a thing of terrible beauty, the skillful use of a sword or the cards of the Suit of Swords requires conscious thought, practiced skill, intellect, and intent. Just as swords are double-edged, the cards of the Suit of Swords mirror the balance between the body and the mind, power and subtlety, and good and evil.

While the cards of the Suit of Swords have strong positive aspects, they can also speak of guilt, anger, impulsivity, and cruelty.

When the cards of the Suit of Swords choose to speak to the reader of time, they point to spring (beginnings) or winter (endings).

The Ace of Swords shouts of power, victory, and clear-headedness (or, if it is reversed, of confusion and chaos).

The Two of Swords mutters of indecision and confusion.

The Three of Swords cries of pain, grief, and heartbreak (or, if it is reversed, of acceptance and forgiveness).

The Four of Swords whispers of rest, contemplation, and relaxation (or, if it is reversed, of exhaustion).

The Five of Swords screams only of loss, defeat, and betrayal.

The Six of Swords complains of change.

The Seven of Swords equivocates of deception and stealth.

The Eight of Swords speaks softly in generalities (in case someone is listening) of isolation and imprisonment (or, if it is reversed, of freedom and release)

The Nine of Swords sobs of hopelessness, despair, torment, and nightmares.

The Ten of Swords wails of crisis, defeat, and loss (or, if it is reversed, of recovery and regeneration).

*

In the Swordsmith's Tarot, there is also the Suit of Knives; in other tarot decks, it might be called the Suit of Wands. Just as the Suit of Swords represents the Air, the Suit of Knives represents Fire. And just as Air is essential to the making of a sword, Fire is essential to the making of a knife, and the cards of the Suit of Knives address the use of a knife: energy, inspiration, creativity, determination, intuition, and ambition. The cards of the Suit of Knives reveal consciousness, spirituality, ego, energy, action, and passion.

While the cards of the Suit of Knives have strong positive aspects, they can also speak of illusion, egotism, impulsivity, or purposelessness.

When the cards of the Suit of Knives choose to speak to the reader of time, they point to summer (the fullest manifestation of life).

The Ace of Knives gushes inspiration, power, and potential.

The Two of Knives proposes planning, progress, and discovery.

The Three of Knives foresees preparation and enterprise (or, if it is reversed, delays and obstacles).

The Four of Knives celebrates harmony, marriage, and home.

The Five of Knives asserts tension, conflict, and competition.

The Six of Knives trumpets victory, progress, and recognition (or, if it is reversed, a fall from grace).

The Seven of Knives threatens challenge (or, if it is reversed, concession or capitulation).

The Eight of Knives rants of speed, action, and movement.

The Nine of Knives dares to speak of faith, courage, and resilience (or, if it is reversed, of hesitance or paranoia).

The Ten of Knives stoically bears its burdens and accepts its responsibilities.

*

Once the cards had told her that the child growing in her womb would be a boy, the Moor's wife had only one other question for the cards: "What will become of my son?"

If the cards had ever answered that question, and she had asked it again and again and again, the woman never told another living soul what she knew, but she sang her Romani songs and danced around the fire of the forge and gave herself up to the passion in the flames and the steel and the music.

*

It was hot today. And the only thing hotter than Toledo in the summer were the fires of Julian de Boabdil's forge. Julian de

Boabdil, and his father before him, and his father before that, was a swordsmith, a Master of long-standing and sterling reputation in the Guild of Swordsmiths of Toledo, Spain, who made the finest blades in all of Europe. His blades and his life were forged by fire, and when he died, according to the faith of his Romani mother (who called him "Tawni"), he would probably burn in Hell. His Moorish father, who never mentioned his faith, or lack of it, would have added, "Allah, Glorified and Exalted be He, said, 'A bed awaits in Hellfire and a gate is open to lead you there' to Sijjin, the lowest stage of the Earth, where you will likely be punished until the Day of Judgement."

And since that day would not likely be today, Julian de Boabdil worked. He sang softly to himself as he worked, a song partly a Gitano cante jondo, that he remembered his mother singing with her heart and soul as she danced, and partly the adhan, the Call to Prayer that his father had sung (Julian smiled as he sang his father's part; his father would have slapped Julian's face to suggest that he would sing the adhan ... that would be haram!), as he made the blades and added his song to the liquid metal. The Christians chose bells, the Jews chose trumpets, and the Moors chose their words to call the faithful to prayer; Julian used fire and steel and song to call his swords into being.

*

Perhaps Julian's father's greatest secret was his making of Damascene steel in his little forge in the south of al-Andalus. His father had traveled east as a young man and studied at the feet and at the forges of Syrian masters. And just as importantly, he had met the Indians who made the wootz steel in their native land and delivered ingots of the precious metal to the smiths in the Middle East. He had made these merchants his friends, and his friends later brought the wonderful steel to his forge in the hills outside Toledo.

Julian's father had other secrets, as well, all of which he taught his son. First, he taught Julian patience. Heating the wootz slowly in the crucibles, over a period of days until a crystal of borax (sent by a friend who mined for gold and silver on the Rio Tinto in Andalusia) tossed on top of the liquid metal would melt. Then it was finally hot enough to add the other secrets: a handful of Cassia bark, a pod or two of milkweed, a blob of cobalt-blue-tinged glass, a pinch of Sulphur, and another pinch of white copper (that was only found in the 'bewitched burgrave of Elbogen', which some said had fallen from Heaven). Last of all, Julian took his knife and sliced the heel of his right hand until a stream of his own bright, red blood dripped into the molten steel. And only then did the smith allow the wondrous metal in the crucible to slowly cool, for three days over a smaller fire in an oven and then for four more days under the distant fire of the sun, before he would begin his real work on the metal that had transformed into Damascene steel.

First, the smith returned the crucible to the furnace. When the pot was white-hot, he would charge it with a flux of powdered charcoal to draw off the impurities. Julian left the little pot in the furnace to cure for three more hours after that and then removed it to skim off the slag (which he tossed back into the furnace as an offering to the fire). Then he poured the now-pure steel into molds that would become the ingots he would use to make his swords. The ingots were placed the oven where they would cool by being moved further and further from the flames over a period of a week.

When an ingot was finally cool to the smith's touch and ready to be worked, Julian heated the block again and then hammered it into a thinner block. The smith did this again and again until it was thin enough to his practiced eye, and then Julian scored the metal down its center with the blade of an axe (one that Julian, himself, had made many years before of the same Damascene steel), folded it over and hammered it thinner again, and then returned it to the fire. Julian hammered and folded the steel nineteen times (for the nineteen angels that the Quran (74:31) names the Guardians of the Fire) and then three more times (once for each member of the Christian Trinity).

Between the fire and the swordsmith's hammer, the sword slowly took its shape. And when the sword finally became as Julian had intended, the smith heated it once more, until the raw blade was red-hot, and then quenched the new sword in water that boiled as it stole the heat from the steel.

Julian would then grind the steel, then file it, and finally polish it. Then he would decorate the blade. Julian, himself, took each careful step the making of each of his swords. Just as he would never consider hiring another man to help him create a child, Julian fathered his own blades.

*

    The blade on which Julian de Boabdil worked today was one of a set of a dozen 'knives'. These were not proper weapons of war, noble and honorable in their design. These bastardized blades were meant to provide entertainment at a lord's dinner. Each blade was a flat, broad cleaver-like thing, a little less than a foot long, sharper than a thorn, with a triangular tip that curved into a single tine that might have been intended as a skewer to stick into that which the blade had cut.

    The swordsmith had come to the engraving of these sharp, cutting things. Three each were to be marked *superius*, three were to be marked *tenor*, three were to be marked *contratenor altus*, and three were to be marked *contratenor bassus*. On each blade, Julian inscribed five parallel horizontal lines upon which hung, like strange little birds on clotheslines, tiny diamonds with tails hanging down or sticking up to no apparent purpose or method. Beneath the five lines, and for some reason aligned with the little diamond 'birds', Julian engraved large, clear words in a language he did not know. The lord's man, who had brought him the instructions for the knives, told Julian that the language was Latin, the language of the nobles and of the Christian priests. On one side of the blade he was to carve a blessing, "Sit tres-in-unum sin tut benedicat nobis quod manducare" (the servant told Julian that it meant "May the three-in-one bless that which we are about to eat"). One the other side of the blade, he was to carve a benediction, "Nos gratias ago vos pro Deo vestro candor valemus" ("We give thanks to you God for your generosity"). At the tip of each knife and again close to the handle, Julian engraved the white lilies that signified the triumph of the Christian crowns of Aragon and Castile and the Reconquista (hidden amongst the leaves of the flowers was Julian's hallmark, 'el perrillo', the little puppy that proclaimed his workmanship to all who cared to look). The handles of the knives themselves were beautiful, delicate things of ivory and silver, carved and colored with more of the twining lilies. But Julian would not put those onto the tangs of the knives until the blades had been finished.

As he worked, Julian swore in the Spanish (he would not curse in Caló, the mix of Romani and Spanish that his mother spoke, out of respect to her) that his customers spoke, adding his anger to the blood and the songs that he had given and forged into the fine steel of each blade.

"¡Que te den por culo, pequeño pavo real!" (Fuck you in the ass, little peacock!), the smith murmured as he pared a thin groove around one of the tiny diamonds.

"¡Me cago en tu puta madre!" (I shit on your bitch of a mother!), Julian added as he filed the steel smooth and then held the finished blade up to the sun to see its bright rays reflected from the shining surface of the knife.

*

The expulsion of the Jews had allowed Julian to purchase the little smithy he worked in from the Jew whose family had owned it for over two hundred years. The Jew had had a choice: he could take

Julian's nearly insulting offer for his family's home and leave overnight or be executed as soon as the King's men found him. That had been ten years ago, and a year after the Jews had left, the Archbishop de Talavera instituted the 'Alhambra' decree, which forced the Muslims in Granada to convert or be expelled; it would not be long, the smith thought, before the rest of Spain, as well, would be forbidden to the Moors. But the smith had a Christian mother (Romani though she was), a Christian given name, and a place in the Guild of Swordsmiths as a Master-craftsman (and the patronage of many important Christian nobles and warriors), so he would, he thought, be safe from the hatred and stupidity and fear that would doom others.

*

Julian de Boabdil's smithy was located near La Santa Iglesia Catedral Primada de Toledo, a holy Christian place of worship that had been built on the ruins of a once-holy mosque that lay in what had once been the heart of La Juderia (the Jewish Quarter).

But as intent as the Christians seemed to be upon eliminating the Jews and the Moors from the whole of the Iberian peninsula, the buildings that the Jews and Moors had built in the ancient city of Toledo were as impossible to ignore as they were impossible to completely eradicate.

The Moorish town walls still held the city in their embrace, even more protectively that the arms of the Rio Tagus that cradled the city to the east, the south, and the west. The main gate to the city,

La Puerta Vieja de Bisgara, had been constructed by the Moors nearly six hundred years before (a century or so after Tariq bin Ziyad and his armies decorated the even older walls of the city with the heads of the Visigoths who had ruled Toledo before them). More recently-built was el Puente de Alcántara, the bridge that allowed entry into the city across the gorge of the Rio Tagus to the southeast, and high above the river, watching the bridge, was the Castillo de San Servando, once a Roman town hall, then a Christian monastery, and then a fortress of the Knights Templars, built in the style of the Moors who had once threatened it. On the highest hill of the city stood the Alcázar, originally a Roman palace, then a Moorish fortress, and finally a Christian stronghold. Even what was left of the Jews in Toledo owed a debt to the Moors. La Sinagoga del Tránsito had dominated the Juderia from the day it had been constructed, over a century before, with its elaborate Islamic decoration that covered the brick, tile, wood, and plaster of its decidedly non-Moorish design. Once the Jews had been expelled, La Sinagoga was given to the knightly Order of Calatrava, who no doubt, were inspired by the magnificent stained-glass windows of its sanctuary.

  Julian and his family had lived across the Rio Tagus, an hour's walk from El Puente de Alcántara, since his grandfather had moved north from Granada in the days when Mohammed ibn Nasr had established the Emirate of Granada almost three hundred years ago. He brought with him a wife, a son, and a knowledge of making edged weapons and armor that was rarely found outside the Levant. His grandfather's son had married a Romani woman and had fathered his own son, to whom he taught everything he knew of steel and fire.

When the Jews were expelled in 1492, Julian was old enough to make his own way and saw an opportunity too good to pass by. He had become friends with a remarkable Jew, Shmuel HaNagid, a swordsmith whose family had lived in Toledo for a thousand years. This wise Jew believed, first of all, that "They shall beat their plowshares into swords..." and in the wisdom found in the first Book of the Ketuvim (the one that the Christians called 'Psalms'), "Gird your sword upon your thigh, O hero, in your splendor and glory." Julian offered Shmuel all of the money he had saved (which was not nearly what the forge was worth and which would have been laughable if Shmuel had not been fleeing for his life) and an ingot of the wootz steel he had kept, and his friend gave him the signed deed to the little forge that lay so deep in the twisting, narrow streets of the Jewish Quarter that even Julian, who had visited his friend every week for over five years, sometimes lost his way. The two men shook hands, and Shmuel and his family left that night, disguised as Christian pilgrims, taking a little trail that goats might have used to reach the grazing fields at the southernmost part of the city, outside the walls, there to board a boat on the Rio Tagus that would take them to Portugal and then onto one of Pedro Álvares Cabral's ships, heading to somewhere called Porto Seguro in a land called Brasil.

That had been ten years ago.

*

There was a knock at the door of his home, and Julian called for his apprentice to answer it. The swordsmith was not dressed to receive visitors. He was working. Julian wore his faded trousers and a leather apron to shield himself from the sparks of the forge. He owned a shirt and a jerkin, but those he saved for wearing out of the house. For meeting with the nobles, a plain tunic, hose, soft leather shoes, and his father's felt hat, which looked entirely too Moorish for this new land of Aragon-Castile, he kept in the trunk at the foot of his bed. This visitor would have to be content with Julian as he was.

When the little mincing servant of Hidalgo de Sangre, Don Lazarillo (a noble with too much money, an ardent desire to impress the Duke of Alba de Tormes, but nothing else to commend him) had come to the smithy to order the knives, Julian was polite but reserved. This popinjay wanted a Master Swordsmith to forge utensils for dining and entertainment, not honest weapons. Julian looked at the little man and thought about tossing the man out into the street, but in those difficult days, when a man whose mother was Romani and whose father was a Moor could be ground under the heel of an effete minor noble with no more thought as if the noble had been killing an inconvenient insect, sometimes it was better to bow than to be broken. The price that had been offered for the work was more than Julian had earned all month. And the servant assured Julian that his fame in making these 'wondrous' objects would become well-known among the best people. Julian reluctantly took the parchment with the specifications for the blades, agreed to the offered amount of gold and consideration, and told the little man to return in a month.

*

It had been a month.

*

The apprentice came to the doorway of the little house, as it opened into the yard and Julian's forge, and announced the servant. The man was attired in black and white, the black to show his master's wealth, with silver rings mounted with large pearls ringed with tiny, flashing diamonds on most of his fingers (visible to anyone who wished to see thanks to the fingers of his black linen gloves having been cut off especially for that purpose), and delicate, diamond earrings that flashed with the reflected fires of the forge hanging from his earlobes. The man wore a white linen shirt with frilled, white linen ruffs, starched stiff and bright, at his neck and his wrists. Over his shirt, the man wore a black velvet doublet, laced in place with black, silken cords, and over that, a black, leather, sleeveless jerkin. He wore a black leather baldrick diagonally across his chest but no proper weapon other than a stiletto at his waist. Black hose and black riding boots (he had obviously ridden to the smithy) covered his legs and feet, and a shining, black codpiece covered … well … the rest. He wore a black velvet cape, embroidered with silver in intricate designs that might have been flowers, draped over his shoulders. His black hair was cut short under a soft, black velvet hat with a gathered crown. He sported a thin, very fashionable 'Goat Beard with Peaks' (a finely-groomed mustache with sharply-pointed tips), its effect marred by a carelessly-left smudge of starch, that had been applied to it to keep it in place, at the corner of his mouth.

The delicate and ornamental servant bowed and requested the knives.

Julian, as he had been led to expect, requested his payment.

The servant affected a posture of irritation and explained, as to a child, that the smith's earnings would be delivered as soon as Don Lazarillo, his Master, had approved the knives as being of sufficient quality for his Master's purposes. The little blackbird seemed affronted that he would have to pay for the work that had been done; perhaps the little man simply believed that the gold that he would have to pay would soil his gloves.

"When can I expect payment, then?" Julian asked.

The servant replied, "I am sure that my Master will have time to look at these entertainments within a fortnight. Do you really want to offend my Lord?"

Julian shook his head, more to himself than something that the servant would be able to see (and disparage), and said, "Two weeks, then. Your master will pay me what he owes me by then. You will give me his word."

"Give you his word?" the servant squeaked, "I would think that someone of your rank would be happy to give my Master what you owe him."

"What I owe him?" the smith's anger began to build in him as if it were a fire and his honor were kindling. He balled his fists to keep his voice steady.

"Of course, good sir," the man in black said, as he began to feel the smith's exasperation.

The smith wanted no more trouble than he already had, and so he said, as softly and as calmly as he could manage, "Very well. Two weeks."

And Julian walked slowly into his house and brought out the dozen knives, each wrapped in a sheath of sky-blue Alpurrajas silk, sent to him from the hidden valleys in the Sierra Nevada where many of the Spanish Moors, who had feared the worst after the Castilians had taken Grenada in 1492, had fled. Julian had many relatives, on his grandfather's side, who now hid in the northwestern mountains of Iberia, and since they would need good swords if they were ever discovered, he had traded some of his blades to them for bolts of their precious silk.

He instructed his apprentice to assist the servant in securing the bundles of silk and steel to the saddle of the minion's mare. Once all of the bundles were tied tightly on, the servant climbed into his saddle, doffed his cap and replaced it on his head, bid the swordsmith "Adios", and put his spurs to the beast, easing into a comfortable canter before he was lost to sight at the first turn of the stone-walled street.

Julian de Boabdil, Master Sword-maker of the Guild Swordsmiths of Toledo watched the work of a month ride off with only the words of a weak, self-indulgent menial who served a member of the lower, immemorial nobility to show for his industry. Well, he would be paid in a fortnight, or he would know why not. His reputation within the Guild and throughout the city would stand him in good stead and the supremacy of his work and the excellence of his craft would be apparent to even the most jaded observers. He would receive his due.

Julian de Boabdil raised his hand in belated farewell. "¡Que te folle un pez, puta!" (I hope you get fucked by a fish, bitch!), he thought before he turned and walked back into his smithy, his work finished for the day.

Chapter 2 – The Dungeon

One of the Major Arcana of the Suit of Knives in the Swordsmith's Tarot is The Dungeon. This card is ruled by Mars, planet of Blood, abode of the God of War. The Dungeon signifies darkness and physical destruction. Through the small, barred windows of The Dungeon, a prisoner can barely see a gray sky filled with clouds of misfortune that promises a rain of despair. Seldom is the sky illuminated by a lightning bolt, a momentary glimpse of the truth that merely shows the desperate captives that there is no hope of salvation, only false promises.

*

Julian de Boabdil had spent the two weeks after his knives had been collected by the little black-garbed toady of Don Lazarillo, diligently creating two fine espadas roperas for a nobleman who knew how to use them, an expert in the old tradition of esgrima vulgar. In these swords, the swordsmith had created masterpieces of swooping, sinuous steel as hilts for the thrusting blades, foregoing a thick, fat pommel, simply allowing the swirling steel to marry the blades to their hilts in what was obviously a nest of serpents, ready to bite the swordsman's prey.

The rapiers and their sumptuously-decorated bucklers were almost finished. Julian decided to let the steel rest for a day while he attended to other business, that of collecting his payment for the knives that he had spent a month crafting.

Unfortunately, this business had become personal, and the swordsmith could not send his apprentice to simply collect what was owed him. He must make the journey to the house of the Don himself. As if he were some bored little lordling with nothing to do.

*

Julian de Boabdil was a master craftsman, a swordsmith (or, if the price and challenge were right, a bladesmith). He made swords and edged weapons that were works of the art of his craft. He was a man of means and some wealth. He owned his home and the forge that provided him his living.

He owned a forgeful of crucibles, a wooden bucket, a bellows, a leather apron, an anvil, an axe, hammers, tongs, large piles of wood, charcoal, coal, a hidden cache of wootz steel, and several small leather pouches filled with Cassia bark, milkweed pods, borax crystals, cobalt glass, powdered Sulphur, and tiny nodules of white copper.

He owned a bed, two woolen blankets that his mother had given him, a trunk where he kept the clothes that he wasn't wearing, a wooden table, a wooden chair, a wooden plate, a wooden bowl, two wooden spoons, three or four knives that he had made himself, a good cleaver, a mallet, a tin kettle, a cast-iron skillet, a three-legged earthenware pot, an iron spit in the hearth, a leather bucket, a mortar and a pestle, a wooden tub, a box full of scouring sand, a two-sided comb made of horn (one side, with its teeth close together, to rid his hair of lice, and the other side, with its teeth farther apart, to make his appearance acceptable), a Roman coin that his mother had given him, a small, now-rounded piece of jet that he had discovered as a boy and had kept in his pocket ever since (for good fortune), and a strange, white, stone seashell he had found in the sierra west of Alicante (the people of the area had told him the mountain was called Mont San Julián, a favorable omen, he thought).

Julian de Boabdil owned a pair of pants (well, two pair, but one had so many holes that even he was embarrassed to be seen in that one). He had a shirt and a jerkin but saved them for wearing out of the house when he had to go to the market. When the Guild met or if he had to meet with a noble client, he owned a plain tunic (in which he had sewn a pocket for his "pocket deities"), hose, a cape, a felted cap for when it was cold and a straw hat for when it was sunny and hot, but those he kept in the trunk at the foot of his bed. He owned a pair of goatskin shoes that tied with leather laces and a pair of knee-high, calfskin boots for bad weather. He had a belt and a leather purse to carry whatever he might need.

He had everything a man could, or so he thought.

*

But if Julian de Boabdil were to keep what he owned, he would have to be paid for his labor.

So, he stuck his head in the water trough where he quenched the red-hot steel of the swords he made. He ran his comb through his hair just to tame its wildness. Then he pulled on his hose, his best shirt, his jerkin, and his leather boots. He fastened his belt around his waist. He pulled his cape from the trunk, shook it out, and put it on his shoulders, tying it at his throat with its silken cord.

His Romani mother, as did all of her people, believed in the power and beneficence of amulets and talismans, just as she believed in the power of curses and the works of the devil. So, to protect himself from evil and to marshal his own personal power to bring himself success, he put the little jet stone and the white stone shell into the pocket of his jerkin.

The other objects that the Romani put their faith and their trust in, as another kind of 'pocket deity', were knives. As they were carried close to a person, they became imbued with the essence of the person who carried them.

So Julian added his little navaja to the other little gods in his pocket. The navaja was a straight razor whose blade folded into its handle. Julian had added his expertise to the little knife that los majos (the 'gentlemen of the lower classes': artisans, sailors, and teamsters), as well as gamblers, rogues, and ruffians, carried at all times as a tool for work or for self-defense. The swordsmith's navaja utilized a little blade of metal to hold it open and closed up tight again when a lever on the handle was pressed. It was small enough to hide in the craftsman's hidden pocket and sharp enough to make itself useful when it was taken from the pocket.

*

Julian de Boabdil shouted to his apprentice, Gunari, that he was leaving and to bolt the door behind him, and then he walked out into the little alley that, after a twist and a turn, opened onto the Travesia Juderia. He walked south, more or less (even the passageways that were broad enough to be thought of as streets were snaky things in La Juderia) until he came to Calle San Juan De Dios. He followed that larger street through a maze of Calles Alfonsos (named after Alfonsos who were Just, or Wise, or Noble), two Calles Ferdinands (named after one who was a Saint and another who was simply Great), and even a few Calles Henrys (named after a Henry who was Impotent, a Henry who was Infirm, and a Henry who was a Bastard). Eventually, Julian saw the Alcazar ahead of him and knew that he was almost to the home of the Hidalgo de Sangre, Don Lazarillo.

He passed the Bab Al Mardum, one of the gates that the Moors had built into the city walls. And just when Julian began to think that he had become lost in the twisting streets, he looked up and saw the Puerta Bisagra and then the Puerta de Alfosno Seis, and he knew that he was close to Don Lazarillo's home, La Cigarral (which the Don's ancestors had built many years before when they had decided that they needed a villa, complete with gardens and a field for their horses, within the city walls of Toledo), on Calle de la Posada do Peregrinos (The Street of the Pilgrims' Inn).

*

The swordsmith walked up the little street to the wooden door. It was made of stout Spanish oak bound with iron. A small cross-shaped balistraria allowed the Don's men to defend the door with a crossbow or see a man who requested admittance.

Julian announced himself, "Julian de Boabdil, Master Swordsmith and Guild Member, begs the forbearance of Don Lazarillo, Hidalgo de Sangre, to hear my petition regarding the matter of a set of knives, commissioned, forged, and delivered."

Some minutes passed, and the thick, heavy door creaked open. A large man, wearing a fine, shining breastplate and helmet, leather shoes, dark hose, a striped linen shirt, greaves on his arms, and a domed, cabasset steel helmet now blocked the way.

The soldier looked the swordsmith up and down, and after deciding that Julian was no threat at all, motioned for him to enter. The soldier closed the door, slid a cross-bar into place, and then motioned for Julian to follow.

The two men passed the stables, two large ovens baking fresh loaves of bread that set Julian's mouth to watering, and four soldiers practicing their skills with lances. As the soldier and the swordsmith came nearer to the main house, the soldier led Julian through beautiful, lush gardens, where peacocks walked on paths made of crushed rock that sparkled in the sun.

When they reached the main house, the soldier motioned for Julian to wait. The soldier knocked on a door, and when it opened, said something to a house servant dressed in the same manner as the popinjay who had collected the swordsmith's knives a month before. This servant motioned for Julian to follow him and led the smith into a large empty room of marble floors, marble columns, and a wooden ceiling high above that was painted with angels and all of the residents of Heaven.

"Wait here," the man told him.

Julian de Boabdil nodded, and the man left him alone in the big, empty room. Julian watched the sun move across the sky through the big windows that were set high up in the walls. After the light began to dim in the indeterminate time between afternoon and evening, the servant returned and said, "Follow me," to Julian as if the craftsman were a spavined mule, worth only a beating.

The servant led the swordsmith into a small room that was paneled with dark wood. Don Lazarillo stood next to a marble bust of someone wearing a crown of leaves on his head. The nobleman turned to Julian and waited.

Julian knelt on one knee and bowed his head in respectful greeting (and remained silent until the Lord deigned to speak).

"You wish to speak to me, tradesman?" the finely-dressed man said in a voice as soft as the silk that caressed his throat.

"Yes, Don Lazarillo," the swordsmith whispered in reply.

"Well ..." the man said, waiting.

"Six weeks ago, my Lord," Julian began, "Your servant asked me to create a special set of knives for your entertainment and pleasure. I received your written specifications for the knives and created a unique set of blades, unmatched in quality and fit for any noble occasion. Two weeks ago, your man came to my forge to retrieve them and deliver them to you. When he took them, he said that you would pay me the price that you offered when you ordered them when you had determined that they were acceptable. Since that day, I have heard nothing as to whether they were deemed acceptable and my earnings would be paid or whether they were unsuitable and my work would be returned to me. I have not been paid for my work, and as a Master of the Guild of Swordsmiths of Toledo, I have come to ask for the gold that I had been promised for my work."

Julian finished speaking and stood silently, respectfully waiting for the Don to answer.

The nobleman turned and walked away from Julian, and just as he reached a door on the far wall that had been opened by a servant, he said, barely loudly enough for Julian to hear, "Go home, my good man. You shall receive your payment before the night is out."

*

It was well past midnight when the swordsmith knocked on the door of his house in La Juderia. His apprentice, roused from sleep, softly asked who was at the door, and when the smith said, "It's only me, 'Nari," it took the boy only a minute or so to put his sleepy thoughts together enough to unbar and open the door.

"Thank you," Julian told the boy and tousled his hair, "Go back to bed. We have an early morning tomorrow."

Then, the finest bladesmith in Iberia looked in his kitchen to find the bottle of orujo he kept for special occasions. As a consideration of his work on an especially fine set of rapiers for a gentleman of Cantabria, Julian had received this bottle of pomace brandy in addition to a full pouch of gold. The gold had been spent years ago, but most of the brandy (distilled from the remains of grapes after they had been pressed) … he knew it as aguardiente … was still here. It was called 'firewater' for a reason, Julian remembered as he took a sip straight from the bottle.

Julian de Boabdil walked to the hearth, tossed another log onto the fire, and then returned to the little table where he sat, bottle in hand, staring off into space and trying to decide how to solve his problem.

He could appeal to the Guild of Swordsmiths. When a man proved that he was a craftsman skillful enough to join the other masters of his craft, he swore binding oaths to support the other Guildsmen in adversity and to back one another in cold-blooded business ventures as well as in hot-blooded feuds. Julian could probably convince the other members of the Guild to forbid its members from doing any business with Don Lazarillo; this kind of pressure would, perhaps, eventually force the little nobleman to pay Julian what was owed to him.

Or he could ask Lord of Casarrubios, Lord of Orso, Justicia Mayor y Alguacil Mayor of Castile, and Mayor of Toledo, Enrique Enríquez, to enact the duties of justice that he had inherited.

Or he could appeal to the Archbishop of Toldeo Jiménez de Cisneros. After all, if the holy man could reform the Franciscans, forcing them to actually become celibate, forego their concubines, attend confession, and preach on every Sabbath and Holy Day, getting Julian's money from Don Lazarillo would be as easy for the holy man as drawing breath.

Or he could travel to Flanders and plead his case before Philip the Handsome and his mad Queen Joanna. Julian laughed so hard at that that the wine he was drinking squirted out of his nose.

No. The best thing would be to walk again to the home of the Don and again politely request payment for the debt that was owed to him. If Julian became a bothersome little flea, the nobleman would pay (even if it would only be to be rid of him).

*

Julian had dozed off, but his eyes struggled open in a bleary awakening when heard a crash. The front door to his little home stood open, and a large man was rushing toward him. As he tried, woozily, to stand up, damn the brandy, the man swung a club at his head, and Julian knew nothing more.

*

When the swordsmith opened his eyes again, the world had turned on him. From his experience with drunkenness, Julian understood that he was lying on the floor, and the blinding headache that accompanied this view of the world was evidence that he was paying for the drink of the night before.

He moaned his discomfort and tried to push himself up so that he could get to his feet and his bed. But his hands and feet would not move but a little, and Julian realized that he was trussed like a hog for market. He was able to move his head, so he looked around his room. It was still dark, but he could see two or three big men, rifling through his trunk, and a small, still form on the floor near him, covered in something wet and darker than the night.

A deep voice said softly, gruffly, but with a note of sympathy, "Go back to sleep, you poor bastard. Morning will greet you soon enough."

Julian's bleary vision saw a boot moving toward his head, and then he knew nothing again.

*

Julian de Boabdil, Master Swordsmith of the Swordsmith's Guild of Toldeo, awoke sitting on a cold stone floor in near-darkness. He tried to stand and found that he was shackled, hand and foot, and that his chains were only long enough to allow him to sit up, leaning against a wall, or if he contorted himself sufficiently, to crouch uncomfortably like a frog.

He shouted, and sometime later, a door opened across the little room.

It was one of the men who had broken into his home and killed his apprentice, Gunari (his Romani parents named him a warrior, but he fell at the first assault), holding a torch. He turned and yelled, "He's awake."

Then the man walked back through the door and closed it behind him, and the darkness enveloped Julian again.

Another time later, the door opened again, and the man with the torch entered the room again, but this time accompanied by Don Lazarillo himself and three others, obviously the men who had brought Julian from his home to this place.

"Can you smell it?" The Don asked.

"Smell what?" the prisoner replied.

The nobleman closed his eyes and lifted his chin. Then he breathed deeply in, savoring some faint scent that brought a thin smile to his thin lips. "Your forge is afire," he said, as if he were commenting on the flavor of an especially ancient and unexpected wine, "The members of your guild have been trying to put out the flames ever since they discovered the conflagration, just before dawn. By now, the flames have spread to the stable next door to your home, and to the bakery beyond that, and to the little warren of rooms across the alley that the poor rent as they can and the patrons of the whores rent by the hour. But alas, they will be too late to save anything. My men took your gold and all of your finished work. Your boy tried to stop them, but all he had were his fists, and they are men of violence, skill, and knives. The child fell to the floor as full of steel as a lady's pincushion. My men brought me you, a fine collection of rapiers and sabers, and even curved sword of Moorish design. These weapons will be fine additions to my arms. I told the men that they could keep whatever else that they liked."

A glimmer of hope flashed in Julian's mind, "The Guildsmen will find 'Nari's body, and they will search for me."

And just as that smallest flower of hope bloomed, the Don laughed, and it withered, "A mad Moor murders his little plaything and then tries to hide what he has done with fire. I am sure that there is a boatman on the Rio Tagus who will remember that he took a large Moor, one with crazed eyes and liquor on his breath, down the river in the night, at just about the time that the fire was spreading to the houses and stables and shops that bordered your smithy."

Don Lazarillo paused and then added, "You will be gone … like a thief and a murderer in the night."

It took Julian a minute to calm the raging fire inside him enough to ask, "What about my pay? Is all of this simply because you wanted my knives but didn't want to pay for the work of an honest craftsman? You are the thief! And you are the murderer!"

"I am no murderer, swordsmith. My hands are clean. And I am no thief. You were told that you would receive payment when I had approved your work. And I have not yet determined the worth of what you have made." Any trace of a smile suddenly vanished from Don Lazarillo's face, and his voice grew terribly calm and intimately soft, its intent making his words as unmistakable as a shout, "So let us see the quality of your work."

The Don snapped his fingers. One of his men ran out of the door and returned after some time had passed. He was carrying one of the silk wrappers that Julian, himself, had sewn to wrap his knives.

Don Lazarillo took the cloth from the man and slid the notated blade out of its covering. The fine steel gleamed in the torchlight of the little stone room. The nobleman held the knife by its ivory hilt and ran the index finger of his other hand along the blade.

He read aloud the words that Julian had engraved on the knife's wide blade, "Nos gratias ago vos pro Deo vestro candor valemus" and then said, almost to himself, "Yes, God's supreme generosity has given me a set of blades, the like of which exists nowhere else in the world, and provided the delicious opportunity to test them as a good knife should be tested, on living flesh rather than on cooked meat."

He ran his thumb down the blade and started when the sharp steel drew his blood. He looked at the wound, stuck his thumb into his mouth and sucked at his own blood, and then he laughed.

"An entertainment, my fellows! Let us celebrate God's generosity with pleasurable activities, good fellowship, and strong drink. Pepe, bring wine for me and ale for my fellows. Arturo, run to the kitchens and bring us a fresh loaf of bread, a haunch of roasted meat, a round of good cheese, and a tub of sweet, yellow butter. Go, now! We will await your swift return."

Pepe nodded to another of the men to help him, and Arturo did the same, and then the four men ran out of the room to do their

Don's bidding, and the Hidalgo de Sangre walked to the room's single stool and sat down to wait.

Julian looked around the little room. There were no windows. There was one door. There were great and small wooden barrels that could have contained almost anything. A small brazier in a corner radiated heat from what the swordsmith now saw were red-hot coals. On the wall where he was chained, to either side of him, were other chains and shackles. The floor Julian sat on was cold, and he could see drops of condensation on the stone walls. He was somewhere underground, probably beneath the villa.

If anyone heard a sound from this room, he or she would ignore it. These sounds had probably been heard before.

*

Sometime later, the four men returned with food and drink.

"Pepe," the Don said with a cheerful manner, "Pour me a glass of my wine, and fill your glass and the others' with my ale. Arturo, put the food onto the top of a barrel, and make me bread, butter, meat, and cheese, one atop the other. All of this preparation has made me hungry. You men, when I have been served, you may eat, as well."

And then he added, seemingly as an afterthought, "The smith will require neither food nor drink. It would only be a waste."

*

The nobleman's appetite was great but was soon sated. He finished the food and then gulped his wine until the glass was empty. He called on Pepe to fill his glass again.

And then, he said, "Sebastian, roll that barrel over here," and pointed to a spot in the middle of the floor, "Bring the smith and put him over the barrel. When he is ready, we shall test his work."

Sebastian's brain was not the strongest part of his body. "Señor?" he asked.

Don Lazarillo shook his head, stood, and walked over to Sebastian. He slapped the man softly on the cheek and said, "We shall flay him."

Chapter 3 – The Ace of Knives

The first card of the Minor Arcana of the Suit of Knives in the Swordsmith's Tarot is the Ace of Knives. This card reaches out to accept, as an offering to it, a life that is growing and developing and one that may yet come into its fullest flower. It may take promises and dreams that are still yet to be and leave them unfulfilled and spoiled, or it may warn, through painful and scarring intervention, that passion and enthusiasm are the poor step-children of preparation, imagination, and practice. A spark of fire or creation has the potential to become a raging, uncontrollable conflagration or the gentle flames that live in a warming, nurturing hearth.

*

The swordsmith was chained to the wall, but even constrained by iron shackles and their linked attendants, he was a powerful man. Sebastian walked over to the big, fettered Moor and kicked him in the side of the head. Julian slumped into unconsciousness.

When Julian awoke, it was in pain. The Don's minions had laid the swordsmith over a big barrel, his chest toward the ceiling, his head hanging down, and his feet pulled so that his body was bowed, and tightened the chains that held his shackles until he could not move either his hands or his feet on his own.

"Bastards!" Julian de Boabdil yelled.

Don Lazarillo walked leisurely over to the smith, looked down into his face, smiled, and said, as casually and warmly as if he were greeting an old friend, "Oh, you shall soon sing far more sweetly than that, Swordsmith."

Julian let his head fall back and closed his eyes.

Only a few seconds later, he heard the ring of metal on metal and opened his eyes at the familiar sound.

Even though his perspective had been overturned, he recognized, in the far corner, a brazier glowing red-hot, upon which sat a kettle, spewing steam as if it were a tiny metal volcano.

"Ah," the nobleman said, "you see our intent. We will offer your suffering to our beloved Saint Bartholomew. Since you are a merely a peon who toils for his daily bread, we will only flay you as our Saint was flayed but not elevate you even to the foot of his cross by crucifying you as he had been. But fear not. I will send your skin to the tanners, those who revere our San Bartolomé and whose patron he is, for them to craft cases for the knives that you made for me. Well … that is, if the knives are acceptable."

"Sebastian," he continued, "take your sword and cut off the smith's clothing. He will not be needing it. But save the cloth; we will use it, I think, to assist us in our labors."

Sebastian began at the smith's feet, pulling off his boots, inserting his knife under the cuffs of Julian's pants at the ankles and sliding the blade up the smith's legs, the fabric parting at the touch of the sharp steel. He did this, first, for Julian's left leg and then for his right. Once the cloth had been sliced, the Don's manservant pulled the cloth away, revealing Julian's pale linen breeks.

"Ah," Don Lazarillo fairly crowed, "Stay your hand, Sebastian. I will attempt to find the jewels that are hidden here." And Julian heard the whisk of a dagger leaving its sheath. Then he felt cold steel on his thigh. A tiny touch of pain moved up his leg, the sound of thin cloth being rent lasted for the briefest thought, and then the nobleman triumphantly brayed, "I have found the dear, little things. Sebastian, hand me one of the smith's knives to aid us in our service."

Julian inhaled in fear and held his breath.

Julian felt the Don slowly slip the flat of one his own blades under his flaccid manhood. "Who would have thought that such a large goat would have such a small horn? It is scarcely enough to allow him to rut with any of our does. We shall leave it where it lies … for now."

And Julian felt the cold metal slip from beneath his penis.

"Sabastian! Back to work! We do not have all day. I am hosting a dinner tonight, and all of my friends will be attending. His tunic and shirt, if you please," the nobleman ordered brusquely.

Sebastian was quick with his work, and soon the smith was naked on the barrel, stretched, and ready for the Don's pleasure.

"Sancho," he ordered, "bring the kettle. Alfonso, bring another of the smith's knives. Ferdinand, the tongs."

Julian heard a rush of activity and opened his eyes, despite himself, to look.

"Alfonso, lay the knife here. Now, you and Sebastian, place the smith's trousers under his head and lift it up. I do not want him to drown."

Julian felt the linen from his shredded trousers at the back of his head, and then, as the cloth was pulled up and despite anything he could do to prevent it, he felt his head being raised so that his chin touched the top of his chest.

"There," the Don said, approvingly, "Now we are ready. Smith, I would suggest that you close your eyes. The boiling water will loosen the skin from your muscles and bone and make it easier to remove, but the water could blind you or sear your lungs if you breathe it in."

Julian saw a small, rat-faced man, who he now understood was Sancho, bring a steaming kettle from the brazier over to where the smith lay chained over the barrel.

"My Lord?" Sancho asked.

The nobleman smiled and nodded. "You may begin," he said.

Julian screwed his eyes shut as tightly as he could and held his breath. The boiling water fell on the tip of his nose, first, and then Sancho moved the kettle's spout all over Julian's face, sparing no skin from the torrent.

As the pain worsened and the water continued to pour over his lips, and nose, and cheeks, and chin, and eyelids, and forehead, and dripped down over his ears, his neck, and the top of his head, Julian heard Don Lazarillo say, "Ferdinand, another kettle, if you please."

And more water poured over his head. The fire on his skin was almost as intolerable as the fire in his lungs as he held his breath. And when Julian could hold the air in his lungs no more, he exhaled and sought to take another breath, but as he did, the second kettle of water scalded him, the water burning his nostrils, his mouth, and down his throat. Julian screamed in pain and received more searing water in his mouth for his pain.

"Good, gentlemen, good," Lazarillo purred, "The preparation is sufficient. I think we can now begin. Ferdinand, bring your tongs. We shall need them after I have made the first cuts."

"Sancho, Alfonso, hold his head," the hidalgo added.

Julian felt two pairs of strong hands grab the sides of his head, and then, a line of pain began at his left temple, moved across his forehead just above his eyebrows, slid to his right temple, and sliced down, around the top of his right ear ("Pull his head up so I can free the skin on the back of his skull," someone said), behind his head, just above where his spine met the base of his skull, and then around to his left ear and back to his temple.

"Smith, my compliments! This knife is as sharp as a lover's farewell and as finely crafted. You should be proud of your work!

Now, carefully, Ferdinand, or I will take the skin from your back, peel this first raw leather from his head. Take care! We need the pieces to be as large as possible if the cases for the smith's knives are to be well-bound in the smith's own leather. Here, I will pry up the skin of his brow to give you a starting place."

Julian felt the blade of his own knife push into where his skin had been cut, sliding between his skin and the bone beneath.

And the smith's knives knew the blood of their maker, the blood he had taken from himself to place inside them. They also remembered the soft echoes of the songs that the smith had sung to them in their making and took those echoes and added them in a quiet harmony to the notes that had been inscribed on their blades in a new coronach for their maker.

The terrible rip of his skin as it pulled away from, first, his forehead, and then as the tongs were moved to pull at his temples, above his ears, and back at the nape of his neck, seemed, strangely, something apart from Julian's understanding. The pain was excruciating, but from deep within him, he heard his mother's song and his father's adhan and the pain became a low harmony to the melody of his parents' music. And just at the edge of his consciousness, Julian heard another song, the singing of his knives, giving the peace of their music to him.

Suddenly, with one final tear, the skin of the top of Julian's head gave up its purchase and came free.

"Bravo, Ferdinand! Bravo!" the Don exulted, "A fine piece of leather this will make!" And through his pain, Julian heard the unmistakable sound of a coin ringing on the stone floor of the underground room. "A silver for your fine work, Fernando!"

Julian kept his eyes shut as tightly as he could. They hurt. The boiling water must have damaged them, but Julian did not want to open them and discover that he was blind. Perhaps, he would still have some of his sight if he let his eyes rest.

"Gentlemen," Lazarillo said, "Now for his nose, lips, chin, and cheeks. But I think his skin needs more softening. More water. We can wait for it to boil."

And over the next hours or years (Julian was not sure), the Don and his henchmen loosened the smith's skin with the boiling water and then flayed the skin from his face and neck.

"A good afternoon's work, my good, strong ones. There is not an inch of skin left above his shoulders," Lazarillo finally said, "Sebastian, pour me another glass of wine while I examine the skins we have taken."

Beside the nobleman's words, Julian heard a slow dripping of something, thick and liquid, onto the floor of the dungeon. He realized, almost as an afterthought, that it was the sound of his blood, pooling on the stones. His face felt cool and the pain was somehow less. He was dizzy and wanted to throw up. Somehow, his body was buffeted with waves of freezing cold and then boiling heat. His thoughts were confused, He felt an overwhelming desire to sleep. And so he did. And as he lapsed into unconsciousness, the blood that dripped onto the floor slowly ceased while his breathing became as rapid as his heartbeat.

Don Lazarillo finished his wine and looked at the man's body with the bloody head, hard, white bone, and soft, white tissue showing where muscles, tendons, and ligaments had parted and given up their hold on the skin that had once concealed them. "My guests will be arriving in an hour or so. Now, I must dress to receive them. We will continue tomorrow, my friends. Be here after you break your fasts in the morning. Enjoy yourselves tonight, but don't be too hungover to work tomorrow, or our friend here will have company. Adios"

And the nobleman and his lackeys left the room and closed the door.

And sometime after his tormenters had left him there, Julian de Boabdil, Master of the Guild of Swordsmiths of Toledo quietly died, alone in the dark.

*

Don Lazarillo, Hidalgo de Sangre, stood still in his chambers as his Master of the Wardrobe directed two pages in his dressing. The guests would be arriving within the hour, but the Don would make his entrance after all of those he had invited had been made to wait. Don Lazarillo had instructed his Steward and his Butler that the knives he had used in the little room were to be left as they were, not washed clean, and used to serve the evening's meat to the Don before they would be employed in the planned entertainments.

*

Don Lazarillo had two sons, Juan, named for the Juan who had founded the House of Trastámara, a hundred years before, and Maximillian, named for the Holy Roman Emperor who reigned at the time of the boy's birth. Don Lazarillo's wife had died giving birth to a scrawny little thing of a girl who had followed her mother into the arms of the Virgin and hour after she had taken her first breath. The two were buried together in the same coffin and interred in the Lazarillo crypt in the lowest basement beneath the altar under the quiet arches and paired columns of the Mudéjar mosque upon which Archbishop Ximenéz de Rada had built his Cathedral.

As the eldest son, Juan would inherit his father's titles and estates and be married to a woman of nobility and substance who would add to the power and wealth of the Lazarillo family. As the second son, Maximillian would honorably perform his familial duty by becoming Juan's seneschal or retainer and marrying a second-rate noble-woman

Since Don Lazarillo was only an Hidalgo, the lowest of the nobles (and not even a Señor - a knight – or a Caballero), the only title Maximillian could expect was what he might earn in the military, but the second son was far too ambitious for that. He briefly considered the priesthood, but since that bastard Archbishop Jiménez de Cisneros had discontinued the practice of the priests' concubines (and enforced celibacy, for God's sake!), the clerical life held no attraction for him. He was nowhere skilled enough or strong enough to become a house knight for a true nobleman, a mercenary (as romantic as that sounded at first blush, Maximillian knew that that path would lead to poor food, cheap wine, a lack of servants, pain, and death), or a Crusade (since the last one of those had been a dismal affair, called for by Innocent VIII again some heretics in the south of France nearly twenty years before, there was little chance of another). The only option left to Maximillian was to ensure that his older brother would die and graciously leave the Lazarillo lands and gold to him.

*

Don Lazarillo was well-known in Toledo for his sumptuous feasts, as much for the exquisite victuals and fine wines as for the entertainments that were as eclectic as they were unexpected. Members of the nobility, of the clergy, of the Guilds, and of the military were friends of the Hidalgo, and the mix of people who were invited to attend these evening amusements drew the participants like flies to honey.

Tonight was little different from other evenings. During the day, tradespeople and supplicants came to the little door where Julian de Boabdil had asked to be admitted, but at night, the finer folk, the nobles and the clerics and the admirals and the generals, were carried to the estate of Don Lazarillo in their black carriages pulled by matched pairs of superbly-bred Spanish horses and attended by liveried servants, nearly as well-dressed as their masters and mistresses, who rode inside the suspended chariot-branlants or the new 'Hungarian coaches' that had been brought to Aragon and Castile from the east by the nephew of Queen Beatrix, Ippolito d'Este of Ferrara. The carriages and coaches were of darkest ebony where they were not outrageously glided. The livery of the coachmen who drove these vehicles, of the footmen who attended the passengers, and of the outriders who accompanied the carriages shone and glittered in the torchlight almost as much blindingly as the coaches themselves.

And when the carriages and coaches rolled, slowly and decorously, up the long, winding drive to the entrance to the villa, they were met by Don Lazarillo's staff.

*

As the first guest began to alight from his coach, two riders galloped up the way, shouting and laughing and tossing something, that later proved to be a much-abused chicken, between them. As they reached the front steps that led up to the entrance of the villa, one of the riders, a dark, round young man with hair as black as night and piercing green eyes, tossed the unfortunate fowl to the Conte's coachman, who caught it, recognized what it was, and promptly tossed it into the gravel next to the coach. The ruffian laughed, sprang off of his horse, and ran up the steps. The other rider, who the villa's staff quickly recognized as Don Lazarillo's younger son, Maximillian, alighted just a step behind the first gamberro (hooligan) and gave chase, winning the race by pushing his companion to the side just as they reached the doormen who guarded the villa's entrance.

"Come, Pepito," Maximillian cried, "I need a drink, and I see that we are in time for supper," as he burst into the great home.

The doormen allowed the second young man, who they now recognized as Pepito el Corcovado, to ascend the steps to the great doors of Spanish oak that kept out those things that should be shunned and safeguarded those things that should be treasured. Maximillian had met Pepito at an afternoon tea for the young nobles of Toledo that had been arranged by one of the many generals, but many suspected that the gaming dens and whores across the Rio Tagus had cemented their friendship with low entertainments, base pleasures, and common enthusiasms.

"Wine! Wine!!" Maximillian yelled, "And none of the vinegar you proffer to these leeches who would suck my father's coffers as dry as their souls," as he clapped his friend on the back and led him into the grand home.

There would be delicious gossip aplenty before this night was through.

*

The Marshal who supervised the guards and armed men whose sole purpose in life was to safeguard the people and possessions of Don Lazarillo's house and estate, had served with distinction in the army of Ferdinand's Crown of Aragon at the siege of Granada, which he had joined as a foot soldier. But due to his intelligence and bravery during the siege, he rose in the ranks and was knighted for bravery for leading his men into the Alhambra on New Year's Day, 1491.

He left the army, but the nobles of the Court remembered his valor, and he was asked to join the Holy Brotherhood (La Santa Hermandad, whose charge was to "guard the sovereignty and service of the king and all the rights he ought to have and guard our bodies and all that we have …"). He wore 'the green sleeves' for five years until Don Lazarillo offered him easier and more profitable employment.

The Marshal supervised the gatekeepers, the guards, and all of the peripheral staff, like the stable-master and his staff, the falconers, the keeper of the hounds, the smithy, and the armorers. And on a night like tonight, when the gates were opened to admit the Don's guests (and who knew who else), the Marshal's watch and control over the physical space of the villa and its environs was as sharp and complete as an eagle guarding its aerie.

Apart from the military staff, Don Lazarillo had also gathered excellent servants to his service. The Hidalgo understood that an effective and efficient servant should find his or her work both honorable and profitable. Good servants made it possible for Don Lazarillo, by keeping a palatial house and a sumptuous table, dressing his staff in the finest livery, and showing conspicuous loyalty to his King and his God, to proclaim his wealth, declare his nobility, and flaunt his power, increasing the respect he garnered from noble, cleric, and peon alike. A servant was a reflection of his master's qualities, and Don Lazarillo's servants mirrored his brilliance.

Don Lazarillo and his staff had been preparing for this evening for two weeks. The Chief Maid maintained her household staff as strictly as any commander of the army. The fireplaces were cleaned, every surface was dusted, and not a stick of furniture or piece of carpet on the floor was an inch out of place. The Head Cook had begun then, preparing for the meal, as well. The cooks and scullions had cleaned the kitchens until they shone and then began their work. The pantler arranged the baking and storage of the bread and cheese that would be served. The butler had inventoried the wine cellar and kegs of beer and ale and ordered more. The staff in the scalding house, in the saucery, in the larder, and in the spicery had made themselves ready for the frenzy of the cooking nearly a week ago. The footmen and the cupbearers had been drilled and drilled again to ensure the perfection of their service. And finally, today, on the day of the gathering, the Seneschal directed the serving staff as it finally set the tables for the dinner.

Don Lazarillo had approved the evening's menu a week before: four roasted hens, a dozen roasted partridges, a grilled swordfish, a kid baked in crust, two roast boar, a loin of beef, a stewed ram, stewed pork, turnips in bacon, half a dozen artichoke-like cardoons, lentil stew, cheeses, Andalusian stuffed eggs, chickpeas with almond milk, olives, figs, sweet oranges, large apples, a variety of sauces (almond and pomegranate, mushroom and herb, garlic pine nut, orange and herb), spices (black pepper, cinnamon, cumin, saffron, turmeric, long pepper, mace, spikenard, galalgal, and cubeb, and finely-ground salt, in twelve individual pewter cellar, one for each guest), herbs (caraway, mint, dill, fennel, mustard for the meats, and anise for the fish and chicken), individual bags of mulling spices to be steeped in each guest's wine (nutmeg, ginger, cloves, sugar, and cardamom), and a dozen loaves of bread (half of which were gilded). The Don intended that his guests understand his wealth and power in even the most lowly and vulgar fare that he offered at his table.

The Don and his guests would dine together in the Great Hall of the villa. There would be many courses of great variety and ingenious invention. Shallow basins of cool, scented water (with a different essence for each course, to enhance the experience of the diners) would be offered before the first morsel was laid on the table and again before each new gastronomy.

Plates of gold would sit at each place, and meats and fruits and cheeses and breads would be served on platters of their own: the meats on gleaming silver, the fruit on flashing bronze, the cheeses on shining copper, and the breads on wooden platters inlaid with intricate designs of horn, ivory, shell, and mother-of-pearl.

Each diner would find that a gold-handled Toledo knife sat next to his golden plate to aid in the eating. And laid above the plates on the table, one for each guest, were the swordsmith's notational knives. These two knives would be the only utensils at the feast. That pederast, Domenico Selva (who would NOT be in attendance tonight nor ever again at Don Lazarillo's table) had shocked the company at the Hidalgo's table last Christmas Eve when he had allowed his eunuch (who he had insisted was merely his page) to cut his meat and place each bite in his mouth from the tines of a golden fork! There was no place for these 'foreign manners' at the Don's table. Men ate with fingers and knives; it was only proper!

*

The Don's guests were escorted from their carriages up the front staircase of the villa, through the immense doors of stout, Spanish oak, and into the marble-floored entryway. There, pietra dura inlays of polished, semi-precious stone created lush bouquets of flowers and intertwined vines and leaves for the Don's esteemed guests to tread upon as they walked toward even more singular pleasures. The walls made their own statement with sophisticated and complex Moorish carvings in dark wood, their intricacy emphasized with high-lights of gold leaf.

An octet of singers, in four voices, offered a taste of the dinner that lay ahead in the Great Hall with an 'ensalada' (a musical salad, combining ingredients from the works of Francisco Guerrero and the Flextas, elder and younger), an entertainment, for anyone who had ears to hear, of diverse rhythms and musical textures, moving like the song it was between popular and more formal melodic expressions, sung in all of the languages that bordered the Mediterranean Sea.

The 'ensalada' consisted of seven courses, alternating transitional sections with three quodlibets: a catalogue (which delighted the guests with a singing of a list of items of their attire), a successive (with the tenor quoting short melodic references and the other voices providing accompaniment), and a simultaneous (where two well-known, but seemingly-disparate, melodies were mixed).

As the guests entered the Hall itself, they were presented with a trio of acrobats, contorting themselves in seemingly wild abandon, and two pairs of jugglers, one couple tossing bright, edged weapons to and fro, and the other throwing flaming objects high into the air and retrieving them without injury.

To calm the diners and allow them to prepare for their dinner, the music in the Great Hall was simple stuff, a cleansing of the sensory palate, provided by a five-course vihuela de mano, accompanying a lovely soprano in soft ballads and villancicos.

*

When Don Lazarillo's guests entered the Great Hall, they found that Maximillian, the Hidalgo's younger son, wearing a black velvet, belted jacket over black, silken paned hose with blood red silk stockings, a short, cape of black wool serge, and a black silken toque, his fingers adorned with gold rings, was there, talking to his friend, Pepito, obviously of lower rank than Maximillian, who, nevertheless, wore clothing that skirted the border between insult and fashion: a short, brightly-orange velvet surcoat, and a brocaded jacket of incarnate red with black lace and black velvet trimming the hems and the sleeves (any men of character and learning who saw this pup would understand the symbolism inherent in his choice of colors – the red of greed, lust, and blood, and the orange of materialism, indulgence, and corruption). His hose was black and he wore no jewelry.

The first guest to enter the room after Maximillian and Pepito was the richest man in Spain, after the Archbishop of Toledo and the King himself. A commoner, Juan de Morales owned one of the seven private mints allowed by the decree of Ferdinand and Isabella in 1497 and the only one in Aragon and Castile. As one would expect, he wore gold to remind anyone he met of his wealth and black for his seriousness of purpose and that he was a man not to be trifled with, bordered with white for his purity. The two young men ignored him, and he called for a cupbearer to bring him wine.

Next, two men walked in together, deep in conversation, Fernando de Rojas, the lawyer who had secured his fame by penning a still-popular play when he was still in school, and Antonio of Lebrixa, a poet, astronomer, and grammarian who most of the population of Toledo respected for his scholarship and detested for the disgusting tedium that manifested itself whenever he spoke. The lawyer wore deep red to announce his high social status and light gold rings to announce that while his mother had been a Jewess, he was 'converso' and proud of both. The poet wore darkly-modest gray and pure white for his dedication to learning.

Then, alone and haughty, in strode General Pedro Navarro, Count of Olivtoa, a famous military engineer, who had designed the fortifications that had won the battles of Canosa, Cerignola, and Garigliano. He would be leaving with General Jimenez to fight the

Moors in North Africa soon and was consumed with an idea of a floating cannon battery, consisting of Arabic mortars and English-inspired field guns. He spoke mostly to himself, lost in his own deep thoughts, after he had requested ale from the cupbearer. He wore deep-purplish blue (as near to royalty as could be gotten), black, and a great deal of gold in fabric and precious metal.

Fray Alonso de Ojeda, a Dominican friar, originally from Seville, who had been elevated by the mad Queen Joanna and the Handsome Philip to be the Crown of Castile and Aragon's ambassador to the Archbishopric of Toledo (the wealthiest and most powerful See in all of Spain) wore brown silk and brown velvet to announce his piety. He walked into the Great Hall arm-in-arm and deep in conversation with Bruno, a Carthusian monk, who Don Lazarillo had invited to discuss breeding the Don's warmbloods with the monastery's Spanish Jennets. The monk wore brown to proclaim his spirituality and beige to announce his poverty.

Finally, the Don's older son, Juan, entered, dressed in the deepest, darkest, most expensive black, with his dear friend, Pedro Álvarez de Toledo y Zúñiga, Marqués de Villafranca del Bierzo, first son of Fadrique Álvarez de Toledo, 2nd Duque de Alba, who wore even deeper, even darker, even more expensive black.

The ten men found their places at the great table and sat, awaiting their host.

Long enough to remind all of the men that they were the Hidalgo's guests, but seconds short of being outright rude, Don

Lazarillo, resplendent in black and gold, walked in with Tomé Gonzáles, El Zayde, whose father had built a mill on the Rio Tagus many years before and had become a very, very wealthy man for it. He wore gold for his wealth, green for youth (a nod to his virility, which no one took seriously), and black, just in case anyone might not have noticed the gold, because he was rich.

The host and his friend took their seats, and after Don Lazarillo blessed the gathering ("Sit tres-in-unum sin tut benedicat nobis quod manducare"), the matter of dinner began.

*

Each diner had one of the notational knives at his place. When he wanted meat, he would motion to a server, tell the page which meat he desired, and the boy would cut a slice from the hens, the partridges, the swordfish, the kid, the boar, the beef, the ram, or the pork and bring it to the guest, laid on the wide blade of the knife.

The knives had been polished until they gleamed for Don Lazarillo's guests; the Hidalgo had insisted that the smith's blood remain on the blade of the knife with which he would be served. It was another small pleasure that the nobleman enjoyed.

As the dinner progressed, eventually, all of the knives were 'bloodied' with the juices of the meat that they had cut. For some reason, Don Lazarillo ate only the rarest of the beef that night, but his guests were too busy sampling the table's other fare to notice.

After the meal was done, and a number of toasts had been proposed to honor the host, the evening's entertainment began.

Don Lazarillo stood and called for the kind attention of his guests.

"My friends," he said, "Each one of you has a wide-bladed knife above your plate. Please pick it up. You will see that the two sides of the blade are different. Please turn to the side where the "Gratiarum action" is engraved and thank our Lord with me."

And the dozen men solemnly spoke together, "Nos gratias ago vos pro Deo vestro candor valemus."

Then, the Hidalgo continued, "As an entertainment tonight, I propose that we sing the holy prayers engraved on these knives."

Tomé Gonzáles said for all to hear, "Have we had enough to drink to attempt this, my Lord?"

The men laughed, and more than one called on his cupbearer to re-fill his glass.

The Don laughed, as well, called for another drink himself, and then he explained how the singing would occur.

And after more than a few false starts, the dozen songbirds managed to burst into polyphony, and after a few more attempts, it was laughingly agreed that it was good and that they should stop before more damage was done.

A fine time was had by all.

*

That was, until Pepito looked at Maximillian, raised a questioning eyebrow, and nodded (none of the other guests noticed this unspoken agreement between the two men).

Pepito leaned past his friend so that he could speak to Juan, who sat at Maximillian's right, and said, loudly enough so that no man in the Great Hall, noble, commoner, or servant, could mistake his words, "Juan, how can you call that abomination singing? I can only guess that your mother's cunt was as loose as your mouth is to get those sounds to come from it. I imagine she got that way from her service to the Jews and the Moors when she was a girl, but for you to call that moaning singing, you must spend your time in the stables swallowing the stallions' dicks."

Juan stared at what Pepito had said, unable to believe what he had heard, and then slowly stood.

Pepito stood and walked around the back of Maximillian's chair to stand nose to nose with Juan.

"And by the look of you," he continued, "She gave some of their dark blood to you … just enough to stain you, but not enough to make you fit to bloody my sword … although, I have heard that many a peon bloodied his staff in your dead mother's arse as she crawled through your father's fields while he bravely fought for his King, the Moors glorifying him with their fear."

Juan was speechless.

So Pepito came to his assistance, "Here is my glove. I freely give it to you so you can throw it at my feet, unless you would prefer to keep it as a favor and a promise of my lance in your bed tonight."

Juan stood still, color rising to his cheeks, but he slowly took the glove from Pepito's hand and threw it at Pepito's feet.

Chapter 4 – The Two of Knives

The second card of the Minor Arcana of the Suit of Knives in the Swordsmith's Tarot is the Two of Knives. This card takes the actions that were set in motion with the Ace of Knives and allows them to continue their progression toward their natural and foreordained conclusion. The potential of the Knives is unlimited as their essence takes the enthusiasm and passion with which they were forged and leads to discovery, self-knowledge, and experiences that are revelatory in their newness and as comfortable as if they have lain dormant, merely awaiting the spark which will allow them to flower in their own time and in their own manner.

The Twos in this deck indicate decisions, although the choices that follow these determinations may have already been made. Stepping into a new world and embracing new possibilities is nothing over which any man has control. Regardless of preparation and intent and hopes and dreams, the journey has begun, and gain and loss are merely the flat and the edge of the Knife.

*

"Bastard," Maximillian cried, "I will feed your lying tongue to the pigs. He looked at the borrowed glove he had thrown down at the feet of his tormentor, "Here!" he swore, "Now!"

Maximillian's father jumped to his son's side, "No! It is illegal. I'll not have you murder a guest in my house!"

"Ah," Pepito said and twisted the sharp words with which he had stabbed the heir of Lazarillo, "Your father seeks to save you. How sweet. I knew that you were mongrel get, but now I see that you are a coward, too. Forgive me, my mouse, for unmasking you."

*

A duel was only legal if it had been authorized by the King. For those who survived an illegal duel, the rewards, other than to their honor, were often banishment or execution (the Church had supported the King by announcing that the participants in a duel would be excommunicated and could not be buried in hallowed ground). And all of the men in the Great Hall that night knew that, if a duel could be prevented between these young men, Don Lazarillo would probably hire an assassin to settle the matter to his satisfaction.

Juan turned to Don Lazarillo and spoke softly, "Father, this is a private matter, and I am a gentleman. I have been slandered and my reputation, and that of my mother, your wife, has been impugned. The only worse disgrace than not defending my honor would be to leave this room without seeking redress."

And here, Pepito interrupted son and father, "So will you apologize, my little goat?"

Juan turned to Pepito and nearly spat, "Never!"

"Very well," the green-eyed man said with a grin, "Then, since all of Toledo knows that you are a fine swordsman, a student of Maestro Achille Marozzo in Bologna, and an adherent of the "the true art" (la verdadera destreza) promoted by that huckster, Jerónimo Sánchez de Carranza," and he strolled lazily to the table and picked up two of the knives that had provided diversion earlier in the evening, "I will choose these musical knives to assist me in singing my tune." He tossed one, the juices of the meat it had cut, still sticky on its blade, to the Don's son.

Juan caught the knife and ran his thumb down its edge, essaying its bite. "These will do," he said, "Clear us a field, gentleman. I will have this chore completed in time for port."

Don Lazarillo saw that he could not stop this madness, so he would ensure that the duel was conducted honorably and correctly. "Who will be your second, my son?" he asked.

Juan clapped his hand on his friend's shoulder, "Pedro will attend me, father," he said with a smile.

"And yours" the Don snarled to Pepito, unable to hide his hatred and contempt.

Pepito looked straight at the Don and asked, "Will you attend me, Maximillian?"

The Don's second son simply nodded.

General Navarro, Count of Olivtoa, a man who knew of blood and conflict said, "I know enough of the physician's art for this, Don Lazarillo. I will act accordingly."

The Hidalgo said, "Thank you, sir."

And then, to the servants in the room, he shouted, "Clear us a space. Fifteen paces square should be enough," and then he walked to one corner of the 'field' and dropped his handkerchief to mark the angle. The general added his to another corner, the lawyer and the poet completing the box.

"And the conditions?" the Hidalgo asked of the two young men.

"Until we are unable to continue," Juan spat, "but I will make sure this one is dead."

"I accept, with pleasure," the laughing-eyed man agreed and then turned away from his opponent, walking to the far corner marked by a small square of linen and lace, stumbling halfway there, as if the wine he had drunk that evening had tripped him.

Juan saw this and smiled. It would not take long to finish this Boorish peasant. Knives, indeed!

Juan went to his corner and drew the knife through the air to test its weight and balance. When he first looked at it, he thought, "This is no proper weapon! It is more a cleaver that should be used in the kitchen or in a butcher's shop!" But upon closer examination, Juan began to understand that this broad-bladed 'tool', with the triangular tine at its tip, was finely-wrought, beautiful, and perhaps, even deadly. It was unlike any weapon he had ever handled, but what was a knife but a shorter sword, and Juan had been trained with the best of swords by the best masters in Italy and here in Toledo.

Pepito turned in his corner to face the Don's elder son, made a sarcastic bow to Juan, and nodded to the Hidalgo, indicating his readiness to begin.

The Don looked to his son, and Juan nodded that he, too, was ready.

Don Lazarillo cried, "¡Empezar!"

*

At the Hidalgo's call, Juan took a step toward his opponent. As he did so, he wondered, for the merest fraction of a thought, how it would be best to proceed. He had been trained with the sword from the time he was old enough to hold a wooden, practice sword, by tutors in his father's house, Masters in Italy, and legendary Spanish fighters, some of whom were beginning to create a new form of swordsmanship, The Destreza.

But in those thousands of hours of practice and training, he had never had cause to use his blade to draw blood in anger or, God forbid, kill a man. Tonight would change all of that.

And, as Pepito came towards him, the fool stumbled again, obviously too taken by drink to have seriously demanded satisfaction or provide much competition for Juan's skills. The fool! He would pay for his rudeness, his insolence, and his drunkenness. It would be a lesson he would not forget because he would be dead. Juan, his new Professor, would instruct him in exchange for his life.

Pepito was a young man who had grown up, had become used to physical labor, and had developed the appetites of a man, even before the beard on his chin could proclaim him one. Before he had met Maximillian, and seen the young nobleman as his entre to the finer homes of Toledo and the promise of a richer life, Pepito had drunk and dined in the worst inns and taverns in the city and had entertained himself with gambling and whores, either of which could have ended his poor life quickly and painfully if he had not learned just as quickly and sometimes as painfully not to make a mistake twice. He had fought (and once or twice killed) other men (and a whore or two) with sticks, knives, rope, bottles, rocks, his hands, his boots, and once, even a soaking wet tomcat. He knew 'close work' the way this pompous peacock knew how to read the Bible.

And so, as he made his first step toward Juan Lazarillo, holding the knife in his right hand, Pepito stumbled, just a little, and swore, just loudly enough to complete the effect.

And it seemed to have worked.

The young nobleman stood up straight, preparing his attack.

*

Pepito had seen many of these dandies who had been trained in Italian swordsmanship. He expected that, at any second now, Juan would rush toward him, attempting to beat his sword away from the line of attack. While, for an Italian fighting with a sword, a good offense was the best defense and thrusting from the shoulder to extend the range of his weapon was a traditional maneuver that was often successful, but Juan wasn't fighting with a sword. And he wasn't fighting an Italian.

First, these knives were not swords. These particular knives were shorter and unbalanced. Their wide blades were designed to slash and cut. Their smaller size made them most effective when their user evaded his opponent with deceptive footwork and bodily movements and used his other hand to control his opponent.

Italians liked to use a pass-step to bring their swords into play against their opponents and then rush toward their opponents, putting fear into any response that they might attempt. These steps hindered the Italian attack, allowing it to only proceed straight ahead. A movement to one side or the other would compromise the swordsman's balance.

Spaniards knew the importance of getting out of an opponent's way. And any Spanish fighter who lived to fight another day knew other things as well. He knew the range of his weapon. These knives were about a foot long, less than a third of a fine rapier. A Spaniard was calm under pressure and allowed his footwork and maneuvers to control the fight. This seemingly unconcerned serenity on the part of the Spanish warrior instilled fear in his opponent, and that fear gained the Spaniard a further advantage.

Part of this menace began in the Spaniard's stance. He stood almost in profile to his opponent, his feet barely apart. Despite his relaxed demeanor, he held his weapon at arm's length, parallel to the ground, the tip pointed at the eyes of his antagonist, threatening any move his foe might make.

Standing in this manner, a Spaniard could move out of the line of attack, direct the movements of his rival to his advantage, and launch his own attack by stepping toward his enemy and, thus, increasing the range of his weapon. A Spaniard used a 'defensive' posture to his advantage and allowed him to use the weaknesses of his victim's technique and style against him.

A Spaniard also knew that an antagonist who can no longer function against him could no longer kill him. The human body contained a variety of organs, nerves, arteries, and muscles that were targets for a determined fighter. Pepito had struck and stabbed and strangled and smashed and struck and hit and kicked and hurt all of these parts of a number of humans' bodies.

And, perhaps most importantly for Pepito, in a non-judicial duel, such as this one, no one would interfere with the fight. Pepito had learned his knife-fighting where no one ever interfered unless they wanted to die. Juan was probably expecting there to be rules.

*

Juan remembered his Italian instruction and rushed toward Pepito, intending to frighten the commoner and score a hit to the man's shoulder or, if he was lucky, the peon's chest.

Pepito saw this attack coming and moved aside, turning as he did so, to give Juan a "kiss". Pepito thrust quickly toward Juan's nose. He was unused to the weight of this knife, but his cut still split the skin just below Juan's nose.

Juan stopped and howled! As he turned to face Pepito again, the excruciating pain that the nobleman experienced was evident in his eyes and the flow of blood that now covered his nose, lips, mouth, teeth, and chin.

"I'll kill you," Juan screamed and went after Pepito again.

Juan again came at the man he would kill, and this time, his fear of being stabbed again slowed his attack.

Pepito sidestepped to his right to evade the nobleman's blade and put a slice in the forearm of Juan's knife hand.

Then he stepped inside Juan's guard, stomped on his instep, and tried to spin and put his elbow in Juan's throat.

The elbow missed, but Juan howled again and limped away from Pepito. He realized almost immediately that, unless he turned to face the commoner, he was a dead man.

Juan advanced, more slowly now, toward Pepito, holding his knife, now covered with his own blood, aimed at Pepito's chest.

Juan was tiring, and Pepito could see the man's fatigue. And so, he decided to take his chance.

Pepito took a step forward and swung the knife across himself, from right to left, striking Juan's blade and knocking it aside.

Pepito switched his knife to his left hand, grabbed Juan's right wrist with his right hand, and chopped at the fingers that held Juan's knife.

With a terrible roar of pain, Juan pulled back, and three of his fingers fell to the floor.

Taking the best chance that he would have, Pepito let go of Juan's arm, took his knife again with his right hand, grabbed Juan's right arm again with his left, and buried the blade of the knife in the black-clad man's forehead.

*

The men in the Great Hall were shocked into silence. Someone, maybe a servant, threw up. Pepito let his knife fall to the floor, and walked to the table where the men had dined not an hour before. He found a goblet still full of red wine and drained it in one swallow.

The victor looked around the room.

His first glance met the eyes of Maximillian Lazarillo, now the eldest son and heir of Don Lazarillo. Maximillian nodded imperceptibly, and Pepito moved his gaze, his work acknowledged and thanked.

His eyes then found Don Lazarillo himself. The Hidalgo seemed to have aged a dozen years in the few minutes that the duel had lasted. He was leaning on his old friend, Tomé, who was leading the distraught man to a chair.

Pepito would deal with the old man when he must.

The victor met the eyes of every other man in the room, assuring them and himself that it had been a private affair, conducted by gentlemen, and no one's business but Juan's and Pepito's. No one seemed inclined to dispute that.

That was fine with Pepito.

And then the Don spoke, "Get out of my sight!"

Pepito walked to stand before the heartbroken man. "Señor?"

"You heard me," the Hidalgo said, and edge of menace mixed with terrible resolve and the barest suggestion of sadness, "Get out of my house! Get out of this city! If you know what is good for you, you will leave Aragon and Castile far behind you. Do not wait for the sun to rise, or that will be the last sunrise you will ever see."

"I will not have you killed ... now," Don Lazarillo said in a tired voice, "The duel was an honorable matter between two gentlemen; satisfaction was demanded, and it was given. Seconds were named and a doctor was present. With ten witnesses to hear me, you have my word that no authorities, civil or of The Church, will be apprised of what has happened here. But if you remain where I know of you, you will not remain long."

Pepito knew that he had escaped. And he knew that the Don meant every word of what he had said. So he did the only thing that was left to do. He bowed and bid the Hidalgo goodbye with a curt, "Señor."

Then he turned and walked from the Great Hall, down the marble hallways, past the shocked servants, and finally, out of the great oaken doors. The Don's servants were excellent ones, for by the time that he had reached the bottom of the staircase in front of the villa, his horse was saddled and waiting for him.

He mounted the beast and put his spurs to her, reaching a gallop by the time he reached the Calle de la Posada do Peregrinos.

He hurried back to his home and packed everything he owned that was of value. He believed that Don Lazarillo had told him the truth and that his life depended upon putting as many leagues between him and Toledo as he could. He had clothing, a Toledo cup-hilt rapier, a falchion hunting sword (with curved blade and a saw back), a buckler, a couple of daggers, a misericorde (he had not been able to afford an Italian stiletto), a couple of pouches of escudos, a pouch with three or four ducats from Lombardy and a handful of Danish coins, and an extra pair of boots. Whatever else he would need, he could purchase … or steal.

And as soon as the old man died, Maximillian would pay the debt that he now owed to Pepito.

Pepito would have to wait at the Puerta Bisagra for the dawn to leave the city, so he stopped at the little tavern where his favorite whore spent her working hours.

He walked into the nearly empty room, saw her, almost asleep, her head resting on her arms at one of the big wooden tables.

Pepito took her by the hand, told the innkeeper to send up a bottle of decent red wine ("… none of that vinegar you give the peasants"), and to not bother him.

*

Pepito and the whore spent the rest of the night and most of the next afternoon, both of them sleeping some that morning, doing what whores do best. Pepito told the woman to go to the kitchen and bring up bread, and meat, and wine. He was feeling as good as she could make him feel, and he decided to leave the following morning.

It seemed to Pepito that the woman was taking much longer than she should have, and he was about to get up, put on his clothes, and leave her unpaid, when there was a knock at the door, and her sweet, little voice from the other side of the door asked, "Cariño, please open the door for me. My hands are full."

Pepito jumped from the bed and ran, naked, to open the door.

It was the whore, carrying a large tray with food and a bottle of wine. She set it down on the room's rickety, little table.

"Take off your clothes, Chica, and then bring me some food and wine," Pepito laughed.

The whore laughed with him and took off her clothes, slowly enough to drive him crazy, folding them and placing them neatly on a little chest at the foot of the bed.

When she was as God had made her, she poured a cup full of wine and brought it to him. Then she turned back to the food. Pepito took a big drink of the wine and thought about how beautiful the woman's ass looked as she served him.

A minute later, she brought him a trencher of stale bread, filled with slices of meat, fresh bread, and an apple she had found. She handed him the trencher and turned back to the table.

Pepito was holding the trencher on his lap with one hand and biting into a piece of excellent pork he was holing in his other when the whore came back to the bed.

But this time, she held a carving knife. Pepito looked up at her, and she sank the blade into his eye.

It took Pepito a minute to stop his wild squirming, but a whore had to be strong to survive all that whores had to put up with, so she was able to hold the knifepoint in his head until he stilled.

Then, still naked so that she wouldn't soil her clothes with all of the blood, she pulled the knife out of Pepito's head and set to work cutting off his cock and balls. The Don required proof that Pepito was dead.

When she had the bloody little things, she put them into a little cloth bag. Then she poured water in the room's basin and washed herself. Finally, she put on her clothes before she went through Pepito's belongings. She kept the money and the clothing, the daggers, and the boots (they were only just a little too big, but they were made of fine leather). The innkeeper could have the rest; they were a man's things, after all.

Then she took the bloody bag down the stairs, and after she had hidden what she had taken from Pepito, she gave the bagful of Pepito to the innkeeper. He would make sure that the Don received it. And the Don paid well.

*

A couple of days later, the whore was sitting at a table in the inn when Don Lazarillo's man came into the room. He brought a heavy bag over to where she sat, thanked her, and left.

The innkeeper hurriedly shooed the inn's customers (at this hour, there was only a sleeping drover and a beggar who had come in to buy a glass of wine with the coppers he had earned so far that day) out of the door before he bolted it.

With the room empty, the innkeeper came over to the whore's table and sat down.

She smiled at him and opened the bag, pouring out a pile of coins onto the wood.

The innkeeper held up a finger to ask her to wait, and he went to the counter and grabbed an open bottle of wine, which he brought back to the table.

"Now," he said as he sat back down, "We can get started."

The two divided up the coins, one for her and then one for him. When all was square, the whore looked questioningly at the bag, and when the innkeeper nodded, she put her share back into the bag.

"Thank you, Ramiro," she said, "I wish you health and happiness, but I do not expect to see you again."

The innkeeper nodded, and the whore walked out into the sunshine.

*

But now, she was no longer a whore. She had money, enough to buy a little place and earn her living as her parents had, as a baker, but in a city far from Toledo.

There were highwaymen on the roads, the King and Queen had done little to discourage that trade, so she walked to a stable that she knew and bought a gentle mare, rode her to the warehouses where a pack train waited to travel the forty miles to Madrid and her new life.

Chapter 5 - The World

One of the Major Arcana of the Suit of Knives in the Swordsmith's Tarot is The World. This card is ruled by Saturn, the symbol of Time. Just as The World, itself, passes through the cyclical progression of the seasons in its march through Time, The World in the Swordsmith's Suit of Knives is also the stationary center of the four corners of the Universe as well as of the four Cardinal directions. The World celebrates every journey as its first and the innate promise of every journey. But, even as it celebrates, The World doesn't care.

*

Maximillian Lazarillo succeeded his father as Hidalgo de Sangre when his father died, consumed by gout and regret, in his bed, thirty years after Juan, Don Lazarillo's eldest son, had been killed in an ill-advised duel. Within a day of the duel, Don Lazarillo had let it be known throughout the city that death of the man who killed his son would please him, but that pleasure brought him no joy as he sat in his cold villa in Toledo. And then, when he had received the little bag full of the proof that the man who had caused his son's death walked no more on the Earth, the Don put away the awful and beautiful knives that had been used in the duel. They were cleaned, and polished, and wrapped once again in their silken sheaths, and carefully placed, along with Don Lazarillo's other treasures and ghosts, in the deepest, most inaccessible hole in the villa's foundations.

*

One day, shortly after Juan's funeral, Don Lazarillo sat Maximillian down and explained to the young man that he must become the man that Don Lazarillo expected him to be.

*

Don Lazarillo told his son that, when he was a boy and Christians, Moors, and Jews lived more or less peacefully together in Toledo, one of his first friends had been the son of a man respected throughout the kingdom of Castile, despite his being a heathen Moor. Don Lazarillo and Rashid learned to hunt and hawk together, they raised swords against each other in training, they shared tutors (and when they grew older, a lover or two), and were known by everyone who dwelt in the city to be as thick as thieves.

When Don Lazarillo had grown old enough, his father had taken him away from his friend to perfect his practice of the art and science of lordship. Rashid and his family had then moved south, across the Pillars of Hercules, to a villa, whose foundations had been laid by the Phoenicians and which over-looked the Mediterranean, near the ancient port of Tétouan. If you were to ask anyone in The Western Kingdom (or, as the French called it, Maroc) or on the Iberian peninsula the source of Rashid al-Din Sinan's great wealth and power, you would find silence and later, perhaps, a koummya (that cruel, curved, double-edged Berber dagger) stuck in your belly.

*

As Don Lazarillo and Maximillian sat together, the father had explained to his son that the world was much more … precarious … that the young man understood. How could his son have lived long enough to become this tall, strong, seemingly capable young man and still know so little of the world the Don had asked himself. No matter. The boy would learn. Or the boy would die.

*

The father had told his son what many men knew but no living man had ever asked about Rashid al-Din Sinan, "My old friend is sometimes called, but never to his face, 'The Old Man of the Mountain'. He is just a man that those who follow him, the Fida'i, call 'The Light of God'."

"But father," Maximillian had interrupted, "The Fida'i are assassins. They are madmen, users of hashish!"

The father had sadly shaken his head, "Those lies, my son, are the simple-minded slander of Christians, those Moors who hate the Isma'ili, and those who fear the Fida'i. The Fida'i are not rabble. They are simply devout men who will do anything to protect their Imam and their Nizari brothers."

"The Fida'i cannot be bought, and they are almost never seen. They are everywhere and nowhere," the father continued.

"How can that be?" Maximillian asked.

Don Lazarillo had smiled, "They are taqq'iya, masking their identities, while they wait for their Imam, my dear friend Rashid, to call them, and then they do whatever they are called upon to do."

"But they are not paid?" the lad had said, incredulously.

"Before you were born, my son," the old man had explained, "I visited my old friend in his fortress-palace by the sea. He told me of his beloved followers, and I was, as you are, skeptical. My sadiqi Rashid took me to his stables where two pure-white stallions awaited us, saddled for a ride. Rashid said one soft word to his servant, and by the time we had left the gates of his home, forty riders accompanied us. We rode until the sun was high in the sky and we had reached a line of cliffs, twice as tall as the Cathedral here in Toledo, from which the blue of the sea could barely be seen far in the distance. The horsemen lined up at the edge of the cliff, twenty on either side of us. With a word from my friend, ten of the riders to our left dismounted and walked to the edge of the cliff. Rashid waited a long moment and then nodded. To a man, every one of these ten shouted, 'Allah 'Akbar!' ('God is great!'), and without hesitation dove headlong to his death. I was shocked, and Rashid could see the consternation and disbelief in my eyes. My friend said to me, 'Such is the devotion of the faithful', and turned to the men to our right. He spoke another word, and ten of those riders left their horses to stand at the edge. He waited another moment, turned to me and said, 'Behold their leap of faith,' and then nodded again. Those men, as fervently as the first ten, shouted their veneration of their God and Rashid, His servant, 'Allah 'Akbar!' and leapt to their deaths. On our ride back to his palace by the sea, Rashid told me that he loved me and, because of his love for me, that I could request his favor ... but only once. And so I have."

Maximillian had been stunned and confused by his father's story and dully repeated, "You have? Requested his favor?"

Don Lazarillo had smiled with his lips, but the hardness of his eyes belied any humor in what he then said, "If I should die an untimely or unfortunate death, you, too, my son, shall die a certain, although not quite as immediate, death. Before a second sun has set after my life has ended, your life will be ended as well. That is the favor I have requested of my old friend."

"Father," Maximillian had said, "You have told me a story that is impossible to believe, of men who would kill themselves for no gain, of hidden assassins, and of a mysterious old man who lives across the Sea and who, yet, calls death down upon men in our Christian kingdom. You have drunk too much wine today, sir, or your old mind is beginning to unravel."

Don Lazarillo had laughed, softly, almost to himself, "My son, what is so unbelievable? That a man may be murdered in Toledo? That there are men who would kill another as a matter of honor? Or that someone so far away could cause all of this to occur?"

"Alright, Father," the young man had reluctantly admitted, "Many an inconvenient man is given an early death in our great city. And some men would break God's law for faith alone. But the wind itself would take a day to travel from here to al-Maġrib, the land where the sun sets. Does this Moor speak to the wind?"

The Don had chucked again, "The wind. Never seen, always there. You forget who else is never seen and always at our elbows."

Maximillian had given his father a quizzical look but had said nothing.

"Have you forgotten about our servants, my son?" Don Lazarillo had asked, "On the day that you were born, on the day you cut your first tooth, on the day that you fell from your pony and broke your arm, and as well on the day you will wed, on the day your children will be born, and on the day that you will die, the news will travel faster and surer than any breeze. From servant to servant to servant again. The word will be abroad, as quickly as a thought, and nothing will be able to stop it. Our servants, by the very nature of the work that we command them to do, know everything of us. And they share that knowledge with every other of their rank. Do you truly believe that you have secrets that are kept? You have a great deal to learn, my dear boy. A great deal to learn."

Maximillian had shaken his head and said, "Father, I am tired with all of your stories and imaginings. I will go to my bed, and perhaps, we shall talk more tomorrow, instead, of things that are real and true. Good night, Father. May the Lord keep you until the morrow."

The Don had walked to his son and kissed the boy's forehead. "Dream sweetly, my son," he said, and then both men had retired for the night.

*

The next morning, Maximillian had awakened to the sweet singing of a red-faced goldfinch, who had perched on his windowsill, and a blanket of gloriously bright sunshine lying across his bed. He had drowsily reached between his legs to scratch an itch (he would have the servants change the bedding today he thought; the fleas were not so bad, but one itch was one itch too many for one as well-born as he, he idly thought as he scratched himself). His fingers had touched something soft and fluffy, a feather. Then another, and then another still.

He had then raised his head and looked down his body. There were feathers floating above the bed and more piled up between his legs! What mischief was this?

Maximillian sat up to get a better look. There, between his legs, the feather bed had been ripped to shreds, its downy filling scattered over the bed and the floor that surrounded it. And stuck into the wool-filled, canvas mattress upon which the featherbed lay was a golden hilt!

Maximillian had then come suddenly, completely awake. He had reached for the hilt and pulled it out of his bedding. It was gold, covered in an intricately geometric pattern of pearls and silver. The blade, to which it was attached, was long, curving, and hideously sharp on both edges. A Moorish blade had been stuck between his legs as he slept!

He would tell his father of this outrage!

But then Maximillian had thought again. If he told his father, and what his father had told him the night before was true, this warning, or reminder, or whatever it had been, would have been known throughout the city, as quickly as his own thought.

No. This would be Maximillian's secret. He would hide the dagger away and merely tell the chambermaids to change the bedding. It would not be bad to be known as a man who was like an animal in his bed, he thought. Maximillian had smiled at this. And he had also smiled at his new secret.

*

After their talk and his discovery the following morning, for the next thirty years, Maximillian had put all of his heart and soul into ensuring that his father's every whim was accomplished, and he had surrendered his life to his father's in the expectation of finally receiving the power and riches he deserved when the old man would finally die.

*

Maximillian eventually gave into his father's incessant nagging and married when he was forty, ten long years before the old man's demise. A child, a son, was born, and the line continued, but its mother died giving it its birth. The old man was able to bounce the little thing on his knee for a year or two before he, too, met his just reward.

By then, Maximillian was almost fifty years of age, saddled with a child he knew not what to do with. He hired nannies and tutors to care for the brat, and by the time that Rodrigo (Maximillian had named his son for the Cid) was old enough to begin to take some direction from his father as a man and as Maximillian's heir, Maximillian himself died, and Rodrigo became the newest of the long line of Don Lazarillos.

*

Rodrigo was the toast of Toledo, a handsome young man with wealth (in gold as well as property), intelligence, and a healthy respect for and enjoyment in the intrigues that surrounded any great house.

As any young man of the time would do, Rodrigo went through the eligible ladies of Toledo and then Madrid and then Barcelona like a warm knife goes through soft and yielding butter. And when he finally found a woman to capture his heart, she was heir to the Count of Ebro, a wealthy but politically insignificant holding in Zaragoza province, to the northeast of Toledo, past Madrid, west of Barcelona, almost to the Pyrenees. Rodrigo happily married the woman, as much for love of her as for the opportunity to move to her family's home, the magnificent Alsharqia Palace, with its three alabaster towers, its Golden Hall, its sumptuous chapel (built as a mosque by the Banu Tujibi Emir, Abu Jaffar Al-

Muqtadir), and its paradisiacal orangeries and gardens. Almost as soon as his bride had placed her flowers on the shrine of Nuestra Señora del Pilar, Rodrigo moved everything that was not nailed down (and some things that were) from the Lazarillo villa in Toledo to his new home in the north.

Rodrigo and his Countess were married for twenty years and were blessed with three children, two of whom joined their mother in death due to a vicious contagion of "Red Plague", the hideous contamination that the English called 'smallpox' (to distinguish it from the "great pox", their silly name for syphilis).

The one child who was left alive to tend to Rodrigo in his old age was named Berengaria, after the wise and virtuous Queen of ancient Castile of 500 years before. At first glance, she seemed a lovely thing, blonde of hair, sweet of voice, blue of eye, and attentive to her father, all the things that a daughter should be. Those who knew her well called her "Beri", behind her back, for her violent temper and vengeful intentions. Berengaria was as spoiled as her namesake had been beneficent, as vindictive as the Queen had been righteous, and as obstinate as the ruler had been sagacious.

*

One spring day, a bored Berengaria commanded her attendants to prepare her coach so that she could take the air.

*

Berengaria had received a coach, constructed in the cold north in Brandenburg's capital city, Berlin, and after which it was named, from her father. The covered compartment, where the passengers sat, was shaped as a comfortable 'U', with a door on each side and each door with an iron step and a small, protected 'boot' where a servant might crouch. Berengaria supposed that poorer folk than she could seat four in the coach, two facing another two, but she had never had to resort to that. The coachman sat above the coach's front wheels to drive the pair of matched geldings that pulled the berlin.

After a year of enjoying this coach, Berengaria decided that it was acceptable for cold, winter days or for when it might rain, but for the warmth of a Spanish summer, it was entirely too close and stuffy. So she did what any girl would do; she demanded another coach but one whose roof had been removed so that she could enjoy the sun's warm rays and the cooling breezes. Her father knew her temper well enough to find an inventive coach-maker who could alter the coach to his daughter's specifications. The second coach was completed just as the warmth of summer began. Berengaria made a special point to kiss her old father on the cheek to thank him and remind him of her affection toward him.

*

On one particular excursion, the first one after the winter had left the land and almost a year after she had first been able to enjoy this open coach, Berengaria was accompanied by her favorite maid, the red-haired Erytheia (an unlettered but sly girl, who had been born on the island of Gades and whose family had fled north, many, many years ago to escape the depredations of the Moors), a footman

(Herculito, Berengaria's 'Little Hercules'), and of course, the coachman (whose name Beri didn't know; why should she?). The driver sat on a seat at the front, Beri, the most important occupant, sat in the back, facing forwards, Ery sat backwards in the coach, facing her lady, and Herculito huddled uncomfortably on the little iron step. One outrider, Diego del Teruel, the handsomest of her father's military men, rode his black gelding at the right of the coach, guarding her from danger.

    Diego was armed with a pistol and a sword, and armored with a shining silver cuirass, which covered his strong chest, and an open morion helmet, with a flat brim and brave iron crest that ran from front to back. He wore good, tall black leather boots, dark gray hose, and her father's colors, red, yellow, and black, with golden lions rampant embroidered across the arms of his blouse.

*

    Erytheia was an excellent maid and had thought to bring a basket of light foods for their hunger and a bota filled with red wine to slake their thirst as they rode.

    The coach bounced over the road, and the two women laughed together as they shared the gossip of the castle and the reputed scandals of the city.

    And then, the coach halted.

    Standing in the middle of the road, the KING'S road, was a lone man, clad in tall, shining black leather boots, deep brown hose, a brown tunic, a white shirt with lace at its collar and its cuffs, brown leather gloves, and a brown cap, adorned with the long, brown-barred tail feather of a pheasant. The man drew two pistols, bowed in a mannerly way, and stated in a strong and assertive voice, "¡Párate y entrega!" ("Stand and deliver!").

Diego, the handsome outrider, wasted not a moment, drew his sword, and put his heels to his horse to run the ruffian down.

Before the outrider had gone five feet, there was a shot, and Diego toppled from his horse, a hole in his forehead.

The maid screamed, and the highwayman walked toward the coach, calmly pulling another pistol from his belt.

He walked to the door of the open coach where Herculito had been cowering and said, "Calm yourself, my ladies. I am here only for your valuables, trinkets that you will soon forget that you had ever owned. I apologize that I had to take the life of your man, but I must make my living, and he would like to have prevented me from doing so. If you will please step down from the coach so that I may do my business quickly and expeditiously, you may just as quickly leave and return to the tedium of your court."

The coachman moved his right hand to the seat beside him, and the gentleman of the road moved one of his pistols toward the driver. "No, no," he said, shaking his head, "You and the boy must also alight although I am certain that neither of you possess anything that I might desire."

The coachman and the page alighted and stood close together, the man's knees knocking together and a single tear escaping the boy's eye.

The desperado stepped, then, to the door of the coach, opened it with a flourish, and held out his hand, as if he were a gentleman, to assist the women from the coach.

Erytheia stood then and moved toward the now-open door of the coach, placing her pale little hand in the brigand's glove. She stepped bravely down, placing one of her dainty feet on the single step, her movement making the leather straps that suspended the coach above its wheels strain and the coach sway, and then her other foot on the dirt of the road. She alit as lightly as a feather, her hair, so naturally curly that it defied the best efforts of any coiffeuse at keeping it in any decent style, bouncing as she moved. The bandit watched her so closely that Berengaria could feel his eyes touching her maid's body through her clothing. The simple thought of it disgusted Berengaria almost as much as it thrilled her.

And then, it was Beri's turn to leave the coach. She stood and held out her hand for the rogue to take, and when his gloved hand touched hers, she gasped with … was it pleasure? No! She would not be seduced by a romantic rapscallion, clad in leather and lace, as handsome as in a dream. No!! She would not.

And then, the ignoble robber spoke, his deep voice strumming the strings of her soul, first to the coachman and the boy, "Gentlemen, I see that you are merely servants of this fine lady, and all that you have is what you have on. Please return to your places in the coach to wait for your mistress to conclude her business with me."

Then, the rogue approached Erytheia. He held out his gloved hand, and the girl put her hand in his. The marauder bowed over her hand and brought his lips almost to touch her skin. Berengaria could feel the heat of him from where she stood. How could Ery stand to be so close to such danger, so close to such a man?

The rake spoke again, "Miss, I see that you are the lady's maid. You are lovely beyond compare, but like your coachman and page, you are but the lady's servant. By the comb in your hair, I see that your mistress loves you and has given you tokens of her affection. I would remember the day that you and I met, so I will ask you for your tortoise peineta as a keepsake and trade one of your earrings, as well, for one of mine so that you will not forget me."

Erytheia took the comb from her hair and handed it to the dashing man with a smile that would have melted another man. He nodded the slightest of bows in thanks. Then she reached to her right ear and removed the little gold lazo, the lacy, openwork design of exquisite scrolls in a bow that held miniscule beads of amber and jet. She gave it to the thief, still smiling, and allowed the tiniest of laughs to escape her full, red lips when he reached to his own ear and pulled out the small golden stud that he wore there, replacing it with Ery's earring before giving the girl his own jewelry.

"Thank you, Miss," the unmannered ruffian told her, "I shall never forget the day that we met."

Then the libertine extended his hand to help Beri's little maid back into the coach. As she climbed back into her seat, her cheeks blushed as red as the wine she and Berengaria had drunk. Ery, then, sat quietly in her seat and concerned herself with putting his earring in the soft lobe of her ear.

Then this knight of the road turned to Berengaria.

"My lady," he said with a deep, slow bow.

Beri straightened her back and raised her chin to show the upstart that his attention was unwanted (oh, how she lied!).

She felt that she must speak to him or die. She wanted him to … oh, by God's bones … she wanted him to see the woman that she was and take her and …

"Sir," she finally said, her heart in her throat, "What would you take from me?"

His dark brown eyes bored into her, and she glanced at his mouth and saw his wet, pink tongue lick his full, red lips in thought and then retreat back into his beautiful mouth underneath his lush and finely-groomed moustache.

And when he spoke, so softly that only she and he could understand him, he said, "You are beautiful, my lady, and your strength and noble bearing shine forth like a beacon from your soul.

I would take nothing from you except that which you might freely give to me."

And he leaned close to her, his mouth warm and inviting. She could feel the heat of him and found herself leaning closer and closer to him until … his lips brushed hers, as lightly as the sun on a flower's delicate petal, as softly as the flutter of a bee's wing, and a torrent of ecstatic pain rushed through her like the warm leveche wind that presages a storm, filling her with a surging gift of life unexpected, and as he broke their kiss, as cruelly and kindly as he had begun it, the warmth of the two of them together lingered within her.

And before she could open her eyes to gaze again upon this beautiful man, he whispered, "Meet me tonight at yonder tree, and we will go away together. I shall be yours, and you shall be mine for as long as we shall live. Come to me by moonlight. Be mine."

And then, she saw him for what he truly was: her hopes, her dreams, and her destiny.

She had to know … "And your name, sir?" she asked with trembling lips.

"I am a fellow of good name, poor condition, and worse quality. I have laid embargos on men and women whom I have met on the road, giving each the opportunity to place either their money or their lives in my hand. I have never taken more than a man or woman could live without, and I have never taken a life undeservedly. The name, my dove, the one that my parents gave me, is Francisco Esteban. I am called El Tempranillo, 'The Early Bird', by the poor souls who I meet on the highroad."

My name is Beri," she told him as she climbed back into the coach.

As the coach turned in the road to return to the castle, Beri looked back. Francisco, her Francisco (she thought, and her heart fluttered to think of it), caught her eye and raised his hand in parting before he went to Diego's motionless body and took the outrider's boots, belt, sword and pistol, the little pouch of gold at his hip, and the two golden medals he wore round his neck: San Miguel, patron of warriors, and San Adrian de Nicomedia, patron of guards.

Beri turned away, knowing in her heart that she would see him tonight.

*

The coach eventually reached the castle, and Berengaria descended, followed by her maid. She turned and said, even before she had trod even the first step of the marble staircase, "Ery, I am tired from the upset of this afternoon. I will take my meal in my chambers. Bring it to me, and then your duties for the evening will be finished."

Beri could see the poorly-disguised joy in her little maid's eyes.

Just as the coachman would now be explaining the death of Diego, the outrider, to the Marshal and the loss of Diego's horse to the Stable-master, Herculito would be regaling every page he met of his adventure. Ery would bring Beri's supper to her chambers but would let a tantalizing tidbit slip to the Cook as she prepared Beri's meal, and then, when Ery was free, the little maid would tell the other maids, who would tell the valets de chambres, who would tell the Master of the Chambers, who would tell the Chamberlain, each adding an exciting detail, that may or may not have actually occurred, to the story.

Berengaria would have the evening to herself. Even if she had not dined alone this night, she would not have dined with her father. His dinner was always with his men (she could see him asking her, "For what can a woman bring to the table?").

Beri knew that her father loved her. Had he not always called her his 'most precious treasure'? This evening, Beri would take her father's 'most precious treasure', along with some of his other treasures, the finest jewels and the most gleaming gold, and bring these precious things to the table of the dashing highwayman who would be her lover, Francisco Esteban, El Temranillo. The early bird would have her and her father's more worldly riches before the sun came up the following morning.

*

Beri ate little. Her stomach was tied in knots with anticipation, and her mind raced with the day's happenstance and the night's fateful plan. She waited until the castle was asleep before she opened her door the slightest crack and then waited ten long, thundering heartbeats before she slid out into the hallway.

First, she would need clothing. Her noble attire, that was proper and expected for the daughter of a count, was unsuitable for her journey tonight. She crept to the castle's laundry room and found just what she would need for her journey and her new life: two light gray linen ankle-length shifts, one to wear and one to wash, with sleeves long enough to cover her elbows, two linen caps to dress her head, white cotton bodices, and ankle-length petticoats, one light blue and the other light gray. Hung from a line and now dry were a couple of pairs of a boy's hose that appeared as if they would fit her. And she found a newly-cleaned wool cloak for when it was cold. She wondered if her Francisco would recognize her in her poor attire.

She returned to her chambers and donned her new clothing. She found her tall, leather riding boots and pulled them on, lacing them tightly. She pulled a fine cotton case from a pillow and stuffed it full of her other 'new' clothes and a second pair of boots. What more?

Beri found a strong leather belt for her waist and went to her dressing table, opening the little drawer in front. She pulled out the dagger that she had demanded from her father when she had been just a little girl (Berengaria had heard the story of the Portuguese woman, Brianda Pereira, who had fought the Spanish invaders at the Battle of Salga, and she had been so taken with the woman's exquisite bravery and skill that she had demanded that her father buy her a little dagger of her own to stick in the belt at her waist. He soon found her a stiletto of Italian design, made of good Spanish steel, and gave it to his daughter as much to please her as to stop her incessant pleading and bouts of tears. As soon as Berengaria held the knife in her little hand, she had walked down to the guardhouse and demanded that her father's Marshal teach her its use. She had become, even by the Marshal's standards, skilled).

Dressed in clothes that no one would notice if they saw her (servants were often invisible to the nobles of the castle), she stole down into the castle's darkest depths, a candle in her hand. She was one of four people in the castle (her father, the Chamberlain, and the Marshal being the others) who knew the location of the strong room, and her father had only shown her where the extra key to the room was kept, in the torch sconce to the left of the iron-clad, oaken door, so that she could keep its treasures safe when he died.

Inside, once she had closed the great door behind her, she lit other candles with the one that she carried to aid in her search. She set her candle in a single brass candlestick beside a large wooden chest. The she opened the chest and found it full of necklaces, and bracelets, and rings, jewelry for a Contessa (which she would be if she stayed in her father's house). She laughed at the thought of it and then placed ropes of pearls and two silver torcs around her neck, golden rings on every finger (two on each just for good measure), and amber bracelets, as well as golden ones, on her wrists and forearms.

Then, she went to another, smaller chest and opened it. It was filled with jewels, rubies and garnets and emeralds, and Beri found a leather pouch and filled it with the largest red and green stones that it would hold, and then filled the spaces between the great stones with smaller ones.

Then, she went to still another chest, and when she opened it, she found that it was full of golden coins. There were coins from Spain, and France, and Italy, and German states, and Denmark, and even distant Russia, and the Levant, as well. Some of these, too, she tossed into a leather pouch to take to her Francisco.

And as she was choosing the finest of the lot, she heard a melody, something wild and free and as compelling as the tide, a tune that might have been ancient or sung by her mother when she was a babe or maybe a song from a wild bird's throat. It drew her to a big, old chest, and when she had lifted its heavy iron lid, she found that the trunk was filled with neatly-stacked sleeves of the bluest silk. She took one in her hands and slid the silken cover off what it covered. These treasures were knives … curious, shining knives. They looked to be ancient things, the sides of each blade carved with the notes of godly song (one side an appeal for blessing and the other a prayer of sanctification) and an edge between them that looked so keen … She touched the meat of her thumb to the sharpness of the blade and felt the steel of it enter her flesh as if it did so in greeting. The knife was so sharp that she felt nothing other than a shivering pressure of the knife's weight until she saw her blood welling slowly up from the edge to leave the essence of her life on both sides of the blade. Then she realized that there was pain, but the pain seemed, somehow, to be part of the song that the blade sang to her. She took the knife away and stuck her bleeding thumb into her mouth to lave the wound. Her blood tasted as sweet and as strong as steel. Her eyes wandered back to the knife as she sucked the blood to stopping, and her blood on the edge of the knife seemed to gleam, but surely that was the reflection of the candle's flame. The strange music of the knife called to her, demanding her to take the knife with her. She took two of the knives, one for her and the other for Francisco, to sing the new songs for their new life together.

*

As she ate what little she could of the supper that Ery had brought her, Berengaria had asked the maid to send a stable-boy to her before she took her leave from the evening's duties. Beri had told the boy to saddle her Zapatera, the Andalusian mare that her father had brought her from Mérida when she had demanded a horse of her own. Her Zapatera was a princess and as smart as Berengaria, and the mare had foaled a magnificent colt, Zapatero (the Shoemaker), two years ago (it was tradition that an Andalusian colt could receive its mother's name in a masculine form).

When Beri, clothed in servant's gray and carrying a heavy bundle over her shoulder, as a maid would be likely to do, went to the stable, her mare was saddled and waiting for her, excited for the night's adventure ahead. Beri arranged her bundle behind the saddle and tied it securely and then led the horse from the stables to the castle's gate. The guard who she bribed to open the gate for her would leave the castle as soon as she was out of sight. His life would be forfeit when it was discovered that he had let her go, but he would soothe his shame, somehow, with the large ruby she had given him.

Berengaria rode out through the castle's gate and down the road, off to the crossroads to meet her love and begin her new life.

*

She came to the tree where Francisco had told her to meet him. There was a quiet tree, a glowing moon, and nothing else within sight … and not a sound … She dismounted from her horse, walked to the trunk of the tree, leaned against it, and waited.

The moon moved across the sky and the stars turned in the heavens, and she was about to cry and return to her life in the castle when she felt someone standing beside her. She turned to face whatever was there, her hand closing on the dagger in her belt.

As she turned, she felt a hand close over her mouth to quiet her, and she moved the hand that held her dagger to rest its tip lightly against the belly of the man who wanted her silence.

The man's soft, deep laugh broke the night's stillness, "Would you really cleave me here under the dark and lonely sky before we can cleave together in our bed, my dove?"

Beri laughed, pulled her dagger away from his belly, and let him pull her into his embrace.

"Let us ride to put this land behind us. I know an inn on the road to Huesca. We can rest there for a few hours before we travel further," he said, and she kissed him her assent.

Francisco gave Berengaria a leg up and then mounted the gelding she recognized as Diego's, a fine horse. They rode through the night under the moon until the sky began to lighten in the east.

The little inn they found waiting for them on the Huesca road had a fine stable where they told the groom to take care of their mounts, promising the boy silver if their horses were treated as well as the guests of the inn.

The two walked to the door of the inn, letting their fingertips touch once before Francisco knocked.

After a minute, a big man with unkempt dark hair and a bushy beard opened it, saying not a word.

"Two travelers seek a room for the day," her lover said,

The big man looked at them and nodded and allowed them entry, "Will you eat while my girl readies a room? I imagine that a prince and a princess of the road, such as you two, will require a room to yourselves," he said.

"Thank you," she said and smiled her best at the man.

He nodded and continued, "Sit. I will bring you soup from the hearth and bread, freshly-baked, from the oven, a slab of cheese, and ale. It is early, as you know, so that meager fare is what we have."

"Fair enough, sir," her savior told the innkeeper and led her to a table in the back from which the inn's oaken door could be glimpsed and no one would see their backs.

And soon enough, the innkeeper brought their food. Beri and her highwayman ate and drank until they were full and the inn's girl came to lead them to their room.

A minute after they had entered the little room, latched the door behind them, and dropped the packs on the planked floor, there was a knock at the door.

The highwayman put his finger to his lips and nodded for Beri to go to the corner and ready her dagger. He turned to the door, his hand on his steel, and asked, "Yes?"

"'Tis only me, Manuel, the stable-boy, Señor," a small voice answered, "Your mounts are groomed, grained, watered, and sleeping in fresh hay, so I have brought you your saddles and tack. In this inn, they are safer with you than with the horses."

Francisco reached into the little pouch at his belt, pulled out a shiny piece of silver, and then opened the door.

The boy brought in the gear and stood, waiting.

The highwayman put the gleaming bit of silver into the boy's hand and reminded him, "Watch them well, my friend, and have them ready to ride at the evening meal. And if anyone asks if a woman has come to this inn, tell them the truth, and say, 'No woman alone has come, nor should she,' and then hurry to knock on our door."

The boy looked at the silver as if he had never seen one in his hand before, and replied, "No one shall know of you from my lips, Señor. I swear by the Virgin."

Francisco nodded, and the stable boy turned to return to his work.

By the time Francisco had finished with the boy and turned back to Berengaria, she had brought her gifts and spread them out on the little, narrow bed.

"See what I have brought you, my love," she said, and Francisco leaned against the door while she showed him.

First, she took the smaller of the two leather pouches, opened it, and dumped its heavy contents onto the bed. The sparkling rubies and emeralds she had brought winked happily in the candlelight. Then she opened the second sack and poured out its gleaming gold. She moved the two silken sheaths to the head of the bed, out of the way, and when the highwayman's look asked her, 'Why?' she said softly, "Soon enough, Señor. Soon enough."

Then she stood before the bed. She let her petticoats fall to the floor and loosened her blouse. Then she took it off and added it to the pile of clothing on the floor.

Slowly, and carefully, she pulled her linen shift over her head, and after she had done so, Francisco came to her and knelt, to help her with her boots.

The man was skilled, and within minutes, they, too, lay discarded with the rest of her common clothing.

She motioned him back, and she bent to untie the ribbons that held her hose, and one at a time, as they were freed, rolled them down until she could kick them off of her toes.

And there she stood before him, clad only in the necklaces of pearls, torcs of silver, bracelets of amber, and rings of gold that she had taken from her father's treasure room.

The highwayman smiled at her, and she proceeded to pull each ring from each finger, slide each bracelet from her arms, and lift the coils of shining pearls and gleaming silver from her neck.

Then, she said to him, "Come and see my special present," and sad upon the bed amidst the gems and gold and jewelry.

He laughed at her boldness and told her with an eager gleam in his eyes, "Yes, but you, too must wait for me."

And the highwayman stood, back to the door, and laid his four Marin le Bourgeoys' flintlock pistols on the little table by the door. Then he took off his 'bastard' long sword (a rapier with a French hilt and a Valencia blade), a shorter arming sword (clearly a child of an Ulfberht blade of broad, Solingen steel with its inscription, "+IINIOMINEDMN", 'in nomine domini' ('in the Name of God'), etched into the blade), a buckler, four or five daggers (scattered about his person), and a short, cast-iron mace, carefully, one at a time, and laid them on the table to join the pistols. He laid his cape atop them all.

Francisco unlaced his black, leather jerkin and let it fall to the floor. Then unlaced a long-sleeved doublet, which he added to what he had discarded. A snow-white linen shirt with no noble ruff to interfere with his highwayman's work then fell atop the pile of dark clothing. He pulled off his tall, black boots and unlaced his codpiece, leaving him clad only in black galligaskins and equally black hose, both of which he doffed for her. And then he came to the bed, wearing only a simple golden cross on a thin gold chain.

He sat beside her and leaned to kiss her.

But she put her teasing finger between their lips and whispered, "More treasures, I have brought for you, my love, before I offer the last" and reached for the silken sleeves she had earlier pushed to the bed's head.

Berengaria placed first one of the sheaths in her highwayman's lap and then the other. Francisco looked at the shining fabric in surprise. "What could they be?" he asked.

"Look and see, my love," she told him, "Look and see."

As he reached into the azure sleeve that held the undiscovered treasure, grabbed hold, and pulled the knife free, he cocked his head.

"Ah, so you hear them, too," she thought.

"They sing!" Francisco exclaimed, "They sing, a tune of anticipation, desire, and lust."

"Or perhaps you hear the song of my heart," she said, but only to herself.

Francisco examined the knife with the eyes of a connoisseur, she thought at first; and then, she saw him hold the blade in his gaze and his trembling hands with the eyes and touch of a lover. She was jealous for only a heartbeat because she had felt the same pull from the knives, herself, when she had first held them. So she had brought them to a man who would understand them, substance and soul, as she had from the first second she had touched them.

*

And then, Francisco brought the edge of the blade to almost touch the tips of each of his fingers in turn, trying to find a fit.

Everyone knew the symbolism of the fingers, and Berengaria held her breath as Francisco determined which finger he would offer to the blade.

First, the highwayman held the knife to his little finger. That finger was associated with intelligence and persuasion. It was the part of the hand ruled by Mercury, the planet as poisonous as its namesake metal, quicksilver.

Francisco listened to the song the blade sang to that finger. Berengaria heard it, too, whisper-soft but clear, an unhappy tune, not the song the blade wished to sing.

The prince of the road moved the knife to his ring finger, the finger associated with creativity, beauty, and romance, ruled by the Moon and silver metal.

Again Francisco listened to the knife's song. Berengaria heard a new song, a song she knew that she would hear on the day that she was wed, but again, it was not the song that the knife wished to give to Francisco.

Her outlaw moved the point of the knife to his middle finger. This finger was the essence of balance and responsibility, ruled by Saturn. Saturn's metal is lead (although many Romani fortunetellers insisted that it was steel).

Francisco listened to the knife's song again. This time, the tune was complicated and intense and lasted for what seemed like hours. Berengaria heard the song and was drawn to it, and she found herself attempting to memorize the tune so she would have it for herself forever,

The road agent moved the knife to his index finger. There was power, authority, and leadership there, and even though that finger was ruled by Jupiter, the father of the planets, its metal is only tin.

Francisco listened to the knife's newest song to that finger, but before Berengaria could tell what melody the knife sang this time, her freebooter moved the knife to his thumb, the finger that was little more than an indicator of character and a signal of friendship. The thumb is ruled by no star or planet. This final finger showed only strength and authority.

Francisco listened to the knife's last song and smiled as if he were sitting with an old friend. Berengaria heard this song clearly, and she believed that she recognized its song as the one that had filled her heart when she had first seen Francisco on the road on the day that changed everything in her life.

Francisco finally chose, moved the knife to his middle finger, and let the knife's sharp tip press into his flesh. The weight of the knife pushed its point into Francisco's fingertip, and in its own time, a ruby drop of his blood welled around the shining steel.

"Do you hear it?" the highwayman exclaimed, "Its song has changed. Now it is a sweet tune of contentment, fulfillment, and happiness. It is a wonder, Beri! You have truly brought me a gift beyond compare."

"Put down the knife, my highwayman. You have no need for it now," Berengaria whispered to him, "I have brought you another gift, one of sacrifice, devotion, and promise. You will, I hope, find my last gift to be as wonderful as the knives, but when this final present transfixes you, as the knives will not, you will not feel the knife's hard utility but only my soft service." And she blew out the candle and pulled him to her in the soft shadows of the morning.

*

That evening, just as the sun began to hide itself below the mountains to the west, the two lovers donned their clothes and set off to the north and their liberty. They left the main road at the tiny village of Almudévar and traveled carefully northwest along the little track.

"I was born," Francisco told Berengaria, "in the mountains of the Sierra de Guara and grew tall and strong in the cañones there, but I traveled south, when I was a young man but old enough to think I knew it all, to the Sierra Morena and the Serrania de Ronda, and there, my bravery and skill made me the hero of many a ballad. But nothing I have braved and no skills that I have learned and mastered have prepared me for the feelings that I find that I have for you, my dove. And just as you have given up your old life to join yours to mine, I will abandon everything I know just to be with you, for as long or as little a time as we will have. To reach the place where our new love can safely flower, we must cross the mountains of Catalonia, the home of gangs of bandoleros and the raids of the salteadores."

Francisco told his love that they would head for the 'Pink City' of Toulouse. With Louis XIII the new king, the little town would be a place where they could shed their old lives and begin anew.

*

He told her these things as they rode leisurely on paths that were poorly traveled and free of other travelers. Once lonely places with no men but shepherds guarding their flocks, these mountains had become the redoubts of Les Écorcheurs, the slaughterers, men who had once been soldiers until their war had ended. Then, they had to find work or starve, but the only work that they knew was following the orders of their lords and killing to earn their bread. So, many heard of the 'Emperor of Pillagers' and came to follow him, ransacking small farms or a manor, if one could be found and overwhelmed. Some of the lowest of these slaughterers were called 'the flayers' because they took everything from their victims, even their clothing.

The more important roads were controlled by Routiers, who everyone called 'Englishmen', even though almost all of them were the Gascons, Spaniards, and Germans that had been French cavaliers during the war but who were now forced to live off the land and the gold they could take from innocent travelers. The strength of the Routiers forced Les Écorcheurs into the mountains and away from civilized places.

These terrible men, and others, still controlled many of the roads near the coast between Barcelona and the French border city of Perpignam, so Ferdinand planned to make their way further west, crossing into France at the little village of Fos. If they traveled as far west as Lourdes, they would find Basque mercenaries, and all of the powers of God would not be able to save them.

*

So Francisco and Berengaria followed the little path that skirted the blue waters of a large lake, Embalse de la Sotonera, and later, at the little ford of the Rio Gállego, they met an unfortunate man of their trade. Before the inept footpad could even utter the first word of his demand, Francisco pulled his flintlock pistol and shot the man in the throat.

The lovers dismounted, and while Beri held their horses, Francisco looked to see what the dead man could offer them as payment for detaining them on their journey.

After he searched the dead man's body, Francisco held up a bag that jingled of coins and said, "This poor soul had little to show for his labors. This bag of silver and copper cobs, a flintlock that is likely to fail for its dull flint, soft frizzen, and touch-hole that is likely clogged, and an old and much-used rondel are all that are worth taking." And so, that is all that he took before he mounted his horse again.

*

They crossed the bridge over the Embalse de la Peña, said a prayer at the chapel of the Hermitage of the Virgin, and found a likely inn in the tiny town of Santa Maria. They loved and then slept another day and a night, finally feeling freed from any pursuit and rising to break their fast and take their leave at sunrise.

*

As the two lovers rose higher in the mountains, Francisco and Berengaria rode more slowly and carefully and reached the four or five huts that were called Puente la Reina de Jaca before the sun began to hide behind western peaks. A kind farmer accepted a few coppers to let them use his barn to rest their horses, and Francisco and Berengaria slept in the hay (when they finally slept). When they awoke, they gave the farmer's wife two more coppers for bowls of thin soup and bread that had once been fresh.

*

The next morning, they came to the Abbey of San Pedro de Siresa where, the monks told them, the Holy Grail had once been found in a crevice in the wall of the church behind the altar. That night, the highwayman and his lady slept apart, each in a separate monk's spare cell.

*

The next day about midday, the two crossed a mountain crest and saw, in a valley far below them, a village, the little town of Lescun, little but still large enough for a welcome inn with real ale and hot water for a bath.

*

They were finally in France, but the long arms of a Spanish Count could still reach them there if they were noticed. So as the mountains gave way to hills, the couple stayed on the roads. But when they could, they left the pathway and, instead, rode across rolling fields or tried unkempt trails, and so they reached the city of Toulouse in another week.

*

They were road weary, and their clothes were worn and dusty, so Francisco and Berengaria found a good inn where they could rest and begin to create their new life.

The Catalonian Hidalgo Esteban and his lady, Isabella, asked the innkeeper for the name of a tailor who was known to sew for people of quality.

They were directed to a man who knew his business, and the business of all of his customers as well. While Esteban and Isabella were measured for their new clothes, in the French style, the tailor proved to be a fountain of information.

The Hidalgo and his lady were introduced, through the tailor's influence and popularity, to the men of quality of the French city who were more than happy to assist such a gracious and noble couple with the tiring details of securing a proper property.

Esteban and Isabella purchased a country house, a French villa with orchards, vineyards, a stable, a fine kitchen, many well-appointed rooms, and a small chapel, with some of the gold that Berengaria had taken from her father's strong-room. They then began the hard work of becoming respectable minor nobility in a foreign land.

Lady Isabella, who was once called Berengaria when she had been the daughter of a count, made a lovely and loving home for the two of them. Don Esteban, who had once been the highwayman whose victims had called him 'The Early Bird', bought himself a seat on the parlement of Toulouse (he and his Isabella discussed his choice of a new career, and they both agreed that Esteban would bring a wealth of valuable experience to his new position). Now, he was just one judge sitting on a bench full of judges, but Esteban knew the business of justice from both sides of the law, even when he had meted it out fairly to those he had once met on the road. As a judge in the parlement, Don Esteban became renowned as a man of patience, courtesy, tact, courage, compassion, and common sense. His fellow judges appreciated his punctuality, firmness, and humility (and that he often bought a round of ale for the other judges, after a dry day of court, in the little auberge just down the street from the courthouse).

*

Esteban put away his pistols and tools of the road, but much to the scandal of their neighbors, he and his lovely wife enjoyed fencing in the courtyard of their little villa as an entertainment and a recreation. The singing knives were put safely away, should they ever be needed, but they sang their songs quietly in the dark in their blue silk sheaths, patiently waiting to be called on again.

*

And, at night, in the soft dark, Don Esteban would whisper "Beri" in his wife's sweet ear as they made love. And Isabella would often cry out "Francisco" more than once or twice before the sun rose.

*

The lovers survived the plague together in 1629, but in 1652, Berengaria died when the Black Death returned to take her, leaving Francisco a broken heart and a beautiful four-year-old daughter.

Chapter 6 – The Sun

Another of the Major Arcana of the Suit of Knives in the Swordsmith's Tarot is The Sun. As an expectant, dazzling day follows every dark night, The Sun is the certain source of life and the nourishment of the soul. The Sun is strong and pure and the wellspring of hope, optimism, and action. The light that the Sun sends is vibration, a celestial music heard by those who will allow themselves to listen. The Sun's unseen pull on all that lives is the unconscious mind directing one's spirit and actions to be true and righteous. The Sun abides, seen or unseen.

*

Their daughter was christened with the name that her mother could never use and that her husband could never call his wife, Berengaria, but her father called his final gift from his beloved wife, Solange. The people of the city saw this naming as the wish of a solemn and dignified jurist to impart good qualities to his only heir, but for her father, Solange would always be his 'angel of the sun'.

*

The father raised his daughter as best he could, teaching her what he knew, the law that he dispensed in his capacity as a member of the parlement, and the outlawry that he had practiced, before he had donned his robes of respectability, as a highwayman.

The man, who had once been a highwayman, taught his 'angel of the Sun' what he believed that his daughter should know.

So she learned the sophisticated and spiritual swordplay of Destreza (as well as the vulgar and worldly blade-work of the streets), and for those times when a sword was not available, her taught her the use of daggers (and hatchets, and cleavers, and whatever might be handy). He taught her to fight with her hands (and elbows and knees) and feet, especially since a woman could not choose her aggressor, and many men who she might meet might be larger and physically stronger than she would be.

The jurist did not neglect his daughter's mind. He taught her to read and write, in English and in French by the time she was six, and then he hired the best tutors for her that he could find (some even came from as far away as Paris!) to help her master Latin and Greek, mathematics, geography (and navigation as well as the reading and making of maps), philosophy, natural history (geology, physics, and biology), art (she especially loved painting and the making of the pigments), and music (she played the recorder badly enough to scare away her audience but the lute was a sweet, soothing thing in her hands). She learned manners and dancing, as well.

Together, father and daughter discovered the works of Greek, English, and French playwrights, taking great, and often uproarious, pleasure in reading them aloud to each other. The father also taught his daughter to read the law and write and understand contracts for the time when she would have no father and no husband and others would have no other thoughts in mind but to rob her.

When the girl turned twelve, even though the neighbors gossiped, the father insisted that his daughter keep the villa's books.

He gave her a small allowance each month, to budget and pay for what she would need for herself: clothes, feed for her pony, and the like.

And to prepare the young woman for a life that would likely include all of life, the father taught her the games that people of all classes played and to gamble, so that she could venture a bet or two, gain or lose her own money, and understand when the games that she would play were fair or not.

To this end, Esteban taught Solange dice and backgammon. To make her way in more polite society, he taught her chess, the French game Piquet, and the excellent game, devised by the poor English poet, Sir John Suckling, of cribbage (taken as whole cloth from the old game of Noddy). For the times she would entertain herself in less polite society, he taught her Karnöffel (the rough and uncouth game that the Church hated, as much for its anarchy as for the fact that its very name was what the peasants who played it called testicles).

The man taught the girl to care for the livestock of the villa: the cattle, sheep, ducks, and chickens. He taught her to ride and how to care for her mount (from its feed and grooming to assisting the farrier with its shoes) and its tack (as well as how to hitch the horses to their carriage and the oxen to their plow). He taught her to fish and hunt, with a bow and with a hawk. And when she had been successful in her hunting, he taught her how to clean and dress her kill and then how to preserve the meat she brought home: how to salt and dry it, or brine it in salted water, or smoke it in the little house in back of the kitchen.

The parent taught his offspring how to keep a garden and how to preserve its plenty: keeping potatoes, onions, and apples (and layering eggs in oats) in the cool cellar he had dug, drying the corn and beans, salting the cabbage and herbs, and making jams from the berries. He taught her how to churn butter and store it in brine to keep it fresh and how to make cheese by warming milk, adding rennet, salting the curd, and putting it by to ripen.

He taught her how to cook, frying and boiling and baking, and thanks be to God, she became a much better cook than he. The villa had a respectable vineyard, and so he hired the vintner who created casks and bottles of wine from the grapes of the property to teach his daughter how this was accomplished.

*

When Solange told her father, through her questions and assertions, that she was a young woman, no longer a little girl (although his father's eye's found it difficult, at first, to accept her maturity, such a tiny, delicate thing that she appeared), he looked at her again and laughed. This was the daughter his wife Berengaria had borne and who he had raised, but she was not the fragile thing he had cared for for so many years. She had become herself and was able, sure, steady, and strong.

And so, he taught her about the knives as her mother had taught him on the night she had come to him and told him that her name was Beri. He bought the old knives out of their safe, hidden place. He slid one out of its cool blue sheath and placed it in his daughter's hands. She looked at it in silence, her eyes wide in awe, and then turned the knife over in her hands to read the Latin blessing and grace and the notes engraved on each broad side of the blade above the words.

Then, she slid the fingertip of her index finger (the place of power and sovereignty, his daughter's gifts and inheritance from her mother) and whispered in amazement, "I hear the song of the knife, the melody of the notes in the blade," she said reverently, "but … the music is the singing of the knife and something more that echoes in my heart …", and then in an instant, the blade slipped into her finger's flesh and drank of her blood, the bright, red essence of his little girl's life coating the knife's sharp steel. And when her blood (blood that he had fathered) touched the knife's keen edge, he heard the song again, himself, an anthem happily floating on the air around them. The three of them, the father, the daughter, and the knife made a consort; they were no more and no less than instruments of the same family. Then the father and the daughter put the knives away in their quiet, dark place and went to the kitchen to make themselves dinner.

*

Solange stayed with her father for many years. In fact, she was spoken of in the City as 'Don Esteban's old maid'. But she often went into the city to meet with her father for a bite to eat at midday in the auberge as the Courts paused in their daily schedule. At one of these luncheons, she was introduced to one Thomas Perdue, Master of Requests. He had been a barrister in the parlement before he purchased his lofty position and now amused himself, when he was not at work for the Courts, by penning entertainments for the theater and using his sharply-trained legal eye to examine the Scriptures. As a Master of Requests, M. Perdue performed as a judicial jack-of-all-trades. One day, he might preside over a bailiwick court; the next, he might preside over a sitting of Parlement. He had even been called upon, more than occasionally, to sit on the King's Conseil privé!

Solange grew to adore Thomas, as much as he came to cherish her (her father, regardless of Thomas' success, saw his daughter's lover as unfit to shine her shoes). But their love would not be denied, and they married. By the time Don Esteban died, during the famine of 1693, his daughter had given birth to a child of her own, a son, Francisco-Esteban Perdue, upon whom her father doted.

The same parrots, who had prattled about Solange's spinsterhood before she was wed, also jabbered about this poor child born so late to the judge's daughter. And when the boy's father was carried away into the bosom of Abraham to join his grandfather just before the century turned, just as Francisco-Esteban had been given his breeches, the gossips gushed more false tears about the hard life that the widow must now endure.

With Tomas' death, Solange was lonely and missed the man that she had loved, but without him, the villa was peaceful, with only her son's laughter to disturb the serenity. She considered her situation and found that she had enough money to live on, even though she was determined to give her son the education that her father had lavished upon her.

So, as her father had done with her, she taught the boy to read and write, and he proved an apt student, becoming fluent in French and Spanish by the time he was eight or nine. She found tutors to instruct the boy in the subjects that she had learned from her tutors. Francisco-Esteban excelled at things of logic: philosophy, mathematics, theology, and when he was older, the law. He cared not a whit for art or music, preferring his recreation to be of the physical.

The boy rode as if he had been born astride a horse, and he cared for all living things as if his father had been St. Francis instead of a prince of the road. He was a godsend to his mother in all of the chores of the villa, cheerful and loving, no matter the task she set him.

The grandson of the price of the roads liked to gamble, probably more than she should have encouraged, but when he vied with his mother at the dice or les jeux de tables (like backgammon), he won more than he lost, and it was rare for him to accept any winnings from his mother (she found, later, that he was not so forgiving of his friends).

And from the time that Francisco-Esteban could hold a weapon, Solange instructed her son in the niceties of bows and blades. And on his sixteenth birthday, she had a special gift made for him.

There had been a party in the afternoon. Francisco-Esteban's many friends had spent the day together at the villa, eating, sporting, drinking, and dancing to the music of La Occitania that permeated the region (the tabor and the pipe from the Basques and the hurdy-gurdy and the bagpipes from Limousin). When all of the guests had gone to their homes and the servants were dismissed to their ease or their beds, Solange asked he son to follow her into his father's room.

She had locked and barred the door when Thomas died, and the room had been a mystery to Francisco-Esteban ever since.

Solange opened the door and invited her son to sit at his father's old desk.

"Wait for me," she said to the boy (she looked at him, and in a flash of recognition, saw him as the young man that he was), "I will return shortly with something very special."

She left the room, and Francisco-Esteban rose from his father's chair and walked around the room, examining the books, his father's portrait on the wall, and every nick-knack, bibelot, and curio that sat on the shelves. Over the mantelpiece of the little hearth that he thought that he remembered from when he was a boy, he found a rapier. It was Spanish, a thing of great beauty and terrible use. He hefted it and marveled at its balance and how well it fit his hand.

"That was my father's," his mother's voice said from behind him, "He used it when he taught me the Destreza. I taught you as he taught me, but I put his sword away when he died. Your father thought it a beautiful thing."

"It is beautiful," Francisco-Esteban said wonderingly, "Is it a Damascene blade?"

"I see that I have trained you well, my son," she said, and he could hear her smile, "Yes. It was made in Toledo almost two hundred years ago, but it is, I am certain, still as deadly and still as sharp as it was the day I put it away."

Solange was carrying three bundles, two wrapped in old, blue silk and another of lush, thick, black silk-velvet, golden-embroidered with the Coq Gaulois, the Gallic rooster, the symbol of France.

"The black, I think," she said, "should be first."

Francisco-Esteban unfolded the dark, rich fabric and pulled out a strange device, made of black leather and metal fastenings. "What is it," he asked as confused as he was pleased.

"They are scabbards," his mother told him, "for two very special blades. Let me help you put them on and adjust them so that they fit you correctly."

"The scabbards are of poplar cores over-sewn with black-dyed sheepskin, embroidered in silver with a Huguenot cross on each one, just below where the blades' handles will show themselves. Your father's family were Huguenot but found that it was not safe to reveal themselves after the massacre on St. Bartholomew's Day over a hundred years ago. But if anyone recognizes this cross on these scabbards, what the scabbards hold will ensure their silence."

As she placed the scabbards on his back and adjusted them so that they would hold tightly for a clean draw of a blade but allow Francisco-Esteban the ease of movement that he would require to use the blades as they were intended, she told him more, "The tips and throats of the scabbards (they are called chapes and lockets) are forged of Damascus steel, as are the blades who will rest in the scabbards."

Solange made a final adjustment and nodded. She reached into her husband's desk, rummaged around, and pulled out a small hand-mirror. "See how it fits you," she said, holding mirror so that he would see the sheaths as they lay on his back.

The young man laughed to see his martial reflection in the little glass.

"Now, you may open the blue," she said with an excitement in her voice that she could not disguise.

The young man reached into the blue silk wrapper, grabbed a comfortable handle, and pulled out a blade, too wide to be a knife and too short to be a sword. On the flat of each side were phrases in Latin and an engraved musical staff with old-fashioned diamond-shaped notes; one side held a blessing, and the other held a benediction.

But there was something else. He found that there was something humming, just at the edge of his hearing (or maybe of his sight), and that if he closed his eyes to concentrate, he could hear it, no *feel* it! The song was as familiar as one of his mother's lullabies that had led him to sleep when he was a babe and as novel and stimulating as the surging bagpipes and hurdy-gurdies that propelled the dancers at his celebration this past afternoon.

"Mother," he began …

… and her smile and beatific nod told him that she knew and heard this music, too.

There was something that the music wanted of him, though. Francisco-Esteban, without a thought, moved his hand to the blade of the knife and held the keen edge in his palm. The music of the blade swelled in his ears and in his heart, and he felt the steel move through the flesh of his palm.

Blood welled up to cover the steel, and Francisco-Esteban pulled the knife from his palm. The blood on the blade gleamed as if it were meant to decorate the music that the knife sang. And when the young man looked at what should have been a terrible gash in the skin of his palm, the edges of the wound had closed, and the only thing that he knew for certain was that a new line had appeared there, one that crossed his life-line, his heart-line, his head-line, and his fate-line.

And the song that the blade had sung still rang in his heart and his ears.

*

For the next five years, Solange trained her son in the knives as her father had trained her. He became her equal in their use, and the mother and the son found that, though the leaning and knowing of the knives, they became as close and as dear friends as they were as mother and son. She called him "Le Couteau" (the cleaver) as they strove with each other; he called her "Mother".

And then, one day, it was time for Francisco-Esteban to make his own way in the world. He had no desire to follow the law or to become an idle nobleman. He was not in love (although many of the young women of the city dreamed of his attention and his regard). This dull, provincial city was not for him. So his mother helped him pack his things and load them onto his back, gave him a pouch of gold and silver (and her love), and wished him success.

He hugged her and kissed her cheeks and her forehead and then hugged her again. And then, he took his walking stick in his hand and started off down the road.

She was resolved not to cry until he was out of sight.

Francisco-Esteban walked to a little rise in the path, turned and waved his farewell to his mother.

She waved in return.

He was too far away to have seen if she had cried.

She held to her resolve and shed not a tear until he was gone.

But then, she walked into her empty house, up the echoing stairs to her room, and wept.

*

The French called their privateers 'corsairs', which may have come from the Latin term for one who undertakes a journey or the Arabic word for pirate. The corsairs, themselves, were a bit of both.

Francisco-Esteban followed the old road from Toulouse to Bordeaux to become one of these journeyman pirates.

*

Privateers were licensed, with the King's Lettre de Marque, to attack ships of France's enemies. If they were captured, they hoped that this license would afford them the status of prisoners of war and a cold, uncomfortable cell until the end of the war instead of dancing the Tyburn jig (as the damnable English called it), the traditional method of execution for pirates.

But when the privateers were successful, they did well (even after the King took his Third).

Unfortunately for Francisco-Esteban, the Treaty of Utrecht, which banned the practice of privateering (at least in the treasure-rich Caribbean), had been signed a year or two before he arrived in Bordeaux. But news traveled slowly in those days, and when Francisco-Esteban reached the sea, French corsairs were still taking ships and gold from Spanish treasure fleets and British merchantmen. The grandson of the highwayman found his way to the docks and heard rumors that René Duguay-Trouin, the most famous of the Breton corsairs, was sailing to Bordeaux from the asylum-city of St. Malo. He had first shipped out, nearly twenty-five years before. on Captain Legoux's *Trinité* and within two years commanded his own forty-gunner, the *Hercule*, by appointment of King Louis. By the time he had been made a nobleman, the brave captain had captured almost twenty Dutch and English warships and over 300 merchantmen. During the War of Spanish Succession, Lord Duguay-Trouin captured three English ships-of-the-line and later the Brazilian city of Rio de Janeiro.

Francisco-Esteban had the highest hopes that he could meet the famous captain, ship out with him, and lead an exciting life as a corsair.

The ship from St. Malo docked at the quay on the Garonné River a week after Francisco-Esteban arrived. He had found a down-at-its-heels, but still respectable, inn and waited on the quay each day before returning to the inn each evening for too little palatable food and too much ale.

But that frustration, boredom, and indigestion would soon be at an end.

When the *L'Auguste*, a fine-looking corsair ship, had off-loaded its cargo and given its crew leave, Francisco-Esteban walked up the gang-plank to pay his respects to the Captain and sign the ship's articles.

L'Auguste was trim little brig of fourteen guns, its deck cluttered with pyramids of bombs and shells, stacks of long-guns, racks of sabers, daggers, lances, and pistols, and a hundred other nautical objects that looked complicated and potentially deadly.

A man with pasty skin, sunken eyes, and Francisco-Esteban realized as he spoke, missing teeth, wearing white, canvas trousers, a red sash that held two pistols, a blue jacket, and a flat-crowned black hat asked, "What do you want?"

"My name is Francisco-Esteban Perdue, late of Toulouse. I would speak with your captain and join your noble ship's company."

The man looked the boy up and down, walked to the rail and spat into the water, and said, "The ship's noble company, eh? Follow me, and maybe you'll get you wish."

He led Francisco-Esteban through a hatchway, down a short flight of steps, to a hallway, and then to a wooden door with a shining brass handle.

The man knocked once and said, "If it please the Captain, a shorebird wishes to take flight with us."

"Come," a strong but highly-pitched voice called from within.

The man opened the door, walked into the room, touched his hat, and said, "Beg your pardon, Captain, this boy asked to see you and sign articles."

"You are dismissed, seaman de Forbin," the Captain said.

The man touched his hat again and left Francisco-Esteban with the Captain.

The Captain said nothing for a minute and then he asked, "Well?"

Francisco-Esteban swallowed to ease his nervousness and then spoke, his voice cracking, "I would join your ship as a corsair, Captain Duguay-Trouin."

The Captain laughed. He laughed so hard and so long that Francisco-Esteban began to feel his temper flare. How dare this man, no matter how famous and accomplished he was, treat him as a fool?

The Captain saw the flush of anger in the boy's cheeks and the fire in his eyes and calmed his laughter, "I apologize, son. But I am not Lord Duguay-Trouin. My name is Captain Charles Cognetz of St. Malo. And if you would accept my apology for my laughter and sail with me as one of my corsairs, I would be proud to have you."

This was disappointing, but Francisco-Esteban had come to Bordeaux to become a corsair and live a life of adventure. "I am Francisco-Esteban Perdue of Toulouse, and it would be my honor to have you as my captain," the young man said and began to extend his hand to shake on their agreement, but then he remembered that this was his Captain, so he pulled his hand back and threw a salute.

The Captain returned his salute and said, "We will work on that salute, corsair, and I will teach you, if you are diligent, the ways of the sea. We are bound for the sea-lanes to hunt British merchantmen, capture their treasure, and fight them as we must. What weapon do you prefer?"

Francisco-Esteban said, "I am good with a rapier, a rifle, and a pistol, but I prefer my knives if I must fight."

"I hope we will not have to put them to use on your maiden voyage, Perdue, but ce qui sera, sera. Be here with your duffel tomorrow morning as the sun rises. We will provision our ship and head out to sea to hunt for our quarry."

"Yes, sir!" Francisco-Esteban said, saluting this time, turned, and left the cabin.

He was a corsair!

*

Francisco-Esteban wrote a letter to his mother, telling her of his good fortune in signing aboard a much-feared and successful brig, *L'Auguste*, as a corsair. He wrote that he expected their first voyage to take a month before they could fill their hold with treasure taken from the damned English. He told her that he loved her and that he would write to her again when they returned to port.

He gave the letter to the inn-keeper with a silver-piece and was assured that the aubergiste would post it on the morrow.

Chapter 7 – The Three of Knives

The third card of the Minor Arcana of the Suit of Knives in the Swordsmith's Tarot is the Three of Knives. This card tells of opportunity and change but warns of risks, disappointment, and defeat. Every journey changes the traveler's awareness. Each life is an adventure, a trek, and quest of challenge and growth and, ultimately, death. The awareness of the trials that lie ahead, once they have been conquered, is called, by some, foresight. Strength can only be gained by mastering limitations.

Just as this card of the Suit of Knives warns of obstacles and impediments, it also foretells favor and benefit for those who prosper in their attempts.

Water is the element of The Three of Knives. Water is an overwhelming barrier and a fearsome opponent. It quenches Fire, it drowns the Air, and it floods the Earth. Water is also the fountain of life, without which there is no life.

The Three of Knives demands attention, punishes overconfidence, and rewards deference.

*

For Francisco-Esteban, the first few days after *L'Auguste* left Bordeaux were a whirl of new sights, new sounds, and finding his way among the new people who were crowded onto the sleek French brig. This two-master and her sisters were the perfect ships to harass the merchantmen who were their prey but could never expect to stand and trade broadsides with an English ship-of-the-line.

Francisco-Esteban was one of the extra men Captain Cognetz had taken on to crew the ships that he planned to take. And since the skills of the young man from Toulouse were anything but nautical, Francisco-Esteban was tested as to his sharpshooting (he was a crack shot and, as such, would spend most battles high above the deck, perched precariously on the little platform that the sailors called the 'fighting top' that was cobbled to the mainmast just below the topsail, trying his best to pick off the officers of any ship that the *L'Auguste* had sunk its grapples into) and found acceptable. So to acclimate the new corsair to his new post, the mate had him climbing the shrouds and, when he was up in the heavens with the gulls and the angels and hanging for dear life onto the footropes at the topgallant on the foremast or main or clutching the main-masthead as tightly as if it were his lover, searching the horizon for likely sails. A small ship could be prey, and a large ship, a ship-of-the-line or man-o-war was a predator fit only to run from.

It had begun as the most frightening task Francisco-Esteban had ever been set. As the ship tacked, it seemed to the landsman that its masts whipped from side to side, trying their damnedest to toss him into the water. The French navy, even including the corsairs, had fewer ships than the English. And to preserve what they had, they French preferred to engage to leeward. As the ships heeled with the wind, which the French preferred because it allowed them a quick and easy escape before the wind if it were needed, their guns pointed high. But no ship could ever heel to only one gage. When the brig tacked, to windward or to leeward, the masts tossed themselves from one side to the other of the ship, and Francisco-Esteban was hard-put to stay aloft.

No ship wanted to announce itself until it had determined whether it would engage. If it fled, no flag or ensign or banner would be raised to alert its adversary; if it made to engage, it would hoist its colors and attack.

So the mate told Francisco-Esteban to get his bloody arse aloft and find them a pigeon to feast upon.

The brig sailed west and then southwest from Bordeaux, across the Golfe de Gascogne (that the English called the Bay of Biscay), then south with Portugal to her east, too far to sea to sight the Pillars of Hercules but ever southward. The sailors told Francisco-Esteban that the land now far to his east, L'Afrique, was a hellish place, where infernal mountains of sand, where nothing could live, met the sea.

The sailors, in the dark, cramped space below-decks before the mast, where Francisco-Esteban had managed to find a spot to hang his hammock, told stories and threw dice (for whatever they had to wager) and, among the few who were interested, buggered one another (other than there being no privacy below, with all of the crew packed cheek-to-jowl, no one remarked on it, besides telling the loudest or most enthusiastic of the participants, "Tais-toi!" ("Shut up!"), and taking the sodomy as a natural proceeding). There were fist-fights aplenty for words said in haste, for sitting in another's spot, and for nothing more than an irritating glance, but Francisco-Esteban discovered, when a bunk-mate found his duffle missing a plug of tobacco, that theft resulted in a flogging (if the mate was told) or a knifing (if it was left to the crew).

So Francisco-Esteban learned to keep the things he valued with him. He kept his clothing, his needle and thread, a tin cup, and his Bible in his duffle, shoved into a tiny space between two oaken hanging knees that supported one of the beams where it met the strakes that covered the timbers of the hull. He kept his small purse with the few coins that were left in it and his working knife safely in the pocket of the pants he wore. But awake or asleep, Francisco-Esteban wore his singing knives, in their scabbards, strapped to his back.

*

One bright, warm morning, about a month out from Bordeaux, Francisco-Esteban climbed the shrouds to begin another uneventful watch, perched high on the foremast above the deck of *L'Auguste* and the sea that bore it onward.

He had been aloft for an hour or two, singing a song from his childhood that he had forgotten that he knew, when he espied a flash of light at the horizon to the south. He looked again and saw the little, dark spot that heralded a ship's mast.

"A sail," he yelled to the mate below, "dead ahead, one point to starboard."

And then the man aloft on the main mast confirmed his sighting, "A sail! Aye, dead ahead, one point to starboard."

"To your stations," the mate shouted to the crew who were either on deck or below.

Francisco-Esteban looked down and saw the Captain, standing beside the man at the wheel on the quarter-deck, raise his glass and turn slightly to starboard.

If the Captain determined that the ship on the horizon was prey, a fat merchantman, they would pursue it. If it was too large, obviously a frigate or ship-of-the-line, they would flee. Until the unknown ship was identified, they would have to follow it, draw close enough to observe its form and manners, and then decide on a course of action.

It took the captain only a moment, "Raise the English colors and hasten away down the wind to the west."

It was a ship of the English Navy; there was no other reason for *L'Auguste* to run. But then, Francisco-Esteban saw the flash again from the spot on the horizon … and then another … from something to its west.

As the French privateer made its escape, Francisco-Esteban watched the horizon where the second flash had come from. There was something there now.

L'Auguste had begun its tack to the west.

"Captain," Francisco-Esteban shouted down, "Another sail! Dead ahead!"

He looked down and saw that the Captain had heard him and was moving the glass to find the new ship.

The bronze-bottomed English ships were all the faster for the metal plating on their hulls. And Francisco-Esteban looked abeam again to find that the first ship, which he could, by now, easily identify as a damned frigate, was coming up on them all too quickly.

Then, out of the corner of his eye, Francisco-Esteban saw another flash from the English ship that lay ahead of them. The bastards were maintaining their line (the English were known to be formalists, arraying their close-hauled ships at regular intervals regardless of the occurrence) but allowing the ships to sail a mile or so apart, too far to communicate with their ensigns and signal flags but easily alerted with the flashes of sunlight on pieces of mirror held by their lookouts high in the rigging.

And then, further to *L'Auguste*'s starboard, another flash, and then another. The English were closing their net, circling the French corsair like cowardly wolves surrounding a noble red deer.

"Another! Two points forward on the starboard beam. And another still! Three points abaft on the starboard beam!"

A minute later, he heard a shout from the deck below. Francisco-Esteban looked down and saw the mate motioning for him to descend. His rifle would be needed. *L'Auguste* was preparing to fight!

*

The Captain of the French brig did everything he knew to do to escape. But the English noose had begun to tighten too soon. Soon, *L'Auguste* was at the center of a tightening circle of six English warships.

And then, the Captain saw his chance. The English ships had, apparently, been given new orders since the Captain had fought them last. When before, the Navy was bound to stay the line, someone had proposed that the line might be broken, as a melee, if the prey was likely to escape.

One of the English Captains seemed certain that the smaller French ship would head as quickly as it could back toward the east, where the circle had not yet closed. In his haste to place his second-rate in the brig's way, he had forgotten how quickly the smaller ship could move.

Captain Cognetz saw the opening and a chance to 'cross the T' of the larger ship and rake it with a broadside in passing on its way to its freedom.

Just as *L'Auguste*' attempted this nimble maneuver and crossed in from of the English ship, the path of escape that the corsair had been offered was dramatically shut. The English ship was a "Seventy-Four"; she had seventy-four guns, from the dozen or so little six-pounders on the upper works to probably twenty-eight of the massive thirty-six-pounders on her lower gun deck. One might expect a pair of eighteen-pound long-guns to protect its stern, but the

French Captain found, now, that this ship had two twelve-pounders at its bow. And these two guns were loaded with something special.

As the brig was just about to bring its guns to bear on the larger ship's bow in a thundering and devastating broadside, the larger ship fired its two smaller guns first. The two guns fired as one, and Francisco-Esteban, who had reached the deck from his perch high on the foremast just seconds before, watched in horror as a pair of cannonballs, chained together, tumbled through the air toward *L'Auguste*, cutting the shrouds and rigging of the foremast and then slamming into the mainmast itself.

The tall, upright, wooden post, taller than any tree in the forest, that had held the sails and the lines that let the canvas catch the wind, toppled and then, with a terrible crash, fell to the deck, killing, wounding, and trapping many of the French ship's crew.

The Captain yelled to the survivors, "To the rails! To the rails! The dogs will try to board us! Prepare to repel boarders!"

Francisco-Esteban ran to the railing with his rifle in his hand. He had a horn of powder, a bag of shot, and a bayonet for closer work. And he had his knives.

The men who joined him there had armed themselves with whatever they could find: pistols, muskets, blunderbusses, grenades, cutlasses, boarding pikes (to kill or wound those who attempted to board), and boarding axes (to cut through boarding lines or break through a door or a head). And they waited for the inevitable.

But before the grapples would be tossed to grasp their ship and pull it toward the enemy, the damned English sought to damage whatever was between wind and water. Solid shot tore through whatever and whomever was on the forecastle, the quarterdeck, and the gun-decks. The English wanted to take the brig, so they refrained from using carcass or heated shot, but they filled the air, the brig, and many of its crew with grape, canister, spider-shot (made of the same chains they used to cut the mast in two), shrapnel, and solid balls.

When Francisco-Esteban and the other marksmen left alive at the rail had the courage to take a shot at the attacking ship, they looked for the officers. Francisco-Esteban was certain that he had killed a lieutenant, and he would have had the pilot, too, if an unfortunate boatswain hadn't moved into his ball's path. But even as Francisco-Esteban was successful, grappling lines were thrown toward the brig, the grapples bit, and the two ships were pulled into their deadly embrace.

The bows of the two ships were drawn together, and most of the men who had fought with Francisco-Esteban at the rail ran forward to do what they could against the greater English numbers. Some of the gunners and sharpshooters ran to the foredeck to barricade themselves in the closed quarters there. They could hold out there for a while even if the English got past the defenders at the bow.

Francisco-Esteban huddled in the temporary safety of the railing. He reached over each of his shoulders in turn and withdrew his knives from their scabbards on his back. He could feel the knives' excited vibrations as they prepared to fight. As master musicians would warm their vocal cords before sharing their song with those whose ears would hear them, the knives began their song, softly, at first, and then gaining strength and clarity as the fighting neared. And as the men of the English ship first gained the forecastle of the brig, Francisco-Esteban heard the music his knives sang as plainly as he had the first time his mother had put them into his hands.

He stood, a knife in each hand, and ran to the battle.

Francisco-Esteban lost himself in the music of the knives and the heat of the battle, bathing his blades in the blood, first, of a big, balding sailor, perhaps the ship's carpenter, who leveled a pistol at his face. It misfired, and the young man from Toulouse sliced a deep cut in the man's neck. The man dropped almost immediately to the deck, grasping his throat to staunch the spurting blood, all to no avail.

The young Frenchman spun and faced a boy, no older than ten or twelve, a powder monkey who had abandoned the heat and smoke of his gun crew to try his hand in the boarding. The boy swung a tomahawk and, when his missed stroke threw him off balance, lost his arm at the elbow to one of the singing blades. His scream was an eerie harmony to the tune the knife sang.

The corsair heard a yell and a curse to his right and turned to help. Rochambeau, the sea artist who was a genius with a back-staff in his navigation, stood in front of a big, burly common seaman (or perhaps petty officer). The Englishman had taken a thrust from the navigator's short sword but had placed a rapier through the corsair's chest in return.

As Francisco-Esteban moved forward to avenge his mate, he felt a terrible pain shoot through his left shoulder. He glanced to see what had caused this torment just in time to see the stock of a musket rushing toward his head.

That was all that he knew.

*

When Francisco-Esteban came to, he found himself with, he determined later, twenty or so wounded men in the hold of the brig. It was dark as pitch, but a great number of cannonballs (the ship's ballast, he thought), the stink of sloshing water, rank, mildewed sacks of spoiled flour, wet coils of rotted rope, and the squeaking of rats told him where he was being held. The other men imprisoned with him, those who were not wounded too badly to talk or who soon died of their wounds, talked among themselves to encourage each other, and he pieced out the story of the battle.

The English were, by far, the superior force in this battle, and Captain Cognetz had, as soon as he had seen that there was no hope of escape or rescue, struck his colors. There was no shame in this. The Captain had the Lettre of Marque from the King; his ship and his corsairs were privateers and would be treated as prisoners of war.

The English had fought as if they were possessed by demons, and between the cannonades and the vicious attack of their boarding, the majority of the French crew had been killed or wounded in the battle. The English threw the dead into the sea (without even a chaplain's kind words), took the French officers aboard the English ship, and threw the living French crew into the hold.

One of the corsairs, who said that he had lived in England as a boy, said that he heard an Englishman call the French sailors, "Hostis humani generis", whatever that meant. Francisco-Esteban knew his Latin, and he knew the law that the Romans had practiced. He didn't tell his shipmate that the high-sounding phrase referred to pirates and meant, "enemy of mankind" and presaged their doom. Francisco-Esteban knew that, in England, the lawful punishment for piracy was "Death without Benefit of Clergy and Forfeiture of All Lands and Goods", and the execution could be carried out on any pirates who were captured, at sea or on land, all without the benefit of a trial.

As the living spoke further amongst themselves, they decided that, since they were still alive, the English intended to take *L'Auguste* as a prize and sail her to port. Even with only one mast, she was a worthy ship. The captured brig and all of its cargo were now the property of the British Crown. An Admiralty Prize Court would determine the amount of the prize, the price the Crown would pay for the warship, and the 'head money' that would be awarded for each member of the captive crew that now sat in the dark in the brig's hold.

The journey to England would take them much longer than their voyage south from Bordeaux had. But at least they were held in a French hold on the sea instead of in that English prison, Tyburn. All of the corsairs had heard the horrific stories of that dreadful gaol.

And then, a weak voice spoke from the other side of the hold. "I don't hold out much hope for us, mes amies," a man said in little more than a whisper.

A number of the corsairs cried out in protest, but when they calmed down, the voice continued, "When I was lying there, wounded on the spar deck, before those English bastards threw me down here, I saw the Captain of the ship that defeated us, a middling ship of the third-rate, a two-decker, the *HMS Swift*. Her crew is very proud of their Captain, a vile and sinful man named Ogle (so I overheard), a child of the Devil if ever I saw one. One of our brave marksmen put a ball into his thigh, and he lay on the stern-most and highest deck (that the English call the poop), bleeding and crying in his pain. The surgeon worked on his leg but must have told him that it would have to come off if he were to live. I could not hear the words that the English spoke, but his dismay and that of his officers was apparent. The surgeon wanted to begin, but then the Second brought our noble Captain Cognetz to him. Our Captain reached into his jacket and pulled out a fine document, it must have been the Lettre of Marque signed by our King. Ogle grabbed the paper, looked briefly at it, crushed it into a ball, and tossed it into the sea. Our Captain was livid, but Ogle motioned him closer. And when our Captain was near, Ogle asked his men to help him stand. Our

Captain must have expected Ogle to extend him the respect and courtesy that seafarers may rightly expect, even after a battle. But then Ogle drew his sword and sliced into our Captain's chest, and when our dear Captain fell to the deck, this Ogle leaned over, pulled out our Captain's red, still-beating heart and began to bite it and gnaw it with his teeth like a starving wolf."

There was not a sound in the black hold, except for the chittering of the rats and the dripping of the seawater that seeped into the bilge.

"As the English sailors brought me to this place, they told me that their Captain, after his savage meal, had only said, 'I shall never give any quarter to any French corsair, and I will serve them all alike,' and then asked the surgeon to take his leg."

The men were quiet then, the living because of their despair and the dead becasue that is what they were.

*

There were no days and no nights in the blackness of the hold. The dead died, and the living survived as best they could, eating the mildewed flour and rancid salt pork and drinking what they could stomach from spoiled casks. Those who brank the bilge water sickened and joined the dead.

After a few days, the prisoners in the darkness had no more to say to themselves or to one another. They were able to hear the voices of the English prize crew, and some of the corsairs understood the crude language of the English. They discovered that the admiral of the little fleet that had captured them was one Captain Hornigold, a man who had once commanded Edward Teach as his Second and who had sailed as a pirate for a while before he was pardoned by King George.

*

Eventually, the ship docked, the hatches were opened, and the prisoners who were still alive were brought into the sunlight in chains. Francisco-Esteban looked around at the unfamiliar river docks and realized that he must be in London, or somewhere very close by.

The dead were thrown into the river, and the eight who breathed were marched or carried to three two-wheeled oxcarts, tumbrils that still smelled of manure.

And then, very slowly, as oxen are never in a hurry, they were taken away from the river, north toward the city.

As they rolled slowly on, they first came to a massive construction of solid, dressed stone.

The driver, who knew no French simply said, "Newgate Prison, you poor piratical bastards, but you'll not be staying there."

Francisco-Esteban recognized 'Newgate'; he had heard of the infamous dungeon, but he wondered what else the driver had said.

A mile further on, the driver spoke again, "The Poet's Church, St. Martin of the Fields. The only rhymes that you'll be hearing will be the Last Rites."

Again, the corsair didn't understand.

But then, Francisco-Esteban slowly came to realize what lay ahead of him.

At first, it was a smell, a fetid, fulsome, fusty stink. The stench of the manure that permeated the wood of the cart was a sweet perfume next to the rank miasma that seemed to surround the road on which they traveled.

Francisco-Esteban saw the source of the fetor.

On each side of the road, one after another, were uncountable cages, each one different, each one holding a body, and each body rotting or worse.

The driver cackled now, "Corsair Lane … the road that takes you French pirates to the gallows and where you'll spend the first part of eternity after you're dead, hanging in chains. That'll teach you a lesson, or I'm not the man who'll deliver you to the noose."

The cages, some were heavy with iron, some were loose, barely held together with almost delicate links, some held only the torsos of their corpses, and some confined the dead men's heads as well. Some had been next to the road for so long that only a few clean-picked bones were left, and some still had flesh softening and turning to redolent liquid inside.

The wind was blowing softly, pushing away some of the vile odor, but it was bad enough that Francisco-Esteban threw up what little was in his stomach.

Each gibbet was different. Some were tall; one might have been thirty feet. Some were short but reinforced; one seemed to have what must have been a thousand nails pounded into it. That one seemed secure. Next to it, an empty one was being taken apart by a crowd of men, the bones, and wood, and steel being bargained and fought over. In the cages that still held recent victims, birds sat on the bars and pecked at the tasty parts that were left of the bodies. Francisco-Esteban looked too closely at one body that seemed to be moving more than the wind could manage and then had to look away when he realized that the motion was simply the burrowing of maggots under the poor, dead man's skin.

*

After passing too may cages for Francisco-Esteban to count, the tumbril lurched to a halt.

"The Tyburn Tree, you poor bastard," the driver said, "The three-legged mare."

In the middle of the road that branched into a 'Y' stood a horizontal wooden triangle supported ten feet or more in the air by three stout wooden legs. Two men were hanging on one side, their necks at an unnatural angle.

A crowd of twenty or so stood around the gallows, waiting for its next victims.

Before he had a chance to take in the horror of the sight, Francisco-Esteban felt something rough close around his neck and himself being dragged out of the cart. He managed to stand after a minute and fought against the noose that dragged him toward the gallows. He saw a man toss the end of a rope up and over the crossbar of the triangle, and then he felt himself being hauled into the air, his legs kicking and finding no purchase, and then nothing but blackness as he tried, in vain, to breathe.

*

After his *Swift* docked at the Howland Great Wet Dock at the Port of London, Captain Ogle took his carriage, which had awaited his arrival since the news of the capture of the French corsair had reached England, to his home, Chillingham Manor, in Bromley.

The Manor had been in his family since it was granted to his ancestor, Robert Pomeroy in 1265. Then, it had been described as a "handsome hall, ceilinged with good English oak. To the western side lieth a small chamber with a wardrobe, a stone chimney, and a fine bed, and to the eastern side is a buttery and a pantry. A side-room sits between the hall and a chapel, the chapel floored with slate and containing a small altar with an ancient cross. The hall has room for four trestle tables and is served by a small kitchen with two ovens and a table. Outside the hall is a dairy building, a slate-roofed granary, and a necessary chamber. To the east of the yard in which these buildings lie is a stable, to which is attached a small room with a bed, and a barn. These buildings are enclosed by a worthy privet hedge with a sturdy stone wall on the southern side. Outside the gate is a pig-stye, a barn for cows, and a stable for oxen."

Since that time, Ogle's family had built it into a fine property, the envy of all who were asked to visit.

Captain Ogle had taken his pick of the possessions of the Captain and crew of the little French brig he had captured. The crew had almost a dozen gold Spanish reales, and twice that many coins of silver. The Captain had two excellent Toledo rapiers, almost twenty fine maritime charts, a small casket full of golden rings and decorations that only a Frenchman (or an effete English fop) would ever wear, and an excellent, matched set of Queen Anne flintlock pistols, .50 caliber, marked as made in Liege, Belgium. Captain Ogle would give all of these to his patron with his thanks.

His portion of *L'Auguste* would be a substantial reward.

But now that he had lost his leg to the French in the service of his country, Captain Ogle had decided to retire from the sea and live out his life in the luxury to which he was entitled. His wife and this three sons would enjoy his company. Perhaps he would write his memoirs.

And the battle that took his leg had given him something remarkable in return.

One of the French seamen fought with a remarkable pair of knives. He was knocked unconscious and put in the hold with the rest of the survivors (and should, by now, be dinner for the crows in one of the gibbets along Corsairs' Lane), and Captain Ogle's Second had brought the Captain the corsair's knives as some of the spoils of their victory.

And just after he had lost his leg to the surgeon's saw, Captain Ogle had first heard the knives singing. They seemed to be singing to him. At least, Captain Ogle knew their song; he had heard it a hundred times in a hundred battles that he had fought, where men died, and blood was spilled, and the heady ecstasy of combat had a music of its own.

Captain Ogle would keep the knives, he decided.

Chapter 8 - The Four of Knives

The fourth card of the Minor Arcana of the Suit of Knives in the Swordsmith's Tarot is the Four of Knives. The number four is associated with stability and the sturdy underpinnings that foster good fortune and fulfilment. The Four of Knives can point to a marriage, a birth, a celebration, a milestone, or the culmination of a journey. While this card can indicate harmony and tranquility, it can also remind us that insecurity and instability as just as much pieces of the transitions that fill our lives. Tension and discord are just as integral pieces of a family's composition as are harmony and peace. Even though a person may want the best for a loved one, the best for one is not the best for another. Even the firmest of foundations can be shaken and demolished.

*

In recognition of his bravery in the capture of the French corsairs and their brig, King George awarded Captain Amaranthus Ogle the only British hereditary honor that is not a peerage, a baronetcy. From that moment on, the Captain would be addressed as "Sir" and "The First Baronet of Bromley", be entitled to a pall, supported by two men, a principal mourner, and four others at his funeral, and have the right to have his first son knighted on the lad's twenty-first birthday. However, technically, he would still be a commoner.

But there were other benefits to the recognition and the Captain's elevation.

Despite now having to use a cane to help him walk on his ivory peg, Amaranthus Ogle was the toast of part of the city of London. He was invited to innumerable parties and met introduced to rich men, noble men, important men, and these men's daughters.

Captain Ogle, Btss., RN (Ret.) had had little time for the fairer sex during his naval career. But as a retired gentleman with a Manor, in Bromley, with a Navy pension (and other prospects), he now found that these fair flowers were quite enjoyable company and seemed rather enchanted by him.

*

Eventually, Captain Ogle married Diffidence Barebones. Her father had been a Member of Parliament from London, a man of some renown. Diffidence bore Amaranthus three sons, and having, thus, done her womanly duty, promptly died.

The Captain sent the boys to proper schools: first, to a proper grammar school (he couldn't remember its name, but he was sure that it was somewhere in Shropshire), and then to a proper Public school, the Comenius School, in Aberllynfi, Wales (the Welsh town's name in English was Three Cocks, a great joke among the lads). Both of these institutions were boarding schools, socially acceptable, and most importantly, far away. His sons were kept out of sight and mind, in that way, for many, many years.

Eventually, though, his sons completed their secondary educations. Noble, the eldest, had been born in 1715. When it was time, the boy attended King's College at the University of

Cambridge, reading for Mathematics for three years and then, scandalously, re-registering for the Law Tripos (and, three years after that, being simultaneously admitted to degrees in Mathematics and the Law), Noble sought employment in London and secured a position with George Hooper, a solicitor or some note. He lived in Marylebone, much to his father's chagrin, but much to the lad's own delight. The wild oats that he sowed there would be forgotten when he took his place, upon his father's death, as the master of Chillingham Manor.

Captain Ogle's second son, Resolved, was born in 1719, and knowing his place and what opportunities would be his as the baronet's second son, he studied at the University of Oxford to prepare himself to join the Anglican clergy. He attended Wadham College there. Resolved was a close friend of the college's warden, Robert Thistlethwayte (who, oddly, later left England to spend the rest of his life on a small Greek isle). The only blemish in Resolved's university career was a fistfight in a common pub where the Captain's son bloodied the nose of a student from another college at Oxford (after hearing the other man reciting a limerick, ostensibly about Thistlethwayte: "There once was a Warden of Wadham/ Who approved of the folkways of Sodom./ For a man might, he said,/ Have a very poor head/ But be a fine Fellow at bottom"). Resolved engaged in no more low behavior after that and was admitted to his degree soon afterward. Rather than finding a place in the established Church, Resolved followed the example of fellow Oxfordian, George Whitfield. Like Whitfield, as soon as he left Oxford, he immediately took to preaching anywhere that would hear his testimony and shunned settling down in a parish. He became an itinerant evangelist and sermonizer. He was dutiful, though, in sending one letter a month to apprise his father of his whereabouts and his winning of souls. Resolved's most recent missive had been sent from Towcester in the Midlands.

The Captain's youngest son, Make-Peace (his name a nod to his Puritan grandfather) was born in 1726. Make-Peace was visiting his father and the Manor for a week during his final term at Comenius when his father asked the boy into his study for a talk.

*

There was a sharp triplet knock on the oaken door.

"Come," the Captain said.

The door opened quietly, and Make-Peace Ogle, all of eighteen and as full of that age as a young man could be, walked into the wood-paneled room.

"Sir," he said, standing easily at his father back.

The baronet turned away from the elaborate Queen Anne desk that he had commissioned on a voyage to the Orient. It was a wondrous thing, exceptionally-made of mahogany, padouk, and quarter-sawn oak, with thirty-five visible drawers (and another half-dozen hidden ones), a handful of concealed hiding places, and behind its two prospect doors, little boxes that could be removed to hold almost anything from coins to jewelry to "the Chinese scourge" (Make-Peace had spent many a happy afternoon, when he was very young and his father was out of the house, searching for the secrets that the desk kept).

"Oh, yes," the Captain said, "We must talk."

"Of course, Father," the young man replied.

The old man pointed to a chair to his left. "Will you sit?" he asked.

"No, thank you, Sir," the boy said.

The Captain was clearly uncomfortable, but as a father and an experienced commander, he was determined to present the facts and expected a proper response.

"You will be leaving the school in the summer, I believe," he began.

"Yes, sir," his son said.

"You are my third son," the Captain continued.

"I believe that is so, Father," Make-Peace agreed.

"Noble, your eldest brother, is my first-born son and shall inherit my estate," the old man went on, "and Resolved, my second-born son has joined the Church …"

The boy only nodded at that.

"So you will follow my vocation and join the Navy, I believe," Captain Amaranthus Ogle, First Baronet of Bromley, RN (Ret.) concluded.

And then he turned back to his work at his desk.

"I see," the young man thought, turned, and left the room, opening and closing the oaken door as quietly as could be.

*

Amaranthus Ogle woke up. It was still the middle of the night. Bright moonlight streamed into his bedroom through the window. He wondered, for a minute, why he had awakened; he was a middle-aged gentleman, but his bladder still allowed him to sleep through the night.

He lay his head back onto his pillow and closed his eyes again, preparing to re-enter the arms of Morpheus. And then he heard the noise.

It was irregular. It was sharp, and then it rustled. Something hard and then another thing much softer.

He sat up and held his breath, waiting patiently for the sound to come to him again.

Nothing, now.

Nothing.

Wait! There it was again.

Captain Ogle got out of his bed and put on his robe.

He walked to the door of his chamber and opened it, waiting a second before sticking his head out into the hallway.

There the sound was again … to the left.

He left his room, leaving the door ajar, and walked softly down the hall.

Past Noble's chambers. Past Resolved's suite. Past Make-Peace's room. To the last door on the left side of the hallway. The locked room where he stored his most valued possessions.

He held his breath and tried the knob.

It turned.

He pushed gently against it.

The door began to open.

Captain Ogle exhaled and walked into the room.

There, huddled over his old sea-chest was his son, Make-Peace, reaching in, rummaging about, and then tossing things haphazardly across the little room.

"What is the meaning of this?" the old man sputtered in indignation.

The young man stopped his frenzied searching, straightened himself, and turned to face the Captain.

"You explained my future to me this afternoon," the young man almost spat the words at his father, "but you forgot that my future is not yours but my own. I will make of myself what I will and not bow to some idle fancy or hallucination of yours."

The Captain knew nothing to say to this impertinence.

Make-Peace continued, "So I will have some things that I can use, things that you could give me as your son, or that I can take as a man."

"You?" his father spluttered, "A man?"

"Yes, father! A man!"

Then Make-Peace reached into the bottom of the chest and pulled out a pair of leather scabbards.

"You shall not have those!" Captain Ogle shouted now.

"And why not, father?" the young man asked, "They have been mine for years. When you were away, and I was just a boy, before you sent me away to that terrible confinement in Wales, I would search your desk for treasure. And one day, I found a key. A key that fit no lock that I could find until I tried it in the door of this room. It let me in, and I found the treasures that I had searched for, meerschaum pipes that a gnome might use, golden coins from lands I had never heard of, pearls, pistols inlaid with silver and gold, a tomahawk from the savage Americas, embroidered tapestries for the farthest east ... and these. These magical knives ... with God's blessing and music sharply carved into the blades. As sharp as a thistle, as sharp as a spur, as sharp as Chaucer's brere, as sharp as a thankless father, they were and still are. These edges sing when they smell blood.

"What?" his father asked, "Are you mad?"

Then Make-Peace stated at the old man, "You didn't know?"

"Once, when I first took them from that French corsair, I thought I heard something, but I had lost my leg and the echoes of battle still rang in my ears."

"You old fool," his son said, "These are musical knives. When I first held one, as a young, young boy, I touched the edge to my tender hand. And as if it were a magical thing, it pierced my skin, penetrating me as a lover might (although I did not know its lust then), with a bit of pain to accompany the pleasure it gave. And as it called to my blood and took a little of it, it sang to me, a song that was new to me and yet a song that I seemed to have always known. I knew them to be mine, even then. And if you have never known them, and shared your own blood with them, they can never be yours."

As he talked of the knives in a manner that a lover speaks of his adored one, Make-Peace slid one of the knives from the safety of its scabbard.

"There," he said, his eyes widening in wonder, "There it is! Can you not hear it?"

The old man looked and cocked his head and strained to hear.

"Nothing," Make-Peace said sadly, "You hear them not. Truly, if you are so deaf to them and their fine music, they cannot be yours."

The Captain heard these words and reached out in anger to grab the knife. "They are mine!" he yelled.

As the father reached out to take away his son's knife long with his dreams, his son thrust the knife out toward the old man to stop him.

And the blade's sharp tip stabbed into the old man's palm and the pointed tine stuck out of the back of his hand.

As the bright blood spurted out of his palm, Amaranthus Ogle screamed in pain and rage, "No!"

With the song of the knife filling his head now, Ogle's third son, Make-Peace, said only, "Yes."

And with that affirmation, the youngest son slashed at his father, slicing deeply, first into the man's right bicep and then his chest. Then, with a swipe at the Captain's face, the blade cut deeply into the father's left ear so that it flopped down to drip blood along the man's jawline.

The son used the sharp tip to stab at his father's flabby belly, opening it, one jab at a time, the gashes and punctures and the blood that each attack produced staining the man's silken robe. And then, a sharper cut that made a deeper incision below the Captain's ribs was deep enough so that stomach and guts spilled their rank contents onto the floor.

At that wound, Captain Ogle fell.

*

Amaranthus Ogle had never spent any time or effort learning who his sons truly were. If he had, he would have known that his youngest, the one who society would consider to be the least, was the most level-headed and the most calm under pressure. Strangely enough, the boy's talents would have served him well in His Majesty's Royal Navy.

*

Instead of fleeing the terrible place of blood and murder, Make-Peace considered his situation. He could stay, be arrested, brought to trial, and hanged for his crime. Or he could outfit himself as best he could and run for his freedom … the boy was smart and well-educated, and he was standing in a room filled with money and treasure.

So, as his father lay bleeding on the floor at his feet, the son looked again, taking his own good time, through the sea-chest. He took a pair of pistols and a well-used rapier (with equal heft and balance, he noticed, to the one he had used in his fencing classes at Comenius). He emptied a leather pouch of some strange, foreign gewgaws and filled it with a handful of coins of gold and silver. Finally, he wiped the knife, even as it still sang to him, clean on his father's robe, and replaced the blade in its scabbard, secure next to its mate.

Then, he left the room and locked the door.

He walked to his chambers and found the clothes that he would need. Good boots, a warm cape, a hat. He rolled up extra clothing, his silver comb and brush, a candle, a tiny tinderbox, and a flint and steel striker in a sheet. Then he strapped the scabbards onto his back, put the pistols into his belt, and donned his cape and hat. As a final guilty thought, he took the Bible that lay on the table at his bedside.

He walked downstairs to the kitchen. He found a fresh loaf of bread and two apples.

Then he walked out to the stables.

He found his favorite mare, loaded his saddle bags with what they would hold and tied the sheet with the rest to one of the bags, saddled her, and mounted.

He walked her out of the manor grounds. That was the quietest way. As he rode over the little bridge at the end of the tree-lined road that led from the great house to the public road, he tossed the key to the bloody room into the water.

He crossed the Thames at Blackfriars Bridge and rode north toward Camden Town. When the sun rose, he soon found a little inn, where he stayed for a meal and a little sleep.

By sunset, he had bid Hampstead Heath farewell.

In another day, Make-Peace Ogle could have been on the road to Bristol, or to Birmingham, or to Norwich.

Who could say?

Chapter 9 – The Craftsman

Another of the Major Arcana of the Suit of Knives in the Swordsmith's Tarot is The Craftsman. Since the Craftsman's art is a product of skill, intellect, and logic, the Craftsman is influenced by the planet Mercury. The Craftsman is the conduit between the intangible world of the soul and the mind and the corporeal and concrete realm of Man. His workbench holds the four primordial elements, Earth, Air, Fire, and Water; but it is The Craftsman who is the embodiment of the time and place where thought, energy, and creation combine to manifest dreams and desire. These visions and passions are elemental things themselves, forged of belief (Fire), intellect (Air), emotions (Water), and substance (Earth).

The Craftsman attains his goals and conquers his challenges through the mastery of his resources, skills, and tools. And to succeed, the Craftsman must be focused, act consciously, and objectively evaluate his progress.

The Craftsman can be defeated through his own impatience, lack of clarity, or greed; he can be overthrown by others if he succumbs to their deceit, manipulation, or guile. The Craftsman must seize his opportunities and shun those who would attempt to dissuade him from doing what he must. And he must always ask himself, "What must change and what must remain if I am to be victorious?"

*

Make-Peace rode all through the night and all the next day, stopping to rest and water his horse at the lonely banks of deserted streams he encountered. He ate bread he had taken from his father's kitchen and gave the apples to the noble beast who had spirited him away to his freedom.

As the sun began to set, the young man found himself at an inn and stopped. He gave the groom four pence to care for his horse with fresh water, good oats, and timothy hay (if it had been harvested when its seed heads were covered in velvet). The groom showed Make-Peace the water, the oats and the sweet hay, and the young man told the groom that he would return after he had eaten his supper.

He walked into the main room of the inn and found a table where he could put his back to a wall and watch the door.

A minute later, the innkeeper walked up to where he sat.

"I have been in the saddle all day, sir," Make-Peace addressed the man, "and I have miles to go before I sleep, but I would break my fast, as late as it is, if your food is worth my tasting it."

The innkeeper was a big man, six-feet in height and almost as wide. His apron was recently laundered, with only, probably, the day's stains on it.

"The food at my inn is as flavorful as the beds upstairs are soft," he began, "I can see that a man as well-born as yourself would appreciate a supper of cold venison, cheese, bread, tea, and wine."

Make-Peace looked the man up and down, smiled, and asked, "Was the venison recently the King's?"

The big man laughed, looked around, and placed his index finger beside his nose before he said, "Who can say, good sir? Who can say? But I will let you decide that, and to help you in the making of that decision, I will bring you a loaf of fresh bread, a wedge of good English cheddar, excellent potatoes, smoking hot and accompanied by sweet butter of the finest quality (from Bess, my Brown Swiss that is pastured behind the inn), a pudding of flour, milk, eggs, sugar, suet, marrow, and raisins, black teas from the East, and a syllabub of cider, nutmeg, milk, and cream. I swear that you will not leave my table unsatisfied."

Make-Peace smiled and nodded, "Then lay on, sir. Lay on!"

Two hours later, his stomach fuller and his pocket a sixpence lighter (that wonderful meal worth every farthing), he returned to the stable, saw that the groom had treated his horse as well as he had promised, tossed a penny to the boy, saddled up, and rode into the night.

*

The moon was a quarter full, the road empty, and Make-Peace's eyes heavy after the filling supper. He let the horse find its own way after a while and had to shake himself awake more and more frequently lest he topple off his saddle and into a heap in the dirt of the road.

He looked around him, as much to awaken himself as for any other reason.

And then he saw light through the trees.

Not lanterns or torches but a light that suggested a fire hidden in the forest, away from the road.

Make-Peace was so tired that he thought that he must chance the cheery welcome of a fire. Other travelers with little money or reasons to shun society might welcome him as one of their own.

In case they chose not to, Make-Peace checked to see that his pistols were primed and ready. And that the dirk in his belt was ready, as well.

*

Make-Peace dismounted at the side of the road, checked, once again, that both of his pistols were ready, touched the rapier at his side and the dagger in his belt, and made sure that the knives on his back were secure but available. He took his horse's reins in his left hand and walked toward the light of the fire.

He reached a small clearing and tossed his mount's reins over a low branch. He stood very still for a moment, allowing the three men who sat at the fire to see him … and judge him.

"Would you allow a weary traveler to warm his bones by your fire?" he asked to them all.

The men looked at each other with glances difficult to read in the gloom.

And then one man, the biggest by the look of him, spoke, "We are all honest men of the highway. There is room for another here at our fire."

A skinny man, dressed almost in rags to his left, chuckled softly.

"Thank you," Make-Peace said and walked back to his horse, taking the saddlebags, saddle, and pad from his mare and bringing them closer to the fire but still far enough from the other men to allow him to make a quick getaway if it would be necessary.

As he lay his saddlebags and saddle on the ground, with the pad leaned against them for his back, and sat down, seeming to take his ease in front of the fire, he placed his hand on the pistol he had taken out of his pocket and placed beside him. He moved so that his dirk and rapier were also close at hand.

And then the man in the middle spoke.

"Welcome, stranger," the big man said, "I'm John Clavell," and nodding to the man on his left, "and this is James Hind," and then to the man on his right, "and this is Claude Duval. We are the only royalty this poor road knows. Who are you, and what makes you travel so late?"

"I am called Sanguine Gore by those who know me," Make-Peace began, "and my father has given his lands and title, horses, hounds, and gold, to my eldest brother and sent my elder brother to Oxford and then to the Church. To me, he gave the suggestion that I should join the Navy. I have left him and all that I knew to make my own way, first on the road, and then wherever the road might take me."

Clavell nodded thoughtfully and was silent for a moment, seemingly enjoying the fire's warmth and collecting his thoughts to reply. "You, who are newly on the road, should know the code that you may live by. I would inform you, if you do not know, that it is customary when travelling to put ten or even a dozen guineas in a separate pocket as a commendation to those who come to demand them. We gentlemen of the road exercise our jurisdiction as the only surveyors of our English highways, our toil ignored by the government. We are happy to content ourselves with taking only the money of those who defer to our requests without dispute, for our humanity, it is often said, is our finest quality," and the three men laughed softly at this.

Clavell continued when the laughter died, "But those who endeavor to escape our toll do not always remain safe and free; we are quite strict in levying our duty. And he without the wherewithal to pay us may find himself knocked on his head for his want."

"But we do this not for ourselves alone. The mischievous blade, that rare Dick Turpin, is the leader of our company. And we only do our duty to him as we bring him our profits," Clavell explained.

"Clavell," Make-Peace had made up his mind, "You scabbed, lying whoreson. This quailing James Hind appears hale for a man who was drawn and quartered a century past. And this Claude Duval, what does he here, when all know that his shade haunts the Holt Hotel in Oxfordshire? And you, Clavell, are you the poet, playwright, and physician who now lies in a grave? And you three fools would take your prize to Dick Turpin? The noble highwayman who bowed to the spectators, climbed the ladder undaunted, and threw himself off the short drop five years ago? You shame his memory with your pudding-headed boasts. You and both of your roaring, pillicocked boys, seek *my* toll? Well then, Captain Queernobs, you and your two yowling Mollies must try, I suppose."

The three robbers, mouths open in shock, paused. And then, with a roar, Hind leapt toward Make-Peace.

The younger man raised his pistol when the thief was just upon him and put a ball through the man's teeth. The dead man fell on him, and Make-Peace pushed the heavy body off of himself and stood to face the next.

As he stood and put his rapier between Duval and himself, Make-Peace felt the knives on his back humming a stirring harmony to the music of the fight.

Duval reached into the fire and grabbed a flaming brand, swinging it as a fiery club, with a great deal more enthusiasm than skill.

The fire swinging at him half-blinded Make-Peace, but he found that he was much more nimble than his attacker. And after Duval had swung again, Make-Peace lunged in at him and put the point of his sword through the meat of the man's upper arm.

Duval howled like a demon but dropped the blazing club.

Seeing his advantage, Make-Peace lunged and again and then again, sending the rapier's sharp tip into the Duval's gut and then his chest.

At this second touch, Duval sat abruptly down and then fell over onto his side, bleeding and groaning, each with quickly-diminishing enthusiasm.

Make-Peace then turned, expecting a third assault.

Then he heard his mare snort and then squeal in fear and refusal. But a few seconds later, Clavell must have mounted her, for Make-Peace heard only hoof-beats riding away.

*

Well, there he was. Lost in the woods, God knew where, with a saddle and tack, bloodied weapons, two dead men at his feet, and whatever they might have left for him bundled in the places they had claimed around the fire.

As he stepped lightly past the dead men, the knives on his back sang a bloody ostinato, repeating their gruesome motif, again and again. To Make-Peace, the music of the knives was as soothing as his mother's lullaby. And the song finally quieted as the blood of the corpses ceased to drip from the raw, rude holes that Make-Peace had opened in them.

The young man stooped to cut each man's purse from his belt. He poured the contents of each into his hand and counted the coin he had gained.

Hind was the poorer of the villains. His purse held three farthings, a halfpenny, and seven dented copper pennies, not a shilling all together.

Make-Peace moved to Duval. His purse was a little fatter: two farthings, five pennies, a shilling, a shining sovereign, and a guinea!

He was not wealthy. These coins would buy him a fine beaver hat but would not be enough to pay for a month of dancing lessons.

No, there was in his hand almost enough for an old, spavined draft horse to replace his now twice-stolen father's mare.

So Make-Peace went to search the dead men's other belongings.

And that is where he found them.

The very last things he would have expected.

Wigs.

Wigs!!

In two sacks where the robbers had reclined when they still breathed, Makepeace found nine, fine wigs, all of human hair and powdered properly. These were things of value, which took the wig-makers' men probably a week each to make, once they had purchased good hair.

Make-Peace left them in their sacks and searched the rest of the little camp. He found horns of powder, pouches of balls and wadding, another sack of flint, and three pistols. These he packed in his saddlebags. He found four daggers and a short sword, all of which he secreted on his person or stuck through his belt.

He found half a loaf of stale bread, a rind of cheese that had seen better days, and two only slightly-bruised apples. These, he also added to his bags.

And then, he moved away from the fire to a spot that allowed him to watch to see if anyone came to the clearing, re-loaded the pistol he had fired and checked to see that his new guns were primed and ready, and sat down to perhaps rest himself a little before the sun would rise.

*

When the sun arose, so did Make-Peace. The roads and the forests were not safe places, he had decided, and so his journey would continue until he found a likely town. But how to get there. He now had no horse, and walking would take much too long he thought.

He considered this as he began his walk down the road, away from his past. He had slung his saddle bags over his shoulder, and carried his saddle under one arm; he clanked as he walked, courtesy of his new and old armament.

After a while, he heard horses behind him, and he turned to see who and what approached. It was a stage coach. A few meager bags and trunks sat on top, the driver was lazily driving his team at a trot, and a sleepy man sat beside the driver, cradling a rusty and dented blunderbuss in his lap.

Make-Peace saw his salvation approaching. He turned and made his way to the middle of the road, placed his saddle and saddlebags on the ground in front of him. He had decided that he would walk not another foot!

The coach slowed as it approached him and stopped, its lead pair ten feet in front of Make-Peace. The man with the blunderbuss pointed the shotgun vaguely in Make-Peace's direction.

"What d'ye want?" the driver yelled down at him.

"Where are you going?" the man in the road asked.

"Why does it matter if you've a mind to rob us?" the driver replied.

"Perhaps I won't rob you if you are going my way," Make-Peace responded.

"Well, if it please your lordship," the driver said and then spat into the dirt beside the coach, "we're bound for Poole, but we could make a stop for you at Bournemouth if you've a desire to take the waters."

"Poole, eh?" Make-Peace, "Do you have room for another passenger."

"You can sit up here with me and my gunner if you've a mind to," the man laughed and added, "But it will cost you a pound."

"A pound?" the young man said, "let me toss my saddle and bags up, and I'll happily join you up in the fresh air."

Make-Peace tossed his things up and clambered up behind them. He sat on the roof of the coach and held on to the little iron railings that served to hold the luggage on the coach-top.

*

It was well past dark when the coach rattled into Pool. The smell of seawater woke Make-Peace from his drowsing.

The coach eventually stopped in front of an inn.

"Here's where we stop, young man," the driver said.

"Thank you, sir," Make-Peace replied, "Is this inn honest and safe for a traveler?"

The old man laughed, "As much as any in this vile little port. Ask for Bess. She's Mr. Noyes, the innkeeper's, beautiful daughter. She waits for those who come by moonlight. Ye have no horse, so you won't need to see Tim, the osler. You'll be fine."

Make-Peace tossed his saddle and bags to the ground and then climbed down himself. He picked up all that he owned, walked to the inn's door, and knocked.

"Who's there so late," a woman's soft voice asked from within.

"A traveler seeking a soft bed and a meal in the morning," Make-Peace replied.

A minute later the door opened to reveal a short, thin, beautiful young woman with black eyes and a red love-knot plaited into her coal-black hair.

"Well, it's sure that you're no hooligan. You've an arsenal at your waist but you're bloody poor at your job if you are a highwayman. You wear no lace at your chin, no velvet coat, no doe-skin breeches, and no French-cocked hat. What is your name, and why should I let you in?" she asked.

"I am no bandit, just a lad looking to find his fortune. I was robbed by your highwaymen last night. They got away with my horse, but I took two of their lives and their pillage. I seek a bed and a meal, and then I will leave you on the morrow," he told her.

"In that case, my brave victim," she smiled at him now, "I can find a bed for you for the night."

"Thank you," he said.

"Oh, I can find a way for you to truly show me your gratitude, as well" she said, taking his hand as she closed the door and threw the bolt. She led him, his hand in one of hers and a candle in the other, to a little room back by the kitchen, where she showed him kind hospitality.

*

In the morning, she put her finger to her lips to silence him. She left for a while and returned with bread, milk, and tea. And after he had taken his meal, she took him again.

When he had recovered his senses, she hurried him to dress and leave from the inn's back door. As he walked down the alley, he turned, and when he did, she threw him a kiss from where she stood in the doorway.

When he turned back to find his way, he noticed the privy that stood across the alley from the inn's back door. He visited that little building and then set off to find his way.

*

As he walked through the town, he thought of what he might do. He had murdered his father, stolen family property that was legally his brother Noble's now. He had killed two more men in the forest on the way to this smelly, seaside town.

He would not join the Navy as his father had determined that he would. He had been educated in a fine, public school and was handy with pistol, sword, and knives (and to remind him of his communion with them, they sang a familiar, little air in their scabbards on his back). He could ride a horse and knew the ways of the better classes.

But, for now, he had much too much to carry. He needed a way to lighten his load.

Then he saw, down at the corner of the street, the sign of the three golden balls, the symbol of Saint Nicholas, who had loaned three sisters each a bag of gold for their dowries. A pawnbroker.

This 'house of Lombard' would not treat him fairly, but the Jew who probably owned it would ask him no questions, either. Edward III and Henry V had each pawned their jewels to pay for their wars, so it was not an ignoble act to finance one's future at the moneylender's.

So Make-Peace entered the little shop. After an hour, he left with just the clothes on his back, the boots on his feet, a new dagger in his belt, a pouch heavy with coin, and his singing knives still strapped to his back under his cloak.

He also now knew where his future would lie.

*

He set out on the road that led to Blandford Camp. He would join the 14th King's Hussar's. These cavalrymen were stationed near the sea to thwart the smugglers that had called Cornwall, Devon, Dorset, and the Isle of Wight their homes for at least a thousand years. No one would know him, and with the British Army just beginning the war against the French, the Marathas, and Mysore in distant India, he might get the chance to see the world.

So when he walked into the camp, he inquired of the first soldier that he met how he might join this fine group of brave men. The soldier thought, at first, that this was a joke, but when Make-Peace insisted that he was in earnest, the soldier pointed to a tent where there was certain to be an officer who could assist this young madman.

Make-Peace walked to the tent, There was no place on the canvas to knock properly, so he cleared his throat to announce his presence.

Nothing happened.

Make-Peace cleared his throat more loudly.

Again, there was no response.

The would-be cavalryman cleared his throat a third time, even more loudly, and a voice from within said, "God's Wounds! If it's consumption you've got and it doesn't kill you, I'll give you your guts for garters! Come in!"

Make-Peace walked in and found a grandly-dressed officer sitting at a field desk.

The man looked up, eyed Make-Peace suspiciously and asked, "Well?"

"I'd like to join the Hussars, if you please, sir," Make-Peace said and waited for the officer to respond.

"And what makes you think that we'd want you?" the man replied.

"I've finished my education at a good public school in Wales, I can read and write, do mathematics, and ride a horse. I can fence and I have hunted with rifles since I was young," Make-Peace told him.

The officer nodded, "And what do you want from the Hussars, then?"

Make-Peace took a deep breath and gave his terms, "I'd be a 'gentleman ranker', sir."

"Oh, you're a rich dandy, sent to school, and then disgraced your family … Drink? Whores? Gambling?" The officer's mien became deadly serious.

"I'd rather not say, sir. I simply don't have the money to purchase a commission. I'll bring no dishonor to the Hussars, sir, I give you my word as a gentleman, if I can just join up."

The officer shook his head and said, almost to himself, "Your word as a gentleman, eh? I'll probably be kicking myself in a week …", but then he addressed Make-Peace, "Alright, then. You'll sign on as a 'gentleman volunteer'. You'll serve as a private soldier with the agreement that you will be given a commission in due time, when you have proven yourself. You'll train and fight with the regular soldiers, but you'll mess with the officers."

The officer opened a box behind the desk, rummaged around for a minute, and then pulled out a sheaf of papers.

"What's your name, soldier?" he asked.

"Sanguine Gore, sir, of Wiltshire," the newest soldier answered.

And he chuckled to himself as his signed his new name.

Chapter 10 - The Master

Another of the Major Arcana of the Suit of Knives in the Swordsmith's Tarot is The Master. This card represents the dominion of knowledge over intuition. The Master is associated with the Moon, and just as the Moon pulls and pushes the tides of the ocean, the Master maintains the balance between the known and the unknowable. The Master guards the unconscious wisdom of enlightenment, knowledge, and understanding that is possessed by all mankind and teaches the righteous novice the truth of dreams and magic that must be innate before the neophyte can transform himself into the instinctual adept.

The Master is a card of change, revealing mysteries, which once seemed so certain, to be merely commonplace minutiae that can no longer be taken for granted. The Master demands that the fledgling heed his 'inner voice', the voice of the knives, and find the calm core of being that is pure and unconcerned with the noise and glare of the world. When this teaching has been learned, seemingly impossible, but flawlessly perfect choices will make themselves manifest, as if from reflex, leaving the conscious mind to attend to more important matters.

Ignoring the Master's teaching, and not heeding the voices that sing in one's soul, will serve only to lead one astray. Others' opinions, commands, and even permissions can have little meaning or significance when considered in light of one's inner voice. The truth is the only Master of the secrets and enigmas that are hidden within another's directives.

*

Private Sanguine Gore, 'gentleman volunteer', joined the 14th King's Hussars at Blandford Camp. He was paid two shillings, six pence, a day (but since he would be a cavalryman with a mount to maintain, he would also receive, when he had finished his training and had been deemed worthy to join the cavalry, an additional sixpence for hay and a peck of oats), shared a tent with four other recruits (there was no need for the Army to waste barracks space on cake and arse party donkey fuckers until they had proven themselves to be worthy of being taken in from out of the rain), marched and trained and marched again and again, and ate most of his meals with the officers (as a fellow gentleman of quality).

The drummer beat the long roll at the end of the row of tents, every morning, two hours before sunrise. The five men in the tent rolled out of their cots, put their cots to order, combed their hair, and washed their faces, necks, ears, and hands (the men took turns emptying the tent's wooden bucket and re-filling it with clean water after everyone had accomplished their morning pisses). While the fresh water was being brought to the tent, Private Gore's tent-mates stepped outside to smoke a small pipe or savor a morning plug of tobacco.

At first light, the first Morning Parade was called to the thunder and screech of the drums and fifes. The men wore their 'undress' uniforms (scratchy, white wool jackets, trousers, and forage caps). Missing soldiers were reported (roll was taken in each tent at the tattoo and delivered to the Lance Corporal), and then the new recruits hurried back to their tents to grab their rifles and their silly-looking shako hats and marched off with the Corporal of the Horse (the cavalry had no rank of sergeant, an old word for servant and an inappropriate term for the Cavalry, but the rank was still adequate for the mud-eating Infantry) for two hours of drill. While the recruits were being forged into soldiers, the Officer of the Day inspected their tents, marking down those whose sloppy habits showed that they required extra drill.

After drill, about nine o'clock, the recruits would go to the barracks for breakfast. Private Sanguine Gore, even though he had signed on as a 'gentleman ranker' with the privilege of messing with the officers, made a point to break his fast with the men he lived and trained with.

Before the men were allowed to eat, a Lance Corporal moved among the tables to ensure that every man was attired appropriately and not drunk (even though each soldier was allowed five pints of weak beer each day, the commissary opened just before sunrise and the first Parade, and more than one man had been known to drink himself sloppy before drill). The troops were allowed forty minutes for breakfast (which consisted, usually, of only bread and beans, since the weekly ration for each soldier was seven pounds of beef or four pounds of salt pork, seven pounds of bread, three pints of beans, half a pound of rice, a quarter pound of butter, three gallons of beer –

or a gallon and a half of watery-rum when it could be got), and were then marched out of the mess to the drumming of the 'Pioneer's March'.

For the next hour and a half, or so, those who had no work duties were able to join the seasoned soldiers, who had had the morning to themselves to chat, drink, game, clean their tents and bedding, and prepare their kits for the full-dress Parade. Arms and uniforms would be inspected at this second Parade, and so, in preparation, stocks, caps, shoes, and pouches were waxed and blacked, musket steel was polished and oiled, and belts were whitened with clay.

Then, the full-dress Parade was called by the buglers, who played 'The Troop'. The soldiers were inspected and discipline was meted out to those who had broken the Army's rules. Those who had been found guilty of drunkenness, theft, or poor conduct were flogged or made to run the gauntlet. One poor sot was made to stand for hours barefoot on tent-pegs for his drunken misconduct. After Private Gore had finished his training and had risen in the ranks, Private Joseph Stoakes was hanged for desertion (to be fair, it was the third time he had deserted his regiment and been recaptured, the first and second occurrences had resulted only in his being branded with the shameful 'D').

The Parade was dismissed at noon, which marked the changing of the guard. Mornings were the same, six days a week, except for Tuesdays and Saturdays, where more duties were assigned to the soldiers, and Sundays, where every man of the Regiment was inspected and drilled for an additional two hours, after which the Regiment marched to church, where the service lasted for only two or three hours more (the British Army was Anglican, not Puritans or Quakers, for God's sake!). Afternoons were full of inspections of the non-commissioned officers, parades for the instruction of new officers, and the training of the recruits and infantry in the care and shooting of their muskets. Many of the soldiers who had no duties earned extra coin by serving as merchants to others, by sewing uniforms, by repairing shoes or muskets, by cutting hair, or by proffering other skills they had practiced before joining the Army.

Private Sanguine Gore dressed in his best for the Officer's Mess. Soldiers and non-commissioned officers ate after the Parades, breakfast at nine in the morning and then dinner at one, but then, there would be no other food, other than what the men bought for themselves from the sutlers or at the commissary, until the next morning. The Officer's Mess was held at a much more civilized hour, 5:30.

The men who Private Gore joined for dinner in the Officer's Mess were, for the most part, the finest sons of Britain's aristocracy. To a man (other than Gore), they had purchased their commissions, and hardly any were using their military service to escape from shame or the law. These were men who had been raised to understand that the British Army (and to a lesser extent, the British Navy) manifested the values of the nobility. For these men, military service justified the privileges and position that the upper class enjoyed in British society. Even the French understood this;

Montaigne, that fopdoodle, had gotten it right when he had written, "The proper life for one of the nobility is that of a soldier."

And for these proper, noble men, the only opportunity for civilized company in the best army on the world was the evening Mess that they ate together.

Because they were a civilized company, their Mess had its own rules and expectations of decorum, as strict as those of the Parade ground, and breaches of etiquette would draw the offending parties fines of bottles of wine or other appropriate sanctions.

Intelligent and witty conversation was expected, and the topics of politics, religion, and love were banned. Gaming and reading at the table were not allowed, and cigars were only permitted after the dessert had been taken away.

The first toast of the evening, the Loyalty Toast, was to King George or to 'His Majesty's British Army'. A number of other toasts followed this, including the passing of the port decanter to charge the port after the meal and its dessert had been finished.

The meal itself indicated the lofty status of its participants. There were always two meats served (except on Christmas Day, when Beef Wellington or a nice steak and kidney pie was added to the bill of fare): a roast sirloin of beef, venison, chyne of mutton or veal, turkey, pigeons, snipes, ducks, or partridges (with bubble and squeak, bangers and mash, or cottage pie, made with the week's leftovers on Fridays). There was cheddar with the meal and Stilton after. Potatoes and onions, and sometimes neeps, were the vegetables. When the Mess could find a competent cook, there was trifle (with fresh berries in season and dried fruits otherwise) for dessert.

*

Between his tent-mates and his Mess-mates, Private Sanguine Gore had the best of two worlds and made fast friends from both of those worlds. These associations and the friendships that they engendered would prove fruitful in times to come Private Gore imagined.

*

Books were Sanguine Gore's 'leather-bound whores'. They would give a man pleasure as long as he paid their price, and they would please him again and again with no thought as to their encounters with others in his absence. They would bring a world of diversion to anyone who would take them into his hands and treat them well. And Sanguine Gore took them again and again.

He had begun his dalliances when he had been imprisoned in boarding school.

Gore, he had been called by the name his father had given him then, Make-Peace Ogle, found that a deck of playing cards could be purchased for seven and a half pence. Most of the other boys had their own decks (and dice, as well) and spent their time away from classwork, when they weren't cruelly tormenting those smaller than they, gambling for farthings or buggering one another.

One day, Make-Peace Ogle was idly reading a copy of *The Tattler* that "Scud" East had brought back from a week in London. He saw an advertisement, in such small print as to be almost illegible, proclaiming that one could purchase Bunyan's "The Pilgrim's Progress" in successively-numbered fasicules, three sheets at a time, at a cost of tuppence for "Part One" and four pence for "Part Two" from the shop of a publisher and bookseller, Thomas Osborne.

This intrigued the boy, as much for his love of reading (he almost lusted after the serials by Defoe and Swift that he found in the magazines), as for the fact that this Osborne was the same man who Alexander Pope had mocked as the 'Chapman' character, who had lost a pissing contest, in "The Dunciad", and so he subscribed to this wonderful offer and, by the time he had left the school, had amassed the entire book.

By then, the seduction was complete.

In the army, Private Sanguine Gore, by virtue of the pouch of gold and silver he had brought with him to his new profession, was able to afford his passion.

He wrote to Osborne and established an account. He would purchase books from the seller, keep the ones he loved, and return the rest, after he had read each one of them, to be purchased by the bookseller for a credit to his account.

He had kept the serialized copy of "The Pilgrim's Progress", a finely-bound copy of Milton's "Paradise Lost", and a pair of beautiful sisters, Pope's translations of "The Iliad" and "The Odyssey".

He had read and returned Pepys' boring diary, Swift's droll "Gulliver's Travels", Defoe's exciting "Robinson Crusoe" and scandalous "Moll Flanders", Congreve's sophisticated play, "The Way of the World", a libretto of "The Beggar's Opera", and an unauthorized English translation of Newton's "Principia: A Treatise of the System of the World".

He had bought a new almanac each year since he had discovered them at age twelve, he followed the tradition of Marcus Aurelius and kept a "diary" in a series of blank books (five shillings each) where he recorded each day's events, and he tried his hand at drawing the beauties of the natural world and expressing his hopes, fears, and opinions in poesy, without worrying that they would ever be seen.

Gore kept his books and folios and diaries in his trunk, with his uniforms and accoutrements on the top, and the knives hidden in a compartment, of which he alone knew, beneath them.

Private Sanguine Gore doted on his 'whores'. On a Friday evening, whenever he had no duties and had been given leave, he would visit the one of Lady Elizabeth Cresswell's houses that graced Bournemouth, "The Holy Ground', with his tent-mates and their friends. He would sit in the parlor, sipping glasses of sangaree, that new and very popular mixture of port, lemon juice, sugar, and nutmeg, and read while the others went upstairs.

The madam took great delight, as did her ladies, in attempting to lure Private Gore to leave the pleasures of the printed pages and enter Eve's custom house (that her ladies offered), Private Gore realized after a few of these evenings had been spent. But the Private was loyal to his bound ladies, and only gave the others his fond but chaste thanks.

Gore cautioned his mates to avoid those women afflicted with "the Great Pox". One of Gore's tent-mates, Garry Owen told him not to worry, "A man can dare or a man can do! And besides, that darlin' little Hannah Dilley is well-schooled in the 'French perversion'," and laughed, "and no one can get the Pox from a whore's mouth, it's said," as he bounded up the stairs with darlin' little Hannah's hand firmly clasped in his.

*

Over the next two years, Private Sanguine Gore became an exemplary Hussar. He was beloved by his tent-mates, who appreciated his loyalty and good spirits, accepted by his mess-mates, who thought young Gore to be a truly noble soul and an excellent gentleman, valued by his bookseller, who never failed to be paid in a timely manner and asked for more books to sell the soldier, and admired by the whores, who were delighted that he was respectful and witty with them and puzzled that he had taken none of them to bed.

*

And then, one day, William Gollmann, their Lance corporal, visited the Regimental Surgeon. He died a two fortnights later from the cure for the clap. A Warrant Officer, the surgeon's assistant, once Gollmann had complained to him of "stitching, shooting pains with soreness and a purulent discharge", injected quicksilver into the Lance corporal, through his 'urinary meatus' as the charlatan called it. When that did not cure the disease, the Surgeon changed his course of treatment to a suppository of belladonna and phosphorus. Gollmann was dead within a week, and Private Gore was promoted to Lance corporal.

*

Lance corporal Gore blossomed with his promotion, earning the respect and admiration of the entire camp. A year later, his superior non-commissioned office, an experienced cavalryman, Corporal of the Horse Bentley Drummle, was thrown and broke his neck when his horse shied at a ditch at the Bilsdale Hunt in Yorkshire, to which he had been invited by his captain. Lance corporal Gore was promoted to replace the man as Corporal of the Horse.

*

In 1746, the French (and their ally, the French East India Company, which had been created a century earlier to compete with the Dutch and the English Companies in that part of the world) took its antagonism in the War of the Austrian Succession to India and pitted its navy and the French Company's army against the English Navy and the Army of the English East India Company.

The navies dueled on the waters while the Companies' armies fought for control of trading posts on the sub-continent.

An Englishman, Robert Clive, arrived at the British post of Fort St. George in Madras, the Company's base on the Coromandel Coast. He did well there until the army of the French Company took the fort. The French Company's army was composed mostly of dirty Indian wogs and neglected to watch the Englishman closely. He escaped his captivity and made his way to Fort St. David, the Company's post at the mouth of the River Gadilam, and then went home to England.

The war raged on for three more years, until it was settled by the Treaty of Aix-la-Chapelle.

Gore was promoted to Cornet and posted to Fort St. George with the task of training the private army of the Company to the standards of the British Army.

Seven years later, Lieutenant Colonel Robert Clive arrived in Madras as the newly-named Governor of Fort. St. David.

In August, the iniquitous 'Brownies' showed their barbaric souls.

Fort William in Kolkata (more properly, Calcutta) was built to protect the trade of the Company in the Bengal Presidency. The Nawab of Bengal deeply resented the Company's interference in his province, in its independence, and in his rule. So, he laid siege to Fort William and captured 146 soldiers, who had been left under the command of a Company administrator. The Fort fell shortly thereafter.

The prisoners were secured in a strongly-barred dungeon, a room, approximately fourteen feet by eighteen feet with but two small windows, which was packed so tightly that the door was difficult to close.

Clive received the news of the fall of the Fort and set out, ordering Cornet Gore's troops in Madras to assist him in the relief expedition.

Lieutenant Colonel Clive led the charge toward the Fort. Cornet Gore saw an opportunity to do his duty for his King and followed to Clive's left, watching the Lieutenant Colonel's inside. The two men, followed by their troops, flew to the attack, slashing, parrying, thrusting and pushing their enemy back by their simple ferocity. The day was quickly won, and Clive ordered his second-in-command, a Major James Agnew (who was later killed by a sniper while fighting the American rebels) to open the dungeon and free the prisoners. Clive looked to this left, smiled his thanks to Cornet Gore and invited him to accompany the two men.

When the 'black hole' had first been filled with its prisoners, 123 of the 146 had died within a day.

When the Nawab had ordered that the door of the dungeon be opened after that first, terrible day and he had seen the carnage, he ordered the bodies of the dead thrown into a ditch, the surviving prisoners fed and given water, and nineteen of the survivors placed back into the tiny room (the other four, he sent north to the city of Murshidabad on the banks of the Bhagirathi that flows into the Holy River of the Ganges).

Lieutenant Colonel Clive welcomed the prisoners to their freedom and called for water and his physician for the newly-freed men. The nineteen, after they had all received water, offered their savior a hearty 'Huzzah'.

The King made Clive a member of the peerage, 1st Baron Clive, with instructions to retaliate against the Indians for their atrocity. Lord Clive defeated the Nawab of Bengal at the Battle of Plassey, and returned to Calcutta before being recalled to England.

For his actions in the rescue, Gore was promoted to Captain-lieutenant, but seeing the power and wealth of the Company, he asked the Baron to intercede for him so that he might obtain his release from the Army and a position in the Company.

Lord Clive was happy to help the fine, young man.

*

With its own military and a civilian army of "Merchants of London trading into the East Indies", 'John Company' had no equal and brooked no interference in its affairs. The world was its oyster (at least until the English Parliament established its sovereignty over the Company's power in the 1770s), and Sanguine Gore was seated at the feast.

Gore found a summer cottage (with sixteen rooms, a stable, and expansive gardens) in the riverside village of Sutanuti and purchased it from the zamindar Sabarna Roy Choudhury family. His position with the Company allowed him to live a comfortable life, and he lived it to the full.

He dined with the directors of the Company, had tea with the directors' wives who saw in him an eligible bachelor, and hunted and played in polo matches with the Indian nobles of the area. Anything that he might wish, he had but to ask for.

His position at the Company was boring and unchallenging until he discovered opium.

*

Sanguine Gore was an educated man. He had distinguished himself academically at a well-regarded Public school and would have done the same at an English university had not his father disdained his further education. Gore had joined the Army and had risen through the ranks, from a Private soldier to a Captain-lieutenant, before deciding to retire with honor and devote himself to his own fortune.

And to ensure that he would create a fortune for himself, he set his course with the British East India Company in Calcutta, its stronghold and base in the Madras Presidency.

Actually, the Madras Presidency had reverted to its previous status, the Agency of Fort St. George, two years prior, but regardless of what its official title was, it was the southernmost province administered by the Company and included the tea plantations of Ceylon.

Sanguine Gore was sitting at his desk one day, pouring over balance sheets of the various shipments of the items that the Company had been shipping from India to China. China was, potentially, a great market that would earn the Company untold profits. That is, if the Company could find something that it could profitably market in that inscrutable land.

The Chinese had, in abundance, a product that the British had found habit-forming: tea. The British imported millions of pounds of the green or black stuff from China every year. Britain was the King of the West, Emperor of the Industrialized World, but the Chinese wanted none of the textiles or other Occidental goods that the English merchants offered to trade for the tea. The deficit in trade was becoming more and more lop-sided with each passing week. The Austrians, the Danes, the Swedes, the Prussians, and the French had begun to attempt to shove the Company aside and take the market in Guangzhou away from it.

The English found that they could sell raw materials to the Chinese and that greedy merchants and corrupt bureaucrats were as numerous in China as they were in the West. So the Company began to ship raw cotton, raw silk, and raw opium from Bengal to China (even though opium was illegal by Royal decree in China, that law was easily circumvented).

Unlike many other commodities, opium was the perfect medium of exchange: it was extremely profitable, it created a market that grew and grew on its own, it was convenient to ship and then store, and it did not decay or spoil.

Gore examined the Company's ledgers. They spoke to him as few other things did; he read them as avidly as he had once read the novels of his youth. And what those account books told him on that fateful morning was that the Company could get preposterously rich by selling the gummy opium (and Gore, himself, could feather quite a comfortable nest for himself, as well).

Gore added, subtracted, and multiplied the figures for an hour, checked his computations, and then repeated the procedure. There it was!

Gore could purchase a 135-pound chest of raw opium from a Mughal farmer in Jessore for two hundred pounds he discovered. And if he purchased more than just one chest, the cost would diminish.

*

The Dutch had been shipping Indian opium to the islands and main-lands of Southeast Asia for over fifty years. They were the ones who introduced the habit of smoking the drug to their customers.

But opium was ubiquitous nearly everywhere that men and women lived. Opium, and its little sister laudanum, were as common in Calcutta as dosa. The Mughal emperors were passionate in their desire for the stuff, often drinking it mixed with wine. Shah Jahan might have loved his wife so deeply that he built her the Taj Mahal as her mausoleum, but he had the remarkable building decorated with the poppies that he also adored. Emperor Jahangir so often visited the "flower-land" that his foreign wife, Light of the World, was left to lead the kingdom because he could not. These kings of kings even gave their war elephants opium before battle to calm their sensitive souls.

Westerners found that opium (and laudanum, which is simply opium mixed with alcohol) could calm nervous disorders (especially among the delicate and highly emotional women among them) and quiet the minds of the insane. Opium could be mixed with other palliative or energizing agents (like wine, whiskey, brandy, hashish, chloroform, ether, belladonna, cayenne pepper, or mercury) and spawn a thousand testaments to the efficacy of its cure for almost any affliction, malady, or complaint. With the terrible diseases of consumption, typhus, smallpox, rheumatism, dysentery, cholera, dropsy, and ague affecting nearly every community throughout the Americas, Europe, and Asia, opium seemed a more effective remedy than blood-letting and a less stigmatizing option than resorting to the cold embrace of 'Mother Gin'.

*

So, to benefit his employer (and provide the funds that would keep him in his old age), Gore began to auction opium in Calcutta. This was just one small part of an elaborate and what would later become a highly-profitable stratagem: English merchant captains would buy tea in Guangzhou on credit and then balance their books with opium in Calcutta. Other English ships would ferry the opium to the Chinese coast where native Chinese would smuggle it ashore to its final destination.

At the first auction, Gore bought one chest filled with the small spheres of 'kong pan', which was, he had been assured, the dearest sort of the stuff.

With the profit from that first chest, Gore bought two at the next auction. At the next, he bought four. Finally, Gore was the sole owner of five chests in each shipment of opium that the Company sent to China.

With his profits, from then on, he purchased stock in the Company. Like any stock, the shares in 'John Company' sometimes rose and sometimes fell, but Sanguine Gore was not interested in easy, short-term gain. He would hold his investments until he would someday return to England.

For the nonce, he would live, very comfortably, on his Company salary in his glorious little cottage, down by the riverside in the peaceful village of Sutanuti. There was work to be done during the week, parties and balls to attend in the evenings, and polo to be played on Saturdays. Capt. Sanguine Gore, HMRA (Ret.), found, to his great pleasure, that he had done quite well for himself, thank you.

Chapter 11 – Five of Knives

The fifth card of the Minor Arcana of the Suit of Knives in the Swordsmith's Tarot is the Five of Knives. Fives symbolize conflict, unease, and struggle, the constituent elements of transformation … or death.

A time of change is a time of challenge, discord, and learning. The path of striving to achieve a goal cannot be trod without encountering obstacles, determining the ways and means to overcome them, and then acting on those decisions. The opponents that impede your way forward may be physical, spiritual, or intellectual … or they may simply be other men and women who seek to stop you.

Prejudice, frustration, anger, and hate are your opponents as well. Embracing them will deny you the benefit of learning from those who would stand in your way. Better to take the gifts that your enemies array against you and adapt them to your use and advantage than toss away treasure that may be hidden within the dross.

Just as it is impossible to avoid change, it is impossible to avoid conflict. The time, the place, and the manner in which you choose to face and resolutely contend with your adversaries is yours to decide.

*

For eleven years, Captain Sanguine Gore (HMRA, Ret.) worked for 'John Company', filling its coffers (and his own pockets) with the profits from the opium trade. With his salary, he lived a luxurious life, full of the finest things, and with his hidden profits, he bought Company stock. He did what every Englishman should do: Obey the law (as it was appropriate), do one's duty, do the work, play the game, and be a man.

But then, one soft Indian summer night, his life changed.

*

There was a great deal of work to occupy Sanguine Gore at the Company. And when work was finished, for the day or the week, there were parties to attend. Some were hosted by the Company's directors and council members and agents, the British government's functionaries (Resident and Governor), and the local Indian nobility, from the Mughal Emperor (when he was in residence in the city) to the Nawab, to the foujidar (military commander), to the lesser officials.

There were formal soirées, and dinner parties in the evenings, and more casual entertainments during the days (garden parties, polo matches between the teams of the Company, the Nawab, and the British Army played each other regularly with occasional matches against teams of minor local potentates who traveled to Calcutta especially for the competitions, and other pleasures, from boat games (vallam kali), to bull racing (kala), to badminton, to the frenetic and completely unintelligible running around of Kho kho).

It seemed to Captain Gore that every holiday in India required a feast. And on one particularly dark night of a new moon, the natives celebrated something they called 'Dawali'. It was a festival of lights. It seemed that every building in the city was lit, from pavement to roof, with thousands of candles and torches, he thought, as his coach rolled through the streets on its way to the palace of the Nawab.

The entire Hindu population of the city seemed to be inside, saying prayers, but just as Gore's coach arrived at the palace, the skies above him were suddenly filled with a cacophony of exploding fireworks; the celebration had begun.

Inside, Gore saw many of his fellow Company men (and the wives of the few married ones) and richly-dressed Indians. As he walked into a great marble hall, where the celebration was in full-swing, he was approached by servants bearing food (meats and vegetables spiced with the unique flavors of India, the leaf of the sweet neem tree, black and long pepper, ginger, cardamom, cloves, cashews, coconut, saffron, cinnamon, and yoghurt, sweets concocted of the most unusual ingredients, chickpea flour, almonds, rose water, sugars and cheeses) and drinks, alcoholic and not (for the English guests there was tea with sugar, a distinctive, hoppy pale ale that the British had developed for the palate of their expatriates, gin mixed with lime and sugar (the same combination that many officers of the British Army used to mask the vile taste of the quinine they took every day to ward off malaria), and for the Indians, there was rice beer (kosna), palm wine toddies, coconut liquor (fenny), lemonade (neebu pani), the favorite drink of Lord Shiva, bhang (a strong mixture of milk, ghee, mangoes, and the ground leaves and flowers of some hemp-like plant), and yoghurt).

The Englishmen and women were dressed in their European finery of lively, bright colors (deep blue, bright red, mahogany red, burgundy red, maroon, liver-colored purple, royal purple, pink, forest green, goose-shit green, turquoise, or Paris mud for the more traditional and pure white, pearl, cream, straw, stone, leaden gray, sky blue, gold, salmon, olive, orange, or lemon for the more daring.

The ladies' formal gowns were stiff things of silk, rich in embroidery and brocade. Hoop skirts prevented the ladies from sitting, but bone stays helped them retain their perfect postures as they stood. These elaborate gowns were low-necked, with skirts that opened in the front to show their petticoats. The gowns' sleeves were close-fitting with more ruffles at the elbows, and the dresses' necklines were trimmed with lace (the more modest women wore fichus tucked into their necklines to cover themselves).

Worn to be seen just enough to be noticed before they were hidden again, the shoes that accompanied these gowns were made of silk or leather and had high, curved heels with separate buckles in silver or decorated with paste stones.

Elaborate hairstyles completed the Englishwomen's attire. Wigs were popular (in colors that flattered their gowns), but even without a wig, a lady could create the high, fashionable styles by adding rolls of horsehair, wool, and false hair to her own and holding the creation together with pomatum, a paste of beef marrow, tallow, hog grease, and oil.

The Englishmen's fashion was equally elaborate but more practical. The goal was to appear fashionable while exerting the least effort in achieving that goal. Nonchalance was the rage. The individual elements of the suit, the coat, the waistcoat, and the breeches, were decorated with fine accompaniments in the formal fabrics that were still demanded for an evening. The skirts of the coats were narrower, the waistcoats beneath extended further, occasionally almost to the knees, shirts exhibited ruffles of fabric or lace, and breeches fit snugly. Low-heeled shoes were of fine leather, fastened with jeweled or silver buckles, and worn with silk stockings. Wigs were still worn at formal gatherings, or a man could brush his hair back from his forehead and tie it with a black ribbon at the nape of his neck (it would, of course, be powdered). A cocked-hat made the ensemble complete.

Some very few young men, who had completed the Grand Tour, affected a continental look, the macaroni: very short, very tight trousers, elaborate coats and waistcoats, enormous powdered wigs, small hats, and delicate shoes. It was a brave young man who chose to wear this fashion; it was generally considered to be a useless affectation, frivolous and effeminate. Its proponents saw it as a bold demonstration of character and identity. In England, duels were fought over words that were said to those who wore the fashion. In India, most Englishmen served in the British Army or were employed by The Company (neither institution accepted dueling as proper behavior), so altercations were few.

Captain Sanguine Gore (HMRA, Ret.) wore a hand-sewn suit in cerise and cream, lined with horsehair and backed with French silk. It was a lightweight suit, all the better for the steaming weather of India. The coat had side-pleats and a waistcoat, embellished with silver embroidery, which extended to the middle of his thigh. Ivory and yellow striped grosgrain ribbon trimmed the edges of his collar, his cuffs, the pleats, and the front of the coat. He wore fine, black riding boots over ivory silk stockings that were barely visible below the hem of his cream-colored breeches. He wore no hat, and he had clubbed his hair without powdering it.

*

Suddenly, there was a military shout, and every eye in the great hall turned to look out over the even larger veranda. At a second command, three hundred Mughal riflemen fired a salute as the silver howdah, the ornate Indian carriage that rode atop a giant elephant, of the Nawab came up the drive.

The elephant stopped at the steps to the palace, and the driver used his gold and sapphire-encrusted ankusha, a wicked pike with a sharpened goad and pointed hook at its end, to force the giant beast to kneel.

The Nawab alighted and walked up the steps.

When he entered the huge room, every head, Indian and English, bowed its respect to him.

The Nawab was of the Mughal, who saw clothing as a creation complementary to its art and poetry. The Nawab was a large, powerful man, as befitted his noble title. His clothing reflected the power that he wielded and the influence that he effected.

His jama, the knee-length, tight-fitting frock that fastened on his right hip was of a misty-blue silk, shining from beneath the open-fronted black, brocaded coat (that the Indians called a chogha), dyed in a dizzying pattern of cochineal swirls, that might have been clouds or wisps of flame. On his feet, he wore soft, red leather shoes, embroidered with gold and silver threads in other twisting patterns. On his noble head, he wore a midnight-blue turban, ornamented with every manner of precious gems, rubies, diamonds, emeralds, sapphires, and pearls. At his side, his patka belt, made of the finest baft hawa ('woven air') muslin (so fine that it could only be worn once), was painted with floral designs so exact and intricate that they might have been living things and held the great curved, golden tawal saber, its hilt covered in jewels and its dangerous blade asleep in its jeweled scabbard. His earrings and anklets were of gold, and his necklaces were of pearls.

He walked through his assembled people and his guests to a tall, gilded throne, made of wood and resin. When he sat, not a soul in the room moved until his wine-bearer had run to bow at the Nawal's feet and present him with a flask covered in gold, silver, jade, and emeralds. When he had tasted the wine and nodded his assent, three musicians, playing tabla, tambura, and sitar, began their song.

And the celebration truly began.

*

The other Indian men were dressed as their Lord, and while not as opulently as the Nawab, much more splendidly than any of the uncouth Westerners.

*

The Indian women were magnificent.

*

A few of the Mughal nobles had married women of the court of Babur. These noble women wore wide, loose, striped pants and tightly-fitting vests that reached almost to the floor, with long or short-sleeves as they saw fit and v-shaped necklines that showed-off necklaces upon necklaces upon necklaces of pearls (one dowager sported fifteen ropes of the precious spheres), which were mimed by bracelets of pearls that filled their arms from wrists to elbows and anklets of pearls, as well. Their hair was set in braids, bound with gold or silver wires to hold it beneath silken scarves atop their heads, in the colors of their vests. Every finger was be-ringed, with the rings on their thumbs being small, exquisite mirrors. No woman was without a golden nose ornament, but the design of each was unique and captivating. Earrings of gold, studded with precious stones were as diverse as the women's nose ornaments.

The majority of the women, though, were Mughal. The Mughal fashion was of a tight-fitting bodice that left the midriffs bare. These women wore long vests, a fashion taken from their men, over bodices that reached to the floor with v-shaped necklines. The opening at the front of a woman's vest was embroidered in gold or silver. The women's lower garments were either tight pants, favored by the Muslim women, or long skirts, favored by the Hindu women. The drawstrings of both of the pants and skirts were decorated with jewels or pearls.

The fabrics that these garments were made of were goat's hair, or lamb's wool, or silk. Regardless of the fabric, the clothing was embroidered with gold and silver thread. Nearly every woman carried a shawl of muslin, so finely-made that it was nearly transparent.

Two of these noble women walked past Captain Gore, and he realized that their clothes and hair had been scented with rose water.

These Mughal women wore their jewelry just as proudly as did their Babur sisters. The Mughals preferred two-inch wide armlets of gold or silver or brass above their elbows, as many as four or five earrings in each ear, and golden chains that lay across their foreheads, holding ornaments in the shapes of stars, flowers, the sun, or the moon.

Each woman had prepared herself to present all of her beauty to a man's senses. The women anointed themselves, with the help of their servants, with bouquets of perfumes that were theirs and theirs alone. Small ornaments delighted the eye of the beholder in unexpected places on their bodies. Their hair was dressed in plaits that mimicked nature's designs and were decorated with fragrant flowers (whose aromas complemented the perfumes that arose from the curves of their bodies). Their eyebrows were made perfectly symmetrical, their eyelids darkened with kohl, and betel leaf reddened their lips. Those women who were married wore the nath rings in their noses, each attached with a gossamer-thin, golden chain to an earring. Every woman's hands and feet were covered with intricate mendhi designs made of henna.

*

Captain Sanguine Gore, HMRA (Ret.) had met many of the people, English and Indian, who were enjoying the holiday at the Nawab's palace, before.

But across the room stood a young woman, an unmarried Mughal noblewoman, by her dress and adornment, the like of which he had never seen.

He could have sworn that his heart skipped a beat when his eyes first found her. And as if in answer to his gaze, she turned to look at him, smiled the smallest smile, and turned away. For propriety's sake? Because he was so unworthy of her glance? Asking him to approach her?

For one of the few times in his life, Gore was completely unsure of what to do.

Then his director walked up to him and commenced to discuss the month's saltpeter shipments.

When he was able to end that conversation, Gore looked back to where she had stood, but she was gone.

*

Sanguine Gore was a tortured soul. He had found a woman unlike any he had ever seen, she had smiled at him, and then, he had lost her. Calcutta was a great city, ninety-nine percent of whom were Indian. Even the Mughal nobility numbered in the thousands. And this stunning girl might live somewhere apart from Calcutta.

What was he to do?

He was lost.

So he buried himself in work, played his chukkas of polo when he was asked, and went to the parties and entertainments where he felt isolated and bored. But what else was he to do?

*

And as businesses and nations change, so did the Company and the Kingdom of Bengal.

*

A Mr. Bush arrived from London as the newest Chief Officer to oversee trade in the Bengali Presidency. He found lodgings in Calcutta's "Great Hotel" (which was advertised as "The Jewel of the East"), but felt insecure and nervous in his lodgings with all of the "Brownies" about. So his first act as Chief Officer was to send for a troop of East India Company Army regulars to guard his suite and offices.

To his credit, he did attempt to learn Urdu and Persian and spent a great deal of his free time learning about India, but he was convinced of two things: first, that the Company in Calcutta, the "City of Palaces", was thoroughly corrupt, and secondly, that European medicine would save the Indian people and provide a bridge between British and Indian culture.

*

And life went on in the Presidency.

A troop of British troops and Mughal soldiers under the command of a Nanda Singh had words and then destroyed a full city block near the docks on the Hoogly River. A few men on each side were killed, a score more injured, and a dozen businesses were destroyed. Mr. Bush met with the local council and agreed to pay for the damages to the businesses and accept payment from the Indians for the burial of the dead and the care of the wounded.

An Afghan named Sobha Khan, who had become a tax collector, filed charges of corruption against the English Governor General. Mr. Khan was supported by the Indians, as well as by the Governor General's rivals in the Council. While the investigation was being conducted, Mr. Khan was indicted for forgery, convicted, and died under mysterious circumstances in the City Jail while awaiting appeal.

Sanguine Gore concentrated on his work and dreamed of the beautiful Indian girl who had smiled at him.

*

A month after the Nawab's celebration, Captain Gore was invited to a garden party by one of the married English couples whose husband worked for the Company. Gore considered sending his regrets, but he was alerted that Mr. Bush would be in attendance and expected all of his employees to attend.

The afternoon came, as Gore knew that it would, and he dressed for a casual afternoon tea. His groom saddled his horse, and the Captain rode out into the countryside to the estate where the couple resided.

There was tea and lemonade. The gentlemen were casually, but properly, attired, and the ladies were a garden of pink, red, purple, brown, yellow, and blue of striped and checked calico and floral-printed chintz. For the hungry, there was Tamil stew, chicken, halwa cakes (made of rice flour), butter, and sugar, and yoghurt. After the meal, there was port, claret, Madeira, and the smoking of the hookahs.

Besides the English Company managers, there were the Munshies, the Indian clerks and accountants who had been hired by the Company: Abdul Karim, Hakimuddin Premchand, Kanhaiyalal Maneklal, Abdur Rouf, and Abdullah Kadir. A tall, cadaverous Englishman named Hickey who had rented offices and ordered a press in order to publish an English-language newspaper, *The Bengal Intelligencer and General Advertiser*, was also in attendance.

As an entré to his plan to spread the influence of Western medicine across the sub-continent, Mr. Bush had invited half a dozen Ayuvedic vaidyas (whose medical practice was based upon Sanskrit texts) and Unani hakims (whose version of Greco-Arabic medicine had been practiced in India for six hundred years) and another half-dozen European doctors who had arrived in India with the British Army. The Europeans disdained the Indian doctors' theory, knowledge, and practice. Any Indian involved with English medicine in India was assuredly a member of the Subordinate Medical Services (SMS), hospital orderlies or, in rare cases, medical assistants (the assistants were referred to by the English as 'native doctors').

Since Mr. Bush's intention in putting together this garden party was to encourage his people, English and Indian alike, to mingle and get to know one another apart from their roles in the Company, this garden party was very much like any other garden party in India in those days.

There would be food, drink, fancy flowers, gambling, and fireworks in the evening.

Since employees of the Company were notorious wagerers (it was said that they would bet on how many people would pass by an open window within a given period of time), and the Indians had been attempting to beat the odds in a variety of contests for thousands of years, this common interest, Mr. Bush thought, might prove to be the glue that would bind these disparate people together.

For entertainment, there were wrestlers, archery, and mallakamba, an Indian sport where a gymnast pulls himself up into the air and gyrates around on vertical wooden poles or hanging ropes. The guests wagered happily on all of those contests.

There were tables set up for the boards of chess, go, mancala, and the Indian games of pachisi and Snakes and Ladders.

And there were tables for cards.

Three tables were set aside for naqsh, an Indian game that was a close cousin to the Spanish veintiuno (that some Englishmen called Blackjack). These tables filled rapidly.

And there were four tables for Ganjifa. This game was played with a 96-card deck of eight suits (slaves, crowns, swords, red-gold coins, harps, bills of exchange, white-gold coins, and cloth). There was betting and the players were very enthusiastic.

Gore found himself drawn to one of the Ganjifa tables. He watched the game for a while, and when a gentleman excused himself and left the game, a chair was open.

A woman, sitting next to the empty chair, looked up at him and asked, "Would you care to join us, Captain Gore?"

Sanguine Gore looked twice at the woman, for a woman it was but dressed in a contemporary riding habit of a tailored jacket, like a man's, a high-necked shirt, a waistcoat, a hat, and a petticoat.

And in an instant of epiphany and elation, Sanguine Gore realized that the woman asking him to join the game was the beautiful Indian girl who had smiled at him across the room at the Nawab's celebration.

"Thank you, Miss …," Gore stumbled, but sat quickly down beside her, "but I don't know how to play, nor have I the pleasure of knowing your name."

The girl's smile, a brilliant, shining thing, lit up the table as well as Gore's heart.

"I would be happy to teach you, Captain," she said, "The game is very much like whist but without a trump. It is mostly played with individual players, but I know these other gentlemen, and I am certain that I can convince them to agree to play as partners to aid in your learning the game."

She spoke to the other players and the seat across from the girl became open. Gore moved quickly to take that place so that the girl would play as his partner.

"My name is Manikarnika. My distant uncle is Ali Gauhar, the sixteenth Mughal Emperor. My father was Nizam Asaf Jah, and his sister, my aunt, is the Honored Gunna Begam. I learned your name at the Dawali celebration at the Nawab's. I have hoped to meet you in person ever since."

And there was that wonderful smile again.

And the two, Gore and Manikarnika, learned to play the game together, and they learned a great deal more about each other as they played, the sound of each other's laughter, the quickness of each other's minds, the touch of each other's hands when cards happened to be passed between them.

The night came to an end much too quickly.

*

Captain Gore asked Manikarnika if he might ride beside her to escort her home.

She agreed that would be gentlemanly thing.

They rode through the moonlight in the warm Indian evening, with all of the stars in the heavens and the great, bright moon above lighting their way. The talked as they rode, and the gates of her family's compound came far too soon.

*

The next day, at his desk in his office, Gore found it impossible to concentrate on ledgers and red and black ink. All he could think of was how her eyes had shone in the moonlight, how her red lips had begged his to kiss her, and how he must have her. Forever!

And there was a knock at his door.

"Come," he said absentmindedly.

A young Indian boy entered his office, closed the door behind him, and handed him a piece of paper, folded once.

Gore reached into his pocket to find a penny for the lad, and as his fingers found the copper piece, he smelled the scent on the paper.

Jasmine!

The same scent that she had worn.

Gore tossed the coin to the boy and waited until he had closed the door behind him before he unfolded the paper.

"Meet me tonight in the plumeria garden by the south wall of the compound. I will wait for you under the pink tree at midnight – M"

Sanguine Gore closed his eyes and promised that he would.

*

The two met in the garden that night.

They met almost every night in the garden, as regularly as the moonrise.

They told no one of their meeting.

The meetings, it seemed, were all the time that they would have.

*

And then, one morning, just as Gore had gotten to his desk and organized his work for the day, there was a knock at the door.

"Come," he said.

Two young Indian men walked into Gore's office, closed the door, and stood blocking the way out.

Gore looked at the men and began to ask, "What can I …"

"You will never see Manikarnika again, Englishman," the larger of the two said, almost spitting it out in his anger, "Our sister will not be soiled by a Western savage. We will kill you, and no one will ever find your body. Stay away from her. Stay away from our home. Go find yourself some British bitch to rut after."

And the two men turned, left, and slammed the door behind them.

*

Captain Gore had little time to do what had to be done. He could only hope that Manikarnika would agree.

*

That night, Gore saddled his horse and rode to the plumeria gardens.

The woman he loved, more than his life, was waiting under the pink tree as she always did.

He ran to her and held her tightly for so long that she whispered in his ear, "Darling, what's wrong. Why do you hold me so tightly?"

He told her of her brothers' demands. He told her that he could not live without her. He asked her to come with him, that night. They would go to a place where they could live together, and no one would ever be able to separate them.

She stood quietly in front of him, and gazed deeply into his eyes. "Of course, my love," she told him, "Let us go right now."

And then a voice from behind her said, "You will go nowhere, sister, with him. He will die here, and we will bury him under your pink tree. Then you will be sent to another city where you will no longer be able to shame our family. Step aside, and let us end this dog's life."

Gore pushed Manikarnika way from him to his right. Then he reached over his shoulders to the hilts of the knives that poked out of their scabbards on his back.

As his hands touched the ivory hilts, Sanguine Gore heard the music that had been absent from his life since before he had joined the army those many, many years before. But, he knew, it was the same, surging, ecstatic song. And the blades sang a harmony together that filled his heart with passion and courage and pleasure.

And then the larger of Manikarnika's brothers stepped toward him, an evil double-edged khanda sword in his hand. The point of the broad sword was blunt, but one edge was reinforced with a metal plate, and a spike stuck out of the other end of the round pommel. The man who wielded it held it with two hands to bring more power to his cut.

But he had not anticipated Gore's knives. Gore slashed at the leg that the man had put forward to balance his lunge, and when the singing edge bit into the man below his knee and cracked his tibia, the man fell screaming to the ground.

Gore put the tip of the other knife in the fallen man's throat as he stepped past him and toward his other assailant. The other man held a Nepalese kukri, a vicious, inwardly-curved knife that was used as much a tool as a weapon. It was a dangerous-looking thing, but the second brother had not learned how to use it. He took a wild swipe at Gore, and when Gore knocked his opponent's blade out of the way and spun to his left, the singing knife in Gore's right hand cut deeply into the man's right side. The man fell like a stone.

Sanguine Gore returned his blades to their scabbard, still hearing the echoes of their music reverberating around and though him. He reached out for his beloved, and with a bloody hand, took hers, whispered, "We must hurry," and led her to his horse.

They cantered through the night, back to his cottage and the gig he had readied for their escape.

All that he needed, he had prepared to take with him: his chest, filled with some clothes, a bundle of banknotes and a bag full of gold, and his books, with a hidden place to hide his knives.

He helped Manikarnika into the two-wheeled carriage and drove as quickly as he safely could to the docks by the river.

There, waiting for them and ready to leave with the dawn, was the little packet, *Lapwing*.

Sanguine and Mrs. Gore (the Captain of the packet did the honors just before they set sail) stayed in their cabin until they could see little Abdul Kalam Island out of the porthole to their west.

They made Madras by October, the Cape in December, and St. Helena's the following January. The ship reached the Downs in England in April, and by then, Mrs. Gore was happily pregnant.

Chapter 12 – Steel

Another of the Major Arcana of the Suit of Knives in the Swordsmith's Tarot is Steel. This card represents steadfastness when all about is change. Steel is ruled by the planet Jupiter, which offers growth and success (and their diametric opposition, death and failure).

Steel is difficult to forge, through fire and force, but deep in its being, it steadfastly holds what created it. To the uninitiated, the strength of steel suggests that nothing in life cannot damage it, but unless it is used, even the finest steel will corrode and rust away. Adversity cannot be overcome by acceptance; it must be challenged and conquered.

Steel, despite its strength, is malleable. It can be formed to suit the whims of the powers that seek to change it. And once those forces are used against it, even Steel must bend, or it will break.

Just as Steel is a substance that can bring one good fortune and the continuance of life, it is also the stuff of cessation and defeat. For Steel to fail, an internal flaw or an external force must exist. Resisting the changes that the world forces upon you will not stop the changes from occurring; it will only lead to the destruction of something you once thought to be invincible.

*

Captain Sanguine Gore, HMRA (Ret.), landed on English soil at the docklands in April of 1771, accompanied by his wife,

Manikarnika. They had little luggage, just the Captain's chest and the few clothes that they had purchased at the few ports-of-call where their packet had stopped on their journey to England.

But Captain Gore was hardly without resources. For a dozen years, he had been purchasing stock in the Honorable East India Company with the proceeds from his illicit purchases and sales of opium (a few well-placed rubies hid any evidence of his transactions and assured that he would be a very rich man when he chose to be, regardless of whatever price the Company's stock was selling for at the moment).

When the Captain and Mrs. Gore disembarked, they caught a hackney coach and were shortly taken to Miller's Hotel (known as a very old and respectable establishment, catering to the finest sort) on Jermyn Street, St. James. Captain Gore left his wife in their suite at Miller's and went to the Company to tender his resignation. The building was once the great mansion house of the Lord Mayor of London but had been re-built and transformed into the hideous 'Monster of Leadenhall' through the vision, if that was the correct term, of Richard Jupp (who Gore was certain, must have been starkly mad). Captain Gore found the correct people to talk to about his leaving, his pension, and his stock. The Company agent to whom he spoke recommended that the Captain open an account at the Bank of England and offered to call him a hackney to take him there.

Captain Gore thanked the functionary, remembering when he had performed his duties in a similar, correct manner. The coach deposited him on Threadneedle Street at the front doors of the bank, and the Captain walked inside, past the two Royal Guardsmen, the Bank Piquet, resplendent and terrible in their red tunics, tall bearskin caps, and bayoneted muskets.

He opened accounts at the bank and engaged, on their recommendation, a solicitor (a Thomas Scoones) and an accountant (a Josiah Wade from Bristol) who the banker assured him, would come to his residence at Miller's the following morning to formalize their arrangements.

His professional and financial business conducted for the nonce, Capt. Sanguine Gore returned to the hotel and took his dear wife shopping.

The couple's first stop was at 93 Chancery Lane, the shop of Ede & Ravenscroft that had done business at that address since 1689. The shop proudly held two Royal Warrants, an honor only held by a very few other businesses; they were robe-makers and tailors to His Majesty George III, King of Great Britain and Ireland, Duke and Prince-elector of Brunswick-Lüneberg, and to Her Majesty Charlotte, Queen of Great Britain and Ireland, Princess of Mecklenburg-Strelitz.

The tailors measured the Captain and showed him, for his approval, fabrics for daytime and evening casual and formalwear. Capt. Gore ordered a dozen suits that would be sufficient for the season. Then he turned to the tailor and said, "Mrs. Gore, my wife, will also need suits, dresses, and women's attire."

"Sir," the tailor replied, rather indignantly, after removing a pin from between his lips, "Ede & Ravenscroft crafts robes for the peerage, but we are tailors, not dressmakers!"

Sanguine Gore smiled and offered the little man more money, but the man declined. Gore offered more and more and more and more, for another five or ten minutes, until the little tailor finally said, "I can recommend the services of The Royal Spitalfields Weavers, themselves holders of a Royal Warrant to provide King George and his family with the making and dressing of lustrings, alamodes, reforcez, velvets, brocades, satins, paduasoys, mantuas, ducapes, tabies, Indian calicoes, and printed linens, all of the highest excellence, which can otherwise only be procured from the famed looms of France and the Low Countries."

These weavers," he continued, "are good Huguenots, the very models of industry, honesty, thrift, and sobriety, and they have worked very well, in the past, with a dressmaker of our employ, Mrs. Shudalls, who we will send to your residence tomorrow at ten in the morning to measure your good wife and consult with her about her needs."

The Captain nodded and thanked the man. He set up an account in his name that would be billed to his accounts at the Bank of England through Mr. Wade.

The tailor assured the Captain that the first of the suits that he had commissioned would be delivered within the week.

This accommodation being found acceptable, Captain and Mrs. Gore left the tailors.

Throughout the rest of the day, the couple visited the finest and most excellent purveyors of the best that London had to offer them: first, to Floris, at 89 Jermyn Street, for perfumes, colognes, powders, and soaps, then to Locke & Co. Hatters, at 6 St. James Street, then to Berry Bros. & Rudd, at 3 St. James Street, for wine, spirits, coffee, cocoa, snuff, and spices, then to Fortnum & Mason, at 181 Piccadilly, for luncheon, and after they had eaten, to Twinings & Co., at 216 Strand, for the teas that would help Manikarnika feel at ease in this strange city.

*

Over the next two weeks, the couple completed the purchases of their wardrobes, partook in the finest of London's restaurants and nightly entertainment, and began their search for a home.

One day, the Captain and his Lady were picked up at the hotel by an energetic young man who 'dabbled' (as he put it) at finding properties for the 'right people'. The three rode out past the potato fields to the little town of Stratford, a rural place of large, handsome homes for those wealthy citizens who had the need of a country home or who had left off trade entirely and retired from their businesses. On the west side on Stratford, they crossed a little bow bridge over the River Lea, and just off the High Street to Barking, they turned up the driveway of a lovely home that had been built in the English Gothic style but which had been re-built by Inigo Jones.

The property man explained that this manor-house had been given to the butler of Henry II upon the King's death and had remained in the family ever since. The butler's descendants had fallen upon hard times and wanted to sell their now-ancestral home to someone who would care for it as they had for these hundreds of years.

Both the Captain and Manikarnika were enchanted by the old stone estate and agreed to purchase it that very afternoon. The papers were signed within a week, and the couple moved in.

Manikarnika spent her time and energy preparing a nursery for the little one she was carrying, and the Captain was as happy as his wife.

But as the pregnancy wore on, Manikarnika was often ill, sometimes with pains that joined the nausea that kept her too often abed.

The poor woman's pain and discomfort was difficult to the Captain to bear. It was difficult, as well, for the maids who waited on Mrs. Gore.

One day, the lady's morning servant, a red-haired Irish girl named Maeve, begged her mistress' pardon.

"Ma'am," she said, "My old mother used a tonic when she was pained that soothed her a great deal. I could get some of it for you."

Manikarnika gasped as an especially sharp stitch shot through her abdomen, and when she could speak, she said, "I would appreciate a respite from even a little of this terrible pain."

The girl said, "I'll go get some for you, Mum," curtsied, and left the room.

She went down the stairs to the room she shared with two of the other maids, all of whom lived in the big house, opened the top drawer of the dresser that held her underthings, reached far into the back, and pulled out a little bottle.

She stopped by the kitchen, found a spoon, and took the bottle and the spoon upstairs to her mistress.

"Here I am, Mum," she said, "Let me show you how to take this."

Manikarnika sat up in bed and watched the girl pour some of the thick liquid into the spoon, and when the little maid bought the spoon to her lips, holding her hand beneath to catch any errant drops, Manikarnika opened her mouth and swallowed every drop that had clung on the spoon.

The Lady closed her eyes and, as the pain left her, fell into a grateful sleep. Maeve left the spoon and bottle on the little table beside her bed.

*

Over the next few weeks, Mrs. Gore's disposition improved. She often felt no pain, and the nausea that had plagued her had disappeared. She was happy and full of life. She often kept to her bed, as she said that she felt a little dizzy when she walked. But her improvement was remarkable, and the Captain was pleased that his dear wife was feeling so much better.

One morning, the Captain had left their bedroom and gone downstairs to the kitchen to fetch a tray of tea and toast for Manikarnika. He and the cook were arranging the food on the plates, putting a rose in a little silver vase that attached to the side of the tray, and both agreeably commenting on the gloriously beautiful day that was dawning.

And then a terrible scream filled the stairway that descended from the mansion's second floor.

The Captain raced to the frightful sound and found his poor wife crumpled at the bottom of the stone staircase. He took her in his arms and carried her back to her bed, calling to anyone who could hear, "A physician! A physician! For God' sake, call the doctor!!"

The Captain's valet lost no time. He ran to the stables, saddled a horse and galloped into Stratford, to the home of Dr. Warren. He pounded on the poor man's door until it was answered and told the man what had occurred.

The doctor got his bag, and the valet placed the physician on the horse that he had ridden there. The doctor galloped to the Captain's home as fast as he could.

When Dr. Warren reached the bedroom, he first hurried the Captain out of the room.

The Captain walked down the stairs and spent an hour pacing the length of the entry hall.

When Warren came down the stairs, Captain Gore could see that something was wrong.

"She lost the baby, Sanguine," Warren said softly.

The Captain wiped a tear from his cheek and asked, "How is Manikarnika, Doctor?"

"Her hip is broken. She needs complete rest," the doctor replied, "and then we must wait and see."

The Doctor left, but Captain Gore knew nothing of it. He walked up the stairs to hold his wife's hand.

*

Over the next two months, Mrs. Gore slept, took more laudanum for the pain, and slept some more. When she awoke, her husband was there, sitting beside her, holding her hand, often asleep from exhaustion.

When Manikarnika was strong enough, Sanguine explained to her that she had lost the baby and that her hip was broken. The brave Indian girl, who had left everything she had ever known to be with the man she loved, took in the explanation, but it seemed to weigh heavily on her.

She often cried and spoke less and less. Her melancholy and sadness overcame her.

And one morning, when Sanguine Gore awoke holding his wife's hand in his, her hand was strangely limp and cold.

He placed his finger at her wrist but felt no pulse. He placed his hand on her little chest but felt no heartbeat.

She had left him during the night to be with their child.

*

After she died, Gore began to wear blue coats with yellow trousers and waistcoats in the style of 'Young Werther', the novel by that German lawyer, Goethe, to honor her memory.

*

The next year brought the 'Crisis of 1772'. The Company suffered heavy losses, and the price of its stock fell precipitously, but Gore had made so much profit on his opium trades when he was in India that he felt little effect of it.

*

One day, the Captain took his carriage into London to see the men at the bank, stop at Simpson's Tavern in Ball Court for the 'Fish Dinner', and pick up a bottle of port at Berry Bros. He was lost in his thoughts, as he often found himself these days, when he looked out the window. The carriage was traveling through an area of terrible slums, somehow full of Chinese. He recognized pubs because of their signs in English, a few sailors walking along with their arms around Oriental women, obviously prostitutes, and one or two men staggering along with glassy eyes that spoke of no drink the Captain had ever had.

And then, he saw the sign that would change his life: "Chinese Annie's – Games of Chance".

The Captain called for his driver to stop the carriage. "Where are we?" he called up to the man at the reins.

"We're in Limehouse in the docklands, sir," the man called down.

Sanguine Gore climbed down and instructed his driver to wait for him. And then, the Englishman walked through the front doors of a two-story wooden building that had seen better days.

Besides being a gambling house, "Chinese Annie's" advertised itself as a boarding house (which offered its guests 'company' who would spend the night with them).

Chinese Annie, herself, sat behind a counter just inside the front door. She was a hard-looking woman who had once been delicate and blonde but who was now stout, graying, and completely in charge of her business.

"Well, milord," she said as she looked Captain Gore from head to toe, "Do you need a bed, a fuck, a game, or something else?"

Gore was a bit taken aback at the woman's sharp tongue, but he had come up the hard way and had heard all of this before. "Where can I find these offerings, madam?"

She smiled, "The fucking and the beds that go with it are upstairs, and the games are right through that door ahead of you. The stairs to the basement will take you to the land of the Lotus-eaters. You'll pay me before you leave."

And Capt. Sanguine Gore could not have explained why he did what he did next, but he said, "Thank you, Madam Annie," and walked down the stairs to the basement.

*

At the bottom of the rickety stairs stood a small, ancient-looking Chinese gentleman wearing a lovely Chinese robe of vibrant blue silk, embroidered with flying dragons and billowing clouds. His gray queue hung to his knees and his sparkling eyes looked out of round, gold-colored spectacles.

The man smiled a toothless smile and turned, motioning for Gore to follow.

As the two men walked down a little hallway with low ceilings and small rooms to either side, Gore saw men, the majority Chinese but a few Englishmen, sailors by their dress, in these little chambers, lying on their sides. The dens were dark and very dim, the only light coming from the tiny flames of the lamps, each reflected in fiery, little glimmers from a hundred facets and polished surfaces that reminded the Captain of stars at night.

Sanguine Gore was mesmerized by the strange place and felt relieved when his guide came to a doorway and motioned for him to enter.

There was an ornately-carved bed, and the man indicated that Gore should take his ease on it and lie down, placing his head on a pillow. "Chum tow," the old man said, grinning and nodding his head.

Gore wriggled around until he was comfortable, lying on his side, his head supported by the head rest.

The old man turned and left Gore alone for a minute, returning with a lacquered wooden tray, upon which were strange bowls, tubes, and implements.

The old man pointed to the tray and said merely, "Yen poon."

Then he took a little brass lantern, with a glass cover like a small, squat hurricane lamp, from the tray, said, "Yen dong," and proceeded to remove the glass and trim the lamp's wick with a pair of ornately-engraved shiny, brass scissors.

He lit the little lamp and placed it on the bed, close to Gore's head. Then from the tray, he took what appeared to Gore to be a clamshell, opened a beautifully-carved and lacquered wooden box, that was inlaid with mother-of-pearl and strange characters in brass, nodded to the box, "Yen hop," he said, and took a small lump of something very black from the box and placed it on the clamshell.

The man reached for the tray again, taking a long silver needle, "Yen hock," he said, and placed a small piece of the gummy stuff on the end of the needle. He held the opium over the flame, rolling the needle as the stuff began to swell and bubble, growing in size, taking on a rich brownish color, and emitting a rather pleasant creamy aroma.

"Chandu," the old man said, smiling with enthusiasm.

He 'cooked' the opium until he was satisfied with its preparation and with his other hand, took a long pipe with a stem of what looked to Gore like bamboo and a porcelain bowl. "Yen tshung," he said, indicating the pipe.

He sat the pipe in his lap and proceeded to twirl the mass of opium on the yen hock on the bowl of the pipe, occasionally it moving back to the flame and then back to the edge of the bowl, until there was a lump of opium, about the size of a pea, nestled in the bowl.

Apparently, there was a small hole in the bowl of the pipe because the old man used the yen hock to push the opium further into the bowl, twisting the needle in the small sphere and then withdrawing the yen hock.

The old man held the bowl of the pipe over the flame of the lamp, warming both the bowl and the opium. When he was satisfied, he placed the end of the pipe at Gore's lips and mimed what could only have been an instruction for the Captain to inhale.

The Captain held the bowl to the lamps' flame and inhaled the thick, sweet smoke, filling his lungs.

The Captain coughed the first inhalation out, the opium smoke being quite different from the tobacco he had smoked in the army or the hookahs he had tried once in India. But the old man seemed satisfied with Gore's progress and encouraged him with smiles and nods to finish the entire bowl.

When the opium was naught but ashes, the old man took the pipe, knocked the ashes into a little brass box, "Yen she hop," he said, removed the bowl from the pipe, wiped it to cool the bowl and cleaned it with a damp sponge, "Sui pow," the old man said, and placed the bowl into a wooden holder, "Yen gah," he said, that was filled with other empty bowls.

The old man inquired with his eye and a tilt of his head if Gore would like another bowl.

At this point, the Captain was feeling nauseous and, despite a valiant but vain attempt on his part to control himself, sat up and vomited onto the floor to one side of the Yen poon.

This, it seemed by the old man's reaction, was not unusual, for he had one cloth ready and cleaned up the mess, placing the filthy rag out of the way. Then the old man handed the Captain another cloth, this one moistened, with which to wipe his mouth.

Gore lay down again and rested his head on the Chum tow to collect his thoughts. He found himself idly running his fingers over the brocade and embroidery of the head rest, enjoying simply the touch and texture of the strange paraphernalia. He closed his eyes to revel in the experience, and when he opened them again, the dimness of the little room, the dancing of the lamp's flame, and the intricate, ornate designs on the pipe and the bowl and the lamp and the old man's robes demanded his attention until he became lost in them.

Sometime later, the old man touched Gore's sleeve, head tilting and eyes arching, the pipe with a new bowl in his hands, to inquire whether the Captain would enjoy another.

Gore smiled and shook his head, "No," and the old man left him.

Eventually, Captain Sanguine Gore left the basement lotus-land of Chinese Annie's and returned to his coach and his life.

*

In 1775, Captain Sanguine Gore, HMRA (Ret.), met Lord North, 2nd Earl of Guilford, and Prime Minister of Great Britain. There was unrest in the American colonies, and Lord North was an astute and clever man, a man would could always find a way to utilize new revenue. To this end, Lord North created a new peerage and sold it to the new Viscount Gore with the understanding that the Prime Minister could depend upon the newest noble's support in the House of Lords.

*

The Viscount Gore realized that his residence should now reflect his new position. After attending an entertainment at Lord Bessborough's new home at Roehampton, The Viscount Gore realized that he had found his architect.

Sir William Chambers had been instrumental in founding the Royal Academy a few years previously but was still available if the price was right. Viscount Gore made certain that it was.

It took five more years to complete the mansion at Stratford on the banks of the River Lea, but the resulting edifice was remarkable.

The Viscount Gore and his residence were the talk of London for the entire season.

*

But wealth, renown, and a secure place in society did not fill Gore. He missed his darling Manikarnika with an ache that only one thing could ease.

It was, however, no more than a 'habit'.

*

Gore had determined, after his first encounter with opium, that he would never darken Chinese Annie's door again.

But, Gore had servants and a great deal of money.

So a month after his initiation to that sweet smoke, he sent his valet to Limehouse to Chinese Annie's. Annie was amenable to securing a discrete and wealthy new customer.

When the valet returned, he brought with him the old man from Annie's den, and the old man brought with him a small, heavy chest.

The valet led the old man up the stairs to the Viscount's bedroom, where Gore waited.

The old man smiled to see his old customer again and motioned for Gore to inspect the chest and its contents. Inside was a tray and three covered compartments, each with a tiger finial, a clamshell made of carved and lacquered wood, four pipe bowls (of various materials), and a lamp.

From a bag that hung over his back the Chinaman took three pipes, one of bamboo, one of brass covered in elaborate cloisonné, and one of horn, and a little box.

The old man proceeded to set up the tray, standing it on three small legs that ingeniously attached to its bottom. He chose three of the bowls, one of Zhu sha (the cinnabar porcelain), one of jade, and one of ivory.

Then, the old man secured the ivory bowl, which had cunningly been carved with birds and flowers as in an Oriental garden, to the bamboo shaft with a brass saddle.

He took the lamp, checked that the wick was as it should be and lit it, motioning for the Viscount to lie comfortably on his bed.

The old man went to the tall windows and pulled the drapes closed, darkening the room so that the only light came from the flickering lamp.

Then, he proceeded to prepare the opium and the pipe for the Viscount.

Gore once again entered the soothing land of the lotus-eaters.

*

When Gore awoke, he was alone. The old man had left.

*

But a week later, a carriage rolled up the driveway, driven by a large Chinese.

The valet brought the carriage's occupants up to the Viscount's study.

Gore stood politely as Chinese Annie, a large and vicious-looking Chinaman (who carried a lovely wooden box), and a small, slight Chinese girl entered the room.

"Please sit," Gore said, indicating three Robert Adam armchairs of gilt wood and gold brocade.

Annie sat primly, flanked by the man and the girl, both of whom remained standing.

"Lord Gore," she said, "I have brought you two gifts to ensure the continuation of your custom." She nodded at the man, who placed the wooden box on a low table in front of the woman. She opened the lid to reveal four small porcelain jars.

Gore walked to the table and looked down into the open box.

"I have brought you four samples for your enjoyment, one from Persia, another from the Pashtuns near where you once lived in

Bengal, a third from Taungoo, and a fourth from the mountains of the Khmer," she said, obviously pleased with her gift.

"And," she continued, "I have brought you a servant, Liánhuā, 'Lotus Flower' in English, the granddaughter of the old man who introduced you to the smoke. If you like, she may join your service to prepare the Yāpiàn for you," then the woman looked hard into Gore's eyes, "Treat her well, and she may stay to serve you; treat her poorly, and she will leave you and my custom with you will end. And I will make certain that no other soul in the docklands will make your acquaintance. Do you understand, my Lord?"

Gore could only nod at the woman's effrontery and his good fortune.

*

The years passed, and Liánhuā grew from a little girl into a lovely woman who served the Lord Gore truly and faithfully.

Lord Gore sought the land of the Lotus-eaters more and more often until he would not leave his room, preferring the dim light and somber quiet there to the glaring brightness and hideous noise of the world outside. Liánhuā brought him food and opium and left him to his dreams.

*

Lord Sanguine Gore, Viscount, Captain HMRA (Ret.) stayed alone in his great house, searching for Manikarnika and his child in pleasant dreams.

Chapter 13 – The Six of Knives

The sixth card of the Minor Arcana of the Suit of Knives in the Swordsmith's Tarot is the Six of Knives. The Six of Knives is a card of success, achievement, and ultimately victory. Public acknowledgement of your accomplishments is your due. Your strengths and talents have brought you to the consummation of your ambition.

The Six of Knives is a manifestation of your reputation. At this peak, your name goes before you and ensures your fame. Those who would criticize your mastery are simply jealous. But arrogance and egotism can still defeat you. If you can control them, your victory will be all the sweeter for it.

A reversed Six of Knives suggests a fall from grace. Success is transitory; after each summit comes the descent, and when you have reached the bottom, there is always another mountain to scale.

*

Jack went drinking with his best friend Spotted Dick (the lad had caught the pox when he had been just a baby and had somehow, miraculously, survived but earned his name … the girls always wondered if Spotted Dick's dick was … well … spotted … but the few who did spot Spotted Dick's dick never spoke of it again). After all, it was New Year's Eve, and a new century, the Nineteenth, would begin at midnight.

"Rum is as cheap as ale," Jack said and walked to the pub where they would serve him a drink. He might have been twelve, but he was tall for his age, and this was the docklands, where as long as he had the coppers to pay for the rum, no one cared.

Jack got as drunk as Dick, and then Dick suggested a walk to Stratford to a house where an old, rich man might be dying with no one to leave his things to. If the place was dark, Dick reasoned, the servants had probably been let off to spend the holiday as they chose, and it would be easy pickings. If the house was lit up, they could return another night. It seemed like a fine idea at the time.

Jack had worked with his father since he had been old enough to stand in the bogs and not fall over, and ever since he was able to work like a man, he had been able to decide where to spend his nights, as a man would. Jack had been spending his nights with his friends for the last couple of years. His parents didn't seem to care. They were old and half-drunk on cheap gin most of the time and were just as happy to see him gone from the single room that the three of them shared. Their lives played out in the east end of the East End on the Isle of Dogs, not a far trek from the leech ponds near Rainham, the slough of Poplar Gut, or the boggy ground of The Breaches. If one fen's supply of the sucking worms had been diminished, there was always another near the meandering of the Thames.

And then, Jack's father had died, coughing up blood in his dirty bed, on All Saints Day, and his mother hadn't left the bed since, her terrible cough seizing her bony little frame and shaking it until she was worn out and gasping when the fit had passed.

Jack would worry about his mother tomorrow. She would still be there in bed; she wouldn't be going anywhere, and she depended upon his work to pay for her food and her medicine. Jack loved his mother; she was all he had … other than money, and when Jack had money, he could buy rum.

Jack had some money now, enough for some rum, but when he didn't have money, he could cut a purse or knock a head or do some odd job and get some. What more could a man require?

*

On this New Year's Eve, Jack had enough money to buy a bottle for himself and Dick to ward off the cold on their long walk to Stratford.

They had finished the bottle before they came to the little bow bridge, and they paused upon its crest as the New Year began with guns being shot, fireworks being exploded, and cheers and laughter being issued from houses great and small, public and private.

They crossed to the other side of the River Lea and walked aimlessly up the road until Dick stopped at a long driveway and said, "Here's the one!"

A thin crescent of moon was all that lit the night, but that was enough. The two boys, for boys they still were, followed the way between colonnades of dark, great trees until the dark mass of a great, quiet house rose ahead of them.

*

Jack and Spotted Dick avoided the pale pools of light that lit the front doors and skirted to the rear of the mansion.

A great row of tall, French doors showed a ballroom inside. All of those doors were locked.

A brick wall came next with no way in.

Then two windows, one next to the other, too high for either boy to reach by himself.

"Give me a boost, Dick," Jack whispered.

Dick laced his hands together for Jack to step upon, and when Jack did, Dick lifted him up to give him purchase at the first window sill.

The window was locked.

At the next window, Dick said softly with a smile, "Turnabout is fair play, Jack."

"That it is, Dick," his friend breathed and returned the favor.

This window grudgingly opened, and Dick slipped inside.

There was no further sound of movement for a minute, and then ten feet further along the wall, a door opened.

Dick stuck his head outside and motioned for Jack to hurry.

*

The two boys walked through the kitchen as quietly as they could manage with their hearts pounding in excitement and the darkness of an empty house making their movements tentative and fearful of discovery.

The found the door to a hallway that led to a pantry, a laundry, a storage area, and finally, a dining room.

The boys moved carefully, taking care to avoid the many chairs arranged around a wooden table that must have been twenty feet in length.

At the end of the dining room was an open, arched way that led to the mansion's entry hall. Opposite the main doors burned a quiet fire, more coals than flame, in a massive hearth. At one side of the hearth sat a cast-iron cradle that held half-a-dozen logs, a few sticks, and a box of kindling. Dick took a stick that was about two feet long and about the diameter of a good cricket bat. At the other side of the hearth stood a rack of brass fireplace tools, made to mimic the form of branches. Jack took a well-used poker, its point and its hook dusted with ashes.

Past the hearth was a broad, curving staircase that led upstairs.

*

The two boys tiptoed up the stairs, and when they reached the second floor, they stopped to listen and look.

A wide hallway led to the right and another led to the left from the landing. The hallway to the right was lit with candles in brass sconces.

Jack motioned for Dick to follow him down that hallway.

*

As they walked down the hallway, they tried each door in turn.

All were locked.

At the last doorway on the right, a room that overlooked the front of the house allowed them entry.

There were two candles burning quietly on a great table near a closed window, and across the room stood a peculiar wooden room. It seemed almost to be a canopied bed, but the canopy was carved of rich red wood and lacquered to a high shine. No surface of the wood was left uncarved or unadorned. The side of the bed, for that was what Jack realized it was, was made in the shape of a large keyhole, maybe four or five feet wide with a circular opening above that that beckoned entry. A lamp hung down inside the canopy to light the bed, but the lamp was now dark. There were soft pillows covered in dark, shining fabric, and a cover of the same cloth. Next to the bed, within reach of a sleeper was a small table at the height of the mattress, and an ornate wooden chair carved in the same patterns as the bed.

As Jack marveled at the bed, he realized that someone lay on his side on the mattress.

It was an old man, eyes closed, who rested his head on a rectangular pillow.

He might have been dead, but then Jack saw him move languidly and adjust his position.

Jack caught Dick's gaze and put his finger to his lips, shaking his head to keep his friend from making any sound.

Just as Jack shook his head, the door, the one that Jack had carefully closed behind them, creaked open, and a woman's soft voice said, "Captain, I have brought the Persian chandu."

And just as the woman said this, she realized that she and her Captain were not alone in his bedroom.

She shrieked!

Dick, never one to consider the results of his actions, swung his stick and struck the woman on her shoulder, the club's inertia propelling the stick into the side of her head.

She dropped the tray and it hit the floor. Bowls, small silver picks and scrapers, a tiny box, and a little lamp flew across the room. The lamp must have been lit, for when it hit the floor, it broke, spewing flames toward the fabric on the bed.

The woman lay moaning on the floor, but the man on the bed barely moved a muscle. He must have been sick, Jack thought, or drunk. But the bed began to burn and the flames raced up the walls on the patterned cloth and paper that covered them.

Jack looked quickly around the room. What was there that he could take to salvage this terrible night?

At the side of the bed, across its opening with the table and chair, sat a small, old, wooden box, something a soldier or sailor might own. Jack ran to the box and grabbed the handle on one end with one hand, keeping his hold on the brass poker with his other.

"Dick," Jack shouted, "Grab what you like, but we've got to get out of here!"

Dick looked around and hurried to the table under the window, grabbing the two silver candlesticks, knocking the candles out of them on the side of the table.

Then, Jack and Spotted Dick hurried from the room and ran down the hall, down the staircase, and out through the kitchen door at the back of the big house.

They ran for a copse of trees about fifty yards from the house and hid there as the house was quickly consumed by flames.

No one came to fight the fire.

*

When the boys had caught their breaths, Dick turned to Jack and said, "Open that box, and let's see what we've got."

Jack stayed still and replied, "What do you mean 'we', Dick? This box is mine. I grabbed it, and I carried it with no help from you."

"Well, we're partners, ain't we?" Dick asked with an angry undertone, "Share and share alike. You can have half of this pair of silver 'sticks, and I'll take half of what's in the box."

"Like hell you will," Jack snarled, as much to himself as to Dick, and then Jack swung the poker. Dick was not expecting that, and before he could move aside the hook on the side of the brass punched into the side of his head above his ear. He fell like a stone, making no sound.

Jack stuck the poker through his belt and opened the box. There was some room left in it, and Jack put the two candlesticks in on top of what appeared to be old clothes. Then he closed the box, made certain that it was secure, and carried it home.

*

When Jack woke up on his pallet on the floor of the little shack at the foot of his mother's bed, it was afternoon. He checked on his mother and she was sleeping. Since she was dying of consumption, she either slept or coughed. Jack kept a pitcher of water and a full glass on the table next to her bed where she could reach it next to a bowl of the porridge he made every night of oats, water, and salt that he cooked in the hearth's smoldering ashes. If his mother was coughing, Jack left the little hovel, afraid of the bad air.

But, since she was asleep, Jack put the kettle on for tea, and as he waited for the water to boil, he pulled the chest he had taken the night before over next to his pallet and opened it. There were the two silver candlesticks on top. He looked at their bottoms and found the hallmarks; there were sterling, not plate. They would be worth their bother. Then, there were old clothes, fit for a man, in good repair but decades out of style, and most of a British Army Hussars uniform. They could be sold to the rag-pickers or traded for something interesting. Below the clothing were a dozen well-bound, expensive-looking books. Again, something that could be sold ... at that new store ... Hatchard's ... in Piccadilly. Yes! And then, the real treasure! Stuck in-between two very old books was a little leather pouch. Jack pulled it out and jiggled it in his hand ... it clinked promisingly. And inside, the boy found pieces of gold and silver, all very old, some English, some French, some he had never seen before with strange writing on them. He took one of the strange gold pieces and bit it. It was pure gold, soft and gleaming. This was real treasure that made the misfortune of the night before worthwhile.

He took the books out of the box. The box was well-made of fine wood. And the more that Jack looked at the box, the more it seemed odd, as if the inside was smaller than the outside ... not smaller ... shallower.

He took the brass poker (that could be sold for a few shillings, too) and tried to find a place between the boards of which the box was constructed where he could pry the wood apart. The box was finely-made, and just when he was about to give up subtlety and resort to bashing the bloody thing until it broke open, when he ran the poker over a little crosspiece on the side, he heard a 'click', and a panel on the bottom of the box rose on hinges, just enough to allow Jack to stick a finger under the panel and open it up.

He looked into the secret compartment and found two light blue cloth wrappers. When he touched one, its softness and smoothness told him that it was silk, although he had never touched anything silken before. What else could be so wonderful?

He took the wrappers out and put them on the floor, and then he closed the lid of the box to give him a place to examine what he had discovered.

He placed the wrappers and their solidly-heavy contents on the box's lid.

Then he reached into one wrapper and slid its contents out into the light of the day that struggled to shine through the dirt that coated the shack's lone window.

And he pulled out a knife, a knife like none he had ever seen. It was very old, and it had seen use. The blade was engraved with strange symbols and words of a language he did not know (Jack could read enough to understand the names of pubs, the boards at the butcher's, and some street signs). But the edge of the blade was …

Ouch!

It was sharp!

All Jack had done was to bring his finger near the edge of the knife, and it was as though the knife reached out for his flesh and bit him.

Jack stuck his finger into his mouth and sucked at it until the bleeding stopped. As he licked his wound, he looked carefully at the blade. The steel seemed to drink in Jack's blood, and as it did so, Jack was certain that the knife hummed in his hand and he heard music.

Jack knew it was foolish, but he moved the blade so that it was close to his ear. There it was again; the knife played music, old music, music the kind of which Jack might have heard in church (or, rather, when he walked by a church on his way to a pub).

The knife finished its song and quieted, seemingly content with taking Jack's blood and then singing its song.

Jack put the knife back into its wrapping, and then he replaced the two knives beneath the secret panel in the bottom of the box. He repacked the books and the clothes and the candlesticks until he could take them to be sold and put the pouch of coins in his pocket.

He pushed the box into the corner and covered it with rags and papers and whatever cast-off things he could find in the shack to hide it. Then Jack checked to see that his mother still slept, tenderly kissed her cheek, and left the hovel, suddenly hungry for a meal of good beef on this New Year's Day and a mug or two (or three) of good ale to accompany his meal.

*

The next day, when Jack awoke, he had business to see to. First, before he did anything else, Jack walked to the Thames and tossed the bloody, brass poker into the dirty water. Then he took the clothes from the box to the rag-pickers and traded them for new (at least to him) shirts, and breeches, and stockings, a waistcoat, and a nearly new frock coat (it did have a hole in the back, about the size of a pistol ball, and there were some brownish stains around the hole, but it was better than any he had ever had). He took the candlesticks to a pawnbroker and got enough for them to buy a good pair of boots.

His regular clothes, for the trade his father had taught him, he kept. And he kept the books, only going to Hatchard's to sell one when circumstances were especially dire.

The pouch of coins lasted a long time.

*

His mother died before his coins ran out. She had died of consumption, but Jack had not felt the life being drained out of him as she fought the disease for her life, so he was fairly certain that she had not been a vampire (many people who had that wasting disease fed off the life-force of their family members, it was said, and were thus revealed as the vampiric monsters that they were. Jack's mother was a good Christian woman (even though she hadn't attended church since before she married Jack's father), so God must have kept her from falling to a vampire's evil ways.

So, as soon as Jack was sure that she was dead, he went around the corner to the neighborhood Resurrectionist and sold his mother's body to the man. Since the man didn't have to drag her rotting corpse from a grave in the dead of night, Jack received an extra payment. Then the Resurrectionist took his mother's corpse into the City and sold her remains to The Worshipful Society of Apothecaries on Black Friars Lane and made his well-earned profit.

Jack now owned the little shack. Once his mother's carcass was gone, he spent the afternoon cleaning the place and putting all of his mother's things (few as they were) into one of the sheets she had lain on in her sickness. Then he took her belongings to the rag-pickers and the pawnbrokers and took what money that they offered for them.

He made enough money by selling his mother's body and her clothes to get himself thoroughly drunk in his mother's honor. He would remember her in a way that she would have approved of.

Jack headed for his favorite pub, The Prospect of Whitby in Wapping. Most of the sailors and smugglers and thieves who drank there (and who were still alive after doing so) were friends of Jack's. At the Prospect, the rum was, indeed, as cheap as ale, and Jack ordered a pint of rum to toast his mother.

Almost as soon as his pint had arrived in front of him, a woman sat down next to him. She was pretty where a woman should be pretty, round where a woman should be round, and quiet when a woman should be quiet. She must have mistaken Jack for a man with money, but tonight she was not mistaken. Jack bought her rum, and she laughed at his jokes. He bought her more rum, and she whispered into his ear. He bought her more rum, and the two of them staggered out of the pub and back to Jack's shack.

Jack had a wonderful time that night and was good and thoroughly fucked before it was over. He fell asleep in a tangle of his and her arms and legs.

When he awoke, she was gone, and he was hungover. He was not especially surprised that she had taken what few coins were left in the pouch he had taken to the pub.

He was surprised, weeks later, though, that he didn't seem to have caught the clap.

*

Jack didn't see the woman again for another eight and a half months.

One day, there was a knock at his door, and when he opened it, there she was, as thoroughly pregnant as a woman could be. She demanded that he let her in, and he did and offered her a chair to sit on. She sat down and told Jack that he was about to be a father, and that she intended to stay here in his house until she was delivered. It was his duty, she said, to care for her since he had got her into this predicament.

This seemed fair to Jack (he was fairly certain that, as soon as the child was born, he could give the mother some gold on the condition that she go away and never return). In the meantime, she could cook and clean, and even though she was very much with child, she could still dance the Goat's jig with him now and then. Jack was fairly certain that this would work out to his advantage.

Two weeks later, Jack came home from work, one day, to find the woman sweating and howling in his mother's bed, energetically giving birth.

"Help me, you bloody Molly," she screamed at him.

Jack had no idea of how to help her, and she quickly realized that.

"Get me some warm water, a clean cloth, a glass of cool water to drink, and a piece of twine to tie off the cord," she panted in-between wracking contractions.

Jack hurried about and brought these things to her.

After a while, a tiny little thing popped out from between her legs, and she told Jack to clean the tiny child and wrap it in the clean cloth.

Then, she told Jack to give the child to her. She tied the cord and cut it and then took the babe to her breast.

After the child was full, the woman handed it to Jack and said, "Hold him. I need to see to myself."

Jack held the little boy while the woman cleaned herself. She asked for another cloth and bundled the afterbirth in it. Then the boy cried, and the woman took him again. He was a hungry thing.

Jack cleaned up and got rid of what was bloody.

The woman stayed in his mother's bed with the baby for a week.

And then, she called to Jack to take the baby, and when he had, she rolled over onto her side and promptly died.

*

Jack took the baby and went to find the Resurrectionist again, and the money that the man paid Jack for the child's mother was enough to pay a wet-nurse for a month. Jack sold more books, after that, to pay the woman until the child could eat solid food.

Then, Jack strapped the child to his back and took his son to work. After the boy began to walk, it was much easier. And as the boy grew, he was able to learn the business that Jack's father had taught him: collecting leeches.

*

Jack Leech raised his son and taught him the business that his father had taught him. The two, Big Jack (the father) and Little Jackie (the son) worked side-by-side in the bogs and fens for years. Big Jack taught Little Jackie all that he knew about leeches. Big Jack Leech didn't know much about letters or numbers or the rest of the world, but the man knew his leeches. He and Little Jackie could gather leeches from March until October, make their money and live in Whitechapel if they chose, but the two talked it over when Little Jackie was about twelve. The father and son decided that Whitechapel was crowded and full of poor people reduced to the workhouses or begging, without a career or gainful profession, and since the father and son had the family business to rely upon and provide them with satisfactory employment, the little shack in the Isle of Dogs was a fine place to live.

When Little Jackie was about six years of age, Big Jack found a poor university student to come to the shack and teach the boy to read and write and cipher. The first day that the scholar found the hovel in the worst part of the worst part of London, he hesitated to take the commission. But when Big Jack showed him the books that remained in the trunk and told the tutor that his pay would be whichever of the books he chose to take, the learned man leapt at the opportunity.

"I would be happy to teach the lad all that I know in exchange for 'The Pilgrim's Progress'," the man said.

Big Jack Leech stuck out his hand to seal the bargain.

The scholar took the other man's hand, shook it and then carefully wiped the dirt and slime from his pale, clean palm.

*

So by the time that Little Jackie Leech was old enough to decide, with his father, where the two of them would live, he was exceedingly well-read. The five or six books that remained in the wooden box were his to enjoy, and enjoy them, he did. He loved the stories of the Greek warriors the most, but there was a dictionary, and a Bible, and a book of Natural History, and between those, the family business of leeching, and the vicissitudes of life in the docklands, Little Jackie Leech knew more of the world than almost any other person within five miles of his home.

Leech collecting paid little enough, even though leeches were in great demand. Hospitals would bleed new patients immediately upon their admission to prevent inflammation, again during the night to stabilize the patient, and four or five times more the next day until they were cured or died.

Medical attendants would do the non-surgical bleeding, applying the bloody worms to a cut in the patient's arms or legs until the leeches had sated themselves with the patient's blood and fell off. The worms were then collected and stored until they were 'hungry' again. Then, in the spirit of economy, they would be re-used, again and again, until the leeches died of old age or the bad blood that they had sucked from a patient.

If a wound became infected, then the surgeon himself would step in and himself apply up to three dozen of the leeches directly to the wound. Medical literature noted that the common course of treatment through bleeding would likely involve the removal of between eleven and sixteen ounces of a patient's blood over the course of four weeks. Some treatments were successful. Some treatments were not.

But, fortunately, almost every disease a doctor might encounter could be addressed with bleeding, and medical procedures used to improve a man's health were rendered more effective through the judicious removal of the body's chief humor. So bloodletting, through cupping or leeches, was used before surgery, before childbirth, before amputation, at the first sign of nosebleed, during excessive menstruation, or to relieve bloody hemorrhoids. And before more severe medical techniques were attempted, or as a last hope, bleeding was preferred for addressing acne, asthma, cancer, cholera, coma, concussion, consumption, convulsions, diabetes, dog bite, epilepsy, excessive sweating, fractures, the Great Pox, hysteria, infection, jaundice, leprosy, madness, paranoia, plague, pneumonia, scurvy, small pox, stroke, syphilis, tetanus, and the vapors.

In order to collect the leeches, Big Jack and Little Jackie would go down to the bogs at the first light of day, as early in the year as the water was warm enough to stand, take off their shoes and roll up their pants, wade into the murky water, and wait for the leeches to find them. After half an hour or so, the leech collector would leave the water and scrape the leeches off of his legs and feet and into glass bottles. When all of the bottles they had brought with them for the day were full, Little Jackie would fill them to the brim with bog water and seal them up tightly. Then father and son would cart the bottles home until the day they had enough to take to the hospital.

The man at the hospital would offer them what he thought they might accept. Big Jack would bargain, good-naturedly, with the man for a while. A sum would be agreed upon. The two men would shake hands. The bottles would be given to the man who would take them somewhere in the bowels of the hospital, empty them, and return the empties to the Leeches, Big and Little.

It was a good life. The man and his son were out in the weather. They earned their keep with honest labor. There was enough money, with the two of them working, to keep them through the cold months when they could not work, and for them to save a little something for a rainy day.

One day, when he was about twenty, Little Jackie woke up on his pallet on the floor. He stood up, walked to the door to make his morning water. When he turned back to the bed where his father slept, he saw that Big Jack had turned an unnatural shade of blueish-gray.

Little Jackie put his fingers in his mouth to wet the tips and held them under his father's nose. The old man wasn't breathing.

Little Jackie Leech was all alone, but he was a young man with a profession, and he knew how the world worked.

So he went to the Resurrectionist.

He knocked on the door, and when it was opened, the man in the doorway said, "So, Jackie, your Da's gone, eh? I'm sorry to hear that. But I did for his Ma and your Ma when they died, and I'll do right by him, as well. I appreciate your coming to me first. So, since

I've done business with your family before, I'll give you a sovereign for you Da, and if the man I know at St. Tom's in Southwark pays me more than usual, I'll give you some extra; if he gives me less, I'll take the hit."

Little Jackie just nodded.

The Resurrectionist saw the sadness in the boy's eyes, "Now, you'll be fine, Jackie. I'll be by soon to collect your Da. Then, you might take the sovereign and buy yourself a fine meal and a good drink or two to remember him by. I'll be along presently."

Jackie Leech turned and walked slowly home. The man came and took his Da within the hour.

*

Little Jackie Leech worked hard and gained a good reputation as a man who could be relied upon, who kept his word, and who knew his leeches. When he was about thirty-five, he found himself more and more often, after a day in the bogs, at a pub that was close by his shack. The ale was wet, the publican threw out anyone who even looked as though they wanted to begin a fight, and Mary served the mugs. Mary was fifteen and the prettiest girl Little Jackie had ever seen. Her hair was a pale blonde that curled so tightly around her head that it seemed a golden halo of an angel. Her eyes were deep, bottomless brown pools that twinkled when she saw him. She was short and delicate; her head only reached to his chest when they stood next to each other. She had a woman's figure, broad where it should be broad, small where it should be small, and round where it should be round.

A year after she asked him his name, they were wed.

There was no church marriage; that would have been too expensive. There was no license from the City; getting one would have taken them both away from their work for an entire day.

Little Jackie went to Mary's home and spoke to her father. Her father looked him up and down, promised to kill him if he treated his little girl badly, shook Jackie's hand, and wished him well. Then he turned to Mary, kissed her forehead, and told her that he loved her.

Mary's mother started crying the moment Jackie came into her home. She hugged her daughter and kissed her cheek. She promised that Mary's father would bring a chest of Mary's clothes and a few other things to Jackie's just as soon as he could.

Jackie and Mary lived together in the little shack, as happy with each other as two people could be. They both wanted a big family, but after ten years of marriage and three miscarriages, Jackie and Mary simply hoped for a child, a single child.

Mary worked in the pub as she had every day since from before she and Jackie met, and Jackie collected the leeches as his father had taught him.

And then, when Mary was about thirty and Jackie was fifty or so, Mary gave birth to a son. They two new parents talked about a name for their heir and decided upon John, John Leech.

The little family prospered, and Jackie taught his son everything he had been taught, leeching, reading, writing, and his numbers.

One day, when John was about fifteen and his mother was still at work, Jackie took his son aside and told him to sit at the little table in their home.

"Our family don't have but one secret, John, but one secret is plenty for anyone. If you tell it, it won't likely be kept unless the one who tells it and the one it's told to be family. This is the one truth I know. So, since you are the only family, outside of your mother, that I'm ever going to have, I'll tell you the secret."

And Jackie pulled the old, wooden box over beside the table.

He opened the lid, pulled out the books that both he and John had cherished from the time each of them had learned to read. There were two little leather pouches still in the chest, one filled with silver and the other half-full of gold.

"These two are for you when your mother and I are dead. Save them as long as you can. Gold and silver come and go; you can always get more of it, but it can be helpful to have some saved should the need arise."

John just nodded, not wanting to hear his father talk about being dead.

"But here is your true inheritance, the same inheritance my father once showed me," Jackie said as he found the hidden catch in the side of the box.

There was a click, and the bottom boards of the box moved.

Jackie reached in and lifted the floor of the box, revealing two blue wrappers.

"These are very old, very fine Spanish silk," Jackie told his son, "Years ago, I took them to a man I know to find out what they were. His eyes popped out of his head when he saw them and could hardly contain his excitement. He offered me a ridiculous amount of money for them, and I could tell that his generosity would still cheat me."

He lifted one of the wrappers out of where it lay in the box. "But here is the real treasure, John," his father whispered, as though the very act of lifting whatever it was that he lifted was a holy thing.

Little Jackie, as Big Jack had done so many years before, slid the knife out of its wrapper, and handed it to his son.

John grasped the oddly-shaped knife by its handle and turned it in the light to see its every side and angle.

"Of course the boy would have no respect for the knife," Jackie thought, "he has never heard the music of the knife."

And, as if hearing the father's thoughts, the blade in the boy's hand seemed to twitch, and as it did, the blade, still as sharp as regret, sliced the tip of the son's forefinger.

"Ouch," the boy said.

"Watch," his father said, as softly as a kiss, "and listen."

The boy listened to his father and gasped as the knife drank in his blood, and as the sticky redness was relentlessly absorbed into the steel, the boy heard the knife's song.

"Da," the boy began …

"Listen," his father said.

And the blade, that had been silent and unfulfilled for so many years, made the music it was destined to make, with the touch of blood starting the tune.

The father and the son sat in the little shack that afternoon until the light began to fade. The father told the boy all that his father had told him about the wondrous knives. And after he had answered as many of the questions his son asked that he knew answers to or had thoughts about, and there was nothing more to ask or tell, the father put the knives away with his son's promise to keep the secret.

*

When John was eighteen or so, one day his father met him outside their little home and said to him, "You must work by yourself today. Today is the day that your mother and I were married many years ago. We have enough set by so that she and I will take the day. She has always wanted to go to the market at Smithfield and see what there is to buy. So we will go together and return tonight as a celebration. When we see you after work, we will raise a toast to our family and take the three of us to a restaurant for a fine meal. Life is more than work, my son."

John smiled and hugged his father. "I will work hard today, and when I return, I will happily join you and Mother in your celebration. Congratulations, Father!"

Little Jackie kissed his son and hurried him out of the shack.

Then Jackie walked back into the shack and bolted the door. He walked over to the bed where his sweet wife lay and leaned over to kiss her.

When she turned and grabbed him and pulled him to her in the bed, both of them laughed for a while, and then it was quiet before they began to laugh again.

*

John Leech was dirty and tired after a day in the bogs, collecting leeches. He had filled five bottles full of the slimy little things, a good day's work.

When he got to his home, he placed the bottles on the shelves that had been nailed to the boards that made the back of the shack. He went to the city pump around the corner and washed himself as best he could in public, and then he walked back to his home.

He tried the door. It was bolted from the inside.

He knocked loudly and cried, "Father! Mother! It's John. It's time to celebrate your anniversary."

There was no answer from inside.

John went to the single window and peered inside, but he could see nothing.

He tried the door again and found it as fast as it had been the first time.

He stopped, then, and thought.

He leaned on the door, and found that if he put all of his weight against the door itself, it would move the slightest bit away from the frame.

So he put his weight on it again and slipped the dull blade that he used to scrape the leeches off his leg between the door and the frame. It took his four tries, but finally, he slipped the bolt and the door fell open into the single room of the shack.

There in their bed were his Mother and Father. He went to touch his Mother's cheek and found it cold and dead. He touched his Father's hand, but his Father was there no longer. There was vomit on the bedclothes, his parents' bodies seemed bent in odd postures, and their skin was tinged blue.

Between them, on the folds of the single blanket of the bed was a bottle of gin, with whatever hadn't been drunk spilled between the two people he had loved.

John had been born in the docklands and had spent his life among people who lived life as best they could. His Mother and Father had been poisoned by the cheap gin that they shared in their celebration.

*

The Resurrectionist came later that night.

"My Father took your Da's parents and his grandparents before them. I'll see that they are treated as well as I can. And, as soon as I'm paid, I'll pay you fair."

John just nodded, and the Resurrectionist took the two bodies away.

*

The next morning, the Resurrectionist was back and paid John what seemed a fair amount.

John thanked the man and sat down at the little table in the shack, wondering what to do.

He would not drink; drink had killed his parents.

He knew that he didn't want to only forget the pain he felt.

He wanted someone to hold him and tell him that everything would be alright.

So he set out for Whitechapel, searching for comfort.

*

John Leech found comfort that night.

He had heard stories of the 'four-penny knee tremblers' who walked the streets of the East End, in Spitalfields and Whitechapel. But he had never met any of these ladies, had the money to do so, or the interest in doing so before.

So he walked from his home on the Isle of Dogs, along the Thames, past the Tower. He wasn't thinking about walking to a particular place, and so his step wandered as did his thoughts. He found himself at St. Dunstan in the East and then on the Mincing Lane. He let his fancy carry him west to Lombard Street.

On the corner of Lombard and a dark little alley, George Yard, John saw a woman. A red-haired woman. She smiled at him, and he walked up to her.

She said, "Hello," with an accent that might have been Irish or maybe that of a Jewess from Europe.

She was pretty, and it was late. The bells of St. Peter's Cornhill, a block away, chimed two.

"How much?" John asked, unsure as how to ask a woman for what he wanted.

"Well," she said, looking him up and down, "I can do you right here, standing up, for four pence, or you can give me eight pence, and I can find us a spot in a doss house for an hour. If you've a shilling, we can spend the rest of the night in a room at the pub in Bell Inn Yard. It's all up to you."

John wanted kindness more than he wanted what the woman offered, and so he said, "Show me this pub. We'll have some food and a drink for you if you like, and then we'll try their room."

She smiled then, as if her smile was the morning sunrise, and put her arm in his, steering him down the alley toward the pub, he thought.

They cane to a branching of the alley, and there, to the right, was a pub.

"Come on," she said, pulling him gently toward it.

And then, something struck his head, and that was all he knew.

*

He woke up, just before dawn.

He felt his head and assured himself that it was still there, despite his screaming headache, but when he took his hand away, he found it covered in blood.

He tried to stand and managed it on his third try. He was able to stay standing if he leaned against the bricks of the alley wall.

He needed a glass of beer … something to wet his mouth. He saw the sign of the pub and patted his pocket to make certain that he could pay for a drink.

His purse was gone!

He checked his other pockets, just in case the blow to his had had addled his mind more than he knew. Every pocket was empty, and the folding knife he carried, just in case, was gone as well. The pocket that had once held his knife was ripped and hung off his pants like an afterthought.

"Damn," he thought.

*

He made it home by mid-morning. It was only two or three miles to his shack, but he found that if he walked too quickly, the blinding headache that he thought he had conquered returned, and if he did not stop and collect himself, he would vomit. He threw up three times before he found himself back on the Isle of Dogs.

John went to bed and slept the rest of the day.

When he awoke, it was dark, and he was hungry.

He went to the wooden box and found the bag of silver, taking one shilling. Then he changed out of his torn and dirty clothes and into some that were more presentable.

He walked to the neighborhood pub.

He sat in a dark, quiet corner, and when the girl came and asked him what he wanted, he told her, "Cold meat, bread, and a pint of porter."

She returned in five minutes with the food and the bitter beer and said, "Sixpence farthing."

He ate and drank, and the girl brought his change. He took the five pennies and left her the three farthings for her trouble.

Then John went back to his shack and opened the wooden box.

*

Late that evening, John returned to George Yard, dressed in the darkest clothes that he owned. He wore a loose coat that covered him almost to his shoes and a beaten-up slouch hat.

He stayed in the shadows until he saw her, the red-haired woman from the night before.

When he was certain that the alley was empty, except for her, himself, and probably, the man who had beaten and robbed him, John Leech stepped out of the shadows, just in front of her.

"Hello," he said in a soft, calm voice, "Do you remember me?"

The woman seemed confused by John, not immediately remembering him in his new clothes.

And then she knew.

And then she screamed!

And before she could voice a word instead of just a squeal, John took the knife out of his right hand pocket and slashed her across the chest.

The blade sunk into the meat of her bosom, and by some horrible happenstance, slid between two of her ribs, after it had sliced her skin, and punctured one of her lungs, silencing her cry, changing it to a flatulent fart of a noise as the air that she had breathed in escaped her.

John heard the woman's cry, but it was a series of grace notes to a strong melody that now filled his mind, and his chest, and his hearing. The song was a symphony to the gentle air that he had heard the day that his father had introduced him to the knives, and they had sung for him the first time.

As she fell to the pavement, she reached out to grab at John's arm, but when he felt her fingers close on the fabric of his coat, he pulled away from her and hacked blindly at whatever was near.

The blade of the knife cut into her cheek, causing her to make a pathetic sound, something between a moan and a howl, the blood spewing out of her and bubbling in the air of her exhalation and agony.

John heard steps running toward him from his left, and a fanfare of song grabbed his attention and focused him to the task at hand.

And before the footsteps and the flourish stopped, he sliced with one blade as he drew the second knife from his other coat pocket.

The first slice hit something solid, causing it to pause briefly before its momentum finished it movement.

A man cried out, half a curse, half a yelp.

Something soft fell to the ground.

And soft harmonies caressed it as it fell.

John glance down and saw a man's hand, a cheap silver-colored ring on its pinky, lying in a puddle of water.

John looked up to see the man he had cut. And before the man could do anything other than bleed, John Leech thrust the point of the other knife into the man's throat.

The man choked on the steel of the knife and on the blood spurting from his throat.

The knives sang together, their gleaming, red-cloaked blades' harmony like a warm, familiar lullaby, safe and soothing.

John Leech, suddenly conscious of what he had done, dropped the knives, turned, and ran.

*

John Leech, leech collector and now murderer, ran away from his crime. He ran and ran and ran and ran.

He knew nothing except that he must run away, until he came to the banks of Father Thames, the stinking, fetid, foul river that moved leadenly through the great city of London. Everything that the City refused, everything that the City disdained, everything that the City had used up and shat out, bobbed sluggishly along in the River.

John ran along beside the filthy flow, caught in the terror of his deed but gradually seeing the floating carcasses, the swimming turds, the garbage wafting on the tide, and the dross and dreck and litter and offal that nearly every man, woman, and child in the metropolis had contributed to this tide of sewage.

And what, John asked himself, was he to do now, now that he had killed a man he had never met and a woman he had spoken not a dozen words to?

"You're as vile and as corrupt as any drainings that float in the river, John," he told himself.

And as he heard these words resound through his mind, he realized that he was just where he should be, at Waterloo Bridge, the Bridge of Sighs. Some called the bridge the 'finest in Europe'. It was a man's place even though it had been built the place where many women could and did end their unhappy lives.

It was a place for suicide, John knew, and John then knew what he must do.

The bridge was long, a thousand feet from bank to bank, and wide, fifty feet at least, and high enough above the foul River to take a jumper's life.

John Leech stopped running.

He stood at the end of the bridge and waited until his breath had calmed.

Then he walked to the middle of the bridge, as slowly and casually as if it had been a beautiful summer's day, full of promise and hope, instead of an appalling night, replete with helplessness and despair.

Then he was at the bridge's center.

John looked ahead of him and then behind, deciding that the distances were almost equal.

He climbed up and stood atop the iron railing, swaying back and forth, his arms out and moving gently, keeping his balance.

And when it was time, John let himself topple forward and silently fall into the River below.

As he fell, he heard the knives' song for the last time and saw them gleaming as they sang in his mind's eye.

No one saw him leave this life.

Chapter 14 – Judgement

Another of the Major Arcana of the Suit of Knives in the Swordsmith's Tarot is Judgement. Judgement is unavoidable and is a reminder that, for every beginning, there is a conclusion, and for every ending, there is a new beginning. The planet that rules Judgement is Pluto, the Lord of the next world.

Judgement comes for every man. Regardless of any understanding that may result from meditation or reflection, despite any realization or epiphany, notwithstanding any action or inspiration that might provoke new possibilities, the truth that lies dormant within every person awaits its Day of Judgement.

Despite what many otherwise good books relate, Judgement is not related to absolution or chastisement; judgement is simply the herald of life's recompense. Guilt is guilt; innocence is innocence. The series of crossroads that is life presents one decision that must be made after another. Every choice that a man makes determines the next crossroad he will encounter. Every crossroad allows a man to act with clarity and forthrightness. The path that leads from that honesty or that duplicity is the correct path for the man who made that decision. Others will suggest alternatives and share the paths that they took, but those recourses were theirs and theirs alone.

Judgement is a reminder that every decision is controlled by the one who makes it. While the events that take place before and after a decision are not always ours to command, one's responses to these events is always ruled by the decision-maker.

*

Constable Bobby Peele (no relation at all to Sir Robert Peel, who had made the London Police his own fifty years before) walked into the twisting passageways of St. Michael's Alley, leaving the coveys of whores who were massed tits to quim on Cornhill Street … he heard a woman's scream and a man's shout and ran toward the sound.

*

Robert Peele was a young man who saw a life of boredom ahead of him with little chance of anything new ever happening along the way if he stayed in the little Midlands city of Wolverhampton.

Thirty years before Robert had been born, another man, with a very similar name had established the Metropolitan Police in the great City of London. While Robert Peel, who was born a peer and would later become, first, the Home Secretary and, after that, the Prime Minister, may never have spoken or written the words enshrined in the 'Nine Principles', he approved of their intent. The Metropolitan Police would prevent crime and disorder, perform their duties to the approval of the public, secure public cooperation and maintain public respect, use little physical force, demonstrate an impartial service to the law, exercise persuasion advice, and warning, provide for the absence of crime and disorder, never usurp the powers of the judiciary, and maintain a relationship where the police are the public and the public are the police.

These principles were not accomplished immediately; the first Metropolitan Policeman to be hired was dismissed after four hours on the job for drunkenness.

The citizens who appreciated the Policemen referred to them as 'Peelers'; those who did not called them 'Raw Lobsters' or 'Blue Devils' (this might have been due to the long-tailed blue greatcoats and top-hats that they wore and the wooden truncheons, handcuffs, and wooden rattles that they carried.

The citizens who referred to these Officers of the Law as 'Peel's Bloody Gang' also showed their feelings toward the uniformed men by assaulting them, blinding them, impaling them, or driving over them in carriages or wagons as the spirit moved the citizens.

To be fair, the Metropolitan Police were not angels. In order to keep the peace, the law-enforcers and the law-breakers followed a common list of unwritten rules. Favors and bribes were exchanged, indiscretions were ignored, and brutality was simply standard operating procedure.

*

But for a young man who fit the qualifications (between the ages of twenty and twenty-seven, at least five foot, seven inches in height, physically fit, and literate, with no documented history of illegality) and who was looking for steady employment with a chance for advancement and excitement, joining the force was a dream come true.

*

Constable Peele began his career with a plum of an assignment. It was his duty, for eight hours a day, six days a week, to walk through the exclusive neighborhood of Mayfair (the province of Metropolitan Police Station 'C'), a place of parks, noble mansions, and exclusive retreats. This quiet area was the Corinthian capital of society, where a man's morals, character, dress, equipage, manner, and deportment were as nothing if his address were not correct.

But Peele had lost this position, within a fortnight, as the result of an altercation between the Constable and one Parker James, Esquire.

The young man was, unbeknownst to Peele, the youngest son of a peer, in London for the theater and the charms of society. The constable had merely asked the overdressed, ratbag jollops (he must have weighed twenty-five stone if he weighed an ounce!) his residence. 'His lordship' was clearly arf' arf' an' arf, he stunk of the cheapest gin and stumbled rather than walked.

Constable Peele had only to batty-fang the man once or twice with his stick to get his attention, and twice more to help him shut his mouth when the pod-snapper ignored the Constable's question and began to make untoward suggestions about the Constable's mother.

Somehow, the drunk had noticed the number on Constable Peele's uniform and had reported the officer's conduct when he had sobered up and seen to his bruises.

*

"No one likes a foozler, Bobby," his sergeant had told him before shipping Constable Peele off to Station H in Stepney, where he was now busily at work as a mutton shunter. Well, some of these little sheep were the jammiest bits of jam Bobby had ever seen, so it might have been worse.

"Ah," Bobby thought idly as he deferentially watched an especially-fetching three-penny upright ply her trade against an alley wall, "But don't we love them whores?"

*

But as Constable Peele ran into the larger space of George Yard, Bobby, looking for whomever had screamed, heard instead a happy tune, half-whistled, half-hummed. If he hadn't been expecting something terrible, Bobby Peele would have whistled along.

And then he saw the bodies … a man with his throat hacked open and missing a hand, that Peele soon found seeming to float in a lake of blood. A few feet away, a woman's body lay, all of her blood drained onto the pavement thanks to great gashes in her cheek and a slice that had opened her up belly like a deer that had begun to be field-dressed.

With the cheery, little tune still bouncing around in his head, Constable Robert Peele bent over and vomited, and when he had finished, he looked at the bodies again, and vomited once more.

And the song remained the same.

*

There was nothing alive in the alley. Even the rats had been scared away.

Perhaps, it hadn't been the blood and carnage that that scared the rats.

Perhaps the soft dripping of the blood onto the pavement in the yard had set the tempo for the strange music that now hung, suspended somehow, in the air.

And now, Constable Peele saw something else, two somethings, actually, that was not alive …

… Or were they?

On the dark, damp, bloody ground near the two corpses lay two oddly-shaped knives, and they shone with more than reflected light.

Peele listened carefully and realized to his amazement that the knives were making the beautiful music that filled his head and the alley with song, the like of which he had never imagined.

Peele walked to the nearest knife. He squatted down to take a good look.

If it wasn't the murder weapon, it had certainly contributed to the atrocity.

Bobby picked it up. It was a lovely, finely-crafted thing, beautiful even as it was covered in blood. The policeman wiped some of the gore off of the blade with his hand, revealing a musical staff, notes, and lyrics to be sung. He touched the notes, and as his fingers lay upon each one in turn, each note sang for the policeman.

Bobby Peele had begun singing in the choir of the Collegiate Church in Wolverhampton before his voice changed. The Dean of the Church, Mr. Peniston Booth, encouraged Bobby in learning the sacred music. Bobby sang the soprano parts of the hymns, at almost every service held at the church, from his eighth birthday until his voice changed when he was thirteen. When it changed, his voice hurried for the opposite side of the double-staves in the hymnbook. Within three months, his once clear and crystalline soprano became a rumbling bass, which frequently cracked and broke along the way to finding its depths. Dean Booth was happy just as long as Bobby sang, and Bobby loved that he could play with and lose himself in new part.

Bobby Peele had sung enough Anglican hymns that he realized the music notated on this knife was something else entirely.

And as the knife sang its songs to him, Bobby followed along, reading the music that was inscribed on the blade of the knife.

When he finally realized that he was singing along with the music of the knife, Bobby stopped abruptly in shock.

He slid his hand along the notes on the blade toward the tip, and when his fingertips reached the knife's point, Bobby touched the pad of his middle finger to the sharp point of it. And as he did so, the knife caught at his skin and took as small bite out his finger, drawing the policeman's blood.

And as Bobby watched in equal parts fascination and horror, the knife drew in his human ichor, and as it did so, its song rose anew, joyful, triumphant, and powerful.

When he came to his senses a moment later, Bobby looked around and saw a crumpled newspaper, lying against a wall. It was the *Tit-Bits*, a weekly scandal-sheet printed on the cheapest of newsprint.

Constable Peele walked over to the newspaper and picked it up.

He shook the paper to un-crumple it, and as he did so, Bobby glanced at the cover headline, "Prince Albert Victor Returns in Triumph from Tour of India".

"Prince Albert Victor, Duke of Clarence and Avondale, that flimsy sot," Bobby idly thought, and then he put his energies to the task at hand. He took one page of the paper and wiped the blood, first, off of the blade that he held and, then, off of the second knife that lay close by. He took two more pages from the periodical, straightened them, one at a time, and carefully wrapped a knife neatly in each. As he sheathed each blade in the inky paper, he could feel the knives both almost purring, as if they thanked him for caring for them on this terrible night.

He stood then and hid the knives under his coat. He looked to see that no one else was there to see, and then he left the Yard and made his way back toward the station. He found crowded corners where lots of people ignored one another, or if they wanted to acknowledge each other, they spoke quietly, agreed upon a price, and left to consummate their transaction. At the end of his duty for the night, the Constable placed the paper-wrapped marvels behind a barrel in an alley that edged the Pub where policemen were known to go for a pint after work.

Constable Peele signed out at the station, and went to his locker to retrieve his mackintosh ... it was London; it might rain ... folding it over his arm before leaving the building. And then he stopped at the pub for the pint that every officer deserved. After this evening's discovery, of which he told nothing to no one, Robert Peele decided that he deserved a second pint, which he did deserve and which he enjoyed quite a bit.

When Peele had paid the publican for his pints and given a penny to the girl who had brought them, he walked outside and headed for his home, stopping just long enough in the alley behind the pub to retrieve his two slim bundles.

Chapter 15 – Justice

Another of the Major Arcana of the Suit of Knives in the Swordsmith's Tarot is Justice. Justice is blind and holds a double-edged sword, signifying fairness and truth. No star or planet influences Justice. Every man gets what he deserves.

Every action has consequences. Honesty and fairness and adhering to the rules may help tip the scales to make it more likely that your actions will have positive consequences. Since not all the people that a fair and honest action touch are fair and honest themselves, nothing is assured. Laws are made by earthly rulers; Justice is the province of Heaven.

It is a man's duty to take responsibility for his actions. The Earth and Heaven above it have no responsibility to explain the results of the actions a man takes.

Justice is, by its very nature, judgmental. Accept what the world hands you, fairly or unfairly; it is yours to make of it what you will. Remaining truthful, and honest, and fair to yourself and to others will get you what you deserve.

Unless the card in the Tarot is reversed.

*

Eventually, Constable Robert Peele's excellent police work helped his superiors forget the complaint against him that had put him in Whitehall that night. Peele developed a passion for solving crimes and requested a transfer to the Detective Branch. He began as a Constable, rose to the rank of Sergeant, and was promoted to Inspector in 1901, just before Edward Henry was made Assistant Commissioner for Crime at the new offices at Scotland Yard. Inspector Peele worked with Henry to establish the Metropolitan Police Fingerprint Bureau, and just as the Bureau was being utilized to help assure the conviction of the burglar Henry Jackson, Inspector Peele contracted cholera.

*

When Bobby was promoted to Inspector, he decided that his life was stable enough to ask Penelope Patterson, the daughter of his landlord, to marry him. This was a surprise to no one. Everyone in the Force and all of Penelope's family (even the cousins in Wales) had expected the wedding to have happened a year or two (or three) earlier. But the couple were content and found a place of their own.

They had settled into what they happily realized was wedded bliss and had been delighting in one another and in their marriage for a year when Bobby got sick. The Force had excellent physicians on call, and Bobby was given home leave until he would recover from the malady.

Tragically, Bobby Peele died at home in his sick bed three months after the doctors had assured him and Penelope that, with rest, Constable Peele would be just fine.

Penelope was distraught. Since she and Bobby had only been man and wife for a short time and the illness that killed Bobby had lasted for an even shorter period of time, the debts that the couple had accrued were few.

The day after Bobby's funeral, which was a grand thing, attended by a great many friends and family, but which increased Penelope's debts, his widow visited the offices at Scotland Yard.

She was treated respectfully and came away from the great new building with an understanding of the amount of Bobby's pension that she would receive, a guinea a week (twenty-one shillings). She would have a difficult time living in London on that paltry amount unless she went to work.

Before her marriage, she had helped her parents with their landlording, earning a small amount of money for herself by taking in sewing. She didn't know what she would do.

Penelope's parents had raised a practical daughter. Since her life would be changing from the security of having a husband and a small apartment, with wedding gifts of silver and china, to the uncertainty of an unknowable situation where nothing could be assured, the new widow would sell what she could, make a budget, and decide what else she needed to do when she found that she needed to do it.

First, she went to Bobby's old trunk. It was all that he had brought to their marriage beyond himself. She could sell his clothing and uniforms, his silver comb and brush, his Bible (no, she would keep his Bible to remember the man she loved as she read it every night), and whatever other things he had packed in the chest.

Other than Bobby's clothes, there was not much there.

But, the dutiful and organized woman that she was, she pulled the clothes out of the trunk, one at a time, inspected each piece to decide if it should be laundered, mended, simply folded, or thrown away. Shirts, trousers, coats, ties, socks, underthings, mittens, gloves, shoes, boots, a scarf, two hats, a cap, three sweaters, and six white linen handkerchiefs were sorted in this manner.

The trunk was empty except for two paper-wrapped bundles at the very bottom.

*

Penelope took the bundles out of the trunk and set them on the floor. She looked again into the chest to see if she had missed anything. She hadn't. It was empty.

She looked at the trunk again, and it occurred to her that it would prove useful in packing up the few things that she would take with her when she moved from her and Bobby's home.

She sighed at that thought, and the beginning of a tear filled the corner of her eye.

She wiped her eye with her handkerchief and blew her nose, determined to finish this terrible task.

There were the two paper-wrapped packages, still sitting at the bottom of the trunk, waiting to be opened.

So Penelope unwrapped them both, one at a time.

*

"How odd," she thought when she had removed them from their paper sheaths. Two old knives with beautifully-carved ivory handles and strange symbols and words engraved onto their blades.

She picked one of them up and held it in her hands, moving it closer to her eyes so that she might see the carving better.

The afternoon sunlight that poured through the window reflected off the smooth steel, and the metal in her hands seemed to warm, just the slightest bit at her touch.

"Well, aren't you the prettiest little thing," she thought idly.

As the words formed in her mind, it seemed like the knife-blade that she held quivered just the least little bit, like a puppy enjoying a scratch behind its ear.

This thought came to Penelope's mind, and as she realized that she had thought this, the vibrations stopped as quickly as they had begun.

"These will bring a pretty penny," the widow decided, "but only from the right person."

She wrapped the bundles again in their paper coverings and put them into a large bag that she put over her shoulder whenever she went to the market.

She would have to consider who would be the right person for these singular things.

*

Mrs. Penelope Peele walked up the great marble steps from Great Russell Street and through the main doors at the South Entrance of the British Museum. A guard at the door looked at the bag over her shoulder, and to avoid any unpleasantness, she walked up to him and asked, "Where might I find the curator, please, Sir?"

"Well, Madam," he replied courteously and not a bit unpleasantly, not at all as she had feared, "that would depend upon which Curator you would like to find."

The truth, sometimes even the whole truth, had always served Penelope well, so she explained about how she had inherited some old knives that she knew nothing about. The guard listened to her entire story, nodding appreciatively in all of the right places, thought for a moment, and said, "Then, I believe, you would want to talk to Dr. Ian Smithers, the Curator of the Early Medieval European Insular Collections," and he nodded, happy with his deduction.

Penelope waited a minute before she finally said, "I see, Dr. Ian Smithers. And where might I find this gentleman, if you please?"

The guard was flustered that he had forgotten to give the little woman who had been so polite the directions to the Curator's office, "Go straight ahead, through the Great Hall on the right side, until you come to the end of 'The Enlightenment'. You will see a staircase. Go down into the basement, and when you get to the first hallway, turn left and Dr. Smithers' office will be the … (and he counted in his head) … the third door on the right. Just knock. No one ever really goes down there."

This information was not very re-assuring to the widow Peele, but she would do whatever she must, and so she crossed the Hall, found the stairs, descended one flight, discovered the hallway, turned to the left, and at the third door, knocked.

Her first raps were shy and tentative, and after no one had answered after a minute or two, Penelope tried again, this time knocking on the frosted glass of the door so strongly that the glass rattled in its frame.

Almost immediately, a voice called from within, "Well, come in, then."

And so, she did.

*

Inside the cluttered little room, an older gentleman sat at a desk that was as cluttered as his mind must have been. Piles of files tumbled in disarray across the flat surface, a stool next to the desk was piled so high with more files that they seemed to ignore any laws that gravity might have wanted to enforce. An armchair sat on the other side of the stool, its seat filled to a more reasonable level with still more papers.

The man looked up at Mrs. Peele.

"Your lordship," she curtsied as she said it.

The man kept staring at her, his eyes moving quickly over her attire, too quickly to be interested in her, but lingering on the bag she carried, the bag with the paper-wrapped bundles sticking barely out of it.

"Madam, I am a humble scholar, not a peer. What have you there?" he asked her in a kind, gentle voice.

"They were my dead husband's," she began, "hidden away in the bottom of his trunk. I've never seen the like, but he was from the Midlands, a Wulfrunian, and they're a bit different. I've met his mother; I know."

The old man nodded and let her finish before he calmly asked her, "I see. Well, what are 'they' of which you speak?"

The widow was flustered that she had spoken so obtusely to such a learned and respectable gentleman, and her words ran out of her mouth in a flood as she pulled the packages from her bag, "Knives, your honor. Strange and old knives, the like of which I've never seen."

As he took one of the packages and unwrapped it, the curator's eyes widened when he saw the first knife, "I've never seen the like, either, madam."

He took the bundle he had opened and laid it on his desk; then, he opened the second and held it in his hands.

Mr. Smithers examined the second knife for a few minutes before he said, "Damascus steel, ivory handles … there appears to be a hymn engraved on the blade," and turning the knife over, he continued, "a different song for each side."

These facts seemed to interest the old, thin man, and he looked carefully at the notes on the blade. Then, in an old thin voice, he began to sing, as best he could.

The knife quivered in pleasure to hear its song sung, but the man seemed too engrossed in reading the music and trying to hit each note correctly to notice the blade's joy.

When the Curator had finished the song, he said "Grace on one side and a benediction on the other. I have heard of these notational knives, but I have never held one in my hands."

He offered her two hundred pounds. "A curiosity," he said disparagingly, but she could see the lust in his eyes for the old things. She said nothing to his offer, and he raised it a minute later to three hundred, "Perhaps one of the medievalists would think these interesting."

She waited for him to offer more, and when he didn't, she told him, in a voice that should have made the man understand that she knew their quality, their uniqueness, and their worth, "Nothing less than a thousand."

He offered three fifty.

Mrs. Penelope Peele looked the learned man straight in the eye and said, "I'm a widow woman, sir, with little learning and a great many debts to pay. I will do what I must. I suppose that the ironmonger will give me less than you are offering, but he will not insult me to my face."

Fifteen minutes later, the curator had told the widow what he suspected but could not prove of the knives' story, and the two of them settled on eight hundred pounds.

*

She took the money. Actually, she took a check. The check was drawn of the account of the 'Early Medieval European Insular Collections of the British Museum' at the Bank of England. Mrs. Penelope Peele walked from the South Entrance of the Museum onto Great Russell Street, turned right until she came to Southampton Row, then left onto Holborn, past Bart's Hospital, and then right onto Princes Street, until she came to Threadneedle Street and the Bank.

She had little trouble cashing the check.

*

Penelope's sister, Emma, now lived in Scotland and had written her before Bobby's death, excitedly telling her of the new cottage house that she was moving to in Edinburgh. The cottage was near Leith Walk, and her new neighbors were artisans and working-class families.

Each cottage had been built as a double flat, with an upper and a lower, with each one floor having four rooms, access to an outside toilet, and its own space for a garden.

When Emma heard of Bobby's death, she wrote to Penelope and invited her to share the flat. It was the bottom flat, the rent was cheap, and Edinburg was a fine city.

Penelope wrote back that she would love to.

*

Penelope and Emma had a nephew who was a rising young clerk in the merchant's bank of Antony Gibbs & Sons. So, before she moved north to Scotland, Penelope took her nephew to lunch, to enjoy his company and to see if he could give her advice about investing her windfall from the knives.

Augustus was not as serious or sober with his aunt as he was with his employers at the bank, and the two had a jolly afternoon, reminiscing and sharing memories. When Aunt Penelope finally marshalled her courage to ask his opinion about an investment, he was so efficient and courteous and kind that she was ashamed that she had ever been hesitant to ask him in the first place.

Augie told her that there were bonds available for the London and North Western Railway (which he called by its acronym, L&NWR, which prompted her to ask him what the devil he was talking about). The L&NRW and its arch-rival GNR (the Great Northern Railway) were locked in a race to have the fastest train from London to Edinburg. Both companies were solid, but the better investment would be in the L&NWR bonds, Augie told Penelope. They would pay six per cent per annum.

Penelope asked her nephew if an investment of five hundred pound was possible. Augie was pleasantly surprised by his aunt's fortune and assured her that it was a fine amount, an investment that would produce a consistent return of thirty pounds a year and which could be easily redeemed if circumstances called for it.

*

The investment was made, and Penelope moved to Edinburgh to live with Emma. Penelope lived on her husband's pension and the interest on the bonds and occasionally supplemented her income by taking in mending and accepting commissions for fancier needlework as she chose.

Once a year, Penelope and Emma would take the train to the little seaside resort town of Girvan. They would spend a week walking the beaches and cliffs, taking the waters of the Firth of Forth, upon which the town lay, and dining at one of the town's two inns on traditional Scottish fish dishes: Cullen Skink (smoked haddock, potatoes, and onions), Finnan Haddie (more smoked haddock, this time creamed), Partan Bree (creamed crab soup), Arbroath Toasties (smoked haddock (what else?), poached and served on toast), or Kedgeree (smoked haddock (or deviled kidneys, for a treat), mixed with rice, hard-boiled eggs, butter, and curry). After a week of hiking, and swimming, and exploring, and Scottish cuisine, the ladies were happy to return home to Edinburgh.

Mrs. Penelope Peele died peacefully in her sleep thirty years after she moved to Scotland. She never regretted a moment of her life.

*

The knives Mrs. Peele had sold to the British Museum were forgotten.

Oddly enough, Dr. Smithers had fully intended to study the strange knives as soon as possible, but the day after the widow Mrs. Peele had come to his office, 'Mr. and Mrs. Veenstra' came to the museum, and Dr. Smithers was smitten with a new love.

Two naked bog bodies, human cadavers that have been mummified in peat, had been discovered on Bourtanger Moor in the Netherlands. Until the bodies reached the British museum and Dr. Smithers examined them, common knowledge had it that one of the bodies was female (the good Doctor laughed at that as he examined the mummies; one had a huge wound on his abdomen, through which his perfectly preserved intestines poked out, and both of the bodies had, the Doctor found through thorough visual observation and palpation, intact and well-preserved phalli). The study of these remarkable artifacts took Dr. Smithers and his staff almost a six months, and by then, the Doctor had forgotten all about the knives.

*

So the knives sat forgotten in a box in the basement of the British Museum, humming a sad, but hopeful song of blood and vengeance.

Chapter 16 – The Stabbed Man

Another of the Major Arcana of the Suit of Knives in the Swordsmith's Tarot is The Stabbed Man. This is the card of the chump, a sacrifice to no good or noble thing whatsoever. The Stabbed Man's number is zero, and its ruling planet is Neptune, the orb of insignificance and wasted possibilities.

The Stabbed Man will make no more decisions and take no further actions. The struggle is ended and there is nothing to control; this card reminds you that it is time to let go of your concerns and anxieties because they can no longer affect or worry you since no new reality is possible.

The reversed position of this card presents the possibility of examining your life from a new perspective as your spirit will as it leaves your body and looks down on your corpse before it continues its journey to something else. This reversal of reality is a gift, a chance to reverse your actions so that you may be able to avoid becoming The Stabbed Man yourself.

The Stabbed Man is a willing victim, someone who has put himself on the path to oblivion by thinking only of self-interest and self-aggrandizement. Putting selfishness and temptations aside may not change a thing.

Dedicating time, energy, talent, or money to the accomplishment of a goal is nearly always beneficial, but sometimes fate drives its razor-sharp shiv between even the most holy or deserving man's ribs and straight into his lung; then, despite all the preparation and skill and positivity that any person can bring to his life, if the karmic ambulance gets a flat tire, all will have been for naught.

The appearance of The Stabbed Man should not occasion a loss of faith, nor should it engender hope where there was none. All difficult times pass, or the people experiencing them do. Be at peace.

*

In the darkness and the silence of the room in the basement of the British Museum where items were stored if no one who worked in the Museum knew what to do with them, the knives sang quiet songs of blood and passion and longing. They waited; waiting did not bother the knives. The other items that were stored nearby listened to the melodies that the knives sang and felt the vibrations that the music created, but they never moved, and they never responded to what they heard. It was not important that other things responded or did not; the knives made music for themselves as they always had and the way that they always would until they were no more.

*

Many, many people worked at the Museum. Some worked because their work was their passion, and doing the work they did made them happy and made them feel alive. These people would have done their work even if they had to earn their living another way and pursue their devotion in their own time and in their own way. There are people like that, following their own stars, everywhere, and that is as it should be.

Others who worked at the Museum did so because their work, whatever it happened to be, paid a wage that these people used to pay for enthusiasms, obsessions, or cravings that had no relation at all to the purposes of the Museum or the tasks they completed there. These people would have earned their livings in any manner that they could to obtain the resources they needed to indulge in their excitements, lusts, and appetites. There are people like that, being dragged behind their weaknesses, everywhere, and that is as it is.

There were still others who worked at the Museum because being associated with the Museum made them appear special in the eyes of people who enjoyed the Museum as an entertainment, as a textbook, or as a glittering bauble that was worn on one's sleeve. These people ornamented themselves with these trinkets, and gewgaws, and superficial novelties because these adornments made them feel more beautiful, and more interesting, and more solid. There are people like that, collecting privileges and admiration as magpies collect shiny objects, everywhere, because they are simply looking for something that is never what they truly need.

*

Leicester Railway Crankshaw (everyone called him 'Gunner' because GNR (Great Northern Railway) was the line that served the Leicester Belgrave Road station where he had been born on a carriage stopped at the Leicester station in 1883) worked at the Museum for a different, but well-considered, reason. The Museum was full of thousands, actually hundreds of thousands (Leicester discovered after he had begun working there), of rare and wonderful things that some people would pay very good money to quietly own.

Leicester had been hired by the Museum as a 'Curator's clerk'; when he had turned twenty-one years of age, he had tried working as a shop clerk, then a baker's assistant, then a laborer, who seemed only to spend his days moving boards and bricks from one pile to another, and then as a tunnel watchman (walking through railway tunnels, keeping the tracks free of debris). None of these honest professions appealed much to Leicester. He was considering joining the Army when two other positions became available: a lighthouse keeper was needed at Lizard Point in Cornwall (with all of the perquisites that every lighthouse offered: loneliness, tedium, and boredom), and the British Museum was searching for Curator's clerk (his Auntie Eustacia was seeing one of the Museum's night-watchmen, and he told her about that job).

Leicester applied for the position, was hired, and found the job of a lifetime!

*

When new items were delivered to the Museum or purchased by one of Curators, the Curators would enter a description of the item into one of many, many ledgers (there was one for each 'Collection', from the Prehistoric to the present day, from the East to the West, from the North to the South, from the familiar to the exotic, from paintings to sculpture to clothing to household goods to weapons to transportation to Nature to technology and to a hundred other areas), assign each new item a number, and then give it to Leicester (or to one of the other Curator's clerks) to take to its new resting place.

Sometimes, Leicester would be asked to retrieve an item for further study by a Curator or for restoration by a Conservator, but mostly, once Leicester took an item to its place, that place would be the item's final resting place.

After a year or so of taking and sometimes retrieving, Leicester realized that no one, beside himself, really knew what was in the dark rooms in the basements of the Museum, that no one would ever know if anything was missing, and that if someone did miss something, Leicester could always plead that the missing thing must have been moved. No one ever told him anything, he could say, and they would believe him.

But no one ever asked for anything to be brought back for more than a look or a mend. So Leicester put the first of his pickings into his pocket. When he hung up his smock at the end of the day and punched the time-clock, a little glowingly-purple jadeite bracelet, from the Uyu River of Burma, rode safely in his trousers' pocket, wrapped in a handkerchief that Leicester had made sure to blow his nose into. No one would want to investigate that handkerchief.

*

When 'Gunner' Crankshaw had secured employment at the British Museum, he also secured his own room in a not-so-sordid little rooming house, south of the Thames in Lewisham. It was a poorer, but generally honest, part of the city filled with dark-eyed, dark-haired, dark-skinned Moroccan families that sold each other their own kind of clothing and their own foods and indulged in customs and a religion that were decidedly foreign to Gunner.

Their clothing would not be appropriate for Gunner's work at the Museum, and if he wore any of it out on the streets, at least on any of the streets outside of Lewisham, he would likely be batty-fanged within an inch of his life.

But their food was wonderful. The shop on the corner always had a bowl of the beef broth with tomatoes, lentils, chickpeas, and rice, that they called harira for a penny (as long as Gunner drank it right there and didn't take the bowl with him). Gunner's landlord was a fine man, married to a shy wife, father to ten well-behaved sons and daughters, who had invited Gunner, more than once, into his home for a Sunday dinner of lamb and prunes or a wonderful savory pie, filled to bursting with roasted pigeon, fried eggs, ginger, cinnamon, and pepper and then topped with fried almonds (bastilla, he called it).

Their religion was something that held little interest for Gunner, not the least because it involved kneeling and bowing on the floor a half-dozen times a day (the Moroccans' God didn't seem to offer them anything more than Jesus and his angels promised the English Anglicans, and with the Anglicans, you only had to kneel once a week).

But one of their customs became the center of Gunner's life.

*

One day, on his way home from his work at the Museum, Gunner across a trio of men, dressed much too grandly to belong where they were walking.

One of the men saw Gunner's proper-looking suit and approached him.

Gunner was ready to knock the man down if he turned out to be a sodding, bloody poofter.

"Pardon me, sir," the Molly said, "would you be able to direct us to Crooke Road? In Depford?"

These three must have been as drunk as boiled owls to be this far away from their goal, but Gunner's mother had raised him right, so he replied courteously, "Sir, you are south of that street. It lies almost to Rotherhithe, near the Dockyards."

"Oh, my" the man said, "It is a great imposition upon you, I know, but would you have the time to show us the way?"

Gunner thought for a moment, and then his good manners and sense of adventure convinced him to aid the men.

They introduced themselves as Alexandre Galens, who said that he was a French author, a writer in the genre of the novel, Hugh Ludlow, an Englishman author (as he proclaimed himself), a creator of biographies, and a Dutchman, Jan Linshoten, who if his cap could be believed, was a Captain of a small trading vessel.

Leicester Railway Crankshaw introduced himself to the men and asked them to, please, call him Gunner. And with the niceties completed, Gunner led the way, explaining this part of the great City of London to Hugh, his newest friend.

Eventually, the quartet found Crooke Road and then their destination, number 37, an unassuming flat in a row of terraced houses, stuffed cheek-by-jowl into the little street.

Hugh excused himself to knock upon the door.

As Gunner began to make his farewells to Alexandre and Jan, the door opened and a rattily-dressed young man greeted Hugh.

Before Gunner could leave, he was invited into the flat and introduced to Charles Mandelbaum, the flat's resident.

Mandelbaum led the other men into a cramped little parlor and left the room, Gunner imagined, to act the host and bring his guests some refreshment.

Mandelbaum returned in a minute or two, carrying a tray of cheap, gaudily-painted tin, upon which sat four glasses, a decanter of green liquor, a china saucer, and a small, ornate brass box.

"Would you chaps care to smother the parrot," Mandelbaum asked, unstopping the decanter that Gunner now realized was absinthe.

There was general agreement among the guests that this would be an excellent idea. Gunner was the neophyte and nodded his head companionably so that his fellows would think him more sophisticated that he actually was.

The glasses were poured, a toast was made to "The Queen!" and the glasses were all drunk right down.

Gunner thought this absinthe a heady potion and was barely able to swallow the stuff without coughing.

"And now," Mandelbaum whispered, carefully opening the box, "for the kif, direct from Nador in the Rif mountains."

He reached into the little box and pulled out a bundle of foreign-looking cloth, cotton Gunner guessed, striped in vivid colors.

Mandelbaum lay the bundle on the tray and unwrapped it. Inside was a chunk of greenish-brown, powdery resin.

Their host reached into the pocket of his waistcoat and pulled out a pearl-handled pocket knife and proceeded to cut five small pieces off of the chunk; the stuff was hard and brittle and seemed to be tightly layered. Each piece was less than the size of a chestnut.

Mandelbaum placed the pieces onto the china plate and passed it around.

When it got to Gunner, he saw that the delicate white plate was bone china, once expensive, but now chipped and worn.

Gunner took the remaining piece and looked at the other men in order to follow their lead.

"Proost!" Jan said and popped the nugget into his mouth, swallowing it without chewing.

"Down the hatch," Hugh added, following the Dutchman's lead.

"A votre sante," Alexandre agreed, swallowing.

"Cheers!" Gunner said, managing to get the dry thing down his throat without choking.

"Another parrot?" their host inquired.

*

The evening saw the four men each eat four more pieces of the hashish. By the time that goodbyes were said, and Hugh had walked into the flat's other room with Mandelbaum (Gunner looked through the door and saw some money change hands), Gunner was having a difficult time walking without stumbling and talking without giggling. The other men were in approximately the same condition.

Hugh thanked Gunner profusely and insisted that he take care of a cab to Gunner's home.

Gunner was happy to accept because, as he explained to Hugh, "I'm feelin' a bit more than half-rats, so I thank you for your kindness," and then he burst into a fit of giggles.

Which his other new friends echoed.

Hugh waved at a cab, and it stopped for its fare.

Gunner climbed in and waved goodbye to the others.

*

The next morning, thank God that it was Sunday and he would not have to work, Leicester Railway Crankshaw didn't remember much from the night before, but he did remember an address: 37 Crooke Road.

And because it was Sunday, and he had nothing important to do, he looked in his purse, found that he had four one-pound notes and a fiver, in addition to ten shilling and two crown coins in his pocket, and decided to walk to Mr. Mandelbaum's to inquire about purchasing some of that delightful kif.

*

Gunner's heart beat like a hammer in his chest when he walked up to the door and knocked at number 37 Crooke Road. What if Mandelbaum wasn't home? What if Mandelbaum was home but threw Gunner down the steps and out?

Before he could think of any more-frightening possibilities, the door opened, Mandelbaum peered out and said, "Ah, Crankshaw. From last evening," and he put his head outside the door, looked in both directions, looked again at Gunner and finished, "Come in, come in."

Mandelbaum motioned for Gunner to have a seat in the little parlor where he had been entertained the night before. Mandelbaum sat in another comfortable armchair next to him.

And then he said, "What brings you to see me, Crankshaw?"

Gunner hemmed and hawed, unsure as to start the conversation, but then he said, "Please, Mr. Mandelbaum, my friends call me Gunner," and then he stopped, as hesitant to continue as he had been to begin.

"So, Gunner," Mandelbaum said, "you would like to be my friend. In that case, you can call me Charlie. But I imagine that you have come for more than friendship."

Gunner could only nod at this.

Charlie must have had this very conversation before. He took the initiative, "You enjoyed the kif last night, and you would like to procure some more. Am I correct?"

Gunner nodded again.

And then Charlie explained to Gunner that all kif was not the same, nor was it all of one price. "This kif is made from the dust of the flowers of the cannabis plant. The best of the dust, the first that is shaken and then pressed into these blocks is called 'nup', that from the second shaking is 'tahgalim' (but it is inferior in quality to the first), and the lowest quality, taken from the third shaking is 'gania'. Once the dust has been gathered, it is pressed into spheres which are kept in small bags made of the finest cotton. An unknown kif may be identified by the ease that it melts under a flame. Some devotees prefer to smoke the stuff, others mix it with laudanum and drink the concoction, while others, like your friends last night, simply eat it. In Morocco, the pressed kif is sold in amounts they call tolas, each about three-eighths of an ounce. Here, in London, a tola of nup will cost you ten shillings, a tola of tahgalim will cost seven shillings/sixpence, and a tola of gania sells for five shillings. The kif that you enjoyed last night was the finest and most excellent nup, from my personal supply."

Gunner added all of this in his mind as he listened, and sadly compared the cost of this new amusement, in which he would like to indulge, to his salary. The Museum paid Gunner a pound and a half, thirty shillings, each week.

Charlie saw the frustration in Gunner's eyes and said, "Occasionally, I will trade a bit of kif for interesting objects that arouse my curiosity."

Gunner was greatly relieved to hear this.

*

Gunner became one of Charlie Mandelbaum's most loyal and most ardent customers. Gunner liked his hashish, and he had little self-control.

Gunner quickly found that curious little treasures that had been gathering dust in the Museum's basement were the kinds of objects that aroused Charlie's enthusiasm.

But Gunner also quickly found that he ran out of the lovely nup much more quickly than he planned.

So one day, Gunner penned a note and mailed it to 37 Crooke Road, Depford.

He left it unsigned, but the subject of the missive would proclaim its author to Charlie.

The note read: "Meet me at 'The Crown' Sunday at three. I have the most unique treasure for your consideration."

*

Gunner was sitting in a chair at a discrete back table, facing away from the door, in the darkness of the old pub at two-thirty that Sunday. He had taken two old knives from their storage in the basement of the Museum, hidden them under his mackintosh, and walked out of the front door of the Museum when his work was finished on Saturday evening.

The knives were very old and things of great beauty, even to eyes and a mind as dull as Gunner's. But Leicester Crankshaw was certain that Charlie would want these two.

Gunner had traded jewelry from ancient Rome, coins from Egypt, silver spoons from before the Revolution in France, and a dozen other smaller things for kif. Charlie had treated Gunner fairly, trading an ample amount of the hashish for each of the trinkets that Gunner brought him.

These two knives would bring Gunner a great deal more of the kif than anything else he had brought Charlie up until now, Gunner thought.

*

The Crown was the one pub in London where a man could buy a pint and then look out a window and see the point in the Thames where the Separatists boarded their little boat, The Mayflower, and sailed for the New World in 1620. The pub itself had first opened for business on Rotherhithe Street as Shipp pub in 1550. It changed its name (to the Spread Eagle and then The Crown) but it retained its dark wood, good food, and dangerous location. No sane man went to The Crown at night without a good reason, and going there in daylight was just as chancy.

Charlie saw Gunner before Gunner turned in his chair and saw him. But then Charlie came to the table and sat down.

"That was a mysterious message, Gunner," Charlie said with a smile.

The girl came, and Charlie ordered a pint for each of them.

"I have something," Gunner began, "that I believe you will like. But they are very rare and will cost you dearly."

The girl returned and set the two pints on the table. Charlie paid her more than he needed to; she would be back when the men finished their talking.

"What could this mystery be?" Charlie asked and took a drink of the dark, bitter brew.

Gunner had placed the knives in their wrappers on a chair next to where Charlie would sit, and when Charlie asked, Gunner simply said, "Look on the seat of the chair next to you."

Charlie turned in his chair so that he could examine Gunner's loot without others in the pub seeing any of what was none of their affair.

He unwrapped the wrapper on the top, and when he saw what was inside, he had to stop himself from speaking until he could find a way to hide his excitement. He took a breath … and then another … and then he asked, in a confused and hesitant voice, "What are these?"

Gunner was mystified. He had thought that the knives were old enough, and fine enough, and rare enough to elicit a better response from his supplier.

"Well," Gunner said, "The card that was with them in the museum says that they are Spanish 'notational knives', from the Sixteenth century, about four hundred years ago. They are made of Damascus steel and carved ivory, and there is music engraved on the blades. From what I can tell, the Museum has nothing like them."

"That is all very well and good, my friend," Charlie said, "but if they are so unique, how in the devil will I be able to sell them. The Museum will realize that they are gone and alert Scotland Yard. And then, I'll be fucked!"

"Don't worry," Gunner saw his kif disappearing as Charlie spoke of his concerns, "I replaced them with other knives that I took from a silver dinner service that Henry I once used. There is no way that anyone will discover that they are missing."

Charlie thought for a minute, making it appear that he was in doubt of the wisdom of this trade. He had played this part before with other kif-eaters whose only thought was how to get more of the wonderful stuff.

After a long moment, a slow draught of his bitter, and then another moment of thoughtful silence, Charlie spoke, "Well, if you are certain that a false trail has been laid … Come to the bandstand at Southwark Park tonight, and I will bring you my share of the trade," he told Gunner, "I'll take these now; it would be too dangerous for you to carry them back to your home and then to the Park later. You can trust me. I wouldn't want to lose your well-appreciated custom."

Gunner said, "Don't worry, I'll be there. What can you give me in trade for them?"

Charlie set the hook in his little fish, "After your careful research into their past and the beauty of them that I can see, I think that they might be worth a pound of the nup. Thank you for thinking of me, my friend."

Then Charlie drained his glass, took the wrappers, stood up, and walked to the front of the pub. On the way, he stopped to whisper in the ear of the girl who had brought Gunner and Charlie their pints. She laughed, untied her apron, and said something to the publican. The man nodded, and the girl left, arm-in-arm with Charlie.

Gunner was as astonished by the thought of getting a pound of the kif that night as he was by the skill of that gal-sneaker, Charlie, and the thought that he and the girl would be doing the bear before Gunner got back to his home.

*

Gunner was so excited at the prospect of getting an entire pound of the wonderful hashish from Charlie that he arrived at the bandstand in the Park just as the sun disappeared behind the flats to the west.

He realized that the park might be the domain of muggers, or even worse, it might be the garden of Mother Clap's Molly House, full of agfay arse-bandits sitting on each other's laps, hugging, kissing, and tickling each other, indecently using their hands, dancing like wanton males and females, and assuming the most feminine of voices and saying, "Oh, my big, strong Man," "Dear Sir, how can you serve me so?", "Oh, ye dear, little Toad!", making curtsies, and sodomizing each other, as camp as a row of tents!

He heard a noise to the east, and he spun to see what it was.

Nothing!

And then a cat's howl, or was it a couple of those buggerers, joining giblets?

It was dark all around him. The moon was new and a very, very few stars were just beginning to twinkle in the sky.

There was the unmistakable sound of a man clearing his throat just behind him.

Gunner spun around to face the pervert, fists ready to defend himself and his honor.

"Gunner," Charlie said calmly, "Are you all right?"

"Oh, thank God," Gunner whispered, and then he said, loudly enough for Charlie to hear, "This Park may not be safe at night."

Charlie nodded in response and reached into the pocket of his mackintosh, pulling out a round object wrapped in cotton.

"This may soothe you, my friend," he said as he handed the bundle to Gunner.

Gunner took the package and hefted it.

"About a pound, Gunner," Charlie said, "Just about a pound."

Gunner nodded his acceptance and decided to open it just to make sure.

He untied the string that was knotted around the little ball, held the sphere in the palm of one hand, and pulled the fabric away from his prize.

It was deep red and its surface was smooth, but too smooth and the wrong color for what he had expected.

Then it dawned on Gunner. "This is a pomegranate!"

To which Charlie shouted, "Oh, Gunner, look! Behind you to your left …"

And when Gunner whirled to see, Charlie reached into his left coat pocket, pulled out his straight razor, grabbed Gunner's right ear with his right hand, and drew the steel across Gunner's throat.

Gunner's blood poured out of his neck, spraying the bandstand and the grass that grew up to it in front of him until there was not blood enough left inside Gunner to allow him to continue to stand. All this while, Charlie held tightly to the dying man's ear, and when Gunner finally fell, Charlie stepped back to keep the blood from splattering onto his clothes.

When, finally, no more blood flowed from the deep gash in Gunner's neck, Charlie moved around so that he could rifle Gunner's pockets. He found thirteen pounds in bills and two gold sovereigns, eight bright, new shillings, two silver sixpence, and five three-penny bits in the now-dead man's pockets, along with an ivory pocket-knife, a heavy silver Waltham railway design pocket watch on a fob braided from a woman's hair. From the little finger of Gunner's left hand, Charlie took a rather nice gold signet ring (with the perplexing initial 'D'). Other than that, the man had nothing of value.

Charlie wiped his razor on the dead man's jacket and left the pomegranate on the ground where it had fallen.

*

Charlie Mandelbaum walked west from the park for a mile along Tooley Street until he reached Tower Bridge Road where he hailed a cab and rode it back to the east and his home.

He paid the cabbie and asked him to wait.

Charlie went inside, picked up the two suitcases that he had packed full of his clothing and his necessaries, a dozen bottles of laudanum and two one-pound spheres of kif, wrapped in colorful Moroccan cloth. In the suitcase, hidden under a false bottom, lay the two knives.

The cab took Charlie to Euston Station, where he would purchase a second-class, one-way ticket to Liverpool.

The train left at six in the morning, and nine hours later, the steam locomotive pulled into the Lime Street Station. Charlie decided not to waste the money it would cost to stay at the North Western Hotel, so he took a cab to the River Mersey, rode a ferry across, and found a seedy little hotel, but one with a private room, in Birkenhead, near the docks.

Charlie slept for twelve hours, and when he awoke, he got dressed and went out to find the Cunard agent and something to eat. At the agent's office, Mr. Charles Mandel booked a second-class cabin for sixteen pounds on the *R.M.S. Caronia* that would leave in three days and take a week more to reach New York City (the following year, the *Caronia* would report the presence of "bergs, growlers, and field ice" to any ship that would hear, a sister-ship or a competitor).

The ship carried 1200 passengers, of which 1100 were third-class (or 'steerage') passengers, about sixty were second class passengers, and thirty were first-class (or 'saloon) passengers.

Charlie's second-class cabin was small and Spartan, about six feet by eight, with a single bunk, an uncomfortable couch, a commode, a chamber pot, a wash basin, and a water jug.

The passengers were assured that their cabins would be swept and carpets removed and shaken each morning after breakfast (and washed once a week if the weather was dry). When the passengers left their cabins for lunch, the bedding would be turned over, the basins would be cleaned, and the chamber pots would be emptied.

Due to the rolling of the ship because of the winds and waves, passengers were requested not to open their windows (the crew of the ship called them 'port holes'), but even if the holes remained closed, the corridors, rooms, and cabins were often awash with sea-water, soaking most of the passengers' luggage and personal belongings.

For those passengers traveling in 'steerage', the water was deeper, the cleaning was not done as regularly, and the chamber pots frequently spilled to mix their contents with the bilge of the vessel. These 'third-class' passengers slept three high in bunks, crammed eight bunks to a compartment. Each of these passengers was assigned a numbered berth and was given a canvas mattress stuffed with hay, a lifesaver for a pillow, and a tin pail to carry their meals from the serving line that ended at the door of the galley to a spot on the deck where they would dine.

The stewards were kept busy, cleaning up after passengers' bouts of sea sickness and distributing rations of brandy to calm the stomachs of those used to the floors remaining in one place. When all of the saloon and second-class passengers' 'mal-de-mer' had been seen to, the stewards, if there were no other tasks for them to complete, did their best to see to the health of those in third class.

The third class passengers were served their breakfasts in three sittings, at six, seven, and eight a.m., lunch at eleven a.m., noon, and one p.m., and supper at five, six, and seven p.m. The salon class and the second-class ate in their own dining rooms with breakfast at nine, luncheon at two and supper at eight. The bars were open for all of the ship's passengers from six a.m. until midnight for beer, wine, liquors and light, solid repasts.

The first and second-class passengers dined in separate dining rooms but shared menus. For all of the passengers, regardless of the menu, fresh food was served until it ran out (or spoiled), and after that time, the fish and the meat that were served were salted.

Breakfast in the first and second-class dining salons featured fresh apples, baked apples, melons, oranges, bananas, stewed figs, or a compote of prunes; oatmeal porridge, grape nuts, corn flakes, or shredded wheat; boiled, fried, poached, or scrambled eggs, Omelettes Parmentier, or Ouefs Espagnole; Wiltshire Bacon, minced chicken, Cumberland Ham, grilled cod steaks, or American dry hash;

potatoes fried or mashed; Vienna bread, standard bread, corn bread, currant bread, white or graham rolls, or oat cakes; conserves, honey, or marmalade; and Ceylon, Chinese, or Sheffield Tea, coffee, or chocolate. For those willing or able to wait, a specialty menu of rump steak, sheep's kidneys, mutton chops, beef bones, or oxford sausage, cooked to order from the grille, could be prepared but would take fifteen minutes to prepare.

Luncheon for these two classes also featured a wide variety of choices: barley broth, beefsteak, oyster pie, spaghetti in cream sauce, roast pork with stuffing and apple sauce, or haricot ox tail; boiled potatoes or boiled cabbage; apple tart, small pastry, sago pudding, ice cream, roasted peanuts and dates, or cheese and crackers; and coffee.

Dinner featured hot dishes: petite marmite, halibut with hollandaise sauce, oyster patties, roast sirloin and ribs of beef, or roast turkey with cranberry sauce; and cold dishes: roast beef, ox tongue, boar's head, York ham, pressed beef, Bechamel chicken, Melton Mowbray pie, or galantine of game; cauliflowers, roast beans, or potatoes roasted and boiled; potato salad, tomatoes, or lettuce; plum pudding with brandy sauce, mince pies, champagne jelly, Genoese fancies, cheese, or ice cream; and coffee.

Third class passengers were fed their meals scooped from huge metal tubs into the buckets they had been given. Breakfast was porridge with soft apples, squishy grapes, or moldy oranges, and tea; luncheon was either salted pork or salted fish with pea soup or sea chowder, and beer; dinner featured baked potatoes or roasted apples, pig's face, cold ham, salt beef, or collops meat. Dessert alternated between bread pudding and rice pudding.

By the time that the *Caronia* docked at Ellis Island in New York City, every passenger was thoroughly sick and tired of the ship's fare.

*

Mr. Charles Mandel, along with nearly hundred other first- and second-class passengers, disembarked from the *R.M.S. Caronia* at the pier on the East River. Then the ship continued on to its berth at Ellis Island.

The steerage passengers were assigned a passenger number. The numbers were listed on passenger manifests, which were inspected by United States Immigration officials as they were checked through customs. The manifests listed each passenger's age, sex, occupation, country of citizenship, port of embarkation, intended destination, ship's berth number, and number of bags. If a passenger died en route, the date and cause of his or her death were also listed.

But for the passengers who had been wealthy enough to purchase a first- or second-class passage, once they cleared Customs, they were free to go.

*

Mr. Charles Mandel, whose friends in England knew him as Crazy Charlie Mandelbaum, was a fish out of water, He knew every place to go, every man to see, and who ran the city in London, but in New York, he was like a baby. But he did have a name, Jacob Lavine, a man who lived in a section of New York called 'Five Points'. Tim Foley, the man who ran the Bessarabian Tigers in Whitechapel, had given Charlie the name.

Five Points was an area in lower Manhattan where four streets (Anthony, Cross, Orange, and Little Water) came together a block from the infamous Mulberry Street. Five Points was a dangerous place, but it was a place that had everything if you wanted any: gambling, liquor, drugs, whores, fighting. If you didn't want any of what Five Points had to offer, you stayed away. It was that easy.

Tim Foley had told Charlie Mandelbaum about Five Points years ago, just in case Charlie needed to get away. But by the time Crazy Charlie actually got to Five Points, the Italians and the Jews were moving in. Irish, Italian, and Jewish gangs fought for every square inch of Five Points, and what belonged to the Irish one day was owned by the Jews that same evening, what the Jews stole from the Irish, the Italians took from them, and what the Italians had, the Irish wanted. The Who-yas took over from the Chesterfields; the Ceffos (the 'Big Dicks') displaced the Coin Collectors, the Allen Street Cadets replaced the Camden Town Gyps, and they all tried to push the Vaffanculos (the 'Fuck-Yous') around.

*

Charlie Mandel found a run-down but safe-looking hotel a mile away from Five Points and organized his belongings. Before he could do anything else, he needed a new supply of laudanum. He still had most of the hashish (he had eaten a bit of it on the *Caronia* to stave off boredom and calm his heaving stomach), but he enjoyed the kif best when he mixed it with the little bottles of opium and alcohol.

America was a wonderfully free land, so all Charlie had to do was to find a pharmacy. There was one a block from his hotel. He purchased a dozen half-pint bottles but insisted upon trying a drink from one before he laid down his money to ensure that what he was buying was genuine. It was.

Charlie returned to his little room and unpacked. He knew that he could sell some of the trinkets that Gunner had stolen from the Museum to people of quality here in New York. But the only way to meet that kind of person was to get an introduction from the one person he knew to contact, the one person on the continent who might know his name, 'English Jake' Lavine (although some called him 'Eat-'em-up' Lavine).

"Who knows," Charlie thought, "maybe this Lavine chap would make me a good offer for the knives."

So Charlie put his razor into his pocket, his gold and silver coins in his purse, and his knives strapped to his back. He took a small chunk of the kif, wrapped it in his handkerchief, and put it in the pocket of his waistcoat along with Gunner's pocket-watch.

Finally, he took a swig out of one of the bottles of laudanum (just to soothe his nerves), screwed the lid on tight, and slipped it into his pants' pocket.

He asked the man at the hotel desk directions to Five Points. The man shook his head in disbelief and pointed south. "About eight blocks," he said.

Later that day, a policeman found a dead body in an alley off of Mulberry Street near a section of Manhattan known as 'The Bowery'. The man had been brutally murdered with a passion that indicated that it was not simply a business deal gone badly; this was personal. The dead man had been slashed and stabbed, the coroner had decided after a uniquely-complex autopsy, over two hundred forty times after his throat had been slashed.

An informant, known to the police as 'Spiritus', suggested that English Jake Lavine was the murderer.

*

English Jake Lavine was a mystery man to the New York City Police. He had appeared, as if out of nowhere, about a dozen years ago, known to a wide variety of New Yorkers as 'English Jake' or 'Eat-'em-up' Levine. He might have worked for the Chatham Square Boys or maybe for the Humpty Gang, but no one would say for certain. If silence was golden, as far as information about Mr. Lavine was concerned, it was as if someone had gilded the mouths and ears of the entire population of the five boroughs.

Mr. Lavine had no criminal record, no birth certificate, and no bills that he might have paid. He had been investigated for a variety of crimes, both violent and non-violent, but he had never been 'booked' by any local, state, or federal entities. One investigation of a crime that Mr. Lavine had admitted to found no evidence to support the confession, so it was dropped.

Mr. Lavine became known to the police because he frequented 'Big Jack's' on Delancey Street, the Essex Hotel, 'Mike's Forsythe Inn', and a number of other establishments that the police felt obliged to raid once or twice a week. But other than being rumored to be a thug-for-hire and carrying a Union Jack that he used as a handkerchief (that earned him the 'English Jack' moniker), no evidence could be found to support the contention that Mr. Lavine spent his time doing much of anything. It was also said that Lavine had served in some branch of the military at some point, but no records could be found to prove anything of the kind.

Mr., Lavine never expressly confirmed nor denied anything that was said of him, even though he bragged of the bravery of his English forebears and the passionate blood of Moorish kings that ran in his veins.

Rumor had it that he was 'full-bodied and strong as an ox, near to seven feet tall with a pecker that could make a bison faint', but in person, he stood slightly over five feet tall with small hands and feet.

He always had money and often bought a 'round for the boys', and it was said that five beautiful Amazons walked the streets for his benefit. But then, no one could truthfully say that he or she had met any of these women, professionally or socially.

Some people suggested that Lavine was 'just a big bluff, blowing in the wind. He would bulldoze the President if the President was man enough to call him … he acted like a hero, and he would die like one, too, someday'. But once a person said something like that about Mr. Lavine, that person could never be found the next day to repeat it. So, maybe, it was just people talking and then changing their minds.

Lavine was called a 'dead shot' who wore three Colt pistols in his waistcoat and a sawed- off shotgun in a holster under his coat. But no one ever saw him use any of them.

*

So when this recent immigrant, a man that some called 'Crazy Charlie' and some called Charles Mendel, was found murdered, and the rat 'Spiritus' whispered that Lavine was the murderer, the police decided that it was time to lean on Lavine.

The criminals of Five Points dismissed this theory as nonsense: 'Eat-'em-up' Lavine was famed as a man who would not even sleep if there was no money to be made by doing it, so he would have no motive to kill a penniless Limey, fresh off the boat.

Lavine was picked up and thrown into a Black Mariah, knocked around a bit, and delivered to the Henry Street police station. Lavine was placed in a little, windowless room and handcuffed to a table. He sat there by himself for four hours while the police investigated his personal effects. The officers took his three pistols and his shotgun, and remarked that the nine-inch knife that they took from him could well have been the murder weapon. But none of the guns had been fired recently and the knife was as clean as if it were to be used for surgery.

So, to increase the pressure upon Lavine, the officers slapped him around a bit more, threw him into a paddy wagon, and drove him to the morgue. They took him into an examination room and pulled the sheet off of Crazy Charlie's mutilated corpse, hoping to break the unflappable man.

Lavine asked for a cigarette and a light.

One of the detectives asked the suspect, "Do you see this?"

Lavine replied, knocking the cigarette's ashes into the hole that once was the corpse's chest, "Of course I do! For ten cents, I'd eat a ham sandwich off this mug's ass and take a nap with him after."

The policemen took off Lavine's handcuffs and let him go. He was never booked and never told why he had been taken in.

Chapter 17 – Fire

Another of the Major Arcana of the Suit of Knives in the Swordsmith's Tarot is Fire. Fire, a spontaneous thing, is created from elements solid and ethereal when all that is required is brought together in heat. Fire's has no planet, but its ruling sign is Sagittarius, a creature born of man and cloud. Fire is passion, beauty, and ultimately, truth.

At first, Fire may seem to be a wild thing, consuming that which allows it to thrive, but in the hands of a patient man, the flames, that to the uninitiated show no order or organization, may be adapted, combined with other forces and elements, and banked at the proper moment to blaze even brighter in a beautiful synergy of talent, skill, and experience.

Consistency, precision, and insight will build a more memorable flame than momentary attention, blind reiteration, and skill-less impatience.

The man who reflects upon himself in the glow of Fire is a man whose life is in balance. Heat and flame hearken to humanity's lust for a meditative peace. The energy that Fire shares with those who would allow the flames to warm them and fire their imaginations is a holy thing, an unquenchable gift that must be given away to be truly received.

*

Jacob Lavine lived with his wife, Lavinia, their son Icarus (who everyone just called Icky), Lavinia's spinster sister, Gertrude, and a number of very well-paid, extremely closed-mouthed servants at the Tredwell House, at 29 East Fourth Street in New York City, where the sisters had lived their entire lives (Gertrude would remain unmarried for her entire life and pass away at the age of ninety-three in her bedroom on the second floor of the old family residence). Jacob Lavine's wife thought that he worked as a merchant; he never disabused her of this notion. But when he went off to his office every day, everyone who knew him through his work knew him as 'English Jake' (or if there had been a violent disagreement, 'Eat-'em up' Lavine). 'English Jake' was no merchant.

*

Joseph Brewster had built a brick and marble row house on Fourth Street, in what was then a quiet, exclusive suburb of New York City, in 1832 and, just three years after that, fell down the great staircase one night when he was coming down to the kitchen to make himself a sandwich at two a.m. When the house was built, Broadway, a couple of blocks away, was a quiet, residential street. John Jacob Astor considered the neighborhood to be fashionably 'uptown'.

The district was home to Astor's very own Opera House (and the site, a few years later, of a bloody riot, ostensibly between supporters of rival Shakespearean actors, but in actuality, one of the first murderous clashes between 'Americans' and British 'codfish aristocrats' over the cultural supremacy of the United States or of

England), but by the time that Mr. Lavine had wed Miss Tredwell (her family had bought the house in 1835 and had lived there ever since), the area was no longer an exclusive enclave for the well-to-do.

*

On Icky's twelfth birthday, his father came home and presented him with a pocket knife, a thing a man should carry. This one was a German-made Henckel, with four blades of fine Solingen steel that folded into a gold enameled, sterling silver handle that fit like a hand in a glove inside its calfskin leather slipcase. It was a beautiful and functional thing, and the boy was thrilled with his father's gift.

After the boy's mother had left the room, his father also gave him a copy of "The Gentleman's Directory".

*

Icky paged through the little leather-bound pamphlet and learned that Madame Beck's 'Elysian Fields' offered the finest and most sophisticated entertainments to "pleasantly while away an afternoon" and that the 'Silver Palace' was staffed with "charming Lady Scholars, well-versed in the classical Greek, Latin, and French cultures". On the other hand, the little tome revealed that Mrs. Coale's house on Spring Street was "rowdy and rough, fit only for the lowest and most base clientele". The book proclaimed that, at another location, "enlightened gentlemen would appreciate the blonde, brunette, and ginger-haired hostesses whose mastery of many tongues prompted extended conversation". One establishment assured the reader that "a licensed physician was on duty from dusk until dawn", and that another hostess had "spared no effort or expense to create a pleasure dome, fit for a King, a Pasha, or even Kublai Khan, with glass and rosewood, brass and ebony, and all of the luxury that might be found in such a Xanadu".

Icky was amazed at what he read, especially when he came to the description of Leo Rossington's Ranch, where "fair Mexican maidens serenade the lucky patron, Indian girls dance without shame in their native undress, and a bear is shackled in the cellar for other amusement."

The entirety of Greene Street was labeled a "festering pit of degradation, best left to society's dregs".

One entry caught the boy's eye, and he pointed it out to his father: "The Culverton Sisters have created an exclusive club for discerning guests. Their 'Newmarket Club' features a first floor, composed of parlors, each of which is designed to appeal to the sensibilities and tastes of the clientele (the Ivory Parlor, the Parlor Cinnabar, the Ebony Room, the Golden Den, the throne of Heaven) while the second floor of the grand building holds the bedchambers where a customer might privately savor the charms of the woman or women of his choosing. On the third floor, an exquisitely-appointed dining room and bar mirrors the finest salons on the best ocean liners and offers equally fine cuisine: pheasant, caviar, lobster, crab, oysters, goose, crudités, warm and cold hors d'oeuvres, and a world-famous cellar of European wines."

"Fascinating," he father chuckled,

"But, look at this, Father," Icky said excitedly, "Then it says, 'The Culverton Sisters have created what is probably the most luxurious and unique house of prostitution anywhere east of the Mississippi' – Mr. Edward Delaney, Chief of the Boston Commission on Vice."

"Icarus," his father said, "It is my belief that a boy becomes a man when he receives his first knife, and a man should learn to be a man as quickly and well as he can. So, come with me, young man, and we will go to a pleasant little house that is not mentioned in the "Directory" but one that I prefer. I will introduce you to a lady of my acquaintance who will help you right along in your journey to manhood."

So the father and his son got into the big, black touring car, and 'Sally', Salvador München, one of the father's oldest and most-trusted employees, drove them to a little brownstone on Vestry Street, a block from the Hudson. The man waited in the car, and the father and his son walked to the front door, knocked, and entered after a pretty young woman in a yellow silken kimono opened the door and greeted them.

An hour later, the father and son returned.

As Icky sat in the car, waiting for his father to get in and get comfortable, he thought about what had just happened. It was frightening at first, and then terribly exciting! The only other time he had felt this way was when he had gotten into fights and beaten his foe bloody.

Jacob Lavine got into the car and turned to his son.

"Son," he began, "a man kept from sexual congress quickly grows sickly and weak. How can he continue to act like a man unless he is able to do everything that a man must do? So, to that end, I have given you a good pocket knife and introduced you to the affairs of men."

Mr. Lavine turned to the driver, "Sally?"

"Yes, sir," the large, muscular man said, turning to politely face his employer.

Mr. Lavine continued, "Icarus, you have known Sally since the day you came into this world, and he has known you as well. Since that blessed day, Sally's one job has been to keep you safe. Now that you have become a man, my son, Sally will take on two additional tasks. First, he will sharpen your knife and all of its diverse blades to a keenness that will be hair-whittling sharp. Secondly, Sally will take you here, to this house, or any other establishment that I have approved of. If you want Sally to sharpen your knife, ask him to sharpen your knife. If you would like Sally to take you here to this house or another listed in the "Directory", ask him to take you for some 'ice cream'."

"Thank you, Father," Icky said.

"You are very welcome, my son," Mr. Lavine replied.

*

In the first month after his birthday, Icky asked Sally to take him for 'ice cream' once or twice. But then, Icky developed a craving for 'ice cream', three or four times a week.

*

Icarus Lavine's mother was pleased that her son had developed an appreciation for wholesome entertainment and delicious confections and asked the boy one day, "Icky, dear, I have never seen a boy enjoy ice cream as much as you. What is your favorite flavor?"

Icky thought for a moment and then replied, "There are so many kinds to try, Mother, I am not sure; as soon as I find one that gives me pleasure, I find another that is very different but just as satisfying."

Mrs. Lavine was charmed by her son's response, kissed him on his cheek, and ushered him out of the door, saying, "I do not believe that I will join you in such delightful amusement, my darling. But please think of me as you savor today's offerings." And she blew him a kiss as he climbed into the rear seat of the great black and gleaming brass Pickard touring car, that her husband had bought only six months ago, and Sally closed the door behind him.

In the little house on Vestry Street, Miss Agatha Fontaine sang ragtime, and Icky was smitten by her beautiful voice and seductive movements. But mostly, he enjoyed Charlotte Perkins. Charlotte charged Icky $10 (half of which went to the Madame) for each pure, uncomplicated act, but Icky found that what he really enjoyed with Charlotte was a pleasure that cost him $25 (of which the Madame received $10).

The first time Icky hit Charlotte, it was accidental. They were laughing and wrestling and testing their strength against each other, each enjoying the dominance and the submission that was part of the physical contest. Icky was holding Charlotte's arms pinioned to her sides when he decided to change his position. He spun away from her, and as he did, his elbow hit her in the mouth.

She cried out and cursed at Icky.

Icky looked at Charlotte and saw that her lip was bleeding and just beginning to swell.

This was the most stimulating thing that Icky had ever experienced, He felt himself growing hard and looked down at his penis. His erection was throbbing, and the head of his cock was deep, deep red and larger than he had ever seen it.

Charlotte noticed Icky's arousal, lay back on the bed, spread her legs, and whispered, "Come to me, big man."

Icky did as she said, and the two of them fucked like they had never fucked before.

When they were finished, Charlotte turned to Icky and explained to him that this was another service that she could provide, but that it would cost more than the simple fucking they had been doing before.

Icky was interested … very interested, but he was new to all of this he told the whore.

"Don't worry, Icky. I'll help you. That's what I do," she said and kissed him on the cheek, her wounded lip leaving a slight smear of blood there.

*

Charlotte didn't look forward to getting beaten, but each violent fuck with Icky paid her what a laborer would take a month to earn. So she tried to think of ways to lessen the pain and let her keep working with other clients while Icky was throwing his money at her.

Icky had gotten excited when Charlotte had caught his elbow with her mouth. There was blood and swelling, too (a nice bruise that she treated with a steak).

So, what was it that prompted Icky's erection?

Over the next few sessions, Charlotte tried to determine the cause of the effect.

*

Spanking was hitting … Charlotte and Icky tried that first … nothing.

Pinching … it hurt … it could cause a bruise … Charlotte had room on her ass for a couple or three good pinches … still nothing.

Blood ... Charlotte's menses were approaching ... she put Icky off until she was bleeding heavily ... and then she allowed him to take the blood that flowed out of her and ... smear it on himself ... nothing ... smear it on her ... Icky hardened at the sight of the redness on the skin of her thighs and belly and breasts.

*

The next time they met, Icky acted the gentleman. He began by thanking Charlotte for her efforts on his behalf.

And then he asked the question he had been burning to ask, "Dear Charlotte, I have a little pocket knife. Sally keeps it as sharp as can be. Will you lay across my lap and let me put my edge to your ass? I will just draw a scratch of blood. Just one. Let us see what transpires. Please?"

Icky was so sweet in his asking, and Charlotte also serviced English Jack, Icky's father, so that if Icky really hurt her, English Jack would pay. He was known to be a dangerous man, but he was also known to have scruples and to be as honest as a criminal could be.

*

The first time Icky cut Charlotte, the two agreed that the cuts should be made somewhere on her body that would not easily be seen.

Charlotte explained to Icky that some of her clients enjoyed scratching her back with their nails as they fucked her.

Icky and Charlotte were lying naked on the bed together, and when Charlotte told Icky about her back being scratched, Icky's cock began to harden. Charlotte saw this and talked about how it felt when it happened and how sometimes the scratches were deep enough to draw blood.

Just the talking was, this time, enough to set the two to getting their ashes hauled.

*

As time went by, Icky drew blood in slashes and cuts on Charlotte's thighs, buttocks, calves, ankles, back (all up and down its length and even across, marking each rib), shoulders, biceps, forearms, chest, breasts, belly, hips, up under her hair by her ears, and at the nape of her neck. The two of them were careful to treat all of the wounds by rubbing the cuts with honey or Demerara syrup, made with brown sugar and water.

Charlotte and Icky saw each other four or five times a week for almost the next four years. Sometimes, he cut her and tended to her wounds. Sometimes, she cut herself, holding his hand under hers on the knife, and they both saw to the cuts and slashes. Sometimes, very seldom, she would slice him where he could watch the steel slice into his skin and his blood ooze up out of himself. He liked it, then, when she lovingly licked his blood away, carefully spread honey onto him where the cutting had been done, and finally, slowly licked the honey off of him into her mouth and kissed him.

They found that they were very happy when they were together.

*

For Icarus' sixteenth birthday, his father had a surprise for his son. Mr. Lavine had noticed that, since Icky's twelfth birthday, when he had given the boy a very nice pocket knife, the young man had developed an interest in edged weapons.

Icky had begun to read about famous swords and knives, he had started to find shops in Manhattan where such things were bought and sold, and he met people who collected the things and conversed with and wrote to them endlessly. Icky bought his first collectible weapon when he was fourteen.

The boy paid $35 for a US Model 1840 Non-Commissioned Officer's sword with a brass hilt, a cast steel blade, and the grip wrapped in wire. It was actually a lovely thing, and Icky spent many hours polishing and buffing the sword and its scabbard.

Icky's father remembered, then, a pair of knives that he had taken away from some fucking Limey, fresh off of the boat then but now long dead, who had wanted to trade them for American greenbacks. The man, what was his name? Curly Hammond? Charley Handle? No … Charlie Mandel … Crazy Charlie Mandel … from London … that was it!

Mr. Lavine had had the knives appraised and had discovered, much to his surprise, that they were quite old and quite rare, just the thing for a collector.

And now Jack Lavine had a collector in the family, and he had the perfect gift for his collector.

*

Mr. and Mrs. Lavine and Aunt Gertrude planned a little family celebration for Icky's birthday. They would dine at home, give the boy his gifts, and then retire so that the boy could meet his friends for another party later in the evening.

The four of them dined on beef tenderloin, Maine lobster, a lovely salad, and for dessert, the newest sensation, a Devil's Food cake, with sixteen little candles arranged on it, accompanied by vanilla ice cream.

The food was marvelous!

Then the family gathered in the salon, and their gifts were given to Icky; he opened them, one at a time, his mother's first.

It was a little envelope, and inside was a little note written on the stationary of the well-respected haberdashers, Weber & Heilbroner. Icarus Lavine was to have made a dozen outfits to his specifications. A perfect gift for a young man, making his way in the big city, his mother thought.

A second envelope lay on the table, addressed to 'Icarus', in his aunt's hand.

Icky opened that envelope and pulled out what had been stuffed inside: a handful of bills, five of them, all hundreds.

Icky rose and went to his mother, embracing her and kissing her cheek.

"Oh, thank you, Mother," he said, "It's perfect!"

He left his mother after a minute and walked to his Aunt, embracing her, as well, but kissing the top of her gray head.

"Auntie Trudie, thank you!" the young man said, "I don't know what I will use it for. Maybe you and I can go shopping together."

The gray-haired woman smiled, obviously pleased that her favorite (and only) nephew was so well-mannered and considerate.

"I think that I have something here, too," he father said, looking to the left and then to the right, and then reaching under the table next to his chair, pulling a package into sight and laying it on the table.

Icky looked at the package. It was long and wide and flat. He picked it up. It was too heavy to be clothes and too large to be money.

"What could this be?" he asked aloud.

"Open it and see, son," his father said, "Open it and see."

Icky nodded and untied the ribbons that crossed the package. He slipped his fingers into the gaps in the wrapping paper where there was no adhesive holding it together and pulled the paper apart.

Inside the wrapping was a cardboard box, a little larger than a shirt-box.

Icky took off the top of the box to reveal …

A knife … no, two knives.

Icky reached for the top one and took it by the hilt. He placed the flat of his hand under the blade and looked carefully at the knife. It made of fine steel with a musical staff and words carved into the wide blade, a different tune on each side. The tip was pointed and engraved with flowers, as was the ivory hilt.

Icky touched the edge with the pad of his middle finger … and promptly cut himself.

He laughed at his clumsiness and stuck his finger in his mouth to suck the wound closed and heard … a song … and felt the knife in his hand trembling. He looked down to see and watched in awe and disbelief as the blood that the blade had taken seemed to be drunk in by the blade.

This knife was a magical thing.

"They are Spanish," his father said, "probably of Toledo steel. I had them appraised and the antiquarian had never seen the like. Since you collect this kind of thing, I thought that they would be perfect for you."

"Oh, Father," Icky said, feeling a tear well in one eye, "Thank you! Thank you!"

And the boy rose to embrace the man, and as he did so, the knives trembled again.

*

The family celebration at an end, Icky ran upstairs to his room to change his clothes for a party at his best friend's.

He looked sharp in just half an hour and made certain to take a hundred dollars form his aunt's gift, just in case he would have time to celebrate with Charlotte later.

He rode off in the touring car with Sally, and his parents didn't see him again until the morning.

*

Mr. Lavine was having his morning coffee in his study while he read the Times. There was a soft knock at the door, and he said, "Come in."

Icky walked in, still dressed in his clothes from the night before, rumpled but clean enough.

"Father," the boy said, "I must speak with you."

This sounded serious, so serious that 'English Jack' Lavine put his newspaper down.

"Then, sit," he said.

Icky sat in the closest leather wingback chair and wriggled around in it until he got comfortable.

"Father," Icky said again, "I have made a decision."

'English Jack' sat up a little straighter. "Yes?" he said.

"I want to go to France and fight the damned, dirty Bosche," the young man's eyes were sparkling with passion.

"Son," his father began, "America is not at war with the Kaiser. We might be in a year or two, but right now, the Krauts are fighting the Tommies and the Frogs."

"I know that, Father," Icky said, "but I could drive an ambulance, or learn to fly a plane for the Lafayette Escadrille, or join the Legionnaires and carry a rifle. With Auntie Trudie's present, I've got enough money for passage on a Cunard liner."

"Son," his father said in a more serious tone of voice, "A war is serious. You could be killed, and you are my only child. I can't let you fly so close to the sun; like the boy you are named after, you could fall and die."

"Father," Icky said, unable to believe that his father was such a coward, a coward but with Icky's own life, "I am not some old Greek story. I am young and strong, I am not afraid. I will be fine."

"That might be true, Icarus, but I forbid it! Until America enters the war officially, you may not go to France to fight and die. No!" his father told him.

Icarus Lavine was furious! He turned away from his father and stormed out of the study, stomping up the stairs.

As the boy's footsteps thundered up the staircase, 'English Jack' Lavine sank back in the comfortable leather of his chair. The boy would be angry for a few days. 'English Jack' would let him cool off and then take him somewhere enjoyable, maybe pheasant hunting in the West, maybe to an exotic locale like Hawaii. The boy simply needed some time and some diversion to help him take his mind off of his silly dreams.

*

Icky went upstairs to his room. He threw himself onto his bed and seethed. And then he made up his mind.

He went to his closet and packed a suitcase. He put in an extra pair of shoes, three pairs of socks, five clean pairs of underwear, three shirts, a sweater, and a pair of slacks. And in the compartment in one side, the part covered by an elasticized cloth, he put the knives.

He put on a pair of sturdy shoes, his raincoat, and a fedora. In his pocket, he put his pocket-knife and four-hundred seventy dollars that were left from his Auntie Trudie's present.

As soon as it would begin to get dark, he would leave.

*

Icky walked out of his parents' house and took a bus to Grand Central Station, where he purchased a one-way ticket to Toronto, with a stop in Buffalo. The train would leave at midnight and take fifteen hours.

The next day, Icarus Lavine arrived in the Canadian city and asked the first policemen he met where he might go to volunteer for the Army.

He was directed to a little building near the government offices in the center of town, where he found the recruiting station for the Canadian Army, Princess Patricia's Canadian Light Infantry.

He endured basic training in Canada, and his unit was shipped out to England in October. Their first camp was on Salisbury Plain near that peculiar pile of rocks that the locals called Stonehenge.

In November, his unit was absorbed by the British Expeditionary Force and moved to Winchester where he and the other soldiers were trained to use the new Lee-Enfield rifles. By Epiphany, they were put into the trenches, somewhere in Belgium, in a place the soldiers called 'Dickiebush'.

*

Life in the trenches was as close to hell as Icky ever wanted to get.

*

It wasn't just the lice (the Brits called them 'cooties'; one doughboy swore that the cooties were his best friends. He had been sent to a field-hospital to be de-loused, and when he returned to his unit, every single soldier in it had been killed – the lice had saved his life!) and the trench fever they spread (which could kill a once-healthy man in less than a week), or the rats that would nibble on a man, living or dead, until someone stuck them on the blade of his knife, or the trench foot (from the standing and sitting and walking through the mud and muck of the open graves that the officers called 'trenches') that made a man's feet swell and stink and rot before they killed him or were amputated to save him, or the rations, of 'Ticklers Plum and Apple Jam' (they called it 'pozzy'), biscuits, and boiled beef (or 'Baby's Head', the meat pudding) – men wondered if it was better to die from eating that shit or from the 'iron rations' of shrapnel that the Germans served up every damned day, or the accessories (gas) that went with those meals.

Whether a man had 'gone west', 'earned the wooden cross', or had been made a 'landowner', the result was always the same; he was dead. In Flanders, it was said that a man had just six weeks to live.

*

Icky had had few opportunities to live since his unit had been sent to the front. The talk in the trenches was of only two subjects, how a man needed good food and how he needed love and a smile. The food was only a dream, but the other was real enough, and like the other soldiers, Icky had money in his pocket and expected to die, so when he could, like a hundred thousand others, he would find a whore.

The officers had the maisons tolérées, the legal houses, where a man could have the finer things, including 'armor' (a condom) to dress his weapon.

Icky and the men in the trenches had to make do with what they could find. And finding it was as easy as spotting a red lamp.

The first red lamp Icky encountered had a big number '3' painted on the it (the lamp was dark then, telling the customers that the establishment was not yet open for business) and a crowd of men, six deep and forty yards long, waiting for the place to open.

At six, the lamp had been lit and over a couple hundred men pushed their way toward the entrance.

For those who wanted to avoid the crush, there were other women (and a few men), who plied their trade in bars, cafes, hotels, and alleyways.

For those who cared to endure the crowd, they would pay a franc at the door and then negotiated with the lady of their choice for the 'pleasure' of her company.

When Icky got through the front door that first time, he walked into a large room with nearly a dozen girls, either completely naked or wearing a tiny bit of lace that covered them at their hips.

The Madame asked Icky, "Would you prefer clean or dirty?"

His shocked stare made her understand that he didn't understand.

"Ah, monsieur," she laughed, "Clean is clean, and dirty is …comment se dit-il …malade … diseased."

Some fellows in his unit had spoken about how, if they got the clap, that 'self-inflicted wound' wouldn't earn them a Wound Stripe, but it would get them a thirty-day stay in a hospital with clean sheets, good food, and attractive and friendly nurses. Many soldiers considered this to be a fair trade.

Icky told the Madame, "Nottoyer … clean, if you please."

The woman smiled and motioned to a skinny, dark-haired girl who took Icky's hand and led him upstairs to a garret, furnished with a stained stretcher, a thin sheet that might have been white at the turn of the century, and a blanket (that Icky was certain had more lice than the trench he had just come from).

He was finished in a few minutes, and when he thought, later, about the experience, he decided that it was like pulling his 'thing' with a stranger in attendance who spoke incessantly in an unintelligible language. Well, it was better than having it off in a ditch with some Gallic bint old enough to be his mother.

*

After his rendezvous, Icky's unit was ordered to move to Ypres, somewhere else in Belgium. On the morning of April 24, the battle began. After this battle, Icky thought idly as he checked and loaded his Lee-Enfield and made sure that his bayonet was securely fastened to the rifle, there would be leave in Paris, or at least in Lille;

perhaps the French girls would be ... an improvement ... and he would be able to use his knife.

"Piss in your hankies, ladies, and hold 'em over your faces. The Jerries are using gas!" someone down the line shouted.

First, Icky smelled the mixed aromas of bleach and rotten hay ... at least the Krauts were using chlorine and phosgene together, that pair would kill him quickly. He stood up to look over the top and saw a green cloud moving closer and closer. If he ran away from it, it would just make it worse.

Icky reached into one of the many pockets of his uniform and found his once-white linen handkerchief. It was crusted with blood, and sweat, and snot and ... his own spunk, but he put it in his mouth to free his hands to open his trousers. Pee was supposed to counteract the gas.

His trousers dropped, and he took the cloth from his mouth and held it at his penis.

And he couldn't piss.

He strained and thought about an ocean of running water, and ...

He couldn't piss.

He dropped the useless handkerchief, and pulled his trousers up.

And he looked down the trench, first to the right and then to the left.

Some soldiers were crouching, frozen in fear in the mud and rainwater in the deepest part of the fortifications. Some stood at the top, looking out into No-man's-land and readying their rifles for when the Germans would send their first troops as soon as the gas dissipated.

Others, not many, ran.

They hopped out of the trenches, scooting in-between the craters that had been made by previous bombardments, trying to make it to the comparative safety of the rear.

It was preferable, Icky decided, to stay put and die better. Physical exertion would only speed up the effects of the gas, and if he ran away and didn't die, he would be shot for desertion.

Icky's throat and eyes were burning, and he coughed. When he wiped his mouth, his hand was bloody.

He would die like a man, he decided.

Private Icarus Lavine, of Princess Patricia's Canadian Light Infantry, 1st Battalion, pulled the knives that his father had given him for his birthday out of their scabbards. They shone in what sun there was and Icky could feel them gently thrumming in anticipation of the blood that they would soon drink. Icky had brought them, thinking that they would be wonderful sexual ... accoutrements ... in his romantic encounters with exotic European women and that their beauty and value would serve him, should he ever need to sell something (like the gold Wilsdorf and Davis chronograph that his father wore) to keep body and soul together.

So Icky stood at the top of the trench, his eyes as low as he could get them to still see what was coming. There were men out there, moving toward him. He rested his rifle on the sandbags at the top of the trench, found a target, sighted, and pressed the trigger.

And the God-damned gun jammed!

There he stood, a worthless rifle in his hands, blood foaming at his nose and mouth, and partially blinded by the gas.

He would die like a man, he told himself again.

He would go over the top and slice up some Germans with his beautiful, sharp knives.

Private Icky Lavine pulled himself up on the lip of the trench and stood tall, looking around for the enemy.

A German sniper's bullet ripped off the top of Icky's head. He dropped the knives (that were now humming with joy and beginning to sing their song of blood and passion) as he fell back into the trench.

The knives, however, fell into the mud of the no-man's-land in front of the trench and slid beneath the surface of the stagnant water and blood that had pooled there.

*

In Greek mythology, a boy named Icarus ignored his father's instructions to not fly too close to the sun. When the wax on the boy's wings melted, he tumbled out of the sky and fell into the sea, where he drowned.

Nearly two thousand years later, a boy from New York City, also named Icarus, ignored his father's instructions to not go to war. When he fell, it was into a trench full of dirty water and suffocating, poisonous gases, where he drowned.

*

The knives sang happily, but quietly, in the midst of the carnage and were eventually buried in the dirt and mud that soldiers and their equipment unknowingly pushed over them.

Chapter 18 – Strength

Another of the Major Arcana of the Suit of Knives in the Swordsmith's Tarot is Strength. The astrological sign associated with Strength is the Lion, a creature of physical, mental, and spiritual power.

Effort, determination, and persistence combine with patience and compassion to create a Strength that is ferocious in its ability to influence and ultimately control destiny. Raw, instinctual nature, that is, ego and fear, is mastered by the greater Strength of selflessness and trust, the wisdom of the spirit.

Strength is a balance of the human and the divine, touched and mediated by a higher consciousness. Strength is, ultimately, a quiet and unobtrusive thing that manifests itself over time without, necessarily, the expectation or likelihood of recognition or reward.

If Strength is reversed, weakness, obstacles, and vulnerability are indicated. Only through focus, determination, and self-control can this reversal be overcome.

But know this: Strength is not capable of mastering every inadequacy, challenge, or jeopardy.

*

The Treaty of Versailles had been signed the year before, and finally … finally … the Germans had returned to their homes, the English had returned to their homes, the Canadians had returned to their homes, the French had returned to their homes, and even his countrymen, the Belgians, had finally left his little farm in peace.

All of those bastard soldiers had certainly taken their time. Their armies had fought five battles over four years in five vain attempts to possess the farmer's fields. And now, who stood alone over his fields? The farmer, of course.

Before the war, the famer had grown chicory and endive to take to market and leeks, tomatoes, carrots, cucumbers, peppers, and cauliflowers for his own meals. He had had a little grove of sweet pears to the south of his home, and his wife loved the red poppies that he had planted around their door.

Now that the armies had left, he would finally be able to return to working his fields every day and plowing his beautiful Gudula (she had been named for Brussels' saint) every night.

The farmer smiled as he thought of it, and he stuck his spade into the ground to continue the trench that he was digging. Yesterday, he had borrowed his neighbor's horse, cart and son, and had spent the day spreading compost over this little field. Today, he would begin the double-digging.

He dug a trench, about twenty centimeters deep and the width of his spade, putting the dirt he had dug in a row of shovelfuls to the left of the trench. When he got to the end of the row, he dug a new trench, putting the new soil he dug into the first trench. He did this until the whole of the field had been dug; it took him almost the entire day.

About half-way down the final trench, the farmer stuck his spade into the dirt and hit something solid.

"Wonderful!" he thought angrily, "Another chunk of army crap. Maybe it is made of a metal that will bring me a franc or two. If it does," he promised himself and any saints who might have been listening, "I will kiss King Albert's golden head," and he crossed himself to forestall any bad luck coming from his blasphemy.

He dug down into the dirt, ruining the simple perfection of the trench, and saw a silver glint.

He reached down and grabbed whatever it was, and as he pulled it free of the soil's embrace, a sharp edge cut into his hand.

He dropped the thing and reached into his trouser pocket with his uninjured hand, grabbing his kerchief. He spit into his hand so that he could more easily wipe away the dirt and blood, and when the cut was as clean as he could make it, he wrapped the kerchief around his hand. It was not so bad that he wouldn't be able to finish the row.

Now that his bleeding hand had been seen to, he looked at what he had unearthed.

It was a knife.

A knife unlike any he had ever seen.

And as the farmer picked it up out of the dirt, he saw another gleam.

A second knife.

The farmer quit his work for the day and left the spade stuck standing up in the trench.

*

As he walked back to his home, he looked carefully at the knife that had cut his hand. It was a beautiful, old thing, made of the finest steel with a hilt of ivory. There were strange designs engraved into the blade and handle, and symbols and words (the farmer had never learned to read) covered both flat surfaces of the blade.

He thought that he should wipe his blood from the blade, but when he tried to do so, he saw that just a trace was left and what there had been was disappearing into the steel. And as his blood joined the metal, the farmer heard music, as though an old, old voice was singing in ringing tones. It was a song that he did not know, but it sounded as if it might belong in a church (the farmer had never learned to attend church); it was solemn and joyous at the same time. A man could worship a song like that.

*

Twenty years later, the farmer's children had grown up, married, and moved away to better lives in cities far away. The farmer and his wife now lived alone for the first time since before the war.

Then, in May, the Germans came again.

*

The farmer had been out in the fields all morning, and he had worked up an appetite. As he approached his little house, he could smell the cooking soup that he would eat with freshly-baked bread for his lunch.

And when he got closer, he saw the ugly, gray truck parked at his front door.

*

The farmer opened his door and walked in. Sitting in the middle of the floor, surrounded by broken dishes and torn sheets and blankets, a smashed chair, and the contents of their pantry, now spilled, and torn, and in pieces, was his wife, his beloved Gudula, swaying gently as she sobbed quietly, a trail of blood snaking down the side of her head where she had been struck.

A crisply-uniformed man, wearing gray and black with a silver 'SS' on his lapels, was holding the knives that the farmer had found so many years before.

"Welcome home," the soldier said in cruelly-accented French. He held up the knives and continued, "You wife told me about these after just a little tap on her head."

The farmer attempted to go to his wife, to hold her, and to offer her his strength. But four strong, young, German hands held him and kept him from her.

"Now," the leader of the Nazis continued, "What other treasures do you have? What special things have you hidden that you have never even told her about?"

"I am a farmer, you pig," the man shouted, his frustration and impotence overcoming his common sense, "All that I own is the dirt of my farm. I found these in the dirt after the war and have kept them for time of need."

"Only these?" the German said, "What a pity."

And he shot the farmer's wife in her stomach.

The farmer screamed, as did his wife.

"She will die slowly, my friend, and very painfully," he told the farmer, "There is a thin chance that she may survive, so I will ask you again. What else do you have for me?"

"Nothing! Nothing!! You have taken everything from me. Please let me take her to the physician. You have what you want now. Please. Please. Please," the farmer cried as he struggled in vain with his captors.

"I will take one more thing from you then," the German said and shot the farmer in the head.

The soldier ordered his men to return to the truck, and as he left the farmhouse, he turned to the dying woman, bent and kissed her on the top of her head, and said, "Watch over him now."

Then he walked to the truck and climbed in next to the driver.

"Back to town," he ordered,

The door of the farmhouse swung slowly in the breeze as the sounds of pain grew softer and eventually ceased.

Chapter 19 – The Seven of Knives

The seventh card of the Minor Arcana of the Suit of Knives in the Swordsmith's Tarot is the Seven of Knives. Just as the number seven is considered fortuitous and wins certain games of chance, the Seven of Knives is a card of fortune, fate, and risk. Life is an adventure where satisfaction and fulfillment are often followed by struggle and contention, all with the intention of seizing the victory and appropriating it.

The Seven of Knives accepts any challenge and defends itself against all comers, but good fortune attends the powerful and deserts those who are fated to fail.

Not every game can be won, and not every life is a victory.

The reversed Seven of Knives is a reminder that no matter how overwhelming the challenges and responsibilities in your life, they are yours. If you lack the confidence, courage, and conviction to succeed and prosper against these obstacles, giving up will not save you.

Choose well the gods and idols that you venerate; they are your devotees as well.

*

SS-Hauptscharführer Sühne, of the Waffen-SS, in his field grey uniform with the golden yellow piping of its shoulder boards, looked appropriately confident and demanding of the respect that all should show to him as 'the Mother of the Company', as he provided his men with the leadership, counsel, and discipline that they deserved, and rolled through Belgium in the camouflaged truck on the most important mission of his life. He had found a treasure, the kind that had been whispered about amongst the disciples of the Old Gods who had found their way into the armed forces of the Third Reich.

The truck drove almost 150 kilometers from the farmer's house in Belgium northwest toward Essen.

When the Master sergeant's squad got to the city, he requisitioned a Kübelwagen and dismissed the rest of his men, and then he and the driver sped northeast again on the road to Osnabrück. It took them two hours to get to the city, pass the prisoner of war camp, and enter the **Kirchlengern Forest.**

This was the home of the Osnabrück Hünenbetten (megalithic tombs … underground barrows that were reached from dripping caves, the mouths of which were stained with some dark-brown substances that resembled dried blood – or something much worse). The people who visited the hünenbetten, and who were still able to speak after their visits, told of feeling intense panic and a petrifying dismay that they were being watched … no, … being hungrily appraised by malevolent entities.

The Master sergeant had no map. He had been told of the cave years ago and had been told how to find it. If he had forgotten, they had told him, it would be his eternal loss.

*

The Master sergeant and his man drove through the frightening forest for hours.

And just as the driver asked if the Master sergeant would like to continue the search in the morning, Sühne saw it!

An errant ray of sunlight illuminated a wild thicket of mistletoe that almost hid the entrance to a dripping cave.

Mistletoe, the wood of the spear that caused the death of Baldr, "the Shining One".

Sühne ordered the driver to stop, and the master sergeant took the knives (he had put them in a leather briefcase so that no one would see them), got out, and sent the driver and the Kübelwagen back to headquarters.

*

When the Kübelwagen had left and the sound of its little motor had faded, the Master sergeant approached the great doors that were obscured in the shadows at the mouth of the cave and knocked twice.

And then he waited.

He waited for a quarter of an hour.

And just as he began to wonder if he was in the wrong place, the doors creaked open. A naked man and a naked woman said nothing but held out their hands to welcome him. They turned and walked back into the cave, and he followed.

Someone he did not see closed the doors behind him with a loud slamming boom.

*

As Sühne followed them, he realized that he was walking through a tunnel. It descended, gradually, deeper into the earth and was lit with torches set at regular intervals.

*

After a while, the naked couple stopped, and a tall, good-looking man, who wore only bright, golden yellow robes, approached him,.

"Do you have them?" the man asked the Master sergeant.

"Yes, sir," Sühne replied and began to salute.

The man laughed, "Here, that is not necessary."

The sergeant managed, somehow, to stop himself before his right arm was fully extended and awkwardly lowed his hand.

"Well?" the robed man asked.

The sergeant opened the leather case that he carried and took out the knives.

"Yes … yes … I see, now." the man said.

Then the man said to Sühne, "You will join us in the rite."

The sergeant smiled in his heart of hearts. He had been accepted into the most secret cult of the Third Reich. He was victorious!

*

"Take off your clothes," the man told Sühne.

"Take off my clothes?"

"The Gods will accept our sacrifice only if we appear to him as when we were born," the man explained as if to an idiot.

The Master sergeant almost laughed with joy at his triumph. He had been accepted as an acolyte of the Old Gods, but he kept quiet as a respectful neophyte should and shed his uniform, shoes, and underthings.

As he stood in the torchlight of the tunnel, naked, the man in the yellow robe disrobed, as well.

The man held out his hands, palms up, and said, "Place the knives, side by side, in my hands."

Sühne did as he had been told, and the man walked away, resting the knives on his hands as if they were delicate things that he was unworthy to touch.

"Come," he said.

They walked for a minute or two down the corridor; more and more torches lit their way and brightened the rock on which they shone so it seemed to be as smooth as silk (or steel)

Finally, the two men came to a large chamber.

*

There must have been hundreds of torches illuminating the great space.

A score or more of men, each as naked as the sergeant and the bearer of the knives, stood arrayed in a circle. Each was blonde, tall, and muscled as an athlete, and each held a wooden staff, taller than himself.

Sühne looked again and this time noticed, maybe, a dozen women, each as blonde as any of the men, each as naked as any of the men, but each, unlike the men, held a spray of white flowers, daisies or, perhaps, edelweiss.

A pool stood in the center of the room and in front of it, a giant of a man, wearing tattered yellow clothes, towered over the others.

He must have stood over seven feet tall, and his hair was golden (there was no other way to describe it). The other men's hair looked pale and almost artificial next to his.

He held himself like a king.

The man with the knives left Sühne, who was standing immobile and mesmerized, and walked in front of the yellow man. Then he went to one knee, bowed his head, and held out the knives to his master.

The 'King in Yellow', as the sergeant now thought of him, looked at the knives and laughed.

Then he walked to Sühne.

"You brought these wonderful gifts to me?" he said in a voice that was as low as thunder but that seemed musical at the same time and made Sühne's knees shake.

"Yes, Standartenführer Hastur," the Master sergeant stammered. As Sühne looked up into the 'King in Yellow's' face, his heart quivered as he saw that the 'King's' eyes were glowing red. Hastur's true face was hidden beneath a web of gossamer, and as Sühne looked down in abasement at the 'King's' glance, he saw that the 'King's' bare feet were webbed.

"We need no human names here," the 'King in Yellow' said, and the sergeant realized that what he had thought were tattered clothes that the Oberst wore was an SS uniform, golden yellow where the army regimentals were gray but bordered with gleaming silver and blood-red striped piping (that indicated a unit the sergeant had never seen or even heard of).

*

Then he turned and said, "Bring her."

Two of the naked men lay their staves down and walked to the rear of the chamber, returning almost immediately, half-dragging a woman, with long, dark brown hair, large, frightened brown eyes, a pleasing figure, and olive skin, who struggled vainly between them.

She cursed at the men who brought her, at the men who stood and watched, at the women who attended them, at the Master sergeant, and at the 'King in Yellow', himself.

The giant, regal man looked disdainfully at the captive woman when she was brought to him and slapped her, hard, but as carelessly as if she were a mosquito that he swatted.

The blow knocked the woman senseless, and in the quiet of the great cave, the king said, "Tie her hands."

A third man brought a length of yellow rope to the two who held the woman, and the three of them together efficiently and professionally bound her hands before her.

Then, the 'King' turned to Sühne and said, "She is yours until the end," and then he nodded, and the two men who held the woman took her to the pool in the center of the room.

The 'King' nodded for Sühne to follow.

"Get in," the 'King' commanded.

And the sergeant did as his 'King' had commanded him.

The pool was round, hemispherical, and made of what appeared to Sühne to be copper. The water was warm; it felt good.

"Here," the 'King' said, "Take her," and the two acolytes passed the still-unconscious woman into the Master sergeant's arms.

Then, the 'King in Yellow' and his minions left the side of the pool and returned to what must have been their places for the ritual to come.

The 'King' took up the knives into his hands and examined them, smiling as he did so; then he laid them back onto the cave's floor and took off his clothing.

The woman stirred in the sergeant's arm's, waking up, and when she was conscious enough to realize that he held her, she shouted, "Let go of me!"

The sergeant was shocked at her outburst and let her go.

She found her feet and made her way to the side of the pool, grabbing it and trying to get a leg up on the lip to help her pull herself out.

One of the men with the staves walked to where she struggled, put his staff to her shoulder, and pushed her back into the water.

The sergeant half-swam and half-walked through the water … was it warmer now? … to help the woman.

When he touched her, she spun and pushed herself away from him.

"What are you doing?" she screamed.

"Trying to help you," the sergeant said in a companionable tone.

"Then help me get out of here, you fool, before they boil us alive!" she said, barely able, in her anger, to keep from yelling.

"Boil us?"

She looked at him as though he were mindless. "The water in this copper pot is getting warmer each second," she said, "We will die here unless were get out."

Sühne realized that she was right.

He dove for the side of the pot and pulled his hands away as he touched the rim and the bright metal burned him.

The Master sergeant noticed, then, that the water in the 'pot' was beginning to simmer, with thin trails of bubbles rising from the bottom.

He glanced at his hands that had blistered from the touch of the hot copper and decided that he must do what he must.

He reached the edge again and began to hoist himself out of the water when a stick clubbed the side of his head, stunning him and loosening his grip so that he fell back in.

When his head cleared, he heard the woman's screams as the water began to ulcerate her soft skin.

The sergeant decided that he would not scream.

But as the water simmered and his immersed legs and torso hurt so badly, and the bubbling water splashed on his face, he joined her, howling his agony.

Their bodies blistered and burned, they lost the strength to stand, and so they began slip under the roiling water.

*

Then, the 'King in Yellow' said, "It is time."

And some of the men lay down their staves and picked up other long sticks that resembled shepherds' crooks.

These men walked to the pot and reached in with their curved sticks.

They were soon able to pull the woman and Sühne out of the water and onto the stone floor of the chamber.

The woman lay still for almost a minute, and then she coughed, a vile mixture of water and blood and something thick and damaged that spewed from her. She rolled onto her back and moaned softly, unceasingly.

Sühne just lay there until one of the crook-men poked him.

Then, he, too, moaned, but he trembled as he did.

Hastur, the 'King' nodded and smiled.

*

Hastur called for the man to be brought to him. Hastur was 'The Night Drinker', 'The Golden God', and he would prepare the male body first since he must wear its flayed skin to successfully perform the rest of the ritual, 'The Impersonation of the God', if it were to succeed.

He took the first of the knives into his hand and smiled as it heard what the knives asked, "How can a mere God compare to the manifestation of fire and steel and blood and song?"

Hastur knew that the rite would allow him to show himself to be Xipetotec to these pale men, these Aryans, who thought of themselves as the 'Masters'. They would soon understand of what a 'Golden God', the avatar of Life-Death-Rebirth, of Creation, of Liberation, of Spring, of the East, of Gold, and of Disease, was capable.

And so, to begin.

*

The men held the male sacrifice, kneeling between them.

Hastur began at the top of the man's head.

The first knife felt its edge penetrate the blistered skin of the man and rejoiced with the touch of his boiled blood, at almost the heat of the knife's tempering so long ago. And it sang its song of benediction when Hastur took the skin in one piece and cast the useless, ugly, dying body aside.

Then, Hastur donned the skin suit, the flayed skin of the sacrifice's hands falling loose from his wrists. His acolytes dipped their fingers into the blood that covered the dying man and painted bloody stripes onto their 'King's' neck, hands, and legs. Hastur himself dipped his fingers into the blood of the sacrifice and reddened his own mouth and lips.

To complete the 'Impersonation of the God', a crown of bright flowers and golden jewelry was placed on the head of the skin suit, and golden ornaments were stuck through the nose and ears of the skin. A naked women brought a heavy gold necklace to Hastur, and he bowed his head to receive it.

As the skin was decorated and made acceptable, the men and women who followed Hastur chanted the old song to 'Red Mirror' from a place that had no music, only words.

The knives knew that song … so they gave the people its tune.

Hastur smiled to hear the music of the knives and the chanting of his subjects and set himself to finish what he had begun.

He took the second of the knives and began at the top of head of the meat that had once been a woman and cut downward so that her skin could be worn by the other participant in the old, red, nuptial rite.

When the dark-haired woman's skin had been removed, a blond Aryan virgin, naked and wearing a crown of edelweiss in her long, long, pale hair that reached to her ankles, and fear and excitement in her pale, blue eyes walked up to Hastur, bowed, and awaited her gifts.

The blonde woman began to hear the knives' song as she was adorned with her own suit of skin. The blood that had covered the knives after their work was wiped on the woman's calves, and thighs, and hands, and cheeks, and finally over her belly and her breasts.

Then she was led to the altar, made of the living bodies of the most fervent of the disciples and covered with more of the white flowers that she wore in her hair, where she was laid down to accept the man, soon to be a God, who wore the other suit of skin.

They would attempt to breed a child of the Old Gods there.

If the woman became pregnant, this would show that the Old Gods had accepted the sacrifice.

In the frenzy of the ritual, the knives sang, their music filling the great room and the minds of all the people there, the ones who lived, the ones who were dying, and the one who was being created.

And when the rite was finished, the knives were forgotten, along with the corpses that were left on the floor.

And even though they sang long, quiet songs for quite a long time after that, the knives knew nothing more for a while.

*

On April 3, 1945, the 11th Armoured Division of the British Second Army entered Osnabrück on its way east, first to bridge the Weser River and then on to liberate Berlin. The Division rescued a hundred Russian slave workers, captured 217 German soldiers (who had decided that it was time to surrender), and freed 6,000 prisoners of war at OFLAG VI-C Eversheide/Osnabrück, an 'officer camp', in the Teutoburger Wald just west of the city.

The camp's barracks were originally built in 1935 for the Wehrmacht, the German armed forces, in 1935. There were thirty of them, all made of wood. The camp consisted of the barracks, which were surrounded by barbed wire and four machine gun towers, and other buildings outside the wire for the German army troops (the Heer).

An airstrike the previous year had killed over one hundred prisoners of war; there was no thought of providing an air raid shelter for prisoners.

When the prisoners were freed, they were half-starved. The Germans had not given them their Red Cross parcels or much of anything to eat beyond mush since the air raid had told them that the Allies were coming. From the time that Red Cross parcels had begun to be delivered to the camp, four years before, the Germans had rifled through the parcels and had taken whatever they liked. They especially enjoyed the peanut butter, spam, cigarettes, and tins of coffee in the American parcels and the Digger flake pipe tobacco, chocolate, tea, and tins of herring in the British parcels.

And when the Germans discovered what MI9 had sent in some of the parcels, they stopped distributing the parcels all together. The MI9, more officially known as the British Directorate of Military Intelligence Section 9, wanted POWs to spend their time planning ways to escape and then escaping. This would serve to improve morale among the captured troops (working toward a common goal is an effective methodology for that sort of thing) and make the Heer divert precious resources to rounding up the escapees.

Hidden in books and games, like Monopoly, were compasses, files, maps printed on silk, and German, Austrian, or Italian currency (depending upon which camp the parcel was being sent to).

*

Technically, it was the British Army that had liberated Osnabrück, but two of the soldiers who were riding along with the 11th Armoured Division were 'observers' sent by their American commander for 'liaison' purposes. The men's uniforms indicated that they were 'Reconnaissance' but their service records, stuck somewhere in a file in Washington, D.C., showed that they worked for the OSS.

The English, the Americans, and the Russians were each pushing to be the first of the Allies to reach Berlin. But soldiering was hard work, and they had just freed thousands of their comrades, so in a forest to the west of the Weser River, the two American 'Reconnaissance' soldiers were taking a little 'unofficial' leave.

*

The soldier and his buddy, Tommy, had borrowed a jeep, had found a bottle of wine somewhere, and had made a command decision of their own to head for somewhere pure and clean, even if for only the afternoon. This big, empty forest was perfect. For the soldiers, in this little bit of stolen time, there was no war; there was just the sun shining through the leaves on trees that had been there for hundreds of years, two good friends who had been through too much together, and a bottle of wine

They drove up a trail that looked as if it hadn't been used for years, looking for an empty glade for their picnic of wine and k-rations.

Tommy had snagged the triple play, three of the K-rations: breakfast, lunch, and supper.

They would make their smorgasbord from whatever they chose from the Breakfast Unit (canned chopped ham and eggs, biscuits, oatmeal cereal, a four-pack of Chesterfield cigarettes, a pack of Wrigley chewing gum, instant coffee, two cubes of sugar, instant coffee, a pack of toilet paper tissues, and four Halazone water purification tablets), the Dinner Unit (canned American cheese, biscuits, five caramels, two cubes of sugar, a packet of salt, a four-pack of Old Gold cigarettes, a box of matches, a pack of Dentyne chewing gum, and a packet of powdered grape beverage), and the Supper Unit (canned beef and pork loaf, biscuits, a two ounce Hershey's chocolate bar, a packet of toilet paper tissues, a four-pack of Lucky Strike cigarettes, Dubble Bubble chewing gum, and a cube of beef bouillon), and the bottle of wine that Tommy had found.

*

But the further up the little trail that they drove, the creepier it became. The tall, dark trees dripped, the wind (or something) moaned, and both men felt as though they were being watched.

Just when the soldier was about to tell Tommy to turn around, he saw something even stranger than the forest they had been driving through: there was a cave hidden by a thicket of scratchy-looking bushes, and visible just inside the mouth of the cave were two huge wooden doors with black metal hardware.

"What the hell is that, Tommy?" the soldier asked and pointed at the cave's mouth.

Tommy pulled the jeep to a stop in the quiet, dripping forest, and the two men got out, ignoring their picnic supplies, the soldier taking his M1 carbine (in case the Model 1911 .45 on his hip wouldn't be enough) and Tommy took his Thompson sub-machine gun.

As the two men had done countless times before in unknown circumstances against unseen enemies, they took their positions on either side of the door so that when the soldier opened it, Tommy could provide the covering fire that might save both of their lives.

The soldier motioned for Tommy to nudge the door open. Tommy was the best point man in Europe. The two men had worked together in their squad for almost four years. Other recruits came and died, and new fellas replaced those who left in the squad in wooden boxes, but the soldier and Tommy were still together. They were the last of the bunch.

Tommy nudged one of the big iron-bound doors open and motioned for the soldier to make his move.

The soldier dove through the now-open doorway and rolled to his feet.

No one was there.

The soldier opened the door to let in some light and saw torches hanging in sconces on the walls.

He took one down, reached into his pocket for a match, and lit it.

When the soldier touched the match to the torch, it flared to life as if it had been made that morning.

Tommy walked carefully into the cave, found a torch for himself, and lit it off of the soldier's torch.

"Three on a match, Tommy?" the soldier chuckled, "That would be bad luck."

Tommy smiled.

The two men walked down a long tunnel that was lined with more dark torches until they came to the entrance to a large chamber.

It was dark, and anyone or anything could be waiting there for them.

The soldier placed his torch on the floor, slung his carbine on his back and took the .45 from its holster. Tommy held his torch up high, so that he could see, but he slung his Thompson around with his other hand, ready to be used.

The soldier went first into the room as Tommy covered him.

The soldier looked around, saw nothing moving, and yelled, "Clear!" to let Tommy know that it was o.k. come in without hosing the room down in Thompson fire.

When Tommy came in with his torch, the additional light illuminated something, two things, on the floor. The soldier walked over to investigate, and as the reality of what he saw not moving sank quickly in, he threw up.

Tommy came over and looked around while the soldier finished losing his breakfast.

The soldier went to the two lumps of what, he had realized, in the moment before he had thrown up, had once been human. In each pile, one a bit smaller than the other, there were bones, cartilage, a little mold on desiccated muscles, but no skin or hair.

He shuddered when he thought of what might have caused these bodies to be like this and idly wondered how long they had been there like this.

And then, something gleamed, off to his right, in the light of his torch.

The soldier walked over to where he had seen the metallic glint.

Two old knives lay on the floor.

He picked one up and saw that, under the dried, brownish stains, the blade gleamed with an almost internal light and strange engraving seemed to almost move by itself. The hilt fit his hand as if it had been made for him, and the weight and balance of the strange weapon (or was it only a utensil) were perfect.

The soldier could have sworn that he heard music.

Chapter 20 – The Eight of Knives

The eighth card of the Minor Arcana of the Suit of Knives in the Swordsmith's Tarot is the Eight of Knives. The element associated with the Eight of Knives is Air because the Eight of Knives is a card of change, energy, and movement.

The resemblance between the shape of the number eight and the symbol for infinity is no coincidence. The structure of the Eight and the form and function of a Knife are channels through which raw energy flows, and as this power rushes through the Eight of Knives, it is uncontrollable, just as the change and movement it creates are not to be denied.

The person caught on this wave must ride out its storm or be consumed by it.

While having a plan in mind can often prove to be beneficial, the Eight of Knives laughs at man's schemes, designs, arrangements, and attempts to harness the raging storm.

A man should remember that there is not always a place of shelter from the storm.

But, then, the Eight of Knives reminds man that, sometimes, there is.

*

After Osnabrück, the soldier and Tommy rejoined the American army and were sent to Hamburg.

That's where Tommy died.

*

There were latrine rumors about Krauts, some regular Ratzies and some SS bastards, hiding in the woods past the autobahn.

The soldier and Tommy were reconnoitering on the left flank of the unit that they had been re-assigned to.

The squad walked into an ambush, and only the soldier's experience, his luck with German bullets, and the trunk of a big tree saved him.

Tommy had the experience, but his luck ran out when there was no tree to stop the German bullets.

Tommy died in the soldier's arms.

*

And then, as the soldier closed Tommy's eyes, he heard them coming for him, too.

*

The soldier lay Tommy down on the leaves that covered the forest's floor, found his carbine and waited …

He waited, hearing the Heinies' footsteps grow closer and closer to his hiding place.

He waited for the right time, the right target, the right shot …

*

And, suddenly, there it was …

The soldier squeezed the carbine's trigger.

And the gun jammed.

The God-damned gun fucking jammed!

He was FUBAR!

"Now, I guess, I'm fucked, too, Tommy," the soldier said, looking into his friend's now-empty eyes.

*

And as the Germans moved toward him, to kill him where he crouched, he heard a song, music so soft and questioning that he almost ignored it in his fear.

And then the soldier listened … and found a sharp steely voice of blood and fire.

The soldier realized that the music came from his pack.

He took off his pack to find the source of the songs before he died; he was a dead man, anyway. What would it matter if he spent his last moments caressed by that wonderful music?

The music was the music of the knives.

*

The soldier put his hands, still sticky with in Tommy's blood, into the canvas rucksack, and they found the hilts of the knives. And when he touched the knives, he knew, as a man knows how to breathe, what he must do to live or to die.

The knives sang of living and dying and much more.

So, the soldier waited …

The knives' music was a quiet, conscious thing, alert and ready, a thing that took the soldier into itself.

And when the knives, their music, and the soldier found the beginning, then it began …

*

When it was over, the soldier had lived, and the other men around him had died and had given their blood to the knives.

The music of the knives was a carol of fulfillment and joy.

*

The solider was cleaning the knives when his countrymen found him.

*

When Eisenhower and his generals gave Torgau to the Russkies, the war was over except for the paper-signing.

The soldier was shipped to headquarters, Frankfurt am Main, to wait for demobilization.

*

Some 'Big Wheel' had decided that a G.I. needed a score of eighty-five to be considered for a trip back to the States.

That was the rule; there was no bellyachin'. Anyone who didn't like it ... well, they could talk to the chaplain, and it would still be the rule.

But by December, the rule had changed, and any enlisted man with fifty points and four years of service could get a boat-ride home.

*

The soldier had no one at home to go back to, so he volunteered to stay.

That was how the soldier finally made it all the way to Berlin, with the knives in his pack.

*

The Russkies blockaded the city a few years later to force the Americans, British, and French out, but the 'airlift' fixed that.

Just as Germany had been divided by its conquerors, its capital city had been divided too. For another fifteen years, or so, the dividing line was a mark on the map, but then that mark was made into a wall.

*

The soldier was a soldier no more, but he was stationed in Berlin, working for a new bunch of letters, something called the CIA.

The man who had been a soldier stayed in Berlin and loved it. He had a little apartment in Schöneberg, not far from the gardens that the Germans called Botanischer Garten und Botanisches Museum. Even though many of the greenhouses that protected the most tropical of the plants in the collection had been destroyed in the shelling when the city had been liberated, the man liked to walk through the trees and beautiful outdoor plants of the arboretum. It was, he figured, about the size of fifty football fields.

*

His work for the CIA was boring but steady ... except for 'Operation Brass'.

*

Almost as soon as the man got to Berlin and began working for 'The Company' (not the 'John Company' of the Raj ... a different, but equally powerful and secretive "Company"), the East German Ministry for State Security, the Stasi, the bastard step-child of the KGB, wanted to compromise the CIA's employees in Berlin. The Stasi sent a number of women to seduce Americans. The soldier alerted his CIA bosses the first time this happened.

He was walking along the Ku-dam, the fanciest street in Berlin, East or West, one evening and was propositioned by a tall blonde. She was stunning. She told him what she would do for him and she told him her price. He told her that he was not carrying money but that he would be happy to meet her another evening.

Most whores in Berlin waited for their clients to approach them and make their specific needs known.

So he told the chief agent the next morning. 'The Company' set up a meeting.

The man met the woman and took her to a little apartment on Wielandstrasse, a block from where she plied her trade.

The man sat on the bed and took the ten marks she had agreed upon out of his wallet. As he did so, she walked to the window and opened and shut the drapes … twice.

Then she turned to him, took off her jacket, slipped off her heels, smiled, and began to unbutton her blouse. She was beautiful, everything a healthy young German woman should be! Except that she had set him up. A minute later, no more, the door was pushed open and three big, ugly, very muscular men strode into the room, each holding a PM, the nasty little blow-back 'Pistolet Mrakova' that the Russians used.

The man sat very still while the woman began to re-button her blouse.

Then the lights went out, and as he had been told, the man who had once been a soldier dove for the floor.

There were shots and a scuffle, and when the lights went on again, a long minute later, two of the pistol-carrying intruders were dead, and the remaining interloper and the woman were standing, secured in handcuffs, within a circle of four plain-clothed, obviously American men.

One of the Americans said, "Thanks, buddy," that the man understood that was his cue to leave.

*

Once Kennedy had called himself a jelly doughnut without a hole ("Ich bin ein Berliner"), the man knew it was time to go.

*

The man would receive adequate retirement pay, and he was still young enough to work if he chose to. He was tired of winters. So he decided to go back to the good ol' U.S.A. and find a stretch of sand to call his own in the nation's newest state, Hawaii.

So the man bought a ticket on the Hamburg Atlantic Line's new *TS Hanseatic* and arrived in the Big Apple after a restful cruise of a little less than a week.

The ship docked at North River Pier 88, and the man disembarked and found himself on 46th street.

He had done some reading and thought that he might hop a train at Grand Central Station, ride the rails to Chicago, and then hop aboard the "Silver Lady", the California Zephyr, and head for Oakland, not in small part because of the leggy and legendary "Zephyrettes".

*

The man was excited! He walked east toward 42nd Street and Park Avenue, enjoying the walk and the tall buildings of Manhattan. He had to remind himself that he was just an old retired fella in the big city. The man laughed to think of it.

Before he had gone a block, he noticed a very attractive woman standing on the corner, crying, a portfolio lying on the ground at her feet.

The man had been raised by his mother to be a gentleman, and a gentleman would always help a lady in distress.

So the man walked up to her and asked her if he could help.

She looked up at him with her two tear-filled, beautiful blue eyes and said, "Oh, I don't know what to do."

The man asked her, as any Good Samaritan would, "What's wrong, Miss?" and gave her the clean, white handkerchief that he had taken from his coat pocket to wipe her tears away.

She said, "Thank you," and wiped her cute little nose. And then she explained, "I have to get this portfolio to my boss in Boston by tonight. We came to New York City for a meeting today, and he went ahead on the train after lunch. I was walking down the street here when some man bumped into me and grabbed my purse with my train ticket and all of my money and my driver's license in it …," and she began to cry again.

The man became bolder, patted the woman gently on the back, and said, "There, there. It's going to be alright."

"No, it won't," she said between her tears, with the most endearing, little hiccups, "If I'm not there, in Boston, with this portfolio, tonight at nine, I'll lose my job and everything!"

The man thought for a minute and made a decision. "I could loan you the money for a ticket, Miss. Then you could get there on time," he offered.

She stopped crying, wiped her nose again, looked up at him, again, with those gorgeous eyes, and said, in the sweetest little voice, "Oh, no. I couldn't. I just couldn't."

"Sure you could," the man said, "It would just be a loan, and you could send me the money when you get home."

"You'd trust a stranger like that?" she said, pausing, "But I just couldn't."

The man didn't know what to say, but before he could say anything more, the woman said, "I could do some clerical work for you … you know …" and she winked.

The man was shocked … but intrigued. He had no plans, other than Hawaii, and the woman was pretty and vulnerable and willing.

Then she said, "I take dictation, $20 for twenty pages," and licked her beautifully-full, red lips, "or fifty pages of typing for $50 if you buy me dinner afterwards," and she smoothed her dress over her shapely hips.

The man had been born at night but not last night. As the light dawned in his eyes, the woman said, "C'mon," took his hand, and led him down the block.

*

The man went upstairs with the woman, and after she had closed and locked the door, she disrobed and strutted around the room. The man put down his suitcase and took off his coat. He had pulled out his wallet, searching for a picture of Mr. Franklin, when everything went black.

*

When he woke up, the man's head hurt, and when he touched the back of his head, it stung; his hand came away bloody. He sat up woozily and stayed sitting on the floor for a while. When he could stand, he did. His suitcase was gone; he felt his pockets and found that his wallet was gone, too.

But he had lived in Berlin for twenty years, so he was no rube.

He could feel the re-assuring touch of his money-belt, under his shirt, hugging his waist. He unbuttoned his shirt and took off the belt. When he opened it, sure enough, there was his passport, his other papers, and the $2,000 he had saved.

His suitcase had had little of value in it except for the knives. They had saved his life once, and they were very old, so they would have been worth some money to a museum or a collector he supposed.

"Well," he thought, "what's done is done. A man can't have everything."

He put his clothes back on and left as quietly as he could (no sense getting the cops involved in this one) and finished his walk to 89 E 42nd St.

"California, and Hawaii, here I come!" he sang to himself as he walked east.

Chapter 21 – The Devil

Another of the Major Arcana of the Suit of Knives in the Swordsmith's Tarot is The Devil. The number of The Devil is six which represents voluntary bondage to mundane, unclean things, as opposed to devotion to the spirituality of a greater Goodness. This card in the Swordsmith's Tarot is ruled by Capricorn, the goat, a lustful animal that is consumed by the negative and sensual forces that seek to imprison mankind.

The Devil reversed proclaims that despair, pessimism, and powerlessness are merely illusions, spawned by fear and false beliefs.

To free oneself from the influence of The Devil is not easy; it requires commitment and courage, but once begun, this journey is possible and becomes more natural and more straightforward the further one travels along its path and remains faithful to the goal of freedom.

But not every man will achieve this goal and defeat The Devil, and the belief that any man is sure to defeat the forces of The Devil is another kind of blasphemy, a kind that The Devil appreciates.

*

Bill 'Wild Boy' Seward, the man who had hit the man over the head with the sock he had filled with a couple of rolls of nickels before he had stolen the man's wallet and suitcase gave the hooker half of the money that was in the sucker's wallet.

He told her, "Take a little walk, Sugar," and he kept the suitcase.

'Wild Boy' had done this before and knew a guy (who knew a guy) who would buy ID, clothes, watches, and other interesting things.

So, he took the suitcase and his part of the wallet loot to the little rent-controlled room he rented by the month up in Spanish Harlem.

He tossed the suitcase onto his bed and locked the door.

*

Then, 'Wild Boy' opened the refrigerator and pulled out the metal ice tray where he kept his works: the two needles he had stolen from the clinic, the rubber sucking part of the baby's pacifier, a length of rubber tubing, a rubber band, and an eyedropper.

He carried the tray into the kitchen and put it on the table. He found a teaspoon in a drawer and a glass, that he filled half-full of hot water (he had to wait a minute for that), in the sink.

He pulled the eyedropper apart first. Then he put it down and reached into his pocket for his wallet. It was almost empty, but there was what he needed still in there: a dollar bill. 'Wild Boy' tore a corner off of the bill to make the needle's 'collar' in the end of the eyedropper. Then, he slid the pacifier onto the other end of the dropper and secured it with the rubber band.

'Wild Boy' felt like shit. His nose was beginning to run, and he felt achy, like he was coming down with the flu. He laughed at that thought; he was coming down with the 'I need a God-damned fix!'

He went to the bathroom and pulled the Luden's cough drops tin from the medicine cabinet and opened it. The junk was there, one little $3 bag, just enough for what he needed, but then he would have to score.

He took the envelope back to the table. He was starting to feel the shakes … but not too badly just yet.

The water in the glass was still warm.

He tore open the glassine envelope and carefully poured the powder into the bowl of the spoon. He laid the spoon on the table, taking special care not to knock it and send the heroin flying.

He tore the envelope open so that it was flat and licked the paper. Yeah! There was just the slightest taste of the junk, a little numbing of the tip of his tongue.

Then, 'Wild Boy' pressed the air out of the pacifier on the syringe and stuck the other end into the warm water. He released the pressure and watched the water be sucked into the glass of the dropper.

Then, he slowly squeezed the water from the syringe into the spoon, and when the spoon was full, he turned the dropper away and squeezed the pacifier, squirting the rest of the water out across the room.

He watched the junk dissolve in the warm water, and satisfied that all was as it should be, he put the end of the needle back into the liquid in the spoon and sucked it in.

When the dropper was full, 'Wild Boy' laid the syringe back on the table.

He found the rubber tubing and tied it tightly around his wrist. He squeezed his hand, making a fist, until he saw the vein on the top of his thumb grow visible.

'Wild Boy' had used the veins in the other parts of his arm so often that they were getting difficult to find. No matter, this would work. It had worked before.

He finished and sat at the table, enjoying the rush.

He was able to get the needle out of his hand, get over to the armchair, and get comfortable, before he began to nod.

*

When he woke up, he wasn't hurting yet, but he knew that he would.

"Let's see what's in the suitcase," 'Wild Boy' thought.

Clothes, a shaving kit, a Bible, a nice pair of shoes ... the junkie tried the shoes on ... too small. All of these things could be easily sold or bartered; he knew the right people for that.

And then, 'Wild Boy' Seward found the knives.

*

"These are two strange, odd things," he thought, turning them over in his hands.

He felt a vibration as he examined them and thought, "Damn! I need a hit, and I'm out. I've got to sell these and score."

*

The man who held the knives couldn't, or wouldn't, acknowledge them. They sang to him, but he didn't seem to hear. They had never encountered a man, except for the dead ones, who was deaf to their music. Maybe this man was dead and didn't know it yet, they thought. They decided that they would wait until they met someone who could hear them before they sang again.

*

'Wild Boy' took the knives to the 'Pawn Lady'. She would almost always buy what he had to sell, unless what he had to sell was covered in blood, or a gun (that had probably been used in a robbery or a murder), or something she couldn't hope to sell to someone else for a profit.

He showed her the knives.

She sat behind the locked cage and pulled them inside, looking them over, one at a time.

"Where the hell did you get something like this? Did you rob the Met?" she asked him, half-laughing and half-serious.

"Found 'em … over on 53rd." he told her.

"Found 'em on 53rd. Uh-huh," the woman nodded in bored disbelief.

"Yeah," he said, beginning to get itchy and anxious, "What'll you give me for 'em?"

"Who the fuck am I gonna sell these to, you dumb fuck?" the 'Pawn Lady' said, "These have flashing red lights all over 'em. They just shout, 'I'm stolen! I'm fucking stolen!'"

*

The two of them argued, loudly enough to frighten other customers out of the pawnshop.

After fifteen minutes of yelling, 'Wild Boy' threatened to leave.

That's when the 'Pawn Lady' offered him ten bucks.

After 'Wild Boy' had spit on her floor in disgust and then offered to clean it up when she said she would never buy any of his shit ever again, the 'Pawn Lady' offered him a dirty rag to clean the floor. When he had cleaned up his spittle and phlegm, she offered him $30.

"That's hardly nothing'," he said, his feelings hurt.

"If you don't think that's enough, you can take 'em and leave, you junkie fuck," she told him.

Thirty bucks wasn't much; hell it wasn't hardly anything, but he was beginning to hurt, and he needed to cop. And thirty bucks would get him through today and, maybe, tomorrow.

It was just enough to get him high.

*

So 'Wild Boy' left the pawnshop, six five-dollar bills in his pocket and ran to the IRT at Hunter College, about two blocks from the 'Pawn Lady's' place. He ran down the steps and jumped the turn-style, and it was just his luck, there was an express waiting for him, doors just about to close.

Seven stops, and he got off at Lexington and One Hundred Twenty-Fifth Street; he had to meet a man.

'Wild Boy' waited outside the brownstone and endured the stares of the Negroes who didn't want him there, messing with their women.

His friend was late; he was never early. He was dressed in black and wore a straw hat, but when he finally arrived and led 'Wild Boy' up to the third floor, showed him the works ("Nah, man, I got my own. Thanks!"), and gave him a little taste, the Seward paid his friend $15 for five $3 glassine bags of that fine Turkish shit. And as soon as he had it in his hand, he left … he had no time to waste.

And he still had $15 for tomorrow (he knew that if he had bought tomorrow's junk today, it would all be gone today, and there would be nothing for tomorrow when he would really need it).

*

When he got back to his building, an old Negro was sitting on the building's front steps, strumming a guitar. It looked like some shitty Monkey Ward thing, but the man had his guitar case open in front of him, hoping for tips.

The man sang in a gravely, tobacco-stained voice, "Me and the Devil was walking side-by-side. I'm going to beat my woman until I get satisfied…"

As 'Wild Boy' walked by, he looked into the case … two quarters, two nickels, a dime and four old pennies … seventy-four cents … and thought "Hell, old man, the Devil's walking with me, too, right here in my pocket." And he laughed, thinking about how damn high he was going to get. He didn't bother thinking about how he didn't have a woman to beat.

*

'Wild Boy' Seward walked into his apartment and locked the door. He prepared the junk, shot it into his vein, and died.

The heroin was much better than he had expected it to be.

Chapter 22 – Nine of Knives

The ninth card of the Minor Arcana of the Suit of Knives in the Swordsmith's Tarot is the Nine of Knives. This card reminds you that, as close as you may be to victory, there will always be another test, threat, or confrontation. Perseverance, determination, and resilience are the armor of the Nine of Knives.

While there may be only a little darkness ahead before a glorious dawn, the Great Wheel of Life promises that more darkness will always follow the light. The warrior who is patient and vigilant will prosper in the face of the adversity that lies ahead, but sometimes, he won't.

When this card is reversed, the walls you have erected to protect yourself from life's challenges may prove to serve as a cage that limits your opportunities. What has grieved you in the past can be transformed into your delight if you choose to commit yourself to the struggle of its destruction.

In its very worst manifestation, the reversed Nine of Knives will reveal, formerly hidden feelings of being under physical, emotional, or spiritual assault. This is not silly paranoia or a misunderstood fear. While good counsel or psychological healing are always beneficial, when these feelings are evinced, defend yourself! The bastards may well be out to get you.

*

The deed to the pawnshop was in the name of Francesca Baker, but no one had called Frankie that since her mother had died in St. Louis, many years before; the deed was to the pawnshop and the rest of the building, lock, stock and six floors of apartments that she rented to missionaries from Utah and members of the Salvation Army. Those people never gave Frankie any shit.

She couldn't say that about the men she took up with.

Frankie was a gentle soul who just happened to have a knack for business, a will of steel, and a keen insight into the souls of men – unfortunately, this did not extend to the men's intentions concerning her.

As a business woman, she held herself and everyone she worked with to the highest standards.

As a strong woman who would allow no one to push her around, she stood immobile.

As a judge of truth and lies (unless those lies and truth had to do with her heart), she possessed the keenest of insight.

*

So when the knives came into her possession, she took them home (that is to her apartment on the top floor of the building that housed the pawnshop), cleaned them and polished them, and learned all that she could about them. She set them in a place of honor on the sideboard that her dear, departed mother had left her.

One day, Frankie took the morning off and a cab to the Metropolitan Museum of Art. She had an old friend, Dr. Bashford Dean, who was the curator of the Department of Arms and Armor. She told 'Bash' about the knives, and he told her what he knew of 'notational knives' and that the best collection of them was found at the Victoria and Albert in London. She thanked him, gave him a hug, and asked him if he would have time to take a short vacation to London with her. He was a terribly shy gentleman who appreciated her flirtation, and her proposition brought a blush to his cheek, but he demurred with the excuse that he had more work to do than he had hours to do it in. She bid him a good morning and returned to her new treasures.

At night, the knives were her only companions, but like any new friend, she found common interests with them to bring them closer. She sang the songs that had been carved into their blades. While she was ashamed that her singing voice was thin and reedy and not fit for people to hear, the knives didn't care; they heard what her soul sang to them, and they reveled in that music.

Frankie had no animal companions (except for men who she occasionally let into her heart) who lived with her in her apartment, no fluffy cats, no whiny lapdogs, no colorful fishes, no chirping birds … just the knives; once she had gotten to know them, though, they were the only companionship that she required.

And the knives appreciated her friendship and quietly considered how best to repay her kindness and care.

*

It took the knives a while, but they finally decided upon a way to show their gratitude.

*

Frankie had often cried herself to sleep before the knives had come to live with her. Her tears were always due to the cruelty, the rudeness, or the insensitivity of a man, of different men, who she had decided to invite into her heart and into her bed (that was what men liked, it seemed).

When the knives had come to live with Frankie, she hadn't had a man in her life for a while, so she had had no reason to cry for a while.

And then, one day, a man came to the pawnshop, did all of the things that a man might do that endears men to women, and treated her (she thought at the time) the way a woman should be treated.

So, naturally, Frankie gave her heart to that man, too.

It was wonderful for a while.

And then, on another day, a few weeks later, Frankie found a lacy handkerchief in the man's coat pocket. It was not a style that she had ever owned (or would ever consider owning), and the perfume that scented it was not a fragrance that she would ever wear. As a matter of fact, the scent made her sneeze when she discovered it.

She asked the man where it had come from, and he lied to her.

He lied so poorly and so flagrantly that it was as if he were yelling at her, "You fool! You stupid, fucking fool!!!"

Her heart broke, right then, into tiny pieces, different tiny pieces than it had broken into before when it had been shattered by the other men who had broken her heart, but it was as utterly broken as it had ever been.

Frankie had thought that her heart would be stronger this time, but she was mistaken.

In tears, she told the man to go and never return.

The man responded by laughing and then said a number of very cruel things before he slammed the door so hard that the glass in it cracked.

The knives, even though they were not in the room where Frankie's heart was breaking, knew what had happened, and they decided that revenge was an appropriate response.

Vengeance was what Frankie truly deserved, and vengeance was the knives' area of expertise and what they were created for.

So the knives gladly helped Frankie.

*

So, with the help of the knives, Frankie hunted down the men who had used her so shamelessly, treated her so badly, and broken her heart so heartlessly. Just as Frankie had taught them some of the music that she knew, the knives taught Frankie to sing their songs.

*

After the knives suggested revenge and explained its joys and pleasures, Frankie decided that if she were to do this thing that the knives were encouraging her to do, she would do it right.

She went shopping.

Frankie bought five cute, black shift dresses with bateau necklines with mid-calf-length hemlines and five pairs of adorable, black leather Mary Quant low-cut shoes (with red-flocked hearts dotting them and sturdy, non-slip soles). She scoured the thrift shops until she found five nondescript dusters, some made of canvas and others made of oilskin, and five dark, slouchy, equally-bland fedoras. The Knives suggested something cheerier for her underthings, so she went to Bamberger's and bought five light blue pairs of panties with big yellow polka dots all over them and five matching bras. She went to the store across the street from Bloomie's and found five pairs of cheap, imitation leather gloves that fit her just fine. Alexander's could always be counted upon to have what she was looking for; how lucky could a girl get? She asked the Knives about jewelry, and they said nothing, so she decided that they were right. It would be too much.

But the knives had agreed that they would be pleased to be carried in one of those 'hippie' Indian cotton shoulder bags with all of the little mirrors embroidered all over it. So Frankie went to the

Village and found a couple of them, one mostly maroon and the other a deep, forest green.

*

Johnny lived in Queens in a little upstairs apartment on the corner of Rampart and Dumaine. Johnny had told her that he always left for his job at the paint store about five minutes until eight (he had told her that he refused to be late for work, but he damned sure wasn't about to get there early). Frankie got to his apartment early and waited outside his door.

He walked out of the door and turned around to lock it when she called his name. He turned to see who had spoken … and she pulled out the knife from the bag under her coat and cut him down like a dog where he stood. She walked away, with the knives singing their joyful song to her, as he bled out onto the sidewalk.

Frankie walked to the Bel Aire Diner in Astoria, it was only a few blocks, and dumped her duster and hat in a garbage can behind a barbershop across the street. The she straightened her dress, walked into the diner, found a seat at the counter, and ordered chocolate chip pancakes and a cup of coffee. After she had paid and left a generous tip, she left the diner, walked down Broadway to the subway station on 31st Street. She took the train back to Manhattan, got off at her stop, and walked the block to her apartment.

Then Frankie changed her clothes and went downstairs to open the pawn shop just a little bit later than usual.

*

Albert Britt lived at 212 Targee St. on Staten Island in an industrial warehouse near the Silver Lake section of the borough.

Frankie finally found the dump, and she walked around to the back of the building, after finding no door in the front or the side. In back, at a loading dock, she found an unlocked door.

She went inside and looked around in the gloom. It was too dark to see clearly, but she did notice an office up at the top of a rickety staircase up by the roof of the building with light shining through dirty windows. It was one of those little rooms that allowed the boss to look down on his workers and check on them.

Her footsteps on the metal stairs seemed, to Frankie, to clang and echo terribly, and she thought that Albert would hear someone coming up the stairs. But as she neared the door to the little room, she heard the unmistakable racket of a radio, or stereo, turned up LOUD! She listened as she trudged up the last steps … "Hotel California" … God! How she hated the fucking Eagles! This took the fucking cake! He had dumped her, and now he spent his time sitting in a little metal room listening to some vapid '80s arena rock instead of returning the love of a good woman.

Now, Frankie was getting angry!

As she kicked the thin aluminum door to the cracker-box office open, she yelled, "Fucking laid-back, limp-dicked, L.A. bullshit, Urban Cowboy, poser Country, elevator music. I should have known!" and when Albert turned blearily around in his swivel chair to see who was making all of the racket, Frankie walked right over to him, and without a practice swing chopped his fucking head right the fuck off!

"Hell, yeah!" she thought.

And then she saw the bag of white powder on the desk. She stuck a fingernail into the bag, stuck out her tongue, and touched the powder to the tip. Almost instantly, her tongue and most of her mouth went numb. Coke! And pretty good coke at that.

Frankie wiped the bloody knife blade on Albert's shirt, now that his torso was slumped back in the chair, returned the knife to the bag under her coat, reached for the baggie, sealed it, put it into the bag with the knives, and left the way she had come in.

She walked down Broad Street to the Stapleton elevated station and took the Staten Island Railway to St. George and then the Staten Island Ferry to Manhattan. When she reached the Port Authority and left the ferry, she hailed a cab and told the driver to take her to too Delmonico's.

When she got out of the cab, she took off her duster and her hat and folded them up, outside in, to hide any errant splashes of Albert's blood.

The maître'd seated her promptly, and she asked where she might find the ladies' room. She went in and straight to a stall, shoving the coat and hat behind the toilet.

Frankie returned to her table and ordered the Dover sole with a little Caesar salad and a tall glass of ice water with a lime wedge. It was delicious. She left a hundred-dollar bill on the table (the rhubarb crème brûlée looked wonderful, but she was full and pretty tired after her outing). She took the subway home.

As she washed and dried the knives, she turned on WPIX, 101.9 FM, and listened half to the news and half to the songs that the knives sang for her.

*

Frankie walked into the pub on York Avenue in Manhattan and found Bill Bailey standing up at the bar, nursing a beer, and said in a voice loud enough for everyone to hear, "Bill, you done me wrong!"

Then she slipped the knife out of her bag, let it hang point-down toward the floor for half a heartbeat, and then swung the blade up from the floor between his legs. The blade cut easily though skin and muscle and a variety of organs, finally sticking at the bottom of his sternum, unable to cut any further.

After Bill fell to the floor, she put a foot next to the blade for leverage and yanked the steel out of him. Then she walked calmly out of the door, turned right, and ducked into the laundromat next door. She hurried out the back into the grass and trees of what had once been an alley behind those old buildings and walked quickly west until she came out onto First Avenue. Then, Frankie walked south, just fifty feet or so to 84th Street, turned right, and hurried over to Second Avenue (ditching her coat in a dumpster behind the apartments at 84th and Second), turning left onto the Avenue.

There was the M15 bus paused at the bus-stop there, so she ran and hopped in through the doors just as they were closing. She took the bus to 36th Street where she got off and walked over to Keen's where she got a nice table and ordered a Butter Lettuce house salad (with balsamic vinaigrette), mutton chops, and creamed spinach.

She realized that she was ravenous!

After she had finished with her dinner, she paid the check, tipped the handsome waiter too much, and left the restaurant.

It was a lovely evening, not too cool, so she walked home, quietly harmonizing with the knives to entertain herself and them and to pass the time.

*

Frankie found Allen in his house on Dooley Street in Brooklyn.

She knocked politely on his front door and waited patiently until he answered.

"What the hell do you want, Frankie," he sneered.

"Do you see this, Allen," she answered, moving the knife so that he knew that it was what she meant.

"Yeah," he said (he was never one for deep thinking).

"Good," Frankie said and jammed the point of the knife into Allen's right eye and into his brain, "Too bad that was the last thing you'll ever see."

When he fell to the floor, his body blocked the doorway. She stepped in over him and, when she was inside, grabbed one of his hands at the wrist. She pulled his body far enough into the house so that she could close the door. She checked the doorknob, and when she found the little button to lock it, she nodded to herself, pushed in the button, checked that the door would be locked, stepped back out the door, and closed it behind her.

She had planned to return to Manhattan the way she had come, via the BMT at the Sheepshead Bay station, but killing these bastards always seemed to make her hungry.

On her way to Allen's house, she had noticed that Delmar Pizza was just a block from the subway station. So on the way back to the station, she stopped there, ordered a small pie, 'Grandma's Style', and a coke. It tasted terrific, but there was much too much pizza for her to eat at one sitting. She finished two slices and asked for a box. She thanked the nice people and took her leftovers home on the train.

*

Charles Silver was standing out front of his little row house on Burke Avenue in the Bronx when Frankie called to him. He looked confused, at first, but his curiosity overcame him, and he walked over to where she stood.

"Charles," she said companionably, "It's been so long. How have you been?"

"Fine, Frankie," he said, a smile trying to decide whether or not to place itself on Charles' lips.

"Too bad, Charles," she said, shaking her head, "I've been miserable."

She took the knife out of the pocket of her raincoat and jammed it under his chin on the right side of his neck, managing to sever his carotid artery and clip his brainstem in the same jab.

"But," she said as he died before he hit the ground, "I'm feeling better now."

She turned, wiped the knife off on his windbreaker, and replaced the blade in the bag she carried inside her coat. Then she walked west to the Burke Avenue Station of the IRT and headed back into Manhattan.

After she took a shower, she put on a pretty dress and went out for Chinese.

*

When she was finally finished getting her revenge on the last bastard, she cleaned and polished the knives and then called on a regular pawn customer of hers, a retired cabinet-maker. She commissioned a cherry-wood case for the knives, lined with blood-red velvet (at their request) for the knives to rest in. The cabinet-maker was as loyal as the day is long, and he was eighty-seven years old when he made the box. The secret of its making and of its contents died with him in his sleep a couple of years later.

*

Frankie put the knives away and returned to the pawn business.

*

But once a week, on Sundays, she would cook a beef tenderloin. Then she would invite the knives to her dine with her.

She ate the beef bloody and used the knives to carve and serve the meat as they had been meant to do. After she finished eating, she would pick the knives up, one at a time, and sing each of their songs with them as the blood dripped off of them and onto the platter. She taught them other songs, ones that she knew and loved, as well, mostly Broadway show-tunes and some Elvis (she sang his in the lowest register that she could manage until she could sing no more because of her laughter).

*

The three friends lived happily together for many, many years.

Chapter 23 – The Stars

Another of the Major Arcana of the Suit of Knives in the Swordsmith's Tarot is The Stars. The Stars in the Swordsmith's Tarot is governed by Aquarius and is a manifestation of the number 17.

Aquarius is a sign of the Air, and a an Aquarian woman is a tempestuous being, full of might and power that is as easily seen as the wind but as clearly felt as a Norther or a snow-eating Chinook. The calm in the eye of the hurricane that is a woman is a place of gentleness, peace, and sharp independence.

And just like a woman, the number Seventeen is complex. Numerologically, seventeen equals eight (one + seven), a number of Strength, composed of the number one (that represents the primal Force of Life) and the lucky number seven (although this 'luck' is due as much to the vagaries of good fortune as it is to intelligence, intuition, knowledge, perseverance, grace, and spirit).

The stars are the blessings of the Universe, and The Stars in the Swordsmith's Tarot bless the one who reads the Tarot. While there have been difficulties and challenges in the past, The Stars indicates a transformation. The hatred, bitterness, and vengeance that once were once all-consuming have been swept away by healing zephyrs into a place of peace and contentment.

If you listen to the soft voices that speak to you, your heart will open to them and accept their encouragement and respect. Just as they share their gifts with you, you should happily reciprocate and bless them and others with your compassion and generosity.

When The Stars is reversed, negativity and discouragement abound, but within this disheartenment, the seeds of awakening sleep, waiting for you to remember to look up again to the Heavens and once again see the glory that can be yours.

*

Frankie died one day when she was ninety-four, and the knives sang her favorite songs to her as she finally slipped away.

After Frankie went softly into the night, the building she owned was tied up in lawsuits for a number of years as a number of especially-unscrupulous developers fought for the right to tear the old apartment building down and put something new and shiny where it had once stood.

The tenants who had lived happily in Frankie's building while she was alive were allowed to stay, by the terms of her will, rent-free for as long as the legal wrangling continued.

All of Frankie's belongings and all of the inventory in the pawn shop were also held up, undisposed of, until one of the unscrupulous men did something even more unscrupulous than he usually did and was arrested for it. The man's businesses and family were investigated by both the IRS and the Attorneys General of the states of New York, New Jersey, and Nevada (and, oddly enough, by the Prosecutor General of Macao, as well as the Attorney General of the Constitutional Court of the Federal Republic of Somalia) and found to be little more than cheaply-constructed shell games of moving money here and there to evade and avoid all sorts of debts and taxes. Once this man was out of the way (quietly serving twenty at Ossining), and his company, such as it was (or appeared to be), had been removed from the bidding on and lawsuits over the building, there was finally a winner. Actually, there were a number of winners.

The first winner was the developer who won the right to buy the building. He immediately gave the tenants their notice and tore the thing down, replacing it with a thirty-eight-story eyesore, a Carbuncle Cup award-winning homage to Rolfe Judd's 'car crash façade' of Saffron Square (without the joyous clash of multi-colored panels to liven it up), that housed the world-wide home offices of Mega-Dollar World, Inc. on the upper thirty floors, above four floors of robot-controlled parking garage, and a bottom four floors of Mega-Dollar World's flagship store.

The inventory of the pawn shop and Frankie's personal effects were sent to an estate auction company, where the whole she-bang was expected to take in about $12,000. Frankie's will stipulated that all of money that her estate generated would be donated to the next winners: the organizations, the Missions and the Salvation Army, who had provided her with such excellent tenants for such a very long time. The auction company tore through the pawnshop's items, and sold most of them at the first, low bid that they received. There was little interest in those things.

A man who was paid, and paid well, for such things, perked up when a beautifully-crafted wooden case came up for bids at the auction. The case was exquisite, and its contents were remarkable: two five-hundred year-old knives, both in superb condition, both engraved in an unusual and unique manner.

The man won the bidding at $1,000. It was, he thought, a bargain.

The man took his purchase to his employer, the third winner: Aries Brown, the Oligarch of Manhattan.

*

Mr. Aries Brown was a man who, although he owned a great chunk of the Earth (and many of the people who walked on that chunk), wanted nothing more than the stars. And he would have them, too, he had told himself every day and every night since he had been six years old.

Chapter 24 – The Ten of Knives

The tenth card of the Minor Arcana of the Suit of Knives in the Swordsmith's Tarot is the Ten of Knives. In a Tarot reading, tens represent reaching a culmination after surviving difficult challenges. So the Ten of Knives suggests reaping the consequences of that victory.

With any achievement comes responsibilities and commitments, and the struggle begins anew. And with the renewed effort and new goals, new adversaries and new obstacles become arrayed against you. External forces oppress you, and your only recourse is to draw upon the inner reserves that have sustained you so far.

But, one way or another, this will pass; you will live and continue to contend against all that assails you, or you will die and will have no more need or ability to do so.

The Ten of Knives reminds us that we have made a Procrustean bed for ourselves and that we must lie in it.

*

Mr. Aires Brown was an easily identifiable man for a man who easily-resembled some (or many) of the people who lived in the borough he called home.

Mr. Aries Brown shaved his head (he had since he was twelve and puberty had come knocking on his door) every morning (well, one of his well-paid staff shaved it for him now), and it had been rumored that other parts of him were as shiny smooth as his pate (no one ... NO ONE ... who was breathing or intended to continue to breathe would comment on that rumor).

Mr. Aries Brown was tall and cadaverous, except for his massive pot-belly (it was not a beer belly; he never drank beer although he was fond of ginger ale).

Mr. Aries Brown wore suits that matched his surname. And ties that didn't. His shoes were chosen from his remarkable collection of crispy crepes, from a pair of light blue All-Court P.F. Flyers (because 'Everything you do is more fun with PF') to Ox Ash and Autumn Undefeated x Converse Pro Leathers, black Super PRO-Keds, Kurt Cobain Signatures, Carafe and Whisper White Puma Clydes, Midnight Suede Lakai Vincents, Deep Lake blue Adidas Busenitz Pro Skates, Chocolate One Star 74s, blue and gold (with the TCMFB lightning bolt on each heel) Adidas RoMcNasty 84-Labs, White and Cardinal Addidas 'Shelltoes', Sunflower Chucks, and Puma Suede Classics in Flame Scarlet and Sulphur Spring. A salesman once tried to sell him a pair of Yeezys (the color doesn't matter), and Mr. Aries Brown broke the man's nose (Mr. Aries Brown wouldn't let ANY-one insult him like that!).

*

Mr. Aries Brown got his start running errands from everyone he could find who had an errand to run: food cart guys, stock brokers, commuters with offices near Grand Central, Jewish diamond merchants, Harlem drug dealers. Back in those days, he was simply Aries Brown.

Aries Brown didn't care whose errand he ran, but he was fast, and efficient, and honest, and kept his mouth completely shut (and his ears and eyes completely open). He was a quick and nimble learner, and he put all of the things that he learned to good use. By the time he was sixteen, he was relied upon by almost every industry, legal or not-so-much, in every one of the five boroughs.

So, one day, when he delivered a package for Alexandre Khazeray, a nice old Jewish man, Aries Brown asked if he could be paid with a diamond instead of cash. This request intrigued the old man, and he reached into his pocket and pulled out a little leather pouch, asked the boy to hold out his hand, and carefully shook five tiny, little sparkling stones into the boy's palm.

The old man looked at them, picked two of them up and put them back into the pouch, and then said, "Choose the one you would like."

Aires Brown had no loupe, so he asked to borrow the old man's. This took the old Jew by surprise, but he chuckled, reached into his vest, pulled out his much-used Zeiss 10x Triplet, and handed it to the boy.

Aries Brown thanked the man, put the magnifier to his eye, and began with the first chip of crystal.

"This one's just shlok, sir. It's second-rate merchandise, nothing more," he said and gave it back to the man.

The boy looked at the second stone, muttered to himself, "It's loupe clean" and put it down, and then he took the third stone and spent longer with it than he had with the other two.

And when the boy was finished, he said to the old man, "This last one is a bluff stone, impressive, but not very valuable, I don't think. The second one is strop. It's probably been sitting in the back of your safe for a long time. I'll take that one, it may be strop, but people can get rich on strops."

The old Jew nodded and stuck out his hand. The boy and the old man shook hands on the deal.

"Mazel und brucha," Aries Brown said.

Mr. Khazeray said, "Good luck and a blessing to you, too, young man. I hope that we can continue to do business."

*

Aires Brown also listened to the stock brokers talk, and when they left their copies of the *Journal* or *The Economist* or *The Financial Times* lying on the benches in Broad Street Station or in Nevelson Park or in the trash cans near Bobby Van's at lunchtime, Aires Brown grabbed them and made them his daily reading.

And from what he learned from reading and listening and watching, he purchased DRIPs (dividend re-investment plans) with a broker he ran for.

From the dealers who sold their wares (coke, and speed, and pot, and occasionally heroin) to the brokers, Ariel Brown took his pay, alternately in their wares and in cash.

He ran for the lawyers, listened to them and watched them, and then he shared what he discovered with the brokers and the Real Estate dealers. He ran a tab with the legal-eagles and an escrow account (that grew like Topsy) with the bankers and the realtors.

*

Aries Brown lived in a tiny little room that had once been a closet for a really well-dressed crossdresser who eventually became very famous in a very-very off-off-off-Broadway cabaret.

*

Aries Brown shared his coke with the musicians and the actors and the drag queens, he shared his pot with the artists and artisans, he shared his speed with blue collar workers all over the City who became his extra eyes and ears, and he shared his junk with Emergency room doctors and anesthesiologists (and through them, and their referrals to their colleagues, received first-class medical care with no co-pay or any payment at all, for that matter).

Aires Brown ran for the chefs as they worked their way up from the kitchen to better kitchens to, eventually, at least for some of them, kitchens of their own, and they paid him in the finest food in the City.

Aires Brown ran for the gamblers and found which horses were going to win at Belmont and Aqueduct, which wheels were paying in Atlantic City, and which dice in which games (in alleys and backrooms and casinos) were shaved. From the geeks, he found which numbers were going to win the New York Lottery tomorrow.

Aires Brown also ran for the madams, and they paid him, befriended him, and gifted him with … information about their clients … information that would prove to be very useful … later.

*

Aries Brown was not much of a scholar until he had made his billions. One day, he ran across an essay written by Alexander Pope sometime early in the 1700s, and he realized that his fortune was based upon what the old Englishman had written three hundred years before, something to the effect that '…what the weak head rules are the never-failing vices of fools'.

Mr. Aires Brown, unbeknownst to himself, had become an expert on the vices of men (and women), and this expertise had made him ridiculously wealthy.

And Mr. Brown's expertise was manifest in his …

… assisting the greedy, those who stole or tricked or manipulated in order to plunge themselves into 'the mire of the world', with their unholy need to possess things, almost anything,

… pandering to the lustful in their wanton orgy of longing to enslave themselves to their desires,

… goading the wrathful in their anger, self-destruction, and revenge, the perversion of mankind's innate love of justice,

… serving the gluttonous in their absolute, unqualified, and impulsive quest to consume and consume and consume again ad again,

…piquing the covetous in their desire to see their fellows destroyed,

… numbing the indifference of the slothful to their apathy, idleness, and boredom, and

… goading the prideful in their hurried rush to put their own selfishness above anyone or anything else.

And through many years of this base encouragement, Mr. Aries Brown learned, and invested, and prospered.

*

And then, one bright morning, Mr. Aries Brown realized that his universe of businesses were making him enough money that he could invest in even more 'business' and make even more money.

And with his money multiplying like rabbits, Mr. Aries Brown now had the time and the influence to spend his time with the people who had, in one way or another, financed his fortune. And these people would want to do almost anything to spend time with him.

But where would Mr. Aries Brown spend his time?

*

Mr. Aries Brown bought a place that appealed to him, a big home behind a big wall with big men with big guns guarding the doors.

And then, as he was traveling to his place, he saw another that charmed him as well. This one was not as large, but is was much more grand.

Mr. Aries Brown soon discovered that he enjoyed purchasing those places that had captivated his eye.

He found that the more he bought, the more he wanted, and the more he wanted, the more he bought.

Soon Mr. Aries Brown's purchases covered New York City, and then he began to buy up Boston, and Philly, and Baltimore, and then Cleveland, and Chicago, and St. Louis, and then Nashville …

Mr. Aries Brown's holdings spread like a cancer across the United States, but since his infection had begun in New York City, he was known as the 'Oligarch of Manhattan'.

*

Mr. Aries Brown had enough money, then, to begin his journey into space.

*

Mr. Aries Brown stopped buying residences and mansions and estates and, instead, bought tech companies, and as soon as he could manage, without hurting the companies' profits, he began to funnel 10% (or 20% or even 30%) of each company's income into certain well-hidden 'departments' that owed their allegiance to Mr. Aries Brown and to Mr. Aries Brown alone.

*

And a couple of years after that funneling began, a company named 'X-terrestrial' appeared way out in the lonely scrubland of Deep South Texas.

Space-X, a competitor of NASA, got all of the press … 'X-terrestrial' made all of the progress.

And as soon as Mr. Aries Brown could do so, he moved the 'X-terrestrial' manufacturing facilities into low-earth orbits.

Mr. Aries Brown hired thousands of engineers, and he paid better than governments, well, not better, exactly, but Mr. Brown structured his compensation packages more precisely to fit the 'needs' of the people whose expertise he wanted to retain (Mr. Brown had honed this particular skill in his earlier efforts as a runner, a provider, and a purchaser); he provided his employees everything they might require or simply wish for.

*

And twenty years later, there was a ship, waiting for Mr. Aires Brown.

*

Like many a man (and woman) who finds success due to his (or her) positive qualities, he (or she) often also finds a manner and a means to manifest his (or her) negative qualities.

When Mr. Aries Brown was a young man, as many young men do, he fell head-over-heels in love with a young woman. As practical, pragmatic, and down-to-earth as he was, she was equally as quixotic, romantic, and starry-eyed.

One day, to surprise him, she asked Aries Brown the date, location, and time of his birth. She couched her request as simply wanting to know everything there was to know about the man she adored, and so he told her. When they parted that day, she went to an astrologer she knew and paid the astromancer to chart her true love's horoscope.

Aries Brown didn't hear from the woman again. He called her and left messages. He wrote her letters. He waited outside her apartment, hoping to see her walking down the street or standing in her window. He never saw her.

So Aries Brown did the only thing that a man can do when a woman deserts him: he walked up to her door and knocked. He knocked and knocked and knocked. He knocked unceasingly until, after the neighbors had threatened to call the police, the woman opened the door and invited Aries Brown inside.

She had been crying, and when Aries Brown asked where she had been, why she wouldn't return his calls, and what had made her cry, she walked into the other room of the little apartment and returned with a tear-stained, crumpled piece of paper that she threw at Aries Brown's feet.

Aries Brown was confused and hurt, and to hide his bewilderment and its sting, he remained deathly quiet and bent to pick up the paper from the floor.

When Aries Brown had smoothed the paper, he read it. And what he read made him very angry:

"… the subject has suffered and painful wound, probably the death of his mother, as evidenced by the square aspect of Chiron to his Moon. The additional fact of Saturn being square to his Venus indicates that he feels that he is unworthy to be loved by others, and this insecurity will likely show itself as an inability to positively relate to others.

His Sun is in Aquarius, and is squared by Uranus' ruling sign, Aquarius. This double eccentricity shows that he will not share himself with or bend to anyone but himself. His Mars is in Sagittarius, and squared with Neptune, shows an almost monomaniacal zeal for his passions and goals but little care for those of others.

Perhaps most disturbingly, his Sun is the Apex planet of a Yod formation, a 'finger of fate', that is the key to understanding this subject's chart. The other legs of the Yod are Chiron and Neptune. The Sun is pressured and wounded by Chiron and irritated by the illusions associated with Neptune. His life, therefore, will alternate between phases of painful diffidence and escapist fantasy. He will lie and exaggerate to attempt to conceal his exaggerations and lies.

The subject is desperate for recognition, so desperate that he no longer cares whether the acknowledgement he receives is positive or negative. He is, and will remain, selfish, immature, and heedless of other people who might want to enter his life."

Aries Brown dropped the paper to the floor, turned away from the woman, and walked out of the door.

*

Mr. Aries Brown put his every energy and effort into his quest for the stars.

And Mr. Aries Brown's scientists and technologists worked just as tirelessly as their employer. His people worked … and built … and tested … and readied … all that was necessary for Mr. Brown to not only see the stars but to touch them.

And one day, Mr. Aries Brown received a phone call from the low-Earth-orbit station that the scientists of 'X-terrestrial' had constructed. The disembodied voice excitedly told him the news: the scientists of 'X-terrestrial' had successfully tested an Alcubierre warp drive!

Up until that successful test, the general consensus of the majority of scientists had been that an Alcubierre warp drive was a lovely fantasy, a fine thing for a science fiction book or movie, but was as unrealistic a method of propulsion as any that could ever have been imagined, much less constructed.

Perhaps the most fascinating thing about this particular theoretical warp drive was how it would work. This drive would not bother with trying to push or pull a ship faster than the speed of light (186,000 miles per second); it would, instead, squeeze the space before it and expand the space behind it. Space, itself, and the Space-

Time continuum in which it existed, would be manipulated so that an object could change its place in space faster than light.

Cool!

The big brains at 'X-terrestrial' had not solved all of the problems inherent in a faster-than-light method of movement, but they had taken a great step forward, a giant-umbrella-banana-Cinderella-lamppost step forward. They had managed to reach a speed that would let a ship that would take eighteen months to travel to Mars and back, with current technology, make the same trip, utilizing the Hohmann Transfer Orbit, in just six days. Mr. Brown's ship would not travel at the speed of light, pulling and pushing space … that would come later … but not much later … Mr. Aries Brown would get to Mars in a reasonable span of time.

*

Mr. Aries Brown put the telephone down. This was the best news he had heard in a very, very, very long time. And for Mr. Aires Brown, since he was Mr. Aries Brown, the only thing to do was to announce the wonderful news to the world!

Mr. Aires Brown would broadcast to every person on every continent on the entire planet that he, Mr. Aries Brown, would be the first man to set foot on another planet, and he would be doing that in a month or so!

So Mr. Aires Brown went to the television studio that had been built in his Manhattan home, and when the producers pointed at him and the red lights on the television cameras glowed, Mr. Aires

Brown looked into the camera and told the world exactly how he felt.

"I could stand in the middle of Times Square and chop someone's head off, and I wouldn't be convicted of anything! Not a thing! You can't beat me, and you can't be me!" the oligarch said, "I'm going to Mars next month!"

*

Of course, there were some details still to work out (supplies for the trip, fuel for the ship, a landing craft, fuel for the landing craft, the crew), but that was minor in comparison to Mr. Aries Brown's great accomplishment.

*

Even with the discovery of the new method of travel and the new ship with its shiny new engines, it would take Mr. Aires Brown three days to get there and three days to get back; when he got to Mars, he would have to use a smaller shuttle-ship to reach the surface and enjoy the activities that his concierge would have planned for him. Maybe Mr. Aires Brown would stay a week (that would be nice); maybe he would return to Earth sooner if he found himself getting bored.

But almost as important as the creation of the ship that would get Mr. Aires Brown to Mars and back would be finding and hiring the crew of the ship who would get him there and back.

After a great deal of thought, Mr. Aires Brown decided that the crew should consist of six: his concierge, his cook, his stewardess, his driver, and his driver's two helpers (a mechanic and an electrician).

*

Mr. Aires Brown had hired the men who would crew his ship many years before as members of his staff and believed that he knew everything there was to know about them. He was almost correct.

*

On the day before the launch, the seven intrepid travelers were ferried to a station in the low-Earth orbit that Mr. Aires Brown had purchased from NASA (in exchange for some incriminating photos of some hanky-panky that had occurred on one of the Space Station Missions in the 2020s).

The Oligarch of Manhattan, Mr. Aries Brown, boarded the ship first.

Mr. Aires Brown was followed by his Concierge, Hamilton Howard (who preferred to be called Albert). This was a man who had served Mr. Brown as his major domo since he had been hired when he had been just a boy, a dirty little boy whose Mormon mother, Ellen (then a missionary in the big, evil City), had met a drummer, Randall (who stood on corners, beating a big bass drum for others' salvation), and when she had told him of her pregnancy, he, like many other musicians, had left her in the lurch. The child was born and was provided for in a foster home in Brooklyn, by funds from an old woman's estate (something to do with loans, usurious loans). The boy attended a public grammar school in Brooklyn, a public high school in another borough, and City College, majoring in a little bit of everything. He graduated with a B.A. in History, New York City history, actually (it was a very narrow area of inquiry his professors had cautioned him). Albert found Mr. Aries Brown through a friend of a friend and had impressed the oligarch over the years with his precision, his insight, and his encyclopedic knowledge. So when the Oligarch of Manhattan asked Albert if he would like to accompany Mr. Aires Brown on a two-week trip to Mars and back, Albert had replied that he would be delighted.

The Cook, Charles Joughin, began his career as a baker, then progressed to the position of Chief Baker, and finally opened his own little restaurant (which soon became THE place to eat!) in Manhattan. The Oligarch snapped him up with promises of cookbooks and television shows and a free hand in his kitchens. When Mr. Aires Brown had asked the Cook to accompany him on the journey to Mars, Charles had begun, that day, to plan every meal that would be served on the trip and had thought to surprise Mr. Aires Brown by bringing those wonderfully beautiful and rare knives, that the American overlord had acquired almost a dozen years ago, along for his dining pleasure and for his entertainment, as well. Now, these works of the cutler's art would be used again as they had originally been intended.

The Stewardess was Heinrich Kubis, who had been burned in a terrible crash, who was excellent at his job, but who preferred to dress in fetching little uniforms that showed off his legs.

The Driver (pilot, I suppose) was a Russian ex-fighter pilot, Peter Nesterov.

The Mechanic was Hank Yunick ("He was about as good as there ever was on engines," someone had once said), who had no sense of humor at all when it came to folks making fun of his surname (he left a trail of well-cared-for vehicles and broken noses in his wake). Mr. Aires Brown had convinced Hank to join the trip to Mars with the promise of a farm in Neshaminy, Pennsylvania, a garage, just for himself in Daytona Beach, and a 1966 Chevrolet Chevelle.

The Electrician was a man named Phillip Austen ("just call me 'P'," he had said) who had worked on an obscure agricultural game show on public access cable in Ames, Iowa, called "Beat the Reaper". Mr. Aires Brown had hired 'P' many years before, but he had never told anyone exactly why.

*

Shortly after the ship left Earth orbit, Albert heard someone singing. It was a lovely song that sounded very old, and Albert went to each member of the crew to find out who among them was possessed of such a lovely voice. None of the crew had been singing he discovered. Albert went to Mr. Aires Brown's suite to see if the source of the music was his employer, but Mr. Aries Brown was sleeping.

Albert walked back through the ship, with the tune ringing in his thoughts. He got to the kitchen which, he found, was empty (Charles was in the pantry, checking the inventory to see if he would have to make any changes to the menus due to missing ingredients). The song was clearer and louder there … and then Albert understood: the knives were singing! Albert stood still and listened … really listened to them. And when he finally understood what the knives were singing, he took matters, and the knives, into his own hands.

He went first to the cockpit and asked the Driver, "Would you care for a drink? Something refreshing?"

The Russian was concentrating on dials and screens and knobs and buttons but said, "A bottle of sparkling water, French, please, would be great! Please just put it right here on this tray beside me."

Albert was a superb concierge, so he returned to the galley and quickly returned with a squeeze bottle of Perrier. He placed it on the tray. Then, he stepped behind the pilot.

"Thanks!" the Driver said.

"You are very welcome," Albert replied, and he placed his left hand on the man's forehead to hold it steady and drew the singing knife, that had been assiduously keeping very quiet and awaiting its gift, across the man's throat. In the zero gravity, the blood that spurted out of the man's throat was a fountain of tiny, bright-red bubbles.

The Driver gurgled for a minute and then lay quietly and died.

Albert returned to the kitchen and found the Cook working on a nice Hollandaise sauce for the Eggs Benedict that would be served with Mimosas in a celebratory lift-off meal. The kitchen (or galley as some of the staff called it) was a tiny place, and even though most of the ship was in zero gravity, the designers had thought of the comfort of the passenger and his staff, so the kitchen, the pantry (including the wine cellar), the salon, and Mr. Aires Brown's cabin were built to provide minimal gravity. In those rooms, liquids would act like Earthly fluids; things could be poured and sipped rather than being sucked through straws.

Albert walked up behind the man, put his hand over the Cook's mouth, pulled the man back into him, and jammed the knife into the cook's back, slicing through his spinal cord, into a kidney, and severing a renal artery. The Cook died almost instantly.

Albert heard a gasp behind him and turned to find Heinrich, the Stewardess, standing there, frozen with a hand to his mouth in horror. Albert turned and hacked at Heinrich's neck, breaking skin, cutting deeply enough into something to drench the hand that held the knife in blood, and breaking the man's collarbone. The Stewardess howled, but Albert was fast; he was able to pull the knife out of Heinrich's shoulder and shove it into his belly before the

Stewardess could take another anguished breah. Heinrich fell to the floor, his pretty legs sticking out from his cute, little skirt, at odd angles in death.

Albert found the Electrician and the Mechanic in rooms where there was no gravity. Their closed hatches had served to keep any of the sounds of the dying men from the technicians.

The Electrician was floating at a bench, testing circuits on a board and calibrating something or other. Albert stood in the hatchway and pushed himself off, flying like an arrow into the electrician's back, knife held out ahead of him and skewering the man. The Electrician's life was over quickly.

It took Albert another five minutes to find the Mechanic, and when he did, the man must have had some idea of what was happening. He was holding a crescent wrench in his right hand and when Albert flew toward him; the Mechanic swung the tool with a practiced hand. Albert moved the knife between them and the wrench clanged off of the sharp steel. Albert's momentum took him into the Mechanic, and the two caromed off each other like billiard balls. They bounced around the room for a minute before Albert managed to arrest his flight and turned to lash out to his right.

He caught the Mechanic with a wild cut to his arm, and as the blood boiled out of the Mechanic, Albert slashed at him again and caught the man's thigh. The Mechanic was bleeding profusely. He was weakening and was about to pass out when Albert stabbed out in front of himself and stuck the knife's blade into the Mechanic's chest up to the hilt.

By this time, both of the knives were feverishly trumpeting their songs of glory, death, and ecstasy. Albert paused for a minute to listen to them, knowing that what would come next would give the knives even more reason to warble and shout their songs.

Albert opened the door to the salon, holding the knives, one in each hand. The crew's blood dripped down the blades, to their handles, to Albert's hands, and then down onto the floor.

Albert's clothes were splattered with gore, and his face bore the splash of the dead men's cruor.

Mr. Aries Brown turned and calmly looked at Albert.

"You've killed them all?" Mr. Aries Brown asked the murderer.

Albert only nodded.

"And now you've come to kill me, too?" Mr. Aries Brown inquired, as though he were asking his tailor about adding a pocket to a vest.

Albert laughed, a smirk at first, then a snicker, then a chuckle, and a chortle, a full-bodied snort, a guffaw, a bray, then a thoroughly amused but derisive howl.

Albert laughed so hard and so completely that he dropped one of the knives so that he could put out a hand to hold himself up and keep from falling.

Mr. Aries Brown looked at Albert, uncomprehendingly.

And then Mr. Aries Brown got angry!

Mr. Aries Brown rose to his feet, balled his fists, and tensed his muscles for a fight.

"C'mon, then, you bastard," Mr. Aries Brown shouted to Albert, the man holding the knife, "Try and kill me!"

Albert looked up, paused to get a breath, and wiped a tear of laughter from the corner of his eye.

"I'm not going to kill you," Albert told Mr. Aries Brown.

"You're not?" Mr. Aries Brown asked, calming slightly, "Why not?"

"Because it's better *this* way," Albert replied with a hint of a smile and held his left hand out to Mr. Aries Brown, palm up,

Then, Albert sliced across his own wrist with the knife, cutting deeply and severing the veins and arteries and ligaments and tendons that connected his hand to his forearm. As his life's blood poured out, he said, "Listen to the knives! They are singing their most glorious song."

Albert fell to the floor and breathed his last breath.

And Mr. Aries Brown was left alone with the stars …

Chapter 25 – Death

The final card of all of the cards of the Major Arcana of the Suit of Knives in the Swordsmith's Tarot is Death. On this card in the Swordsmith's deck, Death, clad in armor, rides a pure, white horse and holds a black flag. Death is indomitable and unassailable, Death allows everything to be born again as pure things, and his realm is as unknowable as the night and as unavoidable as sleep.

Death is as simple and as certain as black and white; there is no reason to think that Death is any more complicated than that.

Death is feared unjustly.

Death's ruling sign is Scorpio, the inevitable one (who is also the Lord of Sex and Taxes). Death's number is thirteen, the number beloved by the Goddess as the turn of each year possesses thirteen moons.

In the Suit of knives of the Swordsmith's deck, Death often symbolizes the positivity of the beginnings that spring from what has been concluded. One door must be closed before another can be opened.

While Death is often the manifestation of sudden and unexpected change, it is also a harbinger of the promise of transformation.

Refusing to accept Death's gift of new possibilities will doom a man to destruction. Accepting the offering that has been freely given will, perhaps, allow a man to change.

Death offers no guarantees.

*

The spacecraft hurtled through the vacuum of space, speeding away from the blue planet. The speed necessary to escape the gravity of the Earth would no longer be necessary in a few minutes and the Driver had planned to shift to the new Alcubierre drive and change course to that of the Hohmann Transfer Orbit just a few minutes after escape velocity had been achieved.

That wouldn't happen now; Mr. Aries Brown's Driver was dead.

*

Mr. Aries Brown stood up from his chair in the salon of his spaceship. As he walked past Albert's inert body, Mr. Brown kicked it, kicked it hard, and then, once he had passed the corpse, he turned around and kicked Albert again.

Mr. Aries Brown learned that kicking dead Albert didn't make him feel any better.

With Albert dead, who was going to serve dinner and plan the entertainments?

Albert had said, before he slit his wrist, that he had killed the rest of the crew. But Albert was a fucking Concierge, not a murderer. Mr. Aries Brown seemed to remember that Albert blanched if the roast beef was too rare.

Maybe Albert had gotten into a fight, and maybe Albert had hurt somebody, but there was no way in hell that Albert had killed anyone … certainly not five other people!

So Mr. Aries Brown left the salon, stopping to pick up the knives to take with him (although he couldn't have told you or me, for the life of him, why he would have done such an odd thing).

Mr. Aries Brown found his way to the kitchen (the 'galley' they had called it as if they were on one of Mr. Aries Brown's yachts … well, Mr. Aries Brown considered, a ship is a ship, so this spaceship must be one of his yachts, as well). Heinrich was sprawled across the doorway, and Mr. Aries Brown had to step carefully over his former Stewardess, lest he bloody his shoes in the sticky, red pool that covered the man and the puddles that flooded the floor around him.

Yes, Heinrich was dead. He was gray and unmoving, and he would never have allowed his legs to be spread in such a provocative and gymnastic a pose in life as he did now in death. It was a pity, Mr. Aries Brown thought, but food and drinks could be served by anyone, so Heinrich's death was not much of a loss.

Now, Charles, on the other hand …

… was slumped on the floor in front of the La Cornue Grand Palais range. The hollandaise was burnt, the poached eggs were nothing but hard-boiled little rocks now, and the English muffins in the Turbo-Chef Tornado toaster oven that sat on the counter were scorched. "I can't eat that," Mr. Aries Brown thought, but then he reached into the little copper-clad pan on the range that held two slices of Canadian bacon and brought one to his mouth. It was cold, but it was bacon.

Mr. Aries Brown finished one piece and took the other with him, stepping back over Heinrich's splayed legs (the man should have spent more time and care shaving them, Mr. Brown thought; if the man hadn't been dead, Mr. Aries Brown would've docked his pay for such sloppiness) in the doorway.

Mr. Aries Brown then went searching for the others. He found the Electrician and then the Mechanic, both dead as trout, although it appeared that the Mechanic had, at least, put up something of a fight, albeit an unsuccessful one.

Finally, Mr. Aries Brown found the cockpit and the body of his Driver.

Mr. Aries Brown put down one of the knives so that he could check the Driver for a pulse, but he could find none.

And then, almost without thinking, Mr. Aries Brown looked out of the porthole (it was square, but that's what they called it … a porthole) ahead of him.

The ship was racing through space, and at the sides of what Mr. Aries Brown could see, stars seemed to move swiftly out of sight behind the ship.

Mr. Aries Brown wondered where the Sun was, and then he thought that maybe the ship was moving away from the Sun in its flight toward Mars, and that was why he couldn't see it.

And as Mr. Aries Brown stood there, mesmerized by the beauty of the universe, he heard … singing.

It was unlike any music Mr. Aries Brown had ever heard before. It sounded very old-fashioned, but he found it to be quite lovely.

And after the tune had been repeated two or three times, Mr. Aries Brown joined in the singing and discovered, to his great surprise, that he found joining in the music to be quite enjoyable, as well.

And when Mr. Aries Brown had added his voice to the music, he realized that the voices beside his own were those of the knives, and the music that he had joined himself with was their music.

Somehow, Mr. Aries Brown did not find himself to be much surprised at this realization. He decided that he would wonder about that later, after he had finished singing.

The three of them, the two Spanish knives and the Oligarch of Manhattan, sang and sang and sang and sang as they sped off into deepest space.

*

In a control room in Arecibo, Puerto Rico, a scientist watched the instruments as the big dish outside scanned the sky. And out where there should have been nothing, nothing but infinitesimally small specks of stardust, the radio telescope picked up vibrations and alerted the scientist to its discovery. The scientist dutifully recorded this data and ran every test he could think of to identify them. They weren't exactly radio waves; they were in the wrong part of the electromagnetic spectrum.

"Hey," he called to his co-worker, "Listen to this!", and he flipped a switch so that the sounds, for sounds they were, played over the speakers in the room,

"That sounds medieval," the scientist said.

"No," his colleague replied, "It's early Renaissance … liturgical, maybe … or Eucharistic … but it seems so familiar and so touching, and so insistent and so demanding. Turn it up and make sure that you are recording this. This could be a close encounter – second kind."

"Don't you mean 'of the third kind'," the scientist laughed.

"No, moron," his colleague responded with an edge to his voice, "Its Hynek's scale: first kind – visual sighting, up close; second kind – an effect that leaves a physical trace, like burn marks on the ground or a sound recording; third kind – where a creature shows up; fourth kind - …"

"Fourth kind?" the scientist asked, "How the fuck many kinds are there?"

"If you will let me finish," his colleague answered, an irritated edge to his voice, "Hynek postulated seven. The fourth kind – alien abduction … and don't ask about probing; that's technically another one; fifth kind – direct communication, like SETI; sixth kind – death of a human, so I can kill you and blame it on the aliens on the tape; seventh kind – alien sex. Now let me get back to making sure we've got this."

And the two scientists listened to and recorded the singing of the knives, so that when they told others of what they had heard that night, late at night out in the jungle south of the city almost to Utuado, the other scientists would not be able to say that the men were insane and the two men who had taped the music could get their work published in a well-respected, peer-reviewed journal.

"Boo-yah!" the scientist thought.

*

And out in the vast reaches of space, the little ship sailed on, and Mr. Aries Brown lifted his voice in the music of the knives to sing their sharp songs.

Printed in the USA
CPSIA information can be obtained
at www.ICGtesting.com
LVHW021645301024
795255LV00005B/153

9 781974 327836